Praise for the FOUNTAIN CREEK CHRONICLES

"Alexander has written a charming historical romance that features well-drawn characters and smooth, compelling storytelling that will have readers anxiously awaiting the second installment of the FOUNTAIN CREEK CHRONICLES. Highly recommended. . . ."

—**Tamara Butler**, *Library Journal*
(Starred Review)

"It's a pleasure to read this debut book. Rich prose, a realistic setting and characters, and a compassionate story of love will keep you turning the pages long into the night. . . ."

—*Romantic Times* TOP PICK (4½ stars)

"[A] tenderhearted story of redemption . . . Rarely does a debut novel combine such a masterful blend of captivating story and technical excellence. Alexander has introduced a delightful cast of winsome characters, and there's a promise of more stories yet to be told."

—**Kristine Wilson**, *Aspiring Retail*

"Book two in the FOUNTAIN CREEK CHRONICLES is a winner. Alexander deftly portrays the heroine's wounded soul and her struggles with regret while being careful not to reveal anything too soon."

—**Bev Houston**, *Romantic Times*

"This second book in the FOUNTAIN CREEK CHRONICLES reveals the power of love and forgiveness. All of the characters in the story are interesting and complex, even if they play minor roles. A warmhearted inspirational story."

—**Nan Curnutt**, *Historical Novels Review*

"Tamera Alexander's characters are real, fallible, and a marvelous reflection of God's truth and grace. Her stories unfold layer-by-layer, drawing you in deeper with every page."

—**Sheryl Root**, *Armchair Interviews*

Rekindled has been named to
Library Journal's Best Books of 2006 list
and is a nominee for
Romantic Times's Best Inspirational Novel of 2006.

Books by

Tamera Alexander

FROM BETHANY HOUSE PUBLISHERS

FOUNTAIN CREEK CHRONICLES

Rekindled

Revealed

Remembered

TAMERA ALEXANDER

✦ FOUNTAIN CREEK CHRONICLES | BOOK THREE ✦

REMEMBERED

BETHANY HOUSE PUBLISHERS
Minneapolis, Minnesota

Remembered
Copyright © 2007
Tamera Alexander

Cover design by studiogearbox.com
Cover photography by Steve Gardner

Scripture quotations are from the King James Version of the Bible.

Published by Bethany House Publishers
11400 Hampshire Avenue South
Bloomington, Minnesota 55438

Bethany House Publishers is a division of
Baker Publishing Group, Grand Rapids, Michigan.

Printed in the United States of America

ISBN-13:   978-0-7642-0110-3
ISBN-10:   0-7642-0110-7

Library of Congress Cataloging-in-Publication Data

Alexander, Tamera.
    Remembered / Tamera Alexander.
        p.   cm. — (Fountain Creek chronicles ; bk. 3)
    ISBN-13: 978-0-7642-0110-3 (pbk.)
    ISBN-10: 0-7642-0110-7 (pbk.)
    1. Young women—Fiction. 2. French—Colorado—Fiction. 3. Frontier and pioneer life—Colorado—Fiction. 4. Mining camps—Fiction. 5. Birthfathers—Identification—Fiction. 6. Fathers and daughters—Fiction. I. Title.

PS3601.L3563R46   2007
    813'.6—dc22   2007007116

DEDICATION

To Joe, with love

Thank you for Paris.

For my thoughts are not your thoughts, neither are your ways my ways, saith the Lord. For as the heavens are higher than the earth, so are my ways higher than your ways, and my thoughts than your thoughts.

ISAIAH 55:8–9

Cimetière de Montmartre, Paris, France
July 17, 1870

VÉRONIQUE EVELINE GIRARD laid a single white rose on her mother's grave, and bent low to whisper into the afterlife. "If somehow my words can reach you, *Maman* . . ." Her hand trembled on the cool marble. "Know that I cannot do as you have asked. Your request comes at too great—"

An unaccustomed chill traced an icy finger up her spine. Sensing she was no longer alone, Véronique rose and slowly turned.

Cimetière Montmartre's weather-darkened sepulchers rose and fell in varying heights along the familiar cobbled walkway. Rows of senescent, discolored tombs clustered and leaned along meandering paths. Canted summer sunlight, persistent in having its way, shimmered through the leaves overhead and cast muted shadows on the white and gray marble stones.

Movement at the corner of her eye suddenly drew her focus.

There, peeking from behind a centuries-old headstone, sat a cat whose coat shared the color of ashes in a hearth.

Véronique sighed, smiling. "So I am not alone after all. You are the *racaille* skulking about."

The cat made no move to leave. It only stared at her, its tail flickering in the cadence of a mildly interested feline. Cats were common in Paris these days, and they were welcome. They helped to discourage the overrunning of rodents.

"He is not the only *racaille* skulking about, *mademoiselle*."

Véronique jumped at the voice close behind her, instantly recognizing its deep timbre. "Christophe Charvet . . ." Secretly grateful for his company, she mustered a scolding look as she turned, knowing he would be disappointed if she didn't. "Why do you still insist on sneaking up on me here?" She huffed a breath. "We are far from being children anymore, you and I."

Contrition shadowed his eyes, as did a glint of mischief. He took her hand and brought it to his lips. "Mademoiselle Girard, be most assured that it has been many years since I have looked upon you as a child." Playful formality laced his tone even as his expression took on a more intimate look—one Véronique remembered but considered long ago put behind them. "With the slightest sign of encouragement from you, mademoiselle—"

"Christophe . . ." She eyed him, anticipating what was coming and wishing to avoid it.

Gentle determination lined Christophe's face. "With the slightest sign of encouragement I would, mademoiselle, for the final time, attempt to capture the heart of the woman before me as easily as I once won the heart of the young girl she once was."

She stared up at him, not completely surprised that he was broaching this subject again—especially now, after her mother's passing. What caught her off guard was how deeply she wished there were reason to encourage his hopes.

She'd known Christophe since the age of five, when they'd tromped naked together through the fountain of Lord Marchand's front courtyard. Remembering how severe the punishment for that offense had been for them both, she curbed the desire to smooth a hand over the bustle of her skirt. Those escapades had extended into their youth, when after hurrying through their duties, they had raced here to explore the endless hiding places amidst this silent city of sepulchers.

She'd adored Christophe then. Of course it wasn't until later in life that he had noticed her in that way, but by then those feelings for him had long passed and showed no sign of being resurrected.

She repeated his name again—this time more gently. "You know you are my dearest friend . . ."

A dark brow shot up. "*Dearest friend* . . ." He grimaced. "Words every man hopes to hear from a woman he adores."

His sarcasm tempted her to grin. But she was certain whatever rejection he felt would be short-lived. After all, he had said *a* woman, not *the* woman.

He gave an acknowledging tilt of his head. "You can't blame a man for trying, Véronique—especially when such a prize is at stake." Resignation softened his smile. "In light of this, I hereby renew my solemn vow made to you in our twenty-sixth year as we—"

"Twenty-fifth year." Véronique raised a single brow, remembering that particular afternoon five years ago when he'd made the promise as they strolled the grassy expanse of the Champs-Elysées.

"*Pardon, ma chérie.* Our twenty-fifth year." His eyes narrowed briefly, a familiar gleam lighting his dark pupils. "I stand corrected, and will henceforth extinguish the fleeting hope that my *dearest friend*"—wit punctuated the words—"will finally succumb to my charm and consider altering her affections."

With a serious sideways glance, she attempted to match his humor. "You will not regret your restraint, Christophe, for you would not be pleased with me. On that I give you my vow." She shrugged and gave herself a dismissive gesture, secretly hoping her mother could somehow hear their exchange. *Maman* had always enjoyed their bantering, and had loved Christophe dearly. "I am like wine left too long in the cellar. I fear I have lost my sweetness and grown bitter with time's fermenting."

He tugged playfully at her hand, and a familiar quirk lifted his brow. "Ah, but I have learned something in my thirty years that you apparently have not, Mademoiselle Girard." His smile turned conspiratorial.

"And what would that be, *Monsieur* Charvet?"

Truth tempered the humor in his eyes. "That the finest French Bordeaux, full-bodied and rich in bouquet, does not yield from the youngest vintage, *ma chérie*, but from the more mature."

Unable to think of a witty reply, Véronique chose silence instead. Christophe's handsome looks and gentle strength had long drawn the attention of females. Why he still held a flame for her, she couldn't imagine.

A silent understanding passed between them, and after a moment, he nodded.

He gave her hand a gentle squeeze, then bowed low and proper, mimicking the grand gesture used daily among the male servants in the Marchand household in which they'd grown up serving together. "I will henceforth resign myself to the designation I hold in your heart, Mademoiselle Girard, and I will treasure it." He smiled briefly and added more softly, "As I always have, *ma petite.*"

My little one.

Christophe's use of his childhood name for her encouraged Véronique to draw herself to her full height. But barely brushing five-foot-three, she hardly made for an intimidating figure and knew full well she looked far more like a girl of eighteen than a woman of thirty. Her mother had often told her she would one day be thankful for such youthfulness. That day had yet to dawn.

Christophe motioned in the direction of the street. "I've come to escort you home. Lord Marchand has requested a meeting with all members of the household staff." He took a breath as if to continue, then hesitated. The lines around his eyes grew deeper.

Véronique studied him, sensing there was more. "Is something amiss, Christophe?"

This time the quirk in his brow didn't appear fully genuine. "Be thankful I came to retrieve you, *ma petite.* Dr. Claude volunteered to come in my place—that *racaille*— but I would not abide it."

She grimaced at the mention of Dr. Claude's intent.

"You must watch yourself around him, Véronique. Though I have overheard nothing absolute, I believe he deems himself worthy of your hand and has spoken with Lord Marchand about pursuing it."

Véronique pictured Dr. Claude, the personal physician to the Marchand *famille.* "Of his worth there is no doubt, and his rank and situation are far above my own. But—"she made a face—"he is so old and his breath is always stale."

Christophe laughed. "Fifty may be older, yes, but it hardly portends impending death, *ma chérie.*" He shook his head. "Always such honesty, Véronique. An admirable quality, but one that will get you into much trouble if not balanced with good sense."

She let her mouth fall open. "I have perfectly good sense, and while you've always warned me against being too honest, my dear *maman*—may she rest in peace—always said that giving a right, or honest, answer resembles giving a kiss on the lips."

He smiled. "When the answer is one you're seeking, no doubt it is just that." He held up a hand when she started to reply. "But let me say this—if your dear *maman* held any belief that contrasts one of my own, I will instantly resign mine and adopt hers without exception." His gaze shifted to her mother's grave. "For she was a saint among women."

He stepped past Véronique and knelt. Laying a hand on the tomb, near the white rose, he bowed his head.

Véronique watched, knowing the depths of his affection for her mother. She knelt beside him and ran her hand across the cool, smooth stone. Her mother had died slowly. Too slowly in one sense, too quickly in another.

Arianne Elisabeth Girard had suffered much, and there were many nights when, in a fitful laudanum-induced sleep, she had begged God to take her and be done with it. For a time, Véronique had begged God *not* to grant her mother's wish. How selfish a request that had been.

But no more selfish than what her *maman* had asked of her in that final hour.

It had been unfair and carried much too great a cost. Her mother would have realized that under ordinary circumstances, but the fever and medications had confused her thinking. Véronique had heard it said that one could never recover from the loss of one's mother, and if past weeks were testament, she feared this to be true.

Picturing her mother's face, she struggled to find comfort in a sonnet long ago tucked away in memory. Beloved by her *maman*, the sonnet's words, penned over two hundred years earlier, were only now being made to withstand the Refiner's fire in Véronique's own life.

Wanting to feel the words on her tongue as the author himself would have, she chose the language of the English-born poet instead of her native French. "'Death, be not proud, though some have called thee mighty and dreadful, for thou art not so.'"

Christophe spoke fluent English, as did she. Yet he remained silent, his head bowed.

Her brow furrowed in concentration. Her voice came out a choked whisper. "'For those whom thou think'st thou dost over-throw, die not, poor death. Nor yet canst thou kill me.'" Her memory never faltered, but more than once the next passages of the sonnet threatened to lodge in her throat.

John Donne's thoughts had often lent a measure of consolation as she'd been forced to watch her mother waste away in recent months. But instead of affording comfort that morning, Donne's Holy Sonnet seemed to mock her. Its claim of victory rang hollow, empty in light of death's thievery, however temporary the theft might prove to be in the afterlife.

She pulled from her pocket the diminutive book of Holy Sonnets, its cover worn thin, and turned to the place her mother had last marked.

The note at the bottom of the page drew her eye.

Still remembering her mother's flowing script, the artistic loops and curls that so closely resembled her own, Véronique experienced a pang in her chest each time she looked at the barely legible scrawl trailing downward on the page at an awkward angle. But dwelling on her mother's last written thoughts offered her a sliver of hope.

"'Death is but a pause, not an ending, my dearest Véronique.'" Véronique softened her voice, knowing that doing so made her sound more like her mother—people had told her that countless times in recent years. If only she could hear the resemblance, especially now. "'When the lungs finally empty of air and begin to fill with the sweetness of heaven's breath, one will realize in that instant that though they have existed before, only in that moment will they truly have begun to live.'"

Ink from the pen left a gaunt, stuttered line that disappeared into the binding, as though lifting the tip from the page had been too great an effort for the author.

Christophe's hand briefly came to cover hers.

Véronique closed her eyes, forcing a single tear to slip free. She still cried, but not as often. It was getting easier—and harder.

Her gaze wandered to the name chiseled into the marble facing— ARIANNE ELISABETH GIRARD—then to the diminutive oval portrait embedded in stone and encased in glass beneath it. She had painted the likeness at her mother's request one afternoon in early February, shortly before her passing, by a special bridge along the river Seine. Some of Véronique's most cherished memories could be traced back to that bridge.

Memories of a man she'd never truly known . . . and yet had always struggled to live without.

Her memories of him were clouded and murky, much like the Seine. Yet she remembered the feel of her father's hand enfolding hers. The tone of his voice as he used words to paint mental portraits describing how the early morning light played against the ripples of the water, rewarding the observant onlooker with multifaceted prisms of color.

Though only five when he left, she recalled how he'd made her feel as they'd walked the canals together—cherished, chosen, *loved*.

Véronique studied the small portrait of her *maman*. She had sketched the curves of her mother's face from memory, just as she did everything. Another gift from the Giver, her mother had called it. The ability to see something once and commit the tiniest details to memory. To store it deep inside, kept safe as if locked away in a trunk, to be taken out and painted or sketched at a later time.

At least that's how it used to be. She hadn't lifted a brush in months, not since her mother had grown ill.

But she couldn't blame that solely on her mother's illness—unflattering critiques about her work from a respected instructor had contributed. She'd been at the Musée du Louvre, copying portraits of the masters along with other students, and the instructor's criticism had been especially pointed. *"You're merely trying to impress us, Mademoiselle Girard, when you would be better served staying within the bounds of conventional artistry. You are here to learn from the masters, and their techniques. Not give us your interpretation of their paintings."*

His assessment stung. Though the criticisms were not new, and were partly founded in truth, his public declaration that her work was not worthy of distinction and that her talent was lacking did nothing to bolster her confidence.

Wind rustled the trees overhead.

Véronique's gaze trailed the luminous shafts of sunlight as they slanted across the grave, turning the marble a brilliant white against the drab brown of an over-dry summer. As far back as she could remember, a place existed deep inside that remained incomplete, wanting. Surely God had granted her this *gift* of painting with the purpose of meeting that need.

Yet since her mother's death all attempts at filling the void with it had fallen grossly short of the mark.

The emptiness within spawned the jolting reminder of her mother's last request. "I want you to do what I never could, Véronique. Go to him. . . ." Véronique had wanted to turn and run, but her mother's urgency had rooted her to the bedside. "Find him. . . . I know your father is still alive." Her mother's eyes pooled with tears. "Do this for him, for yourself. . . . Your *papa* is a good man."

Her mother's gaze had trailed to the table by the bed and settled upon a stack of letters. Once white rectangles, now yellowed with time and bearing marks of oft-repeated readings, the bundle was tied tight—too tight it seemed—and with a ribbon Véronique didn't remember seeing before. "They are no longer my letters, Véronique. They are yours." A tear had slipped down her mother's left temple and disappeared into her hairline. "In truth, they have always been yours. Take them. Read them, *ma chérie*."

She couldn't refuse her mother at the time, but Véronique didn't want the letters. She didn't need to read them again. She already knew of her father's promises to send for his young wife and their five-year-old daughter once he was settled in the Americas—once he'd made his fortune in fur trading.

But Pierre Gustave Girard had never sent for them.

Christophe chose that moment to rise from his quiet vigil and offered his arm. Véronique stood and slipped her hand through, willing the voiceless question hovering at the fringe of her thoughts to be silenced once and for all.

Paris was her home. How could her mother have asked her to leave it to go in search of someone who had abandoned them both?

Christophe walked slowly down the cobbled path, shortening his long stride in deference to hers.

The shaded bower they walked beneath, courtesy of canopied trees, encouraged the chirrup of crickets long after the creatures should have fallen silent in the summer's warmth. Lichen clung to the graves, frocking the rock surfaces in blankets of grayish green. Iron gates of mausoleums barred entrance to keyless visitors, even as the chains hanging from their doors drooped beneath the weight of their mission.

"How can time move so slowly in one sense, Christophe, when

there seems to be such a scarcity of it in another?" Her question coerced a smile from him, as she knew it would.

"Always the poet and artist's perspective on life." He looked down at her. "Something I have aspired to understand but have failed miserably to do."

"And give up your realism? Your ability to"—she tucked her chin in an attempt to mimic his deep voice—"'see the world as it truly is, not as others see it'?"

Christophe shook his head, smiling. "Oh, for the memory you have, *ma petite*. To so fully capture both phrases and images with such distinguishing clarity. You never forget anything."

"That is not true, and you know it. My thoughts are easily scattered these days, and I often forget things."

"Ah yes, you forget to eat when you're painting late at night." His look turned reprimanding. "Or when you used to paint. You forget to quench the flame as you fall asleep reading"—he snapped his fingers—"whatever foreign poet it is that you're so fond of."

She slapped his arm, chuckling. "You remember very well what his name is."

"*Oui*, I know the master John Donne. But why must he be . . . *English*?"

She giggled at the way he said the word. As though it were distasteful.

Pausing, he looked down at her. "It's good to hear you laugh, *ma petite*." He started down the path again. "Let's see, where was I?"

"I believe you were listing my faults. And none too delicately."

"*Oui*, mademoiselle. But it is an extensive list, *non*?" His tone mirrored his smile. "Just the other day, when you forgot to put sugar in *Madame* Marchand's tea, I thought we might have to convene the parliament to decide your fate."

She smiled while cringing inwardly, thinking of Madame Marchand, the family's matriarch. Six years ago Lord Marchand had transferred Véronique's services to his elderly mother after his only daughter, to whom Véronique had served as companion since childhood, had married.

Madame Marchand had reminded her of the sugar oversight no less than four times the day of her grievous error. And without uttering another word, the woman had prolonged the reprimand in proceeding days through short, punctuated glares—starting first with the sugar bowl then slinking to Véronique.

She sighed and shook her head. "I'm afraid my mind has been elsewhere of late."

"But I have saved the worst of your faults for last." Christophe stopped and she did likewise. "You continually forget others' short-comings even when they've purposefully set you at naught. You extend grace where none is due. . . ." He grew more serious. "And you, along with your dear *maman*, have always given the Marchand household the best of service, regardless of Madame Marchand's ill temper and demanding disposition. The ungrateful, aging . . ."

Her eyes widened at the name he assigned to Madame Marchand, but she would've been lying if she denied having thought the same thing on occasion.

They rounded the corner and she spotted one of Lord Marchand's carriages waiting near the entrance. She had walked the two-mile distance that morning, enjoying the time to think—and to be out from under Madame Marchand's scrutiny. "Is Lord Marchand's requested meeting so urgent, Christophe?"

He kept his focus trained ahead.

The seriousness in his expression caused her smile to fade. "Has something happened?"

He aided her ascent into the carriage, climbed in beside her, and rapped the side of the door; the driver responded.

Véronique wanted to press the matter but held her tongue. Pressuring Christophe had never met with success. Quite the opposite, in fact.

The driver merged the carriage onto a main thoroughfare and chose an avenue running adjacent to the Musée du Louvre and the Seine. The river arched through the center of town, its dark waters murky and pungent from the daily deluge of rituals from the city's inhabitants.

Véronique pushed back the velvet curtain from the window to allow movement of air within the carriage, aware of the shadow stealing across Christophe's face.

He leaned forward and rested his forearms on his thighs. "There are things I must say to you, and I ask that you allow me due course, *ma chérie*, before you offer response." He glanced back at her. "Or I fear I will not be able to complete my task."

His tone held unaccustomed solemnity, which provided ample motivation to fulfill his request. Wordless, Véronique nodded.

"Within hours Emperor Napoleon is to declare war on Prussia. Lord Marchand has secretly received word that Prussia is mobilizing an army even now. No doubt they're finding Spain a willing alliance. Lord Marchand—" The carriage came to an abrupt halt. Christophe glanced out the window before continuing, his voice lowered. "Lord Marchand predicts the dispute will be far reaching. Already our *patron* has made plans to depart for Brussels within the week, and . . . I am to accompany him. His entire family will be journeying with him as well."

Suddenly the reason behind Christophe's reticence became clear. She gently touched his arm. "I don't want to leave Paris, Christophe, now of all times. But if—" The carriage jolted forward, and resumed its pace. "But if Brussels is where the family must go, then I'll happily accompany Madame Marchand. I'm certain it won't be for long, and that this . . . blow our country has suffered will be quickly resolved."

He nodded just as the carriage jolted forward, then resumed its pace.

The look he gave her made her feel like a naïve schoolgirl. "It's not that simple, Véronique, for many reasons."

The lines of his brow deepened, and she sought to ease his worry. "I'll be fine. The trip to Brussels might even be good for me. And once we return everything will be—"

"Madame Marchand has informed our *patron* that she has no plans for you to accompany her."

His voice came out flat and final, and Véronique felt as though someone had suddenly cinched her corset two sizes smaller. She tried to draw breath. "But I . . . I don't understand." She shook her head. "I'm . . . her companion."

Christophe's eyes narrowed. "I've been informed that . . . Madame Marchand has already arranged for a new companion to escort her to Brussels."

Véronique moved her lips but no words would come.

The carriage turned onto the cobbled road leading to the Marchand estate.

The discovery of her reduced rank—whatever her position might be—encouraged the emotion to rise in her throat. Véronique swallowed against the knot of anger and tears, and struggled to find the positive in this situation, just as her mother would have urged her to do. "Am I to assume that the remaining staff will stay and maintain the home's readiness for the Marchands' return?"

He didn't answer. His lips formed a tight line.

"Christophe," she whispered, growing more unsettled by the second. "We have always been honest with each other. Tell me what my new position is."

Staring at the floor of the carriage, he exhaled an audible breath. "After this week, you will ... no longer be employed within the Marchand household. He has secured a position for you in the household of Lord Descantes, and they depart for England straightaway."

When summoned to Lord Marchand's private study that same hour, Véronique gathered her remaining nerve and willed the frenetic pace of her heart to lessen. She always found the formal nature of Lord Marchand's study intimidating, and the latching of the oversized door behind her compounded her unease.

She spotted Christophe standing by the far window, his back to her. Lord Marchand had requested to meet with him first, and relief filled her, gathering that Christophe would remain for her meeting as well.

"*Bonjour*, Mademoiselle Girard." Standing behind his desk, Lord Marchand motioned for her to sit in one of the mahogany gondola chairs opposite him.

She paused long enough to curtsy, and then chose the seat that put her in Christophe's direct line of vision. If only he would turn around.

Lord Marchand said nothing for a moment, his hesitance giving her the impression that what he was about to say required great effort. "Monsieur Charvet has informed me that the two of you have spoken, Mademoiselle Girard. And that you are aware of the change in circumstances."

She nodded, wishing Christophe would look at her.

"Before I continue, let me say that it was of utmost concern to me to locate a position for you that would reflect my appreciation for your years of excellent service, mademoiselle." Regret flickered across

Lord Marchand's face. "As well as for your mother's," he added with surprising tenderness. "Therefore, my request that you be placed with Lord Descantes' family."

"*Merci beaucoup*, Lord Marchand." She coerced a smile, glad that Christophe had confided to her about the Descantes family in the carriage earlier. She remembered having met the couple at a formal dinner once. Lord Descantes, severe in his countenance, was in fact most kind, and his wife his equal in that regard. "I'm greatly indebted to you for using your influence for my benefit."

Lord Marchand held up a hand. "It is not only my influence that gained you the position, but also Monsieur Charvet's. He put his own reputation on the line when he recommended you. You may be naïve to the ways of parliament, but no doubt you are aware of agreements made between alliances."

She nodded.

"Negotiations are reached, deals are struck and sealed, all with a single handshake. Nothing more. The integrity of a man's word is the binding force of that contract. Nothing need be written because the man's reputation, the man himself, is the guarantee. Do you understand what I'm saying to you?"

"Certainly, your lordship," she answered. Whatever had transpired, the position with the Descantes family would be binding. If she chose not to work for them, there would be no other position for her, and it would compromise both Lord Marchand's and Christophe's reputations.

"You're a bright young woman, Mademoiselle Girard. It is one of the reasons I handpicked you to be companion to my daughter all those years ago. Francette never had much initiative on her own. I think it partly due to the loss of her mother at such a young age, but I also blame myself. As her only parent, I gave her too much, too easily."

Véronique had long considered this to be true, but of course had never voiced the thought.

"So I sought to locate a companion who would challenge my daughter, inspire her by example." Lord Marchand's smile held endearment. "And I did not have to look far, for I found that child living right here in my own home. You did those things for

Francette." A knowing look moved over his face. "You did what I never could."

Lord Marchand's last phrase, coupled with something in his expression, made Véronique sit straighter in her chair. "Lord Marchand, I—"

She fell silent at the look he gave her.

"Véronique . . ." A sigh escaped him. His expression became aggrieved. "I would ask that you not interrupt me, mademoiselle, as I lay out the circumstances to you."

Surprised by his informal address and reminded of her place in this home, Véronique nodded, wordless. Twice in one day she had received such an admonishment.

"As Monsieur Charvet informed you earlier today, you do indeed have a position with the Descantes. You will serve as tutor and companion to each of their four daughters. But what he did not know, and what I intentionally withheld from him, is that the family will not be traveling to England."

He paused, and the moment seemed to pause with him.

Véronique stared across the desk at this man she'd known all her life, and yet had never *really* known. Christophe turned, drawing her attention, and the look in his eyes communicated one single overriding emotion—anger.

Queasiness slithered through her midsection. The air in the study suddenly grew thick and moist.

"Your *mère* and I . . ." Lord Marchand kept his gaze confined to the ornate desk behind which he sat. "We often conversed late in the evenings, here in this room. Over the years, we became . . . friends. Nothing beyond that," he added quickly, as though reading Véronique's thoughts. "But I grew to care very deeply about your mother. She loved you more than her own life, Véronique. She shared with me her dreams for you, her hopes. And toward the end . . . her regrets. I made your mother a promise before she died."

Véronique found it difficult to breathe, much less remain seated. Her mother's last request played over in her mind. *"I want you to do what I never could."*

She rose slowly, fisting her hands to ease their shaking. She heard herself asking a question, while somehow already knowing the answer. "To what destination will the Descantes be traveling?"

Lord Marchand rose and came around to her side of the desk. So close, yet maintaining a respectful distance. "They are bound for the Americas, *ma chérie*. They leave for Italy one week hence, and you are to accompany them. Lord Descantes will conduct parliamentary business there for some weeks—perhaps longer, and then you will travel with them to the Americas, to a place by the name of New York City. When you arrive, your service to the Descantes family will be concluded, and someone will meet you to take you the rest of the way."

Véronique looked between Lord Marchand and Christophe, numb with shock, feeling betrayed and yet absurdly protected at the same time. "The . . . rest of the way?"

Christophe stepped closer. His eyes were bright with emotion. "You are strong, *ma petite*. Much stronger than you look, and far stronger than you consider yourself to be."

She shook her head. That's what her mother used to say. "I'm tired of being strong, Christophe."

Lord Marchand's gentle sigh drew her attention back. "Through a connection Lord Descantes has established, I have hired a gentleman who will meet you in New York City. I posted a missive with instructions to him this very morning. Lord Descantes will inform him of your date of arrival once that is determined." A tender smile accentuated the traces of vanished youth about Lord Marchand's eyes. "According to your mother's wishes, and in keeping with my promise to her, this gentleman will accompany you to the Colorado Territory, to the last known whereabouts of your father—a town by the name of Willow Springs."

Near Big Hill, Oregon Trail
March 1871

KNEELING OVER A DESOLATE PATCH of drought-ridden valley, Jack Brennan slipped off his hat and briefly closed his eyes. An early morning sun warmed his back and cast a long shadow over the familiar plot of earth. Slowly, reverently, he placed his right hand over the unmarked place.

Moments accumulated in the silence.

A zealous spring breeze swept fine granules of dust over and between his fingers. Without pretense of a marker, this unadorned spot in southeast Idaho held what had once meant everything to him.

He studied the grave that cradled the bodies of his wife and their only child and welcomed the haze of memories that always huddled close when he came back to this place. The place where it had happened. The memories were brief in the reliving, and yet those precious recollections were what had sustained him through his hardest times.

It had taken years, but healing had come. Finally, and completely.

Gradually his gaze was drawn to the lone wild flower sprouting up right where a headstone might have been placed. Braving the desolate landscape, the delicate petals of the yellow owl's-clover bloom bore the palest shade of its name. Its leaves were sticky to the touch and edged in a fine fur that gave the plant a grayish color. The slender flower lifted heavenward, bespeaking courage and a persistence not easily worn down.

An apt flower to be covering his Mary's grave.

Jack let out a held breath and surveyed the western horizon, far in the distance, where the brown plains blurred with the gauzy blue of sky. "This will be my last visit here, Mary." He spoke quietly, relatively certain she could hear him and knowing that he needed to get these things said. One thing he was sure of—if Mary *was* listening, it was from somewhere other than beneath his feet. Despite knowing that, something had compelled him to return here year after year.

He knew this location as sure as he knew every trail, hill, creek, and riverbed—both dry and running—from here to California and on up into Oregon. He'd traveled the fifteen hundred mile stretch from Missouri to the western territories so many times he didn't feel at home anymore unless he was on the move. Or at least that's how it used to be.

Over time, things had changed. *He* had changed.

In the past thirteen springs of guiding wagons west, he'd made camp at this spot each time, the families traveling under the care of his leadership never having been the wiser. Grief was a private thing. Not something to be hoarded and turned into a shrine as he'd seen others do when they lost a loved one, but rather a formidable adversary to be met head on, without hesitation and with a due amount of respect. Otherwise a man might never find his way through to the other side, where grief became less an enemy and more a venerated, even trusted, teacher.

He scooped up a fistful of dirt and let it sift through his fingers.

Slowly, he stood. "For years, Mary, not a day passed but what you didn't occupy my every thought. I'd be wishing I could hold you close again, that we could . . . make love just once more, like we did the night we made our son." He shifted, and sighed. If not for the faded daguerreotype buried deep in his saddlebag, her exact features might be lost to him now. Time had a way of erasing even that which at one time seemed unforgettable.

"Sometimes I try and picture where you and Aaron are, what you're doing . . . what he looks like now. If he's a young man approaching full grown, or still the little tyke I carried on my shoulders." He glanced behind him, remembering.

He'd long since released the guilt of being unable to prevent the ropes from slipping and the wagon careening downhill, crushing the two people he would have gladly given his own life for. Life wasn't always fair, nor did it repay a person kind for kind. A man didn't live thirty-eight years on this earth and not learn that early on.

Two thoughts had assuaged his grief. First, believing there was something better waiting after this life. And the second, akin to the first, trusting that the good-byes said on this earth weren't meant to be forever.

He breathed in the scent of prairie grass and sunshine, and distinguished a pungent scent of musk on the breeze. For good measure, he retrieved the rifle on the ground beside him and scanned the patches of low-growing brush surrounding the area. The gray mare tethered nearby pricked her ears but gave no indication of alarm.

After a long moment, Jack lifted his gaze skyward. He kept his voice soft. "Things have changed so much in the fifteen years you and Aaron have been gone, Mary. It's not like it was when we first set out. There're forts and stagecoach stops along the way now. Miles of telegraph wire stretch across the prairie as far as the eye can see."

If it was quiet enough, he could sometimes hear the whining hum as messages zipped along the woven strands of copper from one side of the country to the other.

It seemed as though the Union Pacific rarely paused for breath these days. Journeying from Missouri to California used to take four months of slow, arduous travel. Now it took two weeks by rail. Many of the railroad lines, such as the Santa Fe, had built tracks directly over the old dirt trails, replacing them forever. All of these things combined, though good in their own right and an indication of a growing country, signaled the end of his livelihood—and the end of an era.

"This country's changed, Mary, and I've had to change with it." He looked away for a moment. "I used to see your face in a crowd and my heart would about stop right then and there." He shook his head. "'Course it wasn't you. I knew that. It was just someone who favored you."

But that hadn't happened in a long time, which made him even more confident that his decision to return one last time was the right one.

He slapped his hat on his thigh, sending out a cloud of dust, then slipped it back on. "I'll always carry you in my heart, Mary. Same goes for you, son." He thought back to the morning Aaron was born. Losing a wife and losing a child carved deep, but very different, scars. He'd be hard-pressed to define which loss had borne the greater burden through the years, but it went against the nature of things for a parent to bury their child. Of that he was certain.

"Part of me thinks you've been waiting a long time for me to do this, Mary. And that maybe you've even been encouraging it somehow, but . . ." He cleared his throat. His heart beat a mite faster. "I'm movin' on. I sold our land up in Oregon a while back. I just never could settle down there without you and Aaron with me. Didn't feel right somehow."

Mary's soft-spoken ways had made it hard for her to express her feelings the first time their opinions had differed. "You always said my stubborn streak was as thick as the bark on a blackjack, Mary Lowell Brennan." He eyed the wild flower again, smiling. "But you'd be surprised at the patience God's taught me through the years." *And what a difference living with you, even for those three short years, made in my life.*

Bowing his head, Jack offered up a final wordless good-bye.

He walked to the mare and loosened the tether, then swung into the saddle. He sat astride and studied the scene that lay before him, wishing he possessed the ability to capture such landscapes on paper. He'd even purchased a sketch pad and pencils a few years back—to fill up some of the lonely nights on the trail. And though he could draw enough to get his point across, sketching with any sense of artistry was a talent that clearly eluded him, and therefore was one he admired all the more. To be able to capture how the young spring grasses, barely calf high, bent in the wind as though bowing in deference to the One who created them—and how the prairie, though seemingly flat for mile upon endless mile, actually rose as it stretched westward, in gradual measures until finally reaching the foot of the great Rocky Mountains, where a new beginning awaited him. At least that was his hope.

The gray mare shifted beneath him.

Jack leaned down and gave her a firm stroking, smiling when she whinnied in response. "Steady, girl. We're 'bout ready."

When guiding his last group of wagons from Denver to Idaho, then on to Oregon last summer, he'd met a couple by the name of Jonathan and Annabelle McCutchens. About a week into the journey, Jonathan had taken ill, and they'd been forced to leave him and his wife behind. But the day before that happened, Jonathan had asked him to mail a letter, and had told him about the town of Willow Springs.

As Jack turned the mare westward and nudged her flanks, Jonathan's words replayed in his memory as though it were yesterday.

"I didn't find what I came looking for in that little town, but I discovered what I'd been missin' all my life."

Jack urged the mare to a canter and, sensing her desire, gave her full rein. One of the first things he planned on doing when he reached Willow Springs was to deliver the letter in his pocket from Annabelle to a preacher by the name of Patrick Carlson and his wife, Hannah. He'd been given specific instructions to hand it to them personally and had gotten the distinct impression that Annabelle wanted the three of them to meet. He looked forward to it.

The next thing he wanted to do in Willow Springs was to visit the banks of Fountain Creek and pay his last respects to Jonathan McCutchens, who had died on the trail. Passing through Idaho, Jack had taken the opportunity to visit Annabelle and her new husband. Thinking of that visit again brought a smile. He couldn't help but think of how much Jonathan McCutchens would have approved of her choice.

Just as he would approve of Jack's right now.

Something in the way Jonathan had spoken about the town, about what he had discovered there, had kindled a spark of curiosity inside him. Jack needed a fresh start, and he hoped he might find it in a little town tucked in the shadow of Pikes Peak.

Willow Springs, Colorado Territory
April 5, 1871

VÉRONIQUE WAS THE LAST to exit the stagecoach in Willow Springs. She'd scarcely stuck one booted foot out the door before a group of half a dozen gentlemen—and she used that term loosely—were already at her disposal, hands extended, smiles expectant. A bit too expectant.

She chose the one man out of the fray who she knew truly fit the description—the garrulous older gentleman who had served as her escort from New York City all the way to this vast, barren wilderness these Americans had the good humor to call the Colorado Territory. If by territory they meant a vacuous, drought-ridden, desolate piece of God's earth, then they'd chosen the correct term. With one unapologetic exception—

The grand range of rugged mountains so proudly scaling the western horizon.

One peak in particular rose in confident splendor, towering over all else in its shadow until it surely crested the threshold of heaven. The highest summits sat shrouded in a fresh falling of snow, which wasn't surprising with the lingering chill in the air. *Breathtaking beauty!* And she had to admit that the air smelled so fresh it tingled her lungs—quite the opposite of the cloistered air in Paris that trapped the smells of decay and *détritus.*

"Watch your footin' there, miss." Monsieur Bertram Colby grinned as his callused hand engulfed her small gloved one. "This first step's always a mite big for someone your size."

Holding her unopened parasol, Véronique managed to gather the folds of her skirt in one hand and place her foot on the rickety stool. After three weeks of traveling in Monsieur Colby's care, she'd grown accustomed to the man's usual warning and was able to keep her balance with his aid. Though her first impressions of Americans had been left wanting—on the whole she found them to be brash, boisterous, and far too outspoken—she readily admitted that Bertram Colby had proven to be every bit a gentleman, regardless of his rough exterior.

"Thank you most kindly, Mr. Colby." Véronique detected the twinkle in his eyes. "*Merci beaucoup*, monsieur," she added more softly, rewarded with the expected raise of his brow.

He gave a hearty nod. "I sure like it when you talk your own way, ma'am. It's right pretty, and surely becomes you."

Several of the men standing nearby nodded in unison, right before their collective attention moved from being focused on her face to an area considerably lower, and behind—to her bustled skirt.

Véronique glanced down at the ensemble she'd chosen that morning. Though she'd grown more accustomed to the attention her clothing drew, she still felt uncomfortable with it. The jacket with floral appliqués, and the ornately-bowed skirt, once an eye-catching emerald green, had taken on a decidedly duller hue with layers of dust coating it. Numerous women had paid compliments on the bustled style of her dresses. More so the farther west they'd traveled. They had also commented on her feathered *chapeau* trimmed in ribbon and ostrich feathers, which she wore fashionably angled over one brow. Some insisted they'd never seen such elegant fashions.

But the only reaction she'd received from any of the opposite gender were overlong stares. Though much was different in this new country, it seemed some things never changed.

With a tilt of her head, she acknowledged the men gathered round, not wanting to appear rude but neither wishing to encourage future discourse. With a practiced flourish, she opened her parasol, then lightly brushed at the dust clinging to her skirt, with little success. No doubt the skirt and jacket were ruined.

"Don't you worry about that dress, miss." Monsieur Colby delivered a look to the other men saying that she was not to be pursued—a look he'd well mastered—and guided her across the street to a three-story building bearing the name *Baird & Smith Hotel*. He kept his hand beneath her elbow. "There's a woman here in town who takes in laundry. She scrubs the daylights outta my clothes and they come back good as new. She'll have that fancy getup of yours cleaned and fresh as spring—I guarantee it."

Véronique smiled as she climbed the steps to the boardwalk. "I appreciate that, Mr. Colby," she answered, all the while imagining the aforementioned laundress dunking her fine garments in a filthy washbasin and "scrubbin' the daylights out of them," as he had so aptly described it.

With silvered-dark hair and full beard, Bertram Colby was an impressive-looking man, in a rugged way, and was no stranger to this untamed life. Though far from the *gentil*, cultured men she'd known back home, Monsieur Colby's polite character was beyond question. She guessed him to be around sixty, but couldn't be certain. The deep lines of his tanned face bore silent testimony to his countless miles of experience as a "trail guide," as he called himself, in this sun-drenched territory. And one thing was indisputable—Monsieur Colby bore the kindest countenance she'd ever seen. He always looked as though he were waiting for another reason to smile.

He nodded toward the hotel. "You go on inside and get your room. I'll see to all your trunks." Taking the steps from the boardwalk down to the dirt street—not a cobblestone to be found, she noticed—he threw his parting words over his shoulder. "You can get settled and rested up before supper, and then I'll take you to Myrtle's for some good eatin'."

She offered her thanks but doubted he heard her over the noise of the street traffic. Pausing for a moment, she watched him move through the crowds. As he nodded to men and tipped his hat to women, Véronique saw every one of his gestures returned. He had a definite way with people, a natural ease with them. It was an attribute she greatly admired and wished she possessed to a greater degree. She'd grown more reserved in recent months, despite having been relatively confident in her abilities back in Paris.

Never one to second-guess herself before—it seemed now a daily occurrence.

Bertram Colby had proven to be a most satisfactory traveling partner over the past three weeks, even if his informal nature breeched her level of comfort on occasion. She'd found these Americans to be far less inhibited in their conversations, and if there was one thing Monsieur Colby was overly fond of, it was conversation. But as a newcomer to this country, she'd found his stories both entertaining and enlightening, though right at the moment she would have traded every last *pâtisserie* in Paris for a hot bath and a moment absent of chatter and curious stares.

Thoughts of those sweet pastries from home served as a reminder that she hadn't eaten since that morning. The food offered along the stagecoach route had been tasteless fare, either undercooked or over, and unfit for consumption—which described most of the *entrées* they'd been served since leaving civilization back East. Surely her stomach had forgotten how it felt to be full and contented.

Véronique retracted her parasol and entered the hotel lobby, thankful to find the establishment clean and orderly looking. The hotel's furnishings were simple but tastefully coordinated, a welcome change from the roadside inns they'd frequented along the stagecoach routes.

A young girl entered from a side door adjacent to the registration desk. Her arms were loaded with folded bedding, and from her intent expression she was clearly focused on her task. She brought with her a delicious aroma that smelled like freshly baked bread. Véronique's mouth watered at the thought of a warm slice smeared with fresh butter and a side of fresh berries with cream—a treat she and her mother had often shared in the evenings.

She touched the cameo—a gift from her father to her mother—at the base of her throat and felt a twinge of homesickness tighten her chest.

The clerk chose that moment to turn, and reacted with a grin. "Good day, ma'am. Welcome to the Baird and Smith Hotel. How may I serve you?"

Returning the smile, Véronique couldn't help but stare. The girl's flawless skin, combined with long black hair and violet-colored eyes made for a striking combination. To discover such etiquette, not to mention grace and beauty, in this unrefined territory took her by surprise. She'd experienced far less cordial greetings in the finest establishments in Paris, and from older, more experienced staff no less. She approached the desk. "I would like a room, please. And my length of stay is undetermined as of yet."

A long pause, attributable no doubt to the unexpected accent.

The clerk recovered quickly. "Of course, ma'am. We have several rooms available and would be happy to accommodate you, however long your respite with us." The girl couldn't have been more than thirteen or fourteen, but her mature voice and manner—obviously coerced but with a genuine-sounding intent—lent her an older air, and Véronique liked her instantly. "Would you prefer a ground-level room or accommodations on an upper floor?"

Again Véronique detected the slightest touch of rehearsed formality in the girl's tone, hinting that she might be trying to appear older than she looked. Véronique smiled. How well she understood that desire. Feeling adventuresome, she lifted a brow in silent question. "I will trust your recommendation, mademoiselle."

That earned her another grin. "Then I'll be pleased to see you installed into room 308."

Cringing inwardly, Véronique smiled. She should have known it would be the uppermost floor.

The girl made note of the room number in the registry, then turned the leather-bound book around and indicated where to sign. "That's a corner room. It's the hotel's nicest and will give you the best view of Willow Springs. You can even catch the sunset over the mountains if you lean out the window a bit."

Véronique's grip on the quill tightened just hearing the suggestion.

The clerk lifted her slender shoulders and let them fall again. "Plus it doesn't cost a penny more." She quoted the price of the room, which included breakfast served in the dining area off to her right.

"That will be most adequate. Thank you." Véronique signed the register, purposefully leaving the departure date blank. The prices quoted for lodgings were reasonable, and she still had ample funds. Lord Marchand and Lord Descantes had both been most generous in their provisions; the combined amount had more than covered her expenses since parting ways with the Descantes family in New York City.

Before she left Paris, Lord Marchand had explained that additional provisions would be waiting for her in an account at the bank in Willow Springs. He'd further explained that he would continue to provide for her needs on a regular basis. Exactly what "regular basis" meant, she wasn't certain, and she made mental note to visit the bank soon. But for now, her funds were more than sufficient.

Reassurance of her financial standing prompted an odd question in her mind, one she was none too eager to answer—should she have cause to seek employment in Willow Springs, for what kind of position did her skills qualify her to fill?

Though not an accomplished musician, she had learned to play the piano alongside Francette, being the girl's companion. But Véronique anticipated little call for that talent in Willow Springs. The same was true for having learned how to serve as an assistant to the hostess for a formal dinner party of a hundred or more guests, or how to mingle among the elite at political balls and hold intelligent conversation with other companions to wives and daughters of foreign dignitaries—everything considered important to know for the companion to the daughter of a lord in parliament, but seeming of little use in this foreign country. And certainly of no use in this remote territory.

Véronique returned the pen to its holder beside the ink bottle, determining not to dwell on what she couldn't change. Instead, she drew inspiration from the hotel clerk's warm welcome. "My name is Mademoiselle Véronique Girard. To whom do I owe the pleasure of such a gracious greeting this afternoon?"

The girl dipped her head. "My name is Lilly. Lilly Carlson, ma'am." Those violet eyes of hers danced.

"And are you the proprietor of this fine establishment?"

Lilly giggled. "No, ma'am . . ." She hesitated and added more quietly, "I mean, Mademoiselle Girard," mastering the pronunciation the first time. The girl learned with efficiency. "I help Mr. and Mrs. Baird in the afternoons, and some mornings. I'm working to save money for a new t—" She paused and glanced away. When she looked back, shyness clouded her former sparkle. "I help with the laundry and the dishes and greet the guests, on occasion."

Véronique nodded, watchful. "My only hope is that Monsieur and Madame Baird are paying you well, mademoiselle. An employee *responsable* is worth a goodly sum."

Whatever the reason for the girl's hesitancy seconds before, it vanished. Her countenance brightened once again. "I'll go get the key to your room and show you upstairs. And . . ." Lilly paused again, her pretty mouth forming a delicate bow. "Would you like me to draw you a hot bath?"

Véronique wanted to hug the child. "That would be heaven. *Merci.* My trunks should arrive here in a short time."

She nodded. "I'll have them carried up to your room."

As Lilly disappeared back through the side door, laughter coming from outside drew Véronique's attention. She stepped closer to the window for a better look.

Bertram Colby stood on the boardwalk a few feet away, speaking with another man. The stranger's back was to her, but the sound of his deep laughter carried through the open window. She could hear their voices but not the specifics of their conversation.

Standing at least a head taller than Monsieur Colby, the man was broad shouldered and possessed a manner that bespoke familiarity. And kindness. He turned toward her then, and Véronique found her interest substantially piqued.

Monsieur Colby's voice lowered. He looked away, still speaking, and the taller gentleman reached out and laid a hand on Colby's shoulder, nodding. Apparently Monsieur Colby had crossed paths with a trusted *camarade*, and that spoke most highly for the man.

The sound of a door opening brought Véronique's attention around.

"I've got your key and have water warming on the stove for your bath, Mademoiselle Girard." Lilly joined her by the window.

"Thank you, Lilly." Véronique motioned in the direction of Bertram Colby and his friend. "What do you know about that gentleman standing there?"

"Mr. Colby? Everybody knows—"

"*Non, non,* my apologies," Véronique whispered. "I have made Mr. Colby's acquaintance. I was referring to the other gentleman."

Lilly shook her head. "I've never seen him before." A mischievous grin crept over her pretty face. "And I think I'd remember if I had.

He's a mite easy on the eyes, isn't he?"

Although not familiar with Lilly's phrasing, Véronique understood her tone and agreed wholeheartedly, though wasn't about to admit such aloud. She nudged Lilly with a shoulder and gave her a playful smile. "How is it that you take notice of such things, *ma chérie*? That man is far too many years your senior."

Innocence swept Lilly's face. "Oh, I wasn't talkin' about me, Mademoiselle Girard." The tiniest flicker of a gleam entered her eyes as she turned. "I was looking at him for you."

Véronique chuckled and stole a last glance out the window before turning and following the girl upstairs. She felt more at ease on her first day in Willow Springs than she'd ever expected to, especially when the real journey still awaited her. "I think I would be wise to keep *both* of my eyes on you, Lilly Carlson. You are youthful, to be sure, but by no means are you still a child."

Thoughts of Christophe sprang to her mind, bringing memories of home. The longing for Paris was always close. That never changed, no matter the miles distancing her from her dearest friend, or from the Marchand home, or from everything familiar.

What was so foreign in that moment was the sudden and unexpected connection she felt to *this* place—and to the father she'd never really known. She thought of the letters her mother had received from Pierre Gustave Girard, and of a particular missive in which he had informed them he was turning from fur trading to mining. *"The streams and rivers no longer yield sufficient trappings, but there is opportunity in mining in these grand mountains. Many have found their fortune already, and I hope soon to be among their number."* In a subsequent letter he had described his new profession but his words hinted at having been carefully chosen. And even as a young girl, Véronique had gathered that mining was a dangerous occupation.

That envelope, nested with others at the bottom of one of her trunks, bore a handstamp with this town's name, and a date registering almost twenty years ago. But would that letter's journey back to its birthplace prove to be any more fruitful than the years of waiting she and her mother had endured?

Lilly reached the third floor and chose the left hallway.

Formerly lost in her thoughts, only then did Véronique notice it—the girl's irregular gait. Véronique paused briefly on the third-story landing, her gaze dropping to where Lilly's dress swooshed around her ankles. The sole of the girl's right boot was markedly thicker than the left, and badly worn on one side. Lilly managed a smooth enough stride given the variance, but her compensation wasn't enough to completely disguise the limp. Or the brace that framed the heel of her boot and extended up her leg.

From the fleeting grimace on the girl's face, Véronique guessed that the stairs were a struggle for her.

Lilly paused at the last door on the right, and Véronique did the same, wanting to inquire but daring not. Lilly turned the knob and indicated with a flourish of her hand for Véronique to enter first.

Decorated in soft florals of yellow with accents of crimson and green, the room provided a warm welcome, though it wasn't a third the size of her private quarters in the Marchand residence. But it would suffice for now, until more suitable quarters could be arranged. Véronique sighed and stretched her shoulders, both weary and hopeful, but mostly thankful to have finally reached Willow Springs and to be done with that portion of her journey.

"This is the only room in the hotel that has a bay window." Lilly crossed the cozy quarters and pushed open the window, opening the shutters halfway. "Come and take a look."

Véronique didn't budge. "Yes, I am certain it boasts an excellent view, as you claim. Perhaps I'll look another time. I'm rather fatigued at the moment."

"Oh . . . of course. I'm sorry."

Regretting the apology she heard in the girl's tone, Véronique sought to make up for it. "Thank you, Lilly, for giving me such a warm reception. Your kindness has helped to shorten the distance I feel from my home."

"And . . . where is your home?"

"France. I was born in the city of Paris. I have lived there all my life." Véronique ran a hand over the simple blocked quilt covering the bed. "Until now," she added softly.

A look of wonder brightened Lilly's eyes, as did numerous questions. But to the girl's credit, she didn't pursue any of them.

Véronique studied the girl as she crossed to the door. Not only smart, but sensitive as well. Such intelligence and beauty in one so young; yet beneath it all she sensed a fragility the girl kept well *masqué,* most of the time. And what was it the girl was saving for? She'd almost admitted as much downstairs moments ago, before catching herself. Perhaps a new bonnet, or a dress. All niceties a girl of her age would rightly desire.

Véronique laid aside her parasol and reached into her *réticule* for some coins. "This is for you, Lilly."

Lilly stared at her outstretched hand. "Oh no, ma'am. You don't need to do—"

Véronique took the liberty of pressing the coins into her palm. "An employee *responsable* is worth a goodly sum . . . remember?"

Lilly looked at the money, and gave a shy nod. "Thank you, Mademoiselle Girard. I'm much obliged." She paused at the threshold, her hand on the knob. "I'll knock on your door as soon as your bath is drawn. It shouldn't take me long, and the water closet's only two doors down from yours."

Véronique scanned the room, only now noticing that it was without private bathing facilities. Recalling Lilly's comment that this was the nicest room in the hotel, and thinking of the girl's impediment, she masked her true feelings and offered her thanks as Lilly closed the door behind her.

She unbuttoned her jacket and moved to hang it in the *armoire,* then noticed the dust covering the garment. Shaking it out as best she could, she caught her reflection in the mirror. Her hair was still arranged atop her head, minus a few curls slipping free, but there was something else about her image that made her pause.

Stepping closer to the mirror, she decided what it was.

My eyes.

Smoky brown in color, they appeared dull, lifeless. She thought of Lilly's flashing violet eyes and their brilliance, contrasted them with her own, and came up lacking. Truth be told, the girl possessed the exact coloring Véronique would have chosen if the Maker had granted her choice.

Sighing, she turned away and withdrew the few remaining pins from her *coiffure.* Her hair fell down her back. She massaged her neck and shoulders. This journey had been enlightening in so many ways, and humbling in others.

Being employed by Lord Marchand had afforded her and her mother a way of life she'd taken for granted, having known nothing else. The household staff had seen to all of her basic needs. Her clothes, only slightly less fine than Francette's, had been sewn by the Marchands' personal family seamstress and when soiled would disappear only to reappear the next day, freshly laundered and back in her *armoire*. Until forced to leave Paris last summer, she'd never realized how pampered an existence she had lived, and how much she had depended on the security and familiarity of that life to make her feel safe. To tell her who she was.

She moved closer to the window, careful not to get *too* close, and gave the shutters a push to allow the cool breeze greater entrance. That was one thing she'd quickly come to appreciate about this Colorado Territory—no matter how warm midday grew with the coming spring, the evenings summoned a welcome cool. She breathed in and detected a sweetness on the air—a pleasant fragrance, yet unfamiliar.

Then she heard it again. . . . Laughter so rich and deep that the mere sound of it persuaded a smile.

Considering the direction from which it came, she guessed Monsieur Colby and his friend were still standing just outside on the boardwalk, two stories below. She gauged the distance to the window.

White lace curtains fluttered in the breeze, bidding silent invitation—either that or issuing a dare. She hesitated, trying not to think about how the floor beneath her feet projected from the building, supported only by a corbel beneath. But the need to be in control, to prove that she could do something of her own volition, momentarily outweighed her fears.

She forced one foot in front of the other.

For centuries, buildings in Paris had been built with oriel windows, so the architectural design wasn't new to her. She simply tried to avoid them, making an extra effort to do so when they were open, like now.

She braced her hands on either side of the window. *It's only three stories. It's only three stories.* The phrase played like a silent mantra in her head.

Quick breaths accompanied the pounding in her chest as the sides of the window inched past her peripheral view. Finally, her midsection made contact with the sill. She gritted her teeth and ignored a shiver as the street below moved into view.

Closing her eyes, she gathered the last of her nerve and leaned forward. A swimming sensation caused her to tighten her hold on the wood framing. She waited for it to pass, and gradually opened her eyes.

Monsieur Colby and his friend were indeed standing where they had been, below her window, as she'd guessed. Street traffic had thinned as afternoon made way for evening.

Her body flushed hot, then cold. *I can do this. . . .*

One street over, a woman at the mercantile swept the boardwalk while a young boy scrubbed the front windows. A bubbling creek carved its way down the mountains, skirting the edge of town, and a white steeple rose in the distance. She couldn't be certain at this distance, but what appeared to be a graveyard lay alongside the length of the churchyard. Lilly had been right, this window provided an excellent vantage point from which to view Willow Springs.

A flush of lightheadedness made her head swim, and a faint whirring began in the far corners of her mind.

Rouge tinted the western horizon, an *azur* sky offsetting the reddish hue. The mountains glowed in the late afternoon sun, giving the appearance that someone had lit a candle deep within them.

With every thump of her heart, the whirring inside her head grew louder. "*Breathe, Véronique, breathe. . . .*" Her mother's voice rushed toward her from years long past.

Véronique gulped in air and tried to push herself back inside. But her arms refused the command. She teetered. The town of Willow Springs started to spin, and everything became a blur.

CHAPTER THREE

ER BREATH LEFT IN A RUSH. Véronique felt herself falling. But in the wrong direction.

"Mademoiselle Girard!"

Arms came about her waist and pulled her backward.

"Mademoiselle Girard!"

A hard jolt to her backside helped clear the fog in her head, and gulped breaths discouraged the whirring. Véronique blinked several times, aware now of being sprawled on the floor, with someone close beside her.

"Are you all right, ma'am?"

The panic in Lilly's voice unleashed a barrage of emotions. Véronique's throat tightened. She massaged her pounding temples, touched by the girl's concern but also warm with embarrassment. "*Oui*, I am fine. Though I am most grateful you came when you did."

Lilly's arm loosened about her waist even as she hastily repositioned her skirt over her legs. But not before Véronique saw the brace extending up the girl's calf and thigh.

Lilly hesitated, and then motioned to the window. "If I might be so bold, Mademoiselle Girard . . . what were you trying to do over there just now?"

"I think I was trying to look out the window." Véronique shrugged, the order of events still sketchy in her mind. Slowly, the memory of the man's laughter resurfaced. "You were correct, Lilly. This room does provide a nice view. It's—" she paused, wanting to get the phrasing right—"a mite easy on the eyes."

Lilly glanced from her to the window and back again. "Well, I'm not too proud to say that you about scared me to death, ma'am. I knocked, you didn't answer, and I came in to find you hanging out the window."

Véronique considered the two of them on the floor and could barely stifle a giggle. What must this girl think of her?

A gradual smile softened Lilly's shock. "I take it you don't do well with heights, ma'am. Why didn't you tell me? I would've put you in a room on the first floor instead."

"*Non, non.* I do not wish to move. I like this room very much." Summoning an air of nonchalance she'd mastered years ago in defense against Christophe's tireless wit, she shrugged again. "Heights are not that bothersome to me . . . as long as I do not look down."

The boardwalk, deserted an hour earlier when they'd first entered the dining room for breakfast, now teemed with morning shoppers. "Monsieur Colby, I cannot thank you enough for all you have done for me. You have been most kind and attentive." Véronique opened her *réticule* to retrieve the bills, hoping he wouldn't argue the point.

They'd met for breakfast at the hotel. The pancakes, cooked thin and crisp around the edges and served with jam to spread between, reminded her of *crêpes* back home, and the sausages had been plump and delicious. She'd also enjoyed a restful night's sleep, thanks to Lilly having drawn a warm bath for her, followed by the late meal she'd shared afterward with Monsieur Colby. She'd half expected his friend might join them but she hadn't seen the man since Lilly had come to her rescue.

She held out the money. "*S'il vous plaît,* Monsieur Colby, I would like you to have this as a token of my gratitude for your services. You have worked most diligently on my behalf."

"No, ma'am. I'm not takin' that." He took a step back. "That French fella, Descantes"—his pronunciation prompted Véronique to smile—"he already paid me exactly what I agreed to at the outset, and I'm not takin' a penny more. Wouldn't be right. Anyway, I'd hardly call what I did for you real work. It was more like a vacation, what with the railroad comin' clear into Denver now and the stage-coach runnin' the rest of the way. I didn't do any real guidin'—not like I used to. As I see it," he added, throwing in a wink, "my main job was to make sure the menfolk left you alone. And I'll admit, I had my hands full on that count."

Realizing she was fighting a losing battle, Véronique acquiesced and tucked the bills back inside her *réticule*. It had been awkward at first, traveling with a strange man in a foreign country. But she'd grown accustomed to Bertram Colby's gentle manner and attentive-ness, his always knowing what to do and where to go next. She would miss him.

She'd been disappointed upon learning at their outset in New York City that he wouldn't be able to continue in her employ beyond Willow Springs. From her brief glimpse of this small town, she gath-ered that finding a driver with a suitable carriage to take her to the neighboring mining communities would prove to be a more difficult task than she'd imagined.

He tipped his hat. "The last weeks have been a pleasure, ma'am, and I hope you enjoy your stay here. Be sure and take in some of the hot springs if you have a chance. They're mighty nice and have heal-ing powers, some say. I hear there's a fancy hotel openin' soon in a town not too far from here just so folks can come, rest up, and soak for a while."

Seeing the exuberance in his expression nipped at Véronique's conscience. She had not lied to Monsieur Colby, but neither had she been completely open with him about why she was in this country. He believed her to be on a pleasure trip and she hadn't corrected the misassumption. "*Merci beaucoup*. The hot springs. I will attempt to see that attraction during my stay."

Twice she'd been tempted to tell him her real reason, and twice she'd held back. She'd not confided in him, and apparently neither had her benefactors. She'd overheard Lord Descantes conversing with Monsieur Colby in New York City and had also been briefed on the letter penned by Lord Marchand to him. In short, the letter declared that someone of great personal import to Lord Marchand needed safe passage to the town of Willow Springs and that Monsieur Colby was to see to her every need in the course of travel. The amount Lord

Marchand paid Colby was listed in the missive, and her former employer had compensated him well—demonstrating the same generous nature he'd shown her.

"I don't know what France is like, ma'am. But this is mighty pretty country out here. I think you'll like it. The people in this town are good and honest . . . for the most part. You remember everything I told you, you hear?" His expression reflected concern. "'Specially about some of the men."

She smiled. "*Oui*, I will do my best." Though she knew it would be impossible for her to remember everything, given the way the dear man liked to talk.

He'd often warned her about "scoundrels" as they'd traveled together, but apparently he was not familiar with the ways of French men. She could hardly imagine the men here being any bolder when it came to their advances on women. Growing up with Christophe as her closest friend had made her *privilégiée* to insights that might have otherwise remained hidden.

He had been the first to disclose to her the pivotal nature of a man's thoughts, revealing how varied they were from a woman's. Through Christophe's detailed discernments, she'd learned that the two sexes approached situations, as well as relationships, quite differently. That bit of knowledge had proven beneficial on more than one occasion.

"A grown woman out here on her own is one thing, Miss Girard. But bein' as young as you are . . . Well, miss, that's another. You best watch yourself at every turn."

"I will do that. I promise," she answered, knowing he considered her much younger than her thirty-one years. But since it wasn't proper to discuss a woman's age—nor was it important to sway his opinion in this regard—she let it pass. "I wish you all the best as you continue with your responsibilities in Denver, Monsieur Colby, and I hope our paths will cross again."

"I'll be back through here in a couple months or so, ma'am. I'll be sure and look you up, if you're still here. To see how you're farin'."

"I will look forward to that rendezvous." She curtsied. "And I will also look forward to seeing how you are . . . farin'." She tried to pronounce the word as he had, and failed miserably. But the attempt earned her a grin.

Watching Monsieur Colby walk away proved more difficult than she had imagined, and Véronique busied her thoughts with the tasks at hand. She needed to visit the town's depository that morning to ascertain her financial standing, which was based solely on whether Lord Marchand's funds had been deposited as he'd promised her before she left Paris. Then she would visit the town's livery to inquire about hiring a driver and a carriage.

But one thing she feared was certain—the likelihood of finding an escort as capable and honorable as Bertram Colby seemed a dwindling hope.

———

"How kind of you to hand deliver her letter to us, Mr. Brennan." Hannah Carlson lifted the lid from the Dutch oven on the stovetop and gave the contents a stir. "And definitely beyond the call of duty."

"My pleasure to do it, ma'am." Jack savored the aromas as he watched Mrs. Carlson slide a skillet of corn bread into the oven. Home-cooked meals were a rarity for him.

So far, everything Annabelle had told him about Patrick and Hannah Carlson was proving to be true. He'd instantly felt at home and could see why Annabelle had spoken of them with such fondness. When they'd invited him to stay for lunch, he'd gladly accepted. It delayed his trip to the town's livery to speak with a Mr. Jake Sampson about the wagon he'd ordered, but the day was young.

"Mrs. McCutchens and her—" Jack caught himself. "I'm sorry, I should say Mrs. *Taylor* now. She and her husband send their best to you both. And, Pastor"—he glanced across the table at Patrick Carlson—"Matthew sent a special message for you. He said to tell you that he wished the two of you could have another one of your . . . 'front porch interviews,' if that makes any sense."

Patrick shook his head, a thoughtful smile surfacing. "It does indeed. Matthew Taylor's a good man."

"I always had a certain feeling about Annabelle and Matthew," Hannah said, wiping her hands on her apron. "Especially after we got that one letter. Remember, Patrick? Annabelle penned it while they were traveling to catch up with your group last summer, Mr. Brennan. She wrote to reassure us that she and Matthew 'hadn't killed each other yet.'" She laughed softly. "And that's when we knew."

Pastor Carlson shook his head. "No, that's when *you* knew, Hannah. I still didn't trust him."

The pastor's tone was teasing, but Jack sensed a smidgen of truth in it, and he understood. He'd had reservations about Matthew Taylor the first time they'd met on the northern plains, when Matthew and Annabelle rendezvoused with his group heading west. But Matthew had quickly proven him wrong, for which Jack was thankful. After everything Mrs. Taylor had been through—losing her husband, Jonathan, so early in their marriage and so unexpectedly—she deserved some happiness.

And that she'd found it with Jonathan's younger brother just seemed right somehow.

Mrs. Carlson returned to the table with a fresh pot of coffee. "Lunch will be ready in just a few minutes. By chance, Mr. Brennan, did you see Matthew and Annabelle's daughter while you were there?" She glanced at his empty cup with a raised brow.

Jack nudged it forward. "Thank you, ma'am. And I certainly did." His smile felt sheepish. "I gotta admit I was a bit surprised to discover they already had a daughter, but Matthew explained that Annabelle was with child when his brother passed on. I didn't realize that on the trail." Knowing that would have made his decision to leave Annabelle and her first husband, Jonathan, behind on the trail even more difficult. "Their Alice is a cute little thing, and not lacking for love, I can tell you."

Hannah pursed her lips. "Oh, I'd love to see that precious child. Annabelle mentioned in her letter that Sadie was doing well. Did you get to see her too?"

"Briefly." Jack blew across the surface of his coffee and took a sip. "Sadie was real quiet around me, but that's understandable . . . after all the hardship she's been through. They say she's adjusting well."

Jack gathered understanding from the couple's subdued nods and was relieved he didn't need to comment further.

The evening he'd visited in the Taylors' home, Matthew and Annabelle had been open with him about their pasts, and about Sadie's. So many emotions had accompanied his learning that Annabelle and Sadie had both been sold into prostitution as young girls—surprise, disgust, and anger had battled inside him—but he'd also never been more in awe of God's ability to heal and to make new.

The scrape of Mrs. Carlson's chair drew his attention. "I'm not sure if you know this, Mr. Brennan, but Annabelle lived with us for a while before she married. She and I got to be very close during that time." Hannah pulled the corn bread from the oven. "You wouldn't believe how much I still miss that woman. She was such a help to me."

Jack caught Mrs. Carlson's subtle wink at her husband as she set the skillet on a pad in the center of the table.

She covered the corn bread with a towel. "Annabelle used to volunteer to listen to my husband practice his sermons, and let me tell you . . ." Hannah gave an exaggerated sigh, and Jack turned in time to see a mischievous look creep over the pastor's face. "It was so refreshing. There are days I'd pay a fortune to have that sweet woman back." Giggling, she tried to scoot away but wasn't fast enough.

Patrick caught her with one arm and pulled her close. "And you can imagine, Mr. Brennan, how refreshing it was for me to get insights from someone who actually reads her Bible!"

"Patrick!" Hannah swatted at her husband's arm.

Jack laughed along with them, admiring the way they bantered back and forth, and appreciating the home they'd made together.

"The stew's about ready," Hannah said, still grinning. "I'll call Bobby in and we'll be set. Lilly mentioned something about having lunch with a new friend today. She said they might stop by later, but it'll just be the four of us for lunch."

Jack noticed how Patrick's gaze followed Hannah as she left the room. Though it had been many years, he still remembered what that felt like—to be so captivated by one woman that she literally drew your attention, no matter where she was.

In some ways, Hannah Carlson reminded him of Mary. His wife had possessed the same gracious hospitality and playful humor, but Mrs. Carlson was more outgoing than Mary had been. Mary's soft-spoken manner and her determined desire to put others before herself were the things that had first attracted him to her.

Pastor Carlson pushed back from the table and stretched out his legs. "So, Jack, now that you're retired from guiding families west, what are your plans?"

Following the pastor's lead, Jack leaned back and got more comfortable. "I'll be running freight up to the mining camps around this area. I've already got an agreement with Mr. Hochstetler at the mercantile here in town. Met with him this morning, in fact. He has arrangements with most of the suppliers in the surrounding camps. I'm taking the place of his freighter, who was injured recently."

"Injured?"

Jack nodded. "Apparently the guy tried to haul too heavy a load over a pass. The accident happened up around Maynor's Gulch about a month ago. Wagon shifted to one side, wheel clipped the edge, and the whole thing went over. A ledge broke the driver's fall on the way down, but he spent two nights stranded up there before somebody happened along and found him. His leg was busted up pretty bad. Hochstetler said the guy will be lucky to walk again, much less handle a rig."

"Sounds like there's quite a bit of risk involved. You sure you want to get into that line of work?"

Jack smiled, already having answered that question in his own mind. "I think that's one of my main reasons for making this change. The risk in this new job is personal . . . no one else to be responsible for or to look after." He paused. "I hope this doesn't come across as self-centered, but . . . after what I've done all these years, I'm ready to look after only me for a while."

Patrick seemed to weigh that response. "Being responsible for others is a heavy load to carry, and you've borne your share of that for . . . how many years now?"

"A little over thirteen."

Patrick nodded. "It's hard enough finding your own way in this world. But knowing others are depending on you, that they're watching your every step, can be a burdensome thing. Even if it's a job you've enjoyed and a road you've traveled many times." Patrick took a slow sip of coffee. "So tell me, what was life like for you before you took to the trail?" His brow arched. "If you can remember back that far."

Jack sat up a little straighter at the question. It had been a long time since he'd spoken to anyone about Mary and Aaron, but Pastor Carlson had a way about him that invited conversation. Jack hesitated, softening his voice. "I remember life back then pretty well, in fact."

It took some doing, but he gradually told Carlson about Mary and Aaron, the accident, and his recent—and final—visit to their grave in Idaho. "I think traveling that road—many times, like you said—is how I eventually made my peace. God used all those years, and all those miles, to heal my grief."

Carlson's expression grew thoughtful. "I'm sorry for your loss, Jack. But in the same breath, I admire what you allowed God to do with it. You'll never know how many people's lives were changed because of that choice."

Wrapping his hand around his empty cup, Jack silently acknowledged the pastor's kindness with a nod. Then he shifted in his chair, ready for a lighter turn in the conversation.

"So when do you start this new job?"

"I'm supposed to head out Monday morning with my first load, but I've yet to pick up my wagon. I stopped by the livery last night, but I arrived later than I'd planned, and the place was already closed."

"That's because you were out raisin' Cain with Bertram Colby."

Jack didn't even try to hide his surprise.

Pastor Carlson grinned. "Mr. Colby stopped by briefly this morning on his way out of town. He told us you'd arrived and—"

A door slammed at the back of the house and a young boy rounded the corner at breakneck speed.

"Whoa there, Bobby!" Patrick reached out and playfully grabbed his son by the scruff of the neck. Despite the boy's squirming, the pastor easily managed to wrap an arm around his son's chest and pull him close. Bobby giggled as his father tickled him and mussed his hair.

Jack watched the scene between father and son, and a distant thrumming started deep within him that he was helpless to stop. With determination it rose, and he looked away as the thought surfaced—Aaron would've been sixteen this year, had he lived.

In an instant, snatches of memories never made with his son flashed in quick succession, one after the other—teaching Aaron to fish, taking him on his first hunting trip, showing him how to tie knots, instructing him how to read the night sky so he'd know the next morning's weather. The tightening in Jack's throat grew uncomfortable, and he swallowed to lessen it. Being healed of a hurt didn't mean you still wouldn't mourn the loss from time to time—that was another lesson he'd picked up somewhere along the way.

Hearing the young boy's laughter drew Jack's focus back, and gradually persuaded a smile.

"Bobby, I want you to meet Mr. Brennan." Patrick looked at Jack across the table. "And this is Bobby, our youngest. Bobby, Mr. Brennan here is a real live wagon-train master."

The boy stilled from his antics. "No foolin'?"

"No foolin'," Jack repeated, guessing Bobby to be around seven or eight.

"There you are!" Hannah appeared in the doorway, hands on her hips. "You ran off so fast I couldn't keep up."

As though not hearing, Bobby raced around to Jack's side of the table. "Will you tell me some stories, Mr. Brennan? Did you ever kill anybody?"

Hannah lightly chucked her son beneath the chin as she passed. "You mustn't pester Mr. Brennan, Bobby. He's our guest." She shot Jack a look of warning. "Bobby loves hearing stories about life on the trail. I hope you don't mind."

"Not in the least, ma'am." Jack rested his forearms on his knees so he was closer to eye level with the boy. "Besides, what's the good in rescuing a newborn calf from the jaws of a mountain lion if you can't tell someone about it?"

Bobby's jaw went slack.

Patrick rose from the table. "Well, I can see that just about does it. Not only do you have to stay for lunch, Jack. Now you have to move in with us!"

CHAPTER FOUR

VÉRONIQUE SEARCHED THE street corner, then glanced again at the paper in her hand. Lilly Carlson's directions to the livery—penned in block-style letters, strikingly uniform in shape and size—directed her down this particular street. But the street bore no marker declaring its name. Granted, Willow Springs wasn't a large community, but how were newcomers expected to find their way without street markings?

After saying good-bye to Monsieur Colby, she'd located the bank with little difficulty and discovered, to her relief, that Lord Marchand had already made a sizable deposit to an account registered in her name. Ample funds were available to hire a carriage and driver, and to keep her driver employed, at least until the next deposit arrived.

Véronique looked up again and huffed at the lack of proper signs. She committed Lilly's note to memory, and then tucked it inside her *réticule*. Did the people in this town *déconcertant* not believe in displaying placards to mark their thoroughfares?

Parasol poised in one hand, she tugged at her high-necked lace collar with the other. She would've sworn the sun's rays burned stronger here. Already an April sun shone brightly overhead, chasing away the morning's chill. Ignoring the open stares of townspeople, she summoned a confident stride and set off down the street.

She passed the mercantile, where doors stood propped open by barrels of potatoes and onions. Minutes later, she passed a men's clothier, which she made mental note of for later—*Hudson's Haberdashery*. Perhaps the gentleman inside behind the counter possessed the skills necessary to rescue her green ensemble now hanging sadly in the wardrobe back at the hotel.

A low whistle attracted her attention before she caught herself and faced forward again. A group of young men—schoolboys from the looks of them—gathered on the boardwalk outside the barbershop. Their comments were indistinct, but their laughter carried over the rumble of wagons trafficking the street.

Farther down the planked walkway, she slowed her pace and stepped closer to the front window of a shop.

Dresses hung from a wooden dowel, with obvious care having been given to their arrangement. What drew her attention first were the colors, or lack thereof. The materials all consisted of drab browns and dull grays. They looked similar to what the scullery maids at the Marchands' home might have worn, only not nearly as nice. Hoping this wasn't the only dress shop in town, Véronique couldn't ignore the disturbing suspicion that it was.

The livery sat adjacent on the corner ahead, just as Lilly had described. Véronique crossed the street, careful to maneuver a path around the deposits that horses, oxen, and other animals had left in their passing. Didn't this town have people who were responsible for the removal of such . . . occurrences? The bright royal blue of her gown was already covered with road dust; it wouldn't do to be dragged through a pile of—

Her boot sank into something soft.

She took a quick step back, then grimaced and exhaled through her teeth. Not only was her boot covered with it, the hem of her gown was caked in the filthy waste.

She glanced around for a patch of weeds or grass in which to scrape her heeled boots, but apparently God had banished all manner of growth from this accursed scrap of earth. Trusting no one around her spoke French, she continued down the street, taking immense pleasure in expressing her opinion of this town, this territory, indeed this entire country and its inhabitants, beneath her breath.

She paused outside the open doors of the livery. Having never entered this type of establishment before and uncertain of the protocol, she chose to listen for a moment. Lilly had described the proprietor, and Véronique easily distinguished Monsieur Jake Sampson from among his customers. Now to decide what her best approach with him might be.

Men came and went, each giving her a thorough perusal as they passed. Without exception they all tipped their hats and greeted her cordially, but being the only woman in sight, Véronique wished now that she'd asked Lilly to accompany her.

Bits and pieces of Jake Sampson's conversation with his customers floated toward her, and she soon relinquished any doubt that he was the right man to whom she should inquire about locating a driver and carriage. This man appeared to know everything about everyone in Willow Springs.

Waiting until the last customer exited, she took a deep breath and knew the moment had come.

Monsieur Sampson stood by a stone furnace a few feet away, his back to her. He pumped a lever protruding from the side—five, six times—until flames shot up through the throat of the stone structure.

"*Bonjour*, Monsieur Sampson." She raised her voice to be heard over the crackle of the fire.

"Be with you in just a second," he answered, still bent over his task. "Been a busy mornin' and I've had nary a minute to even—" He saw her and fell silent.

Véronique closed the distance between them. "*Bonjour*, Monsieur Sampson. I come in hope of securing your assistance, sir."

He cocked his head. A slow smile drew up the sides of his weathered cheeks. "Well, I'll be . . ." he muttered, barely loud enough for her to hear. His eyes took on a sparkle. "Bon-jour, Madam-moselle."

Caught off guard, Véronique chuckled at the unexpected reply and at the accent with which he butchered the words. But his familiarity with her language was encouraging. Perhaps this would go more smoothly than she'd anticipated. "*Bonjour*, Monsieur Sampson." She gestured toward herself. "*Je m'appelle* Mademoiselle Véronique Eveline Girard."

"Jim-a-pel Jake Sampson," he answered, thumping his chest with pride.

His mispronunciations were endearing, and they coaxed a smile from her. "*Enchanté de faire votre connaissance, monsieur. Je cherche un chauffeur et une voiture pour me porter au—*"

"Whoa there, missy." Sampson held up a hand. "I made out somethin' about you bein' pleased to meet me and then something about a carriage, but I'm afraid there's more there than I can hitch my cart to." He leaned forward. "Can you understand what I'm sayin' to you?" His voice rose in volume as he spoke.

She chuckled again. "Yes, Monsieur Sampson. I understand every word you are speaking."

"Whew! Well, that's good 'cause I only know a handful of your words, and those are a speck rusty."

"When did you have occasion to learn my language, Monsieur Sampson?"

"Let's see . . ." He bit his lower lip, causing the healthy growth of graying whiskers on his chin to bunch out. "That'd be some twenty-odd years ago by now. We had us a lot of French trappers come through these parts back then."

His answer evoked an unexpected response. Véronique worked to keep her hope in check. "French trappers . . ."

He nodded.

"Did you happen to know any of those men?"

"Oh sure, I knew plenty of 'em. They came through here in droves." He crossed to a workbench on the far wall and retrieved a *maillet* before returning to the fiery pit. "Always brought plenty of business with 'em too, just jabberin' away the likes of which you've never heard. You couldn't understand but a few words." His bushy eyebrows arched. "Well, that wouldn't be quite true in your case. Would it, ma'am?"

His laughter rang out hearty and genuine, and she took no offense in it. Somehow the levity made her next question easier to pose. "I know it has been many years, but do you remember any of these men by name? Perhaps a man by the name of Pierre Gustave Girard?"

"Girard," he repeated, looking at her more closely.

"He would have been through Willow Springs in the fall of 1850—perhaps earlier."

"Back in '50, you say?" He let out a low whistle. "That's another lifetime ago for me. . . ."

The wistfulness clouding his features made the twenty-year span feel like a chasm she hadn't the slightest hope of traversing.

"No, ma'am, can't say the name Girard strikes any chord with me. But the first name is familiar soundin' enough," he answered, his voice lighthearted.

"*Oui*, I can understand that." She tried to match his tone, but the pang of disappointment robbed the attempt. Had she expected to simply step off the coach and find her father waiting there for her after so many years? No, but neither had she anticipated the far-reaching breadth and width of this country—the miles upon miles of land stretching east to west, as far as the eye could see. The magnitude of the task before her had grown more daunting with each mile traveled by train or coach, and she felt inadequate in comparison.

The only clue she had to her father's whereabouts was a letter, and this tiny nothing of a town tucked in an obscure part of the world—a part she wished she'd never laid eyes on.

At the moment all she wanted was to be back in Paris, strolling down the Champs-Elysées on Christophe's arm, by her bridge on the river Seine, or visiting her mother's grave in Cimetière Montmartre.

From across an ocean, from the other side of the world, a familiar voice gently beckoned. "*I want you to do what I never could.*"

Véronique bowed her head at the memory of her mother's request, and at the thought that Christophe was no longer in Paris and that Paris was no longer as she remembered. Not according to the contents of Christophe's letter she'd received in New York City upon her arrival. And not according to the newspaper accounts she'd read while there. Weeks old by the time she read them, the reports confirmed Christophe's description of the fall of their beloved city after months of continual besiegement—the citizens of Paris starving, eating all manner of animals just to stay alive—even the rats that roamed the sewers and alleyways.

All of these thoughts wove together to form a cord that snapped taut inside her—bringing her reality to the forefront. She had no other place to go, no one else to whom she could turn.

She lifted her gaze and grew embarrassed at discovering Monsieur Sampson patiently watching her. She took a deep breath and gathered her composure.

"Have I said something to upset you, Miss Girard? If I have, I humbly ask for your pardon, ma'am."

If she wasn't mistaken, Jake Sampson's demeanor had changed

ever so slightly. He possessed a *gentil* quality she had not attributed to him before. "Not at all, Monsieur Sampson." She cleared her throat. "But I do have something to inquire of you. Something that is most important to me."

He remained silent, watchful.

"I am in need of a driver to escort me to neighboring towns in this area. I am willing to pay for the gentleman's services, of course. And if he does not own a suitable carriage, I can afford to pay for that as well."

"A driver, you say." He laid aside the *maillet.* "You mean like a man for hire to take you places?"

"*Oui,* a man for hire. Someone to drive the carriage."

His brow knit, whether from his frown or the smile that followed, she couldn't be certain. "Someone to drive the carriage, huh?"

"*Oui,*" she answered again, this time with less confidence. Why did he keep repeating everything she said?

"I'm afraid I don't know of any men lookin' for a job like that at present, and I'm fresh out of carriages. But if it's a wagon you need, you've come to the right place. I've got one in the back there, ready to go. It's a freighter, made to order. Fella paid half up front and was supposed to pick it up a week ago, but he hasn't showed. Haven't heard from him either." He gave her a discerning look. "How are you at handlin' a team, ma'am?"

"A team?"

"Of horses, ma'am. Do you know anything about drivin' a wagon?"

"Ah . . ." Véronique found herself unable to maintain Monsieur Sampson's gaze. "*Oui,* of course. I have had that *expérience.*" If she counted that one time with Christophe when they'd been riding in the carriage and he'd momentarily handed her the reins. They'd been eleven at the time, if she remembered correctly.

Question lingered in Monsieur Sampson's features. "Why don't you just take the stage, miss? That's a lot easier, not to mention safer and cheaper."

"I have studied this option at length, and the stage route does not encompass where I need to travel." While passing through Denver with Monsieur Bertram Colby, she'd visited a surveyor's office and had procured a list of mining towns in the area surrounding Willow

Springs. According to the map, the communities dotting the landscape didn't appear to be far from each other. She wasn't experienced in map reading but had calculated with relative confidence that the mining operations could be visited in short order.

"And just where are you needin' to go, miss?"

The manner in which he posed the question gave her the impression she was losing his favor, and that was something she could definitely not afford. "I desire to visit your neighboring mining communities, Monsieur Sampson, and I am willing to pay the driver a most *generous* wage."

"Yes, ma'am, I got the generous wage part just fine. But these mining *communities . . .*" He said the last word pointedly, as though it were a question itself. "I don't know what information you're workin' off of but there are no mining *communities* around here—not civilized places where a young woman like yourself ought to be travelin'. No, ma'am." He shook his head. "They're rough and dirty and uncivilized, and I'd hardly call them neighborly. The only drivers that trek up to those camps are rascals who I wouldn't want you goin' with. Not even with me along ridin' shotgun, much less on your lonesome. They'd take advantage of your tender age, and even young as you are I think you're old enough to know what I'm referrin' to." His expression said what his words only hinted at.

Véronique felt her face heat, due in part to the topic of conversation but also at being cast, yet again, as a woman much younger than her actual age. All her life, other people had made decisions for her, and she'd let them, having no choice in the matter. But in past months she had discovered that she did have choices. She liked that difference and wasn't about to surrender it willingly.

"So under the circumstances . . ." Sampson paused. His eyes narrowed for a slight instant. "I'm afraid I can't help you with what you're askin' of me. Not and do it in good conscience. *Je suis désolé*, Mademoiselle Girard," he added, the pronunciation of his apology near faultless.

Véronique couldn't find the words to respond. He'd flatly refused her request, but he'd done it in such a caring manner she couldn't hold him in contempt. So why did her jaw ache so badly? And what was this heat stirring in the center of her chest and spiraling up into her throat? She could scarcely breathe because of it. Monsieur

Sampson's concern for her, however sincere, didn't change her reasons for being there or her determination to see this journey through. Apparently she hadn't made that clear enough.

"Monsieur Sampson, I spent over a month on a ship crossing the Mediterranean Sea and the Atlantic Ocean, caring for four sick children and their *mère* while I myself was ill on more than one occasion. Followed by riding in a train, where I either suffocated from the closed air or choked from cinders and ash blowing in my face. After that *extrême* pleasure, I was stuffed into a coach with five other passengers and jostled for miles in order to get to . . . this place. I have invested much in my journey to stand here before you now." She hiccupped a breath. Her whole body trembled. "And yet you tell me you are intentionally refusing to provide me aid? Might I ask why?"

Fisting her hands at her sides, she waited for him to answer, her words playing back in her mind. Never had she spoken to anyone like this before, much less a stranger and a man as kind as Monsieur Sampson seemed to be.

She bowed her head and kept her attention focused on the caked hem of her skirt. Might Christophe have been right? Was she stronger than she once considered herself to be? But if this behavior could be defined as stronger, should she truly desire such a thing? She fully expected Monsieur Sampson's response to match the *ferveur* of her own, and with good cause. She had spoken out of turn, and to a much older gentleman—no matter that her rank would have far exceeded his in France.

But when she lifted her chin, she saw only kindness and compassion in his eyes.

"When did you last see your father, Mademoiselle Girard?" he asked after a long moment, his voice barely audible over the low crackle of the fire.

Her chin trembled. She couldn't answer.

"Or have you ever seen him?"

She blinked and tears slipped free. "He left for the Americas when I was but a child."

"So he was a trapper."

She nodded. "Before he turned to mining. He was supposed to send for us, my mother and me."

Silence settled between them, unencumbered, as though they'd spoken to one another like this many times before. Something within her told her she could trust Jake Sampson, and she chose to listen to that voice.

"But your father never sent for you, did he. . . . And now you're here, some twenty years later, hoping to find him." Monsieur Sampson's focus flickered past her to the open doors. "Is your mother here with you?"

Oui, in every way but one. She shook her head, her throat tightening. "I left my mother in France," she whispered. "In Cimetière Montmartre."

CHAPTER FIVE

M R. SAMPSON, YOU CERTAINLY do fine work, sir." Having just
come from lunch with the Carlsons, Jack knelt to survey
the undercarriage of the wagon. Reinforcements of wood
and steel crisscrossed the breadth and width of the extra deep wagon
bed, enabling the conveyance to withstand even the heaviest loads he
would demand of it.

He ran a hand along the lower curve of the back wheel and
checked the spokes. *Flawless.* "Bertram Colby recommended you
highly, Mr. Sampson. He said you were this territory's finest wheelwright." He stood slowly, waiting until he had Sampson's full attention. "But I think he was off on that estimation." He hesitated only a
second. "This is the finest built freight wagon I've *ever* seen. And I've
traveled about every mile of trail west of the Mississippi, so I've seen
a slew of them."

Jake Sampson laughed as though the opportunity might not come
around again. "Well, it wouldn't do for me to argue with that, now,
would it, Brennan? I can't be takin' all the credit though. I was just
followin' your instructions, after all." Sampson pulled the checkered
bandanna from around his neck and wiped the layer of sweat from
his brow. "You made the drawings real specific like. I've still got 'em
over there on the bench if you want 'em back."

"What do I need those for? I've got the real thing now." Jack extended his hand. "Thank you for having it ready for me, and I apologize for being a few days late on picking it up. I made an extra stop in Idaho I hadn't planned on."

"I was only startin' to wonder about you. Real worry hadn't set in quite yet." The old man's eyes squinted when he grinned, and his handshake was as solid as his workmanship. "I built this buggy to take just about any grief you wanna give it. But one thing I don't know yet is where you're plannin' on takin' it. You must have some heavy loads and rough country in your sights, son."

"Yes, sir, you could say that." Jack gestured to a bucket of water. "Do you mind?" At Sampson's nod, he filled the ladle and slaked his thirst, speaking in between drinks. "I'll be running the freight service up to the mining towns around here for Hochstetler at the mercantile."

Mild surprise skittered across Sampson's wizened features. "Minin' towns . . . You don't say. I thought some crook by the name of Zimmerman was doin' that."

Jack smiled at the none-too-subtle insinuation. So far not one thing he'd heard about Zimmerman had been complimentary. Made him wonder why Hochstetler had kept the guy on. Jack only hoped his predecessor's widespread reputation wouldn't cast a shadow on him, and he planned on working hard to make sure it didn't. "He did, until he got hurt recently, and then the job came open. I was already looking for work in this area, and Bertram Colby knew it. I had told him where to reach me if anything came open, and he wired me about it. I applied for the job right away." Jack returned the ladle to the bucket. "Hochstetler took me on sight unseen. Colby put in a good word for me, and I know that's what did the trick."

"Colby's a good man. We go way back together. If you're a friend of his, Brennan, you're already one of mine." Sampson considered him for a moment. "You from around these parts?"

"No, sir. I'm originally from Missouri, but I've spent the last several years guiding wagon parties, bringing out new families to fill up all this open space." Something about the way the older man stared at him made Jack wonder if he had something else on his mind. So far Sampson had seemed like a pretty straightforward character. Jack decided to let it play out, give Sampson time to bring up whatever else might be brewing up there.

Jack motioned down the street in the direction of the mercantile. "Hochstetler told me about another couple of storekeepers in the area who are looking to expand their trade. I'll head over and see them this afternoon. I need to leave Monday morning with a full load."

"I might be interested in doin' that, too," Sampson offered. "Let you sell some of my stuff. For the right price, of course."

So that was it. The old man wanted a piece of the pie. "Judging from the quality of your work, Mr. Sampson, I'd welcome whatever you'd like to sell. I'll buy certain kinds of inventory outright and other kinds on consignment, with an agreement that items ordered are ready on the days I'm back in town. I'll also take orders from the miners and work out an agreeable schedule for delivery on your end. Sound fair enough?"

Sampson gave him a calculating look. "How often will you be runnin' up and down the mountain, would you say?"

"I'm figuring at least twice a week. Maybe three times, depending on the distance to the towns and what the weather's like."

"You be travelin' alone, Brennan?"

What was this old codger up to? Was he hinting at wanting to go along? Jack ran his tongue along the inside of his cheek, working hard to hide his grin. "Is there somethin' else you're wanting to ask me, Mr. Sampson? If so, I'd prefer you went ahead and asked me outright. I'll always deal with you that way, sir—straightforward. My word is binding. I'll do what I say I'll do, and I'd appreciate the same courtesy."

A grin split the old wheelwright's face. "That's exactly the kinda man I pegged you for, Brennan." The grin died a hasty death. "Which is why I hate to have to tell you this."

Jack felt a weight drop into the pit of his stomach.

"I had an interested party come by here earlier today askin' about this wagon. Real vocal about needin' it. Willin' to pay cash for it on the spot too."

Jack worked to keep the frustration from his voice. "But this is my wagon. I put a deposit down on it. I sent you the designs, you built it custom for me, just like you said a minute ago."

"I know, I know. That's what makes this so all-fired hard for me to say. . . ."

Jack pulled a wad of bills from his shirt pocket and silently counted. "I have the other half of the payment right here. It's yours." He held out the money. "Mr. Sampson, I need this job, which means I need this wagon." A regular farm wagon wouldn't withstand the load of goods he needed to haul, much less be able to cover the punishing terrain.

Jack took a calming breath, trying to figure out where Sampson was going with this. His thoughts skidded to a halt. "If it's more money you want . . ." He sighed and studied the dirt beneath his boots. He'd invested a sizable amount just to get the wagon and a team of horses. He needed the remainder to cover supplies and inventory, not to mention finding a place to live. He'd hoped to visit the land and title office to see what property might be available. "Listen, Mr. Sampson . . . guiding wagons for thirteen years didn't make me a rich man. You and I had a deal, and in my book the integrity of a man's word is as binding as any contract, written or otherwise."

"Oh, I don't want more money, Mr. Brennan. No, no . . ." Sampson shook his head. "I wouldn't take one penny more than what we agreed on. It's just that . . . we also agreed to a delivery date."

Jack felt the invisible knife in his gut twist a half turn.

"And when that date passed by, well, I think I might've gotten the impression you weren't interested anymore. One thing leadin' to another, I think I might've given that other party the notion that the wagon was available."

"You think you *might've*?" At Sampson's noncommittal shrug, Jack exhaled through clenched teeth and put the money away. "Tell you what, if you'll let me know how to get in touch with this guy, I'll see if I can work something out with him. Maybe he's not in as much of a hurry as I am. You could even use my drawings again and build him the same rig."

Sampson stroked his beard. "We could do it that way, but I got the feelin' that time figured into it for this other person too. Tell you what . . . I think it might be better if I get in touch with them instead, under the circumstances." The old man wriggled his gray brows. "I can be mighty persuasive when I put my whole self into it."

Begrudgingly, Jack made his way back to the Baird and Smith Hotel, hoping Sampson's persuasive talents would work better on the other fella than they'd worked on him.

By the time Véronique met Lilly for lunch, it was half past one. The outdoor restaurant Lilly chose had a dozen or so tables dotting a rare patch of shade beneath the bower of an aging tree. Seeing the blue and white checkered tablecloths fluttering in the breeze, listening to the low hum of conversation and occasional laughter, catching the sweet scent of a pipe, Véronique closed her eyes and, for a moment, was carried back to a street café near the Musée du Louvre.

But only for a moment.

Seeing this place deepened her longing for home—especially when reliving the outcome of her recent meeting with Monsieur Jake Sampson.

But she wasn't about to give up. She'd come too far to simply *abandonner* her plans at the first major obstacle. Drivers with carriages for hire were plentiful in Paris. Not so here, it would seem. But as Christophe had once told her—referring to certain members of parliament around the time when final votes were being cast—money was a powerful motivator. Lord Marchand had been overly generous with her, therefore allowing her to be the same with others.

Surely there existed in Willow Springs one honorable man who would be willing to take her offer and escort her to these towns.

"Do you not like your food?" Lilly leaned closer, her voice low. "I can order something else, if you want."

Véronique blinked, then peered down at the untouched beef still occupying half of her plate. "Brisket" is what Lilly had called it, but the glistening slab of meat slathered in a brownish sauce Véronique could not identify held no appeal, despite Lilly's compliments to the *restaurateur*. "I am certain it is delicious. I . . . simply do not have much hunger at the moment." As if on cue, her stomach growled. Véronique cleared her throat in hopes of covering the sound.

Lilly stopped chewing. The telling lift of her brow indicated she hadn't found the lie convincing, yet the smile immediately following said it was already forgiven. "I can tell something's wrong, Mademoiselle Girard. I don't know what it is, but I'd like to help if I can."

Véronique smoothed the napkin on her lap, considering just how much to tell Lilly. The girl was so young, yet displayed such maturity for her—

Something from the corner of Véronique's vision caught her attention. A man crossing the street directly in front of the establishment.

She recognized him instantly, and even with the scowl he bore, the display of kindness she'd witnessed from him toward Monsieur Colby the night before couldn't be erased from her memory. His determined stride would have easily counted for three of her own, and she followed his progress until he rounded the corner out of sight. She eased back in her chair, staring in the direction he'd gone. What would ignite such anger in a man whose laughter so easily persuaded a smile?

"Mademoiselle Girard?"

Lilly's voice drew her attention back yet again. Seeing concern in the girl's expression, Véronique felt instant regret. "*Je suis désolée,* Lilly. I was somewhere else for a moment."

Lilly repeated the unfamiliar phrase, her pronunciation near perfect. "That means 'I'm sorry'?"

Nodding, Véronique glanced down at her lap. "My compliments on how swiftly you learn, but . . ." She sighed. "I fear I am not good company at the moment. My meeting with Monsieur Sampson at the livery did not bring the resolution I sought."

Lilly paused between bites. "He couldn't recommend a driver to you?"

Wouldn't was more like it, but Véronique didn't wish to disparage the older gentleman to Lilly. His motives—however uninvited and misplaced—appeared to have been rooted in her best interest. "He knew of no drivers currently seeking employment. But he did offer me the sale of a wagon." She summoned a smile. "Unfortunately, my skill in the art of driving is what you would call . . ."

Unable to find the exact word she desired, Véronique reached into her *réticule* and withdrew a tiny volume entitled *Grammar and Proper Usage of the English Language.* At times she still fumbled for the correct English word. And on occasion, her native tongue crept into conversation, especially if the words were similar in the two languages.

She flipped the dog-eared pages, scanning as she went. "Ah! My driving skills are what you would call . . . deficient."

Lilly grinned, but Véronique could see the wheels turning behind those violet eyes. She had yet to confide in Lilly about her reasons for being in Willow Springs. Lilly had assumed, as had Monsieur Bertram Colby, that she was here on an excursion for pleasure with plans to visit the surrounding countryside. What a ludicrous thought—that someone would travel all the way from Paris, France, for a pleasure trip here.

Véronique made mental note of the new word and put the book away. She gave thought to telling Lilly the truth, knowing how far-fetched her reason for coming to America sounded. But she also battled the recurring thought that, even though she'd been a *petite fille* at the time, perhaps she was somehow to blame for her father's never returning to Paris. Her mother had repeatedly assured her that was not the case, but the doubt lingered.

Setting her misgivings aside, Véronique decided to confide in her new friend. And beginning with her mother's last wish, she shared the entire story, feeling her burden lift considerably as the details unfolded.

Lilly listened, never interrupting. She finally blew out an exaggerated breath. "That's one of the most beautiful things I've ever heard, Mademoiselle Girard. I can't imagine what you've been through to get here."

"*Oui*, the past months have been difficult, but the most arduous portion of my journey still awaits. Yet I feel as though already I have reached an *impasse*."

"Something we could try . . ." Lilly leaned forward, using her fork to help make her point. "Is to list an advertisement for a driver at the post office. My papa's done that before. Mr. Brantley has a bulletin board where people post notices for services or supplies they want or need. We could also tack some signs up around town. And we could put your father's name on there . . . to see if anyone remembers him."

Véronique's mood brightened with the suggestions. "*Merci*, Lilly, those are wonderful ideas!"

Lilly scrunched her nose. "Only thing is, I think Mr. Brantley charges five cents for each item you post on his wall."

Véronique waved the comment away. "Is your post office open at this hour?"

"Sure. But first . . ." Lilly's gaze dropped briefly to Véronique's plate. "I'd really like it if you'd try Mrs. Hudson's creamed potatoes."

"Thank you, but—"

"They're delicious . . . I promise."

The lilt of Lilly's sweet voice coaxed Véronique to take one cautious bite. Then another. The whipped potatoes tasted of fresh cream and butter, light and smooth, with not a lump to be found. *"Très délicieuse."* Enduring a look of triumph from young Lilly, Véronique finished the entire serving.

But as they rose, she threw a parting glance of disapproval at the untouched brisket on her plate.

If someone forced her to name one good thing about this territory, without question Véronique would have to answer . . . the sunsets. Pausing outside the boardwalk of the hotel that evening, she lingered for several moments, memorizing the hues of *orange* and *lavande* as they hovered like a vapor over the mountain peaks.

As the sun sank lower, the mingled shades grew paler, spilling down among the canyons and ravines with languid grace until finally the colors gathered among the clefts and crevices in pools of dusky violet and gray. Watching the magnificent display, she felt a rare moment of concession. Silently, she acknowledged that while Paris was still most beautiful in her memory, this was one exhibition her beloved city could not claim.

Her mind went to the trunk in her hotel room that contained her canvases and paints. Christophe had insisted she bring them. The trunk remained securely fastened, the leather straps still cinched taut by Christophe's hand. In her state of mind while packing to leave Paris, she hadn't wanted to bring the items. And her differing opinion had spawned a disagreement between her and Christophe on their last afternoon together.

"You have been given a gift, *ma petite*, and there will come a time when you will want these again. If you leave them here, I fear their ill fate will be secured."

She took the rolled canvases from him and laid them aside. "I have no further need of these, Christophe. We both know what low opinion Monsieur Touvliér has of my talent. I'm fooling myself to think I could ever—"

"You are fooling yourself, Véronique, to believe one person's word over the passion you feel inside when you cradle the brush in your hand. Or when you capture a piece of time and history in your perspective and make it your own." He shook his head, his voice softening. "Do not so hastily discard a dream for one man's opinion, *ma petite*. After all, for whatever else he may be, Monsieur Touvliér is just that . . . one man."

Véronique doubted whether the painting supplies had fared well in the journey overseas, or in this arid clime. She hadn't attempted to paint in over a year, but she had tried her hand at sketching a few weeks back.

Nothing.

Everything she'd drawn had been disproportionate to everything else. Or else lacked any sense of life or movement—or originality. What gifts God had so generously given her before, it would seem He had recalled with equal completeness for some unknown reason.

Her gaze settled on the rocky clefts where deepening purples gave way to expanding darkness. Did anything remain that she could do in order to win back God's favor in that regard? If yes, He held the answer just out of her grasp.

As she crossed the hotel lobby, Mr. Baird, the proprietor, glanced up from behind the front desk. He lowered his newspaper and stared at her across wire-rimmed spectacles. "Miss Girard, I was hoping to catch you before you turned in for the night. A note came for you earlier."

"A note?" Véronique's first thought was that Christophe had written again, but seeing the plain piece of folded paper in Mr. Baird's hand, she quickly dismissed that hope. Perhaps it was a response to the advertisement for a driver that she'd placed at the post office earlier that afternoon. She'd indicated for all interested parties to contact her at the hotel. Which reminded her, she needed to make Mr. Baird aware of that.

He nodded as she explained. "Oh, that's fine by me, Miss Girard. I'll be sure and tell the boss so she'll know to be on the lookout too."

She stared for a moment, not understanding.

Mr. Baird chuckled. "I was referrin' to my wife . . . Mrs. Baird." He winked. "She's the real boss around here. I just do whatever the good woman tells me."

"*Merci.*" Véronique took the note, giving a slight nod. She was gradually becoming accustomed to the informalities so common among the people of this country, even if she didn't claim to understand them. She scanned the brief missive, unsure what to make of it at first.

"Good news, I hope," Mr. Baird commented, returning to his newspaper.

Véronique read the note again, and smiled. "*Oui,* I believe it is. My sincere thanks, monsieur." With a bounce to her step, she was to the stairs before she remembered. "Monsieur Baird, would you be so kind as to draw me a bath this evening?"

"You betcha, ma'am . . . though it might be a while." He pointed directly above them. "Another guest just went in there a minute ago. He should be done soon enough, then I'll give your door a knock."

She sighed, wishing for a bath but even more for bed. "I'm rather tired. Could I request that it be drawn first thing in the morning instead?"

After arranging the time, Véronique climbed the stairs to the third floor. Shared lavatories were not unknown to her. They were common enough in Paris, in the lower classes. But sharing with someone of the opposite sex—that was a new experience. One for which she had yet to develop an *affinité*.

She reached the third-floor landing and a sloshing sound drew her attention. She paused. Looking up, she realized she'd stopped right by the lavatory. Footfalls coming closer from the other side of the door sent her racing down the hallway. Once safely inside her room, she collapsed on the bed and giggled at her overreaction, then glanced again at the note from Monsieur Jake Sampson.

It read: *Mademoiselle Girard, come by the livery first thing in the morning. Your carriage awaits.*

VÉRONIQUE STEPPED INTO the steaming bath and slowly sank down. With her shoulders pressed back against the tub, she stretched out her legs. The hot water seeped into her muscles, tingling, relaxing. *Heavenly*, but for one thing—did Americans have something against scented bath water? Or perhaps they simply hadn't yet learned about perfumed baths from their European cousins.

She still had a good foot of space before her feet touched the opposite end, so she slid down farther and dunked her head, thoroughly soaking her hair. Breaking the surface again, she wiped the water from her face and breathed the moist air deep into her lungs.

Monsieur Sampson's note came to mind. Contemplating what he'd meant by it, she rubbed the coarse block of soap between her palms and smoothed the lather over her arms and legs. The arid climate of this territory was drying out her skin, and this soap certainly wasn't going to help any. She'd used the last of her favorite lemon and sage grass lotion three weeks ago, having carefully rationed it since leaving Paris. Perhaps the mercantile could order—

The latch on the washroom door jiggled.

Instinctively, Véronique sank deeper into the tub, wishing there were bubbles to aid her intent. Had she slid the lock on the door into place? Certainly she had. . . .

The door handle rattled again.

"This room is *occupée*," she called out.

Silence. Then what sounded like the clearing of a man's throat.

"I'm sorry, ma'am. I didn't think anybody would be in there this early. I . . . I just came for my shirt. I think I left it in there last night."

Véronique peeked over the edge of the tub, then back at the door. "*Oui*, I believe you are right. I see a garment hanging in the corner. However, I am . . . unable to come to the door at this moment."

"Ah . . . no, ma'am . . . I mean . . . yes, ma'am. I understand. You just take your time. I'm in no hurry."

Breathing a sigh of relief, Véronique rinsed off and reached for her towel.

"I'm sorry to have bothered you, ma'am."

The sound of his voice sent her plunging again. Water sloshed over the sides and back of the tub. "You have caused me no bother." She brushed a strand of wet hair from her face. "But that is changing quite rapidly," she added softly, certain she heard a soft chuckle come from beyond the door. She waited for the sound of retreating footsteps. Hearing none, she peered over the edge and saw a shadow beneath the door. "I am aware that you are still there, monsieur."

"Ah . . . yes, ma'am. I . . . I'm just going to wait outside here so I can get my shirt."

Rising slightly, Véronique checked for cracks in the door. Detecting none, she climbed from the tub, ran a towel over her body, and then pulled on her dressing gown. The robe covered her adequately, but she blushed at the idea of a strange man seeing her dressed like this. And even more at his apparent lack of trust.

"Monsieur, I am no thief. I assure you, I will not attempt to abscond from the lavatory with your shirt."

Another soft chuckle. This time louder than the first, and affirming what she thought she'd heard earlier. "No, ma'am. You don't sound much like an . . . absconder to me. It's just that I've got something in the pocket there that's mighty valuable, and I want to make sure it doesn't wander off."

Now curious, and emboldened by his lack of decorum, Véronique crossed the room and lifted the shirt from the hook. She peeked inside the front pocket and instantly realized his cause for concern. Glancing back at the door, she had a sudden thought. "What is in the pocket of your garment, monsieur, that is so valuable to you?"

Silence, then the creak of a floorboard. "Are you just about done in there, ma'am?"

Véronique held back a giggle, enjoying being the one with the *avantage*. "*Oui* . . . just about." She returned the shirt to its hook and rushed through her morning ritual. She cleaned her teeth and combed and towel-dried her hair, more conscious of her movements, and of time's passing, knowing he was waiting.

When she was done, she opened the door. And immediately wished she could close it again.

Jack had to lower his gaze significantly just to look the woman in the eye—but it was well worth the effort. She glanced at him, then looked away again, and he got the impression she wasn't completely comfortable with him.

Reasonable, under the circumstances.

He maintained his distance in hopes of putting her more at ease. "I'm sorry for having startled you a few minutes ago, miss. I wasn't expecting anyone to be in the washroom this early."

She briefly looked up before once again confining her attention to the floor. "Thank you. I accept your kind *apologie*, monsieur."

He smiled, realizing he'd correctly guessed her native tongue moments before.

She gestured behind her toward his shirt. "As you can see . . . there it hangs."

Recognizing the familiar fabric and seeing the outline in the front pocket, Jack felt the tension in his gut begin to relax. How could he have been so foolish? But he'd been so upset last night, so frustrated with Jake Sampson and the whole situation, that he hadn't been thinking straight. He stepped to one side, allowing the woman space to exit. The shirt was hanging exactly where he'd left it. He quickly counted the money, and experienced a rush of relief. Fortunate for him that such an honest woman had been first to use the washroom.

"Your garment is safe, monsieur. In the same condition you left it last night, *non*?"

Her expression was all sweetness, yet something in her tone seemed to mock him. But with his money safe in hand again, Jack didn't care. "Yes, ma'am. Looks as if everything is in order, thank you."

He closed the bathroom door behind them, and before he knew it, she was several paces ahead of him down the hall. She walked fast for being so little, but he caught up with her easily, not wanting her to leave just yet. No doubt she knew what was in his shirt pocket—he could sense it. And he rarely misjudged people in that regard. "I appreciate you acting with such integrity, ma'am. Not everyone would have done as you did."

Pausing in front of room 308, she reached into her pocket and withdrew a key. "*Oui*, you should be grateful to me, monsieur. It was a most arduous task."

There it was again, that hint of mockery in her voice. Though he couldn't see her expression, he definitely heard her smile this time.

She tried fitting her key into the lock and achieved success on her third attempt, still apparently unwilling to look at him. The thought that he might be the object of her discomfort both bothered and encouraged him.

The front and shoulders of her robe were slightly damp from her freshly-washed hair. Her belt was cinched modestly tight, preventing any gapping in the fabric, yet her care at swaddling herself so only served to accentuate the curve of her small waist and slender hips. Recognizing the drift in his focus, Jack pulled his attention back and was pleased to actually find her looking at him. Whatever this young woman lacked in height, she made up for in every other way.

She was completely stunning—and much too young for him.

He took a step back. Being thirty-eight years old hardly meant he had one foot in the grave, but he would place her age around twenty years his junior, and that was too big of a difference in his book. No matter what the opinions or practices of others might be. Anyway, he'd been looking forward to lightening his load these days, to being responsible only for himself. Isn't that what he'd told Pastor Carlson? Suddenly those words had a hollow ring to them.

"Well, thank you again, ma'am. I sincerely appreciate your honesty." *And I hope our paths cross again sometime* is what he wanted to add, but didn't. Still, something told him the chances of that happening were good.

Jack walked back down the hallway, fully aware that she hadn't yet shut her door. Once he heard the click of the latch behind him, he retraced his steps, pulled out his own key, and entered the room directly across from hers.

CHAPTER SEVEN

WHEN VÉRONIQUE DESCENDED the stairs to the hotel lobby an hour later, business appeared to be brisk for a Friday morning. At the front desk, Monsieur Baird assisted a couple with two small children while four other gentlemen waited off to the side.

The men didn't resemble the kind of patrons Véronique had seen staying at the hotel. They had the appearance of hired hands, only slightly rougher around the edges, and the way they looked at her sent prickles of warning skittering up her arms and neck. Perhaps Monsieur Baird had engaged their services for a specific task at the hotel. If so, he would be well advised to instruct his workmen to use the back entrance next time.

As she crossed the lobby, one of the men bolted forward, blocking her path.

"Miss Girard, isn't it?" Butchering her name, he thrust out his hand, breaking all *étiquette* in the process.

Caught off guard, Véronique backed up a step. The man addressing her was tall, with a thick build, and had obviously consumed a breakfast *entrée* which included onions as a main ingredient. How did he know who she was? She stared pointedly at his hand until he returned it to his side.

"I'm here to speak with you, ma'am." He cast a glance at the three men behind him. "And I'd like to make it known that I was first in line."

First in line? Véronique didn't know what he was referring to, but she was relatively certain that whatever it was, it could not be of lesser priority to her.

The other men suddenly stepped forward to form a half circle around her, all speaking at once.

"Miss Girard! A word with you, please." Monsieur Baird's voice boomed over them all.

Véronique skirted around the wall of men to see the proprietor striding toward her. He wore a severe expression, and she got the distinct impression he was unhappy with her.

"May we speak in the dining room, Miss Girard?"

Grateful for his timely rescue, she glanced at the clock on the front desk. Jake Sampson would be expecting her at the livery any time now.

"This won't take long, I promise," Monsieur Baird added as though reading her mind, his clipped tone persuasive. He indicated for her to follow him.

Once inside the dining room, he closed the double doors behind them. Monsieur Baird acknowledged the patrons occupying several of the tables, then guided Véronique farther to the back. "Miss Girard . . ." His voice was hushed. "Those men in there are answering the notice you posted yesterday."

Véronique shook her head. "That can't be. . . ." She glanced back at the closed doors, able to picture the men all too clearly in her mind's eye. "None of them fit the description for which I advertised. I specifically requested—"

"My guess, Miss Girard, is that you listed *your* name on that advertisement." His dark brows slowly rose over the rims of his spectacles. "Am I correct?"

Her mind raced, trying to follow the turn of his thoughts and failing to do so. She nodded in answer to his question.

"I realize this is none of my business, ma'am, and you're free to tell me so after I'm done. But seeing as you're quite young and might not be aware of certain things, I feel it's my duty to step in here."

She stiffened at his comment about her age. Always, people were making that assumption. Always, they were making decisions for her—and she was weary of it. Forcing a smile she hoped passed for pleasant, she determined to change that—starting now. "I appreciate your concern, monsieur, but I want to make it clear to you that I am capable of making decisions for myself. I have traveled all the way from Paris, France, to get to this—"

Monsieur Baird held up a hand. "Miss Girard, this has nothing to do with whether you're capable or not. You're a very capable young woman, I've no doubt about that. I also have no doubt as to why those men showed up in answer to your advertisement." His features softened. "Willow Springs is a small town, ma'am. Word travels fast here. Everybody in this town knows who you are."

She frowned. "But I have been here for only two days."

"Like I said, ma'am, this is a small town and . . . I don't mean any disrespect by this, but we don't get many women from Paris, France, through here." He smiled. "And you tend to make a lasting first impression, Miss Girard. But those men in there . . ." He shook his head. "They came here for all the wrong reasons. Trust me on that. And for the record, just because you're capable of doing something, ma'am—like listing this advertisement—doesn't necessarily mean you should."

She wanted to object, but the truth behind his statement wouldn't allow it.

He gave a heavy sigh. "In the end, it's your decision. But I've got three daughters about your age, and I wouldn't dare let a one of them set off anywhere with those men in there, much less up to the mountains. I'm sure if your father were here, he'd feel the same way."

Véronique's breath caught. A stinging sensation rose to her eyes. Monsieur Baird did not know her reason for being in Willow Springs, so there was no way he could know how much his last comment had hurt her. She lowered her face. The obvious love this man possessed for his daughters only deepened her regret over her own father's absence from her life. The reminder of what she'd had—and lost— was keen, and razor sharp.

She cleared her throat, forcing down the rising tide of emotion. "I appreciate what you have said to me, Monsieur Baird," she whispered. "I acted in haste and did not consider with proper care the outcome of my actions." She glanced again at the door, dreading having to face those men again.

He trailed her gaze and then gave her an unexpected wink. "Would you mind if I took care of those rowdies in there? It would do this father's heart a world of good."

Relieved beyond words, Véronique wished she could hug him. But she settled for a curtsy instead and made her exit out the kitchen entrance.

She arrived at the livery later than planned, and just as she had imagined, Monsieur Sampson was busy seeing to other customers. She waited off to one side, giving him a small wave when he acknowledged her presence with a smile. Her nerves were taut, partly from all that had happened that morning, but also from anticipating what Monsieur Sampson was going to tell her.

Finally there came a moment between customers when they could speak in private.

"Good mornin', Mademoiselle Girard." Jake Sampson wiped his hands on a soiled cloth, then made a show of scrutinizing her gown. He let out a low whistle. "I gotta say, ma'am, you're 'bout the prettiest thing I've seen so far today. One of these years I'm gonna have to get myself over to Paris. Does everybody over there dress so fancy, the way you do?"

The question, innocent enough, brought her up short. Particularly in light of Monsieur Baird's earlier comment about her making a "lasting first impression." Véronique smoothed a hand over the lilac fabric, suddenly self-conscious. It was one of her plainer dresses and by far not a favorite. Yet it was a great deal finer than any other garment she'd seen anyone wearing in this town. Studying Jake Sampson's attire, she seriously doubted whether he owned a suit or even a shirt of its equal. That realization prompted an unexpected shyness, and she looked away.

She'd lived such a privileged life in comparison to others. How could she have lived that way for so long being blind to that fact?

"*Merci beaucoup.* You are most kind, Monsieur Sampson. And I think you would very much adore the *ville* in which I was born and raised." It was a safer answer, in light of not knowing what the recent months of war had done to her beloved city. "I offer my apologies for not being here sooner. I was delayed at the hotel but am eager to learn what you have to tell me." She glanced about. "And to see this carriage you wrote about in your note."

He gestured toward the back of the livery.

She turned, only to see the same oversized farm wagon she'd noticed the day before. It hosted no canopy, no plush compartment, and no seating other than the wooden bench the driver would occupy. She tried to mask her disappointment, to think of something to say that would ease the silence growing heavier by the second, and failed.

"I know it's not what you were expectin', ma'am, and for sure not what you're used to. But it'll get you where you're wantin' to go—I promise you that."

The man's tone had taken on a forced quality that caused Véronique's face to heat. She crossed the distance to get a closer look at the conveyance, and to hide her embarrassment. The boards of the wagon bed fit flush together—no cracks for sunlight to peek through—and they were connected with thick bolts, some as thick around as her fist. Though she was unfamiliar with such construction, the careful details of Monsieur Sampson's workmanship clearly bespoke a man who took pride in what he did.

She ran a hand over one of the rear wheels, regretting her initial reaction. "*Au contraire*, Monsieur Sampson. This is one of the most finely built wagons I have ever seen. And it will serve my purpose well. *Merci beaucoup*."

"You're most welcome, mademoiselle," he said quietly. "Turns out a fella came in here yesterday and told me the very same thing, which leads to why I sent you that note. He's new to Willow Springs but comes with high marks from a man I've known for years. And 'til the sun decides to start risin' in the west, you can bet that friend's word can be trusted."

"Does this . . . *fella* have experience as a driver?"

A faint smile curved Monsieur Sampson's mouth. "You're catchin' on real quick to our words. And yes, ma'am, this gentleman's driven his share of wagons, all right. He's been guidin' folks for over thirteen years."

Véronique considered this while wondering how to phrase her next question. Lacking savvy in business dealings, she decided to get straight to the point. "What is the price of this conveyance, monsieur?" Her hand went to her *réticule.* "I can deliver payment to you this morning."

"That's all fine and good, mademoiselle, and I'm sure we can agree on a price. But there's a few things you and I need to get straight before I get you and this gentleman together. First off, I need to let you know that he doesn't—"

"Good morning, Mr. Sampson."

The voice coming from behind Véronique sounded vaguely familiar. And if her *intuition* was correct, she'd heard it before—through a bathroom door that very morning.

M R. BRENNAN!" Monsieur Sampson strode toward the front of the livery, meeting the gentleman halfway. "I wasn't expectin' you back here quite this early."

While she'd hoped to see the man again, Véronique hadn't expected it to be so soon after their first encounter. She smoothed a hand over her hair and thought of how she'd looked earlier that morning. Hopefully, he would consider this an improvement.

Monsieur Brennan shook Sampson's hand. "I was out and just thought I'd stop by to see if you'd heard anything yet." He turned in Véronique's direction and removed his hat. "Ma'am, it's nice to see you again."

"Likewise . . . Monsieur Brennan." Véronique offered a brief curtsy, enjoying having the *avantage* for the second time that morning. As she lifted her head, she watched a slow smile curve his mouth. It softened the strong angular lines of his face and brought out the kindness in his features. His smile captured both the mischief of a boy and the awareness of a man, and she found the effect . . . intoxicating.

"You two know each other already?" Monsieur Sampson's attention darted between the two of them.

"We had the pleasure of meeting at the hotel this morning. Briefly." The subtle tilt of his head made her think he was most likely reliving the details.

Véronique worked to keep her smile as subdued as his. "Monsieur Brennan left something of value behind—" her focus flickered to the telling outline in his front pocket—"and I had the opportunity to provide safekeeping for the item."

"And it was a most arduous task for you, if I remember correctly, mademoiselle?"

"*Oui,*" she whispered, mildly impressed with Monsieur Brennan's pronunciation. But far more with his gift at *repartie.*

After a moment, Monsieur Brennan turned back. "Mr. Sampson, I need a final answer from you, sir. I've got rounds to make to my vendors over the next couple of days. I need to arrange for supplies and get them inventoried and loaded. The buyer in Jenny's Draw expects his delivery from Hochstetler no later than Monday after-noon, which means I need to leave at sunup that day."

Jake Sampson ran a hand over his beard as though giving this news his full consideration. "That sounds like a good plan, Brennan. Yes sir, it does. Mighty thorough on your part to think things through like that."

If Véronique interpreted Monsieur Brennan's expression correctly, he had anticipated quite a different response. She sensed his frustra-tion and, in part, shared it. The thread of this conversation seemed a touch frayed.

"Mr. Sampson . . ." Brennan's posture stiffened slightly. "I need you to tell me outright—is that wagon mine or not?"

It took a moment for the question to register with her. Was the wagon *his* or not? Véronique's attention moved between the two men as she waited for Jake Sampson to tell Mr. Brennan that the wagon was already sold. That it belonged to her, or would, as soon as she paid for it.

But he didn't.

She stepped forward with the intent of clearing up the misunder-standing, but Monsieur Sampson's look of warning kept her silent.

"The problem, Mr. Brennan," Sampson said, rubbing the back of his neck, "is that I'm in a bit of a quandary here. The other person I told you about is still interested in the wagon. In fact, they've told me they want to buy it."

Véronique relaxed at Monsieur Sampson's admission, but she didn't approve of the way he was handling the situation. Why didn't he reveal that she was the person buying the wagon instead of acting like it was someone else? Perhaps it was customary here to spare patrons the angst and embarrassment of bidding for the same conveyance. But they were all adults. Monsieur Brennan would understand that she'd simply gotten there first.

"Did you try speaking with him?" The muscles in Monsieur Brennan's jawline corded tight, much like Christophe's used to do before his temper erupted. "Did you ask if they could wait until you got another one built? Timing is crucial for me, sir."

Monsieur Brennan's voice had deepened with resolve, but still he maintained his gentlemanly decorum, and Véronique's estimation of his character grew immensely. Her mother had always said that the true measure of a person was best observed when dealing with adversity. And judging from the scowl on Monsieur Brennan's face, the situation was most decidedly adverse for him at the moment.

"This person needs that wagon now too, Mr. Brennan." Monsieur Sampson remained firm on his position, yet humble in tone. The two men were well matched in that respect. "They have a lot of traveling to do. And they need to do it before winter sets in. Some of the places they're needin' to get to are treacherous come first snowfall, so timing figures into things for them as much as it does for you. But I got the impression they'd be real open to workin' a deal with you—in exchange for your services."

At the mention of a deal, Véronique's concern was resurrected. Why did she need Monsieur Brennan's services? The wagon belonged to her, not him.

"In exchange for my services? They want me to haul something for them?"

Monsieur Sampson gave a half-hearted nod. "In a manner of speakin'. You'd get full use of the wagon though, whenever you want it . . . at no cost to you."

Hearing that, Véronique readied an objection. How was her driver supposed to escort her to mining towns while her wagon was at Monsieur Brennan's constant beck and call? "*Excusez-moi, messieurs.* I must interrupt—"

"And you'll get all this, Mr. Brennan," Sampson continued, his tone unusually firm, "in exchange for allowin' this person to ride along with you on your trips from time to time."

Poised to argue, Véronique felt an imaginary veil being yanked away. She gradually let out the breath she was holding and turned to look at Monsieur Brennan. *He* was the driver to whom Jake Sampson had referred earlier? The one with all the experience, who came so highly recommended?

With that discovery, she felt a weight lift from her shoulders. God had provided a driver to see her journey to its fruition.

A renewed sense of hope took hold inside. From Bertram Colby's reaction to seeing Monsieur Brennan the other night, she had already guessed him to be an honorable man. He was exactly the type of man she needed to provide her safe passage to the mining towns where she could locate her father, Pierre Gustave Girard. The man her mother had loved in life and to whom she had remained faithful unto death.

Véronique felt it again—the same rising tide of emotion she'd experienced when speaking with Monsieur Baird at the hotel that morning. Only now she knew what it was . . . the fledgling love of a child. Like a tender green shoot, it sprouted from a root in dry and sterile ground somewhere deep inside her—the love for a man she couldn't remember, and a father she might still never know.

Her gaze slowly trailed to the wagon, then back to Monsieur Brennan. She'd never been astute at bargaining, but this was one *négociation* she was determined not to lose.

CHAPTER | NINE

J ACK WASN'T CERTAIN he'd heard the woman correctly. Through
a haze of lingering frustration and anger, he looked down at her.
"You want me to be your *what*, ma'am?"

"My driver, monsieur. I will compensate you well and will allow you
use of my wagon when you are not escorting me on my journeys."

"Escorting you on your journeys?"

She nodded, her smile leaving no doubt that she considered her
offer acceptable, if not overly generous, and that the deal between
them had been struck.

The woman could not have been more mistaken.

"Ma'am . . . mademoiselle," he corrected, making sure he had the
livery owner's attention, "I don't know what you and Mr. Sampson
have cooked up between you, but if you think I'm going to agree to
the two of us traveling up in the mountains together, going to mining
towns, of all places . . ." He sighed and shook his head. "I wish to
inform you as gently as possible . . . that you are mistaken."

Frankly, he couldn't believe Jake Sampson would even propose
such a thing, much less be party to it. He would've thought the older
gentleman had more respect—first for this young woman's reputation, and second for his being a normal red-blooded male.

Jack had to admit . . . if he'd considered this lady pretty before, he
had been wrong. She was captivating.

Her smile faded. Confusion clouded her features.

The sudden change tugged at his sense of honor, until he realized it was his sense of honor that wouldn't allow him to agree to such a cockeyed plan.

"Mademoiselle—" Jack hesitated, realizing he didn't know the woman's name. From the awareness in her eyes, he guessed she was thinking the very same thing.

He could already tell she would be a handful to travel with. Not that he was going to—he wasn't—but he'd seen his share of female travelers through the years. At the outset of a journey, he could pretty well peg which women would adjust to the hardships and make the trip fine, which ones would have more of a problem adapting, and which ones would most likely be the death of him along the way.

She offered a curtsy befitting an emperor's court, gracefully sweeping her skirt to one side. "*Je m'appelle*—" she rose slowly, her smile radiant—"Mademoiselle Véronique Evelyn Girard."

Oh, this woman was *definitely* part of the latter group. Jack couldn't help but smile at that thought, then immediately feared she would misconstrue his reaction.

If the rekindled hope in her expression could serve as evidence, she'd done just that. "I am certain, monsieur, that we can come to some type of arrangement that will be agreeable to you. Your associates speak most highly of you, and your experience in being a driver is extensive, *non?*"

Jack supposed that what he'd dedicated the past thirteen years of his life to could be summed up as a kind of "driving." But the way she said it made his past profession seem far less a contribution to mankind than he would have liked. And he'd always hoped to leave something of a lasting legacy. But that was his pride talking, and he knew it. "Mademoiselle Girard, I am honored that you would entrust me with your safety, but this arrangement is simply unsuitable, for more reasons than I care to number."

She frowned. "You do not know the entire arrangement, as I have not told you what your compensation will be. And yet you find it unsuitable?"

Jack acknowledged the two men entering the livery just then, not missing the object of their stares or what manner of men they were. Another customer wandered in after them. "When I said unsuitable, I wasn't referring to—"

"I have in mind to pay you seven dollars for each day that you escort me to these neighboring communities." She opened her reticule. "I have monies with me now and can pay several days in *avance*, if that is your wish."

"Ma'am, please"—Jack moved to shield the stack of bills from view—"put your money away. It's not safe to flaunt cash in public like that." As if the woman herself wasn't enough of a temptation. . . .

"I was not *flaunting* my money, Monsieur Brennan." Offense cooled her tone, as well as those brown eyes. "I was demonstrating that I am capable of providing remuneration for your services."

Jack hesitated before answering. Seems no matter what he said, he said the wrong thing. "That fact was never in question, ma'am. I was only trying to protect your interests, not . . . correct some social blunder."

She nodded, pursing her lips. "You mean a *faux pas*."

He stared for a second. "Pardon me?"

"A *faux pas* is a blunder of some sort. It refers to either an action or an utterance, and can be made in public or in a personal setting."

Already familiar with the meaning, Jack allowed her to go on dissecting the word limb by limb as he kept a close eye on the two men nearby. Jake Sampson was assisting the other customer, but Jack instinctively knew the livery owner had eyes in the back of his head.

"But the word"—she squinted as if trying to recall something—"in the sense you wielded it, Monsieur Brennan, denotes making a mistake through stupidity or carelessness or ignorance."

In addition to being captivating, the woman must've had one whopping dictionary as a child. Her expression mirrored such pride that Jack almost hated to burst her bubble—almost. "You've missed the point entirely, Mademoiselle Girard. I was explaining to you that when I asked you not to flaunt your money, my motives were rooted in trying to protect you. I was not accusing you of having committed some . . . *faux pas*, as you called it."

"*Oui*, but . . ." She pulled some kind of book from her reticule and began flipping through the pages. She stopped, her eyes widening. "Ah . . . the word *flaunt* means 'to display in a pretentious or disregarding manner.'" She tilted the page in his direction, her finger moving along as she read aloud. "'To obtrude oneself to public notice, or to treat contemptuously.'" She snapped the book shut, both her smile and manner demure beyond question. "Of those listed behaviors, monsieur, I was quite innocent. That is why I felt the obligation to—"

Jack held up his hand, and would've gladly waved a white flag if he'd had one. "Perhaps I should have chosen a different word, mademoiselle."

"Ah," she said again, punctuating the air with a dainty forefinger. "Words carry very specific meanings, *non*? Which is why you must be more careful in your choice of them."

Some fairly choice words for her came to mind at the moment, but Jack kept them to himself. He might've enjoyed her innocent observations under different circumstances, but as he caught a glimpse of his wagon—correction, *her* wagon—he could only think about what this mishap was going to cost him, both in time and money.

He would visit the other vendors in town this afternoon, see if any of them happened to have a freight wagon available for lease—even short term. If not, he'd be forced to visit the mercantile and advise Mr. Hochstetler that there would be a delay in the scheduled pickups and deliveries—something he wanted to avoid if at all possible.

Years of living like a nomad had taught him to remain flexible, to exercise eyes of faith in seeing beyond the crisis at the moment. In the whole scheme of things, not being able to purchase this particular wagon wasn't that big of a setback. It wasn't the loss of someone he loved, or of someone who had been entrusted to his care. Now, if only he could convince Mr. Hochstetler at the mercantile to see things that way.

The two men who had been loitering in the livery—shopping, as it were—finally left. Jack took that as his cue. "Mademoiselle Girard, I wish you all the best in your endeavors, and if you would allow me to be plainspoken with you, ma'am . . ."

What light her expression held slowly receded. "You are refusing my offer, Monsieur Brennan?"

Such innocence. Part of him felt concern for her, and yet, he reminded himself, she was not his concern. "Yes, ma'am, I am," he said quietly. "And I'd be remiss if I didn't at least try to persuade you to stay away from the mining camps. You referred to them as neighboring communities . . . they're nothing of the sort. They're rough and crude— and tend to draw men who match that description. I don't know your reasons for wanting to go, but I can tell you that those camps are no place for females, much less a young woman like you."

"Yet you go to these places." Honest query filled her voice. Not a hint of sarcasm lingered.

"It's different for me, ma'am. It's my job to carry freight to the miners. Plus, I'm a man."

The tiniest smile touched her mouth. "If I were to be a man, monsieur, would you allow me to accompany you?"

"Don't even let that thought take root, Mademoiselle Girard. If there's one thing you could never be mistaken for, it's a man." This young woman was feminine through and through, but he detected a determined will that wouldn't be easily swayed. Perhaps he'd assigned her to the wrong camp earlier.

Her smile was brief. "How will you manage without a conveyance?"

Again, not a hint of gloating tainted her voice. "I haven't figured that out yet, ma'am. But I will."

"If I offered you more money, would you be persua—"

"I told you before, there are many reasons I won't agree to do this. And money doesn't figure into any of them." He'd already guessed from her clothes and the way she conducted herself that she came from wealth. Probably had a rich father somewhere who doled out double eagles to his daughter like they were raindrops in Oregon. The man hadn't done her any favors. "I'm sorry, ma'am, but my answer is still no. I can't state it any plainer than that."

She slowly bowed her head. "There is no need for you to restate it, monsieur. I understand the meaning of that word quite well."

Jack couldn't see her expression, only the way her hands were knotted at her waistline. He intended to be the first to leave, but when she skirted around him, he let her go. He watched her as she walked away.

The crowd of shoppers cramming the street parted at her approach, as though a silent trumpet had blown, announcing the passage of royalty. She seemed oblivious to it, and he couldn't help but wonder if everything in her life had come so easily.

He waited. Giving her a good lead felt like the right thing to do. She wouldn't want to see him again anytime soon.

"You surprised me, Brennan. I expected you to take her up on that offer."

Jack turned at the sound of Sampson's voice. As he watched the old man pick up a saddle and stow it on a bench against the wall, he wrestled with what had just happened, unable to reconcile it. "Then you underestimated me, sir."

"And I don't customarily do that with people."

Jack weighed his next question before asking. "Is it your custom to try and manipulate people into doing your bidding, instead?"

Sampson paused for a second, showing no offense. "No, but I'm not above tryin' to give God a hand when I see something that needs to be done. Especially when I know it's the right thing to do." He picked up a horseshoe and a pair of tongs and carried them to the forge.

Jack followed. "You really think sending me and that young woman trekking all over the Rockies—alone—is the right thing to do? Do you have any idea what mining towns are like? Or what position you'd be placing Mademoiselle Girard in, not to mention what burden of responsibility you'd be saddling me with?"

"I know exactly what burden you'd be saddled with, Mr. Brennan, and I'd gladly strap it on your back right now, if I could!" Jake Sampson shoved the horseshoe into the bed of red-hot coals, sending sparks shooting upward.

Jack had learned long ago that when faced with someone's anger, patient silence served him well. Deciphering the feelings behind the anger went much faster if he wasn't so busy reacting to it.

"She's bound and determined to get up to those camps, Brennan." Sampson laid the tongs aside. "And if she gets hooked up with the wrong kind of man—or men—it won't end up good. We both know that."

"Then you need to find some way to convince her not to go."

Jake Sampson's unexpected laughter was brief and humorless. "I've got about as much chance of doin' that as I have of wadin' out in Fountain Creek and comin' up with pockets full of gold." He eased down on an upturned crate and gestured toward an old chair in the corner.

Jack hesitated, then dragged the chair over and straddled it.

"She wandered in here yesterday sayin' she needed a driver and a . . . carriage." Sampson pronounced the word as Mademoiselle Girard might have, and it drew a smile from Jack. "As if I've got those just sittin' around. She's traveled a long way from home to get here, Brennan, and convincin' her to just turn around and sashay on back to Paris isn't gonna be easy. Not when she's come in search of her father."

That got Jack's attention. "Her father?"

"She says he came through here back in the fall of '50. He was a trapper. Said she was just a wee thing when he left her and her mother behind. I'm afraid there's only heartache in store for the child, even if she does find him, though chances of that happening are next to nothing. I tried to tell her, but somebody's filled her pretty little head with the notion that if she finds the man who helped bring her into this world, she'll find her father. But those two things don't always go hand in hand."

A shadow crossed Sampson's face and Jack couldn't help but wonder what lay beneath it. Yet one thing was painfully clear to him—he'd been mistaken about Mademoiselle Girard, at least in part. And he regretted his hasty judgments. But even if he'd had this information beforehand, it wouldn't have changed his final decision. He still stood by it, however much he sympathized with her. And he agreed with Sampson that finding her father would be next to impossible.

When men wanted to disappear, they chose this territory with good reason.

"I've known my share of Frenchmen through the years." Sampson's focus extended beyond the confines of the livery doors. "A good lot, most of 'em. They sent money back home to their families. Just tried to make a livin' like everyone else. Once the fur market went bust, most of the trappers around here crowded into the streams with the rest of us, lookin' for gold. Most never found so much as a nugget for their trouble."

The jostle of passing buggies and wagons along with indistinct bits of conversation floated toward them through the open doors of the livery. Jack studied the man across from him, sensing there was more to him than he'd originally credited.

Jack leaned forward, resting his arms on the spindled back of the chair. "So did *you* ever find any gold, Mr. Sampson?"

A long moment passed. Then a gradual smile ghosted Jake Sampson's face, and Jack wondered if he'd been given his answer.

The old man kept his attention trained ahead. "You know the trick to pannin', don't you, Brennan? It's knowing when to stop. Greed's a powerful adversary. If you give her a foothold, she'll take back everything she's given, and then some. Learning to be content is hard. But not learning . . . sometimes that's even harder."

Jack looked around the livery—a modest business to say the least. He didn't know what to believe about whether Sampson found gold, but his gut told him the man was telling the truth. Jack smiled to himself, imagining what motivation the man might have for being rich and yet living like he wasn't. Sampson might be a bit odd—even eccentric—but he seemed harmless enough.

"You still have my down payment for that wagon, sir, but I want you to keep it," he added quickly. He stood and carried the chair back to the corner. "I want you to build me another one just like it, as soon as possible. And this time, there'll be no confusion about who owns it." He waited for Sampson's acknowledgment, then turned to go.

"She's lost her mother too," Sampson said quietly behind him.

Jack paused in the doorway.

"Mademoiselle Girard got real teary when she told me, so I figure it wasn't too long ago. Maybe that's the reason she left home when she did. Figured she didn't have anything left to lose, or maybe nothing left to stay for."

Bowing his head, Jack slowly exhaled. "Manipulation is a cheap form of cowardice, Mr. Sampson. I don't respond well to it."

"If I would've asked you outright, would you have said yes?"

Jack looked back, and shook his head.

"Mr. Brennan, you're the only man I know who I trust to do this."

"With all respect, Mr. Sampson, you don't know me."

"I know Bertram Colby. And I know that if you've earned that man's good opinion, you're finer than most. You can argue this point with me all day long, but you've already proven to me you're the right man."

"And just how do you figure that, sir?"

Sampson rose from the crate and took a step forward. "Because after everything she offered you, you still said no."

L ATER THAT EVENING, Véronique stood a safe distance from the open window in her room and watched the sun swath the mountains in a cloak of crimson and gold. How small and insignificant she felt in comparison. And how isolated and alone.

Examining her melancholy, she easily traced its root—Monsieur Brennan's refusal of her offer earlier that day. She still couldn't believe it—even after the offer of more money, he'd remained firm.

Though she hadn't seen him at the hotel again, she assumed that he was a guest, or at least had been, based on his having left his shirt in the washroom. She tried to think of something else she could propose that might persuade him to reconsider. But the somber finality lining his expression earlier told her that her efforts would be wasted.

The hollowness stemming from his rebuff was not easily set aside. How foolish she'd been to pin her hopes so quickly on one man. Surely God had not brought her all this way only to leave her now, but it was beginning to feel as though He'd done just that.

A cool evening breeze rustled the curtains.

Billows of whitish-gray clouds stretched across the western horizon, one atop the other. Wave upon fluffy wave crested, reflecting the last vestiges of light until the sky resembled an ocean churning to meet the shore. Deep within her subconscious, she remembered the rocking motion of the ship that had ferried her across the Atlantic, so far from home. Véronique closed her eyes and recalled the tangy brine of the ocean. She could almost taste the salt spray on her lips and feel the unsettling queasiness in her stomach from the constant pitching and swaying.

She blinked to dispel that last unpleasant memory.

How were Lord and Lady Descantes faring? Were they still in this country? Were their girls practicing the English they'd learned while under her tutelage? She picked up the vellum-bound book on the table beside her—*Le Comte de Monte Cristo*—and turned it in her hands, recalling how much Lord and Lady Descantes' daughters had relished the tale.

As fond as she was of the story by Alexandre Dumas, it held no appeal this evening. She placed the book back on the table.

Men's voices drifted in from outside in the hallway.

She paused, listening. Then startled at the knock on her door.

Opening it, she found Monsieur Baird waiting on the other side, and heard the door to the room opposite hers in the hallway latch closed.

"Good evening, Miss Girard." Monsieur Baird stood a good distance back from the entryway. "I've come to retrieve your dinner tray, if you're finished."

Glad for the company, however brief, she nodded. "*Oui*, I am. *Merci*. And may I send my compliments to your chef?" She retrieved the tray and handed it to him. "The meals I have enjoyed in your hotel have been the most palatable I have experienced while in your country."

His expression warmed. "I'll be sure and pass those kind words along to my wife. She'll smile at hearing them, ma'am. Thank you."

Another thought sprang to mind. "I also wish to compliment you on your hotel staff, Monsieur Baird. Miss Carlson is a most exceptional employee, especially for one so youthful."

"Why yes, ma'am, she is. And we're happy to have her." Monsieur Baird glanced at the tray. "This'll save her a trip up those stairs again tonight, which is always a good thing this late in the day."

Véronique was surprised to hear the girl was still working at this hour. "The stairs are a challenge for her?" She phrased it more like a question and less like the truth she already knew, not wanting to cast a disparaging light on the girl.

He nodded. "More so in recent days, but you'd never know it from Lilly's attitude. She just plugs right along, never complains about anything. She's always been that way. Which makes me hurt all the more when I think of what's ahead of her." He blinked. Looking away, he cleared his throat. "But she's as fine as they come. So's her family. Well . . . I'll say good-night, ma'am. Hope you rest well."

"*Bonsoir*, Monsieur Baird, and I wish you the same." Véronique closed the door and leaned against it, wondering about the proprietor's comment about Lilly's future and if it had to do with the brace on her leg. Had Lilly been born with the impediment? Or was it the result of a recent accident? The girl compensated for it extremely well, which in Véronique's mind ruled out a more recent occurrence.

She crossed to the *armoire* and withdrew her nightgown. She'd spent the afternoon unpacking, a task that had busied her thoughts for a short time at least. The modest *armoire* didn't accommodate half of her dresses, and the rest lay arranged over a wingback chair, awaiting a proper brushing. After pulling the floral curtains framing the open bay window closed, she undressed.

The silk of her nightgown provided scant warmth. She crawled between the cool sheets and pulled the quilt up over her body. Though the room was not extremely chilly, she shivered. Tired but not ready for sleep, she reached for John Donne's *Devotions Upon Emergent Occasions*. The pages fell open at the exact spot she sought.

Her gaze went to the underlined portion. "'No man is an island, entire of itself; every man is a piece of the continent, a part of the main.'"

She paused and reread the sentence again, silently. Slipping past the window, aided by night's quiet, the distant gurgling of what she assumed to be Fountain Creek serenaded the silence.

After a moment, she continued. "'If a clod be washed away by the sea, Europe is the less, as well as if a promontory were, as well as if a manor of thy friend's or of thine own were: any man's death diminishes me, because I am involved in mankind, and therefore never send to know for whom the bell tolls; it tolls for thee.'"

Reading Donne's familiar prose, being reminded that he considered no person truly isolated, or ever completely alone, helped ease the aloneness she felt. And she wondered . . . Did Donne have the slightest knowledge that the words he'd breathed life into so long ago would continue on long after his own heart had beat its last? She liked to think that he did.

"Mademoiselle Girard, I am honored that you would entrust me with your safety, but this arrangement is simply unsuitable, for more reasons than I care to number. . . ."

The words from earlier that day pushed their way into her thoughts with frustrating clarity, as did the memory of Monsieur Brennan's determined attitude. If only she could think of something that might sway his opinion. On further thought, Monsieur Brennan did not strike her as the type of man who could be easily swayed.

She placed the book on the bed table and, with a soft breath, blew out the oil lamp, then curled onto her side. But for a sliver of moon-glow cast across the foot of the bed, darkness bathed the room.

She drew up her legs, wishing for a fire in the darkened hearth, or at least for the bed warmer she'd always found tucked between her sheets in the Marchand household on chilly nights. She cradled an arm beneath her pillow. The bed warmer had always been present when needed, so she'd never questioned how it had gotten there.

But who had warmed the coals for her bed all those years?

As she assisted Francette Marchand in preparing for bed, her own adjoining chamber had been made ready. Servants' faces came to mind but none of their names, of course. They had been house servants, after all, not a companion to a family member, as she had been.

Shivering, Véronique pressed her face deeper into her pillow, surprised at the knot forming in her throat, and at the unexpected desire to convey her appreciation to whomever had faithfully seen her bed warmed for so many years, without a slightest word of thanks from her.

"Sure, I've got a wagon you might be interested in, Mr. Brennan. It's in the back of the barn there. Haven't used it in a while myself, but you're welcome to look at it."

Jack followed the rancher inside the barn, mindful to shorten his stride in deference to the older gentleman's arthritic gait.

Following the fiasco at the livery with Mademoiselle Girard yesterday, he'd spent the previous afternoon scouring Willow Springs for another suitable wagon. And this morning had him following his last possible lead. But from the barn's state of disrepair, Jack was none too hopeful. If this didn't pan out, he owed Hochstetler a visit at the mercantile—and that was one visit he did not want to make.

Starks led the way down a hay-strewn aisle that was flanked on either side by empty, low-ceilinged stalls. Sunlight grew dim the farther back they went and the air more stale, thick with dust and the tang of days-old manure.

A tingling sensation started at the base of Jack's neck. The smell of livestock didn't bother him, yet it gradually became more difficult for him to breathe.

He followed Starks, clenching and unclenching his hands at his sides in an effort to ease his sudden tension. He looked back over his shoulder at the open doors of the barn, and felt his pulse slow.

Starks stopped and turned. "Here she is." He waved his hand, indicating for Jack to step forward. "Take a good, overlong look at her. See what you think."

At a glance, Jack realized he didn't need an overlong look—good or otherwise—to know that this wagon would scarcely make it into town, much less survive a rugged mountain pass. His throat tightened as he became aware of the wall close at his back and of the low slant of the ceiling above him.

Not wanting to appear disrespectful, Jack made a pretense of checking out the conveyance. "She looks like she's been a faithful partner, that's for sure."

"Oh, she was the best. Saw me through many a harvest."

Jack swallowed, trying not to think about Billy Blakely and what had happened the summer they—"How many years have you had her?"

"Going on twelve now. But they don't make wagons like this anymore . . . you can take that to the bank."

The nostalgic look on the rancher's face might have drawn a smile had Jack been able to think straight. He bent down and peered at the wagon bed's undercarriage, already knowing what he would find and needing a chance to clear his mind of the fog.

With a sigh, he rose. He gripped the wagon for support, easing up when the sideboard gave slightly beneath his weight. "Only thing is, Mr. Starks, I need a wagon bed that's reinforced beneath with steel and wood. So I'm afraid this won't work for me."

"Well, that's a shame."

Jack moved so he could view the open doors again, hating the numbing sensation thickening his temples. "But I can clearly see why you've kept the wagon all these years." Wanting to make a run for it, he indicated for the older man to precede him back down the aisle. "Wagons like this get to be like old friends, don't they, sir?"

Starks slowed, glancing back over his shoulder. "They do at that. My missus says it's only good for kindling, but I just can't bring myself to break it apart, not yet."

Once they crossed the threshold into sunlight, Jack drew in a deep breath. The dizzy feeling faded and he began to relax. It'd been a long time since he'd had such a reaction, but confined spaces had always been uncomfortable for him. . . .

He lifted his hat and ran a hand through his hair, then resituated the hat on his head. Sleep had kept its distance until the wee hours last night, what with his brooding over what Jake Sampson had done. The soft spot in that man's heart, however well-intentioned, was creating a rift in Jack's personal plans.

Mr. Starks extended his hand, his smile undimmed. "I hope you find what you're lookin' for, young man. And I'm sorry to've wasted your morning."

"Not at all, sir. I appreciate your time."

Once astride his horse, Jack watched the aging rancher walk back toward the house. Funny how people hung onto things, even when the item's usefulness or practicality had long since passed. While Jack knew he had faults, plenty of them, being tied to "things" wasn't among them.

Years of guiding families west, seeing wagons loaded beyond their capacity at the outset, only to watch those same families cast off furniture, boxes of delicate china, and trunks of fancy clothes along the way, had taught him not to become overly attached to what was staying on this side of eternity.

Heading his mount back toward town, Jack knew the meeting with Hochstetler was inevitable. He only hoped the mercantile owner would be open to discussing alternative arrangements.

CHAPTER ELEVEN

Véronique tacked the last of the notices she and Lilly had made to a board outside the telegraph office, then stepped back to view their handiwork. Lilly's excellent penmanship rivaled every other advertisement posted, therefore drawing more attention to it.

In phrases centered across the page, the script read:

> *Citizens of Willow Springs*
> *Possessing information about*
> *Pierre Gustave Girard (born Paris, 1820)*
> *Or his whereabouts*
> *Are requested to contact*
> *The Baird & Smith Hotel.*
> *Reward offered.*

Simple. To the point. Listing the year of birth had actually been Lilly's idea, in order to give people an idea of how old a man her father would be. Offering a reward had been Véronique's. Commoners responded more heartily when given a monetary incentive—at least that's what Christophe always said.

She headed back toward the hotel, keeping her attention on the path before her. She had no desire for a recurrence of what she'd stepped in on the way to her first visit with Monsieur Sampson.

Besides the four men who answered her advertisement yesterday morning, who had been entirely unsuited to the task—and Monsieur Brennan, who had been entirely closed minded to the task—she'd received no other indications of interest. But the day was young, and the notices she'd posted yesterday and this morning were sure to draw interest from emerging Saturday shoppers.

Véronique rounded the corner. Spotting the hotel up ahead, she slowed her pace. A queasiness expanded in the pit of her stomach.

A group of men—she counted twenty at least—were gathered outside in the street in front of the hotel. She moved to one side of the boardwalk, watching. *It couldn't be . . .*

After a moment, Monsieur Baird emerged from the hotel and made a path through the group. He climbed atop a barrel and nailed a piece of paper to a post. No sooner did he get down than disgruntled shouts rose from the onlookers.

Véronique pressed close inside an angled nook of a shop doorway. Hearing the men's comments from where she stood, she quickly gathered what they were there for. Thinking of the other notices she'd posted, the sick feeling in her midsection expanded to a dull throb. Monsieur and Madame Baird would be *furieux* with her for causing such a—

She jumped at the touch on her arm.

"Mademoiselle Girard! I've been looking for you!"

Lilly Carlson stood close beside her, her expression a mixture of expectancy and remorse. She motioned for Véronique to follow. "You've created quite a stir back at the hotel, Mademoiselle Girard. Or should I say, our advertisement did. Mr. Baird sent me to find you before you came back and got caught in that mess."

"*Merci,*" Véronique whispered, managing a tremulous smile. "Thank you for saving me that embarrassment."

Young Lilly led the way in the opposite direction down the planked walkway. Véronique couldn't help but notice the girl's limp was more exaggerated than before.

Lilly glanced back as they neared the corner. "They've been there for the past hour, waiting for you. Mr. Baird said there's not an upright one in the bunch." She gestured to her right. "Just to be safe, we'll cut down this way and then go up the other street. We can use the hotel's back entrance. Where were you, by the way? You were already gone by the time I got there this morning."

"I was . . . posting the notices regarding my father." Véronique cringed even as she said it, knowing now that she should have checked with Monsieur Baird before doing so. She glanced behind them. "Monsieur and Madame Baird are angry with me, *non*?"

Lilly's eyes widened. "No, Mademoiselle Girard, they're not angry at all, I promise. I explained to Mr.—"

They paused to allow a woman and little girl entrance into a shop. Véronique tipped her head back to read the shingle above the door: *Susanna's Bakery and Confections*. The treats in the window tempted her appetite and reminded her that breakfast had long since passed.

"I explained to Mr. Baird," Lilly continued, "that I encouraged you to write that notice and that neither of us ever thought of something like this happening."

"And how did Monsieur Baird respond to this explanation of yours?"

Lilly paused on the boardwalk. Her expression grew unusually serious. "He said that if we were going to take part in a man's world then we needed to learn to think like men."

Véronique's mouth slipped open. She couldn't believe kind Monsieur Baird would utter such a thing. Then she noticed the firm lines of Lilly's mouth begin to twitch.

"I'm only joking, Mademoiselle Girard!" Lilly laughed. "He said to tell you not to worry for one minute, but for us to please resist posting any more notices." She leaned closer. "At least until after he's cleared the lobby of men."

Relieved, Véronique smiled and nudged Lilly's shoulder. "I am still needing to learn when I can believe what you say and when you are playing with me."

"My papa would say that if my mouth is moving, you'd better beware!" She smiled. "But this does mean we probably need to go around and collect the notices we posted."

They spent the next hour doing just that before heading back in the direction of the hotel. Véronique glanced at Lilly walking beside her. It was good to have a friend—however much younger—here in this place, especially since she'd been missing Christophe.

She hadn't heard from him since receiving his letters upon her arrival in New York City. She determined then to write him again this week. But was he still in Brussels? Or had he returned to Paris with

Lord Marchand and his *famille*? She decided it would be best to post the letter to the Marchand family address, entrusting that their grand home still stood unharmed.

"If you're not busy tomorrow"—Lilly yanked a notice down from a post by the dry goods store—"my parents would like you to join us for lunch after church. They're eager to meet you."

Véronique paused to offer a deep curtsy. "I am most pleased to accept your invitation, Mademoiselle Carlson. And I look forward to meeting your *famille*."

Lilly grinned. "Would you teach me how to do that, please?"

Realizing what she meant, Véronique looked down, thinking of the girl's brace. Just as quickly, she drew her gaze upward, not having meant to stare. "You want me to . . . teach you how to curtsy?"

Lilly nodded. "It looks so pretty when you do it." As she held Véronique's attention, awareness moved into her eyes. "If I bend my leg just right, I don't think my brace will get in the way. I've got real good balance too. Even Doc Hadley says so."

Véronique felt her face heat and her heartstrings pull taut. "*Je suis désolée*, Lilly. I did not mean to imply that—"

"No, it's okay. I've lived in Willow Springs for a long time." She shrugged. "Everybody knows."

That answered one of Véronique's questions. "You compensate for it very well, *ma chérie*."

Lilly dipped her head. Her smile faded, but only a bit. "I've had a long time to learn."

Véronique lifted her chin. "I will teach you how to curtsy, Lilly Carlson. And I will teach you my language, if that would please you."

The girl's violet eyes took on a sheen. "That would please me very much, Mademoiselle Girard. *Merci beaucoup*."

"And we will get started today, but first . . ." Véronique looked up. "May we visit this establishment for a moment?"

"The mercantile?" Lilly shrugged. "Sure. I'll check with Mrs. Hochstetler inside—she and her husband are the owners—to see if she has anything to be delivered to the hotel. That'll save the Bairds a trip over here."

Véronique worked to imitate the serious expression Lilly had fooled her with earlier. "Lilly, you are a sweet and kind girl, but I would encourage you, *ma chérie*, to be more considerate of others in your life." Véronique slowly let her smile bloom and tapped her chest. "Namely . . . *moi*!"

Content at seeing Lilly's wide-eyed grin, she hurried inside.

Riding by the hotel on his way to the mercantile, Jack couldn't resist a quick glance up to the third-story bay window. It was open, but he didn't see any sign of her.

Parts of what Jake Sampson had told him yesterday replayed in his mind. Mademoiselle Girard's father had been through Willow Springs roughly twenty years ago, and she had been a little girl when her father had left Paris. He quickly did the math. That would make her around twenty-two, twenty-three at the most, if he had the dates right. Older than he'd originally guessed, but not by much.

Movement drew his eye—something fluttering in the breeze near the front door of the hotel. The piece of paper wasn't tacked along with others on the door, but was affixed to a front post, making it more noticeable. He didn't remember it being there earlier that morning. Curiosity got the better of him and he retraced his steps.

The paper curled in the breeze. Jack gripped a bottom corner so he could read it. Then he read it aloud a second time, unbelieving. "'The position of driver for Mademoiselle Girard has been filled. No further applications required.'"

He immediately recalled the two surly-looking men who had stopped by the livery yesterday, the ones who had given Mademoiselle Girard a thorough perusal. He didn't have to guess long at their intentions if they were the ones she'd hired.

Jack couldn't imagine a young woman like Mademoiselle Girard being in their company here in town, much less out there on her lonesome. She was far too young and naïve to be traveling with men of such shallow character. Men like that wouldn't hesitate in the least to—

He shuddered to think of all that could go wrong.

The blur of possibilities running through his mind suddenly fell away, and a single thought rose to the surface. After he spoke with Mr. Hochstetler at the mercantile, he would head back to the livery and speak with Mr. Sampson about this new development. Surely

Sampson could talk some sense into the woman—regardless of her already having made her decision.

Thinking of her setting off into the mountains with men like that was almost enough to change his mind about accepting her offer—almost.

The mercantile was crowded. Jack waited in line, hat in hand, with others at the front counter. Finally his turn came. He assumed the woman behind the counter was the owner's wife but wasn't certain. "Is Mr. Hochstetler in? I'd like to speak with him, please."

The woman gave an exasperated sigh and wiped her forehead with the back of her hand. "My husband's in back."

"Would you kindly tell him Jack Brennan is here? I need to speak with him about a business matter."

She stared, unmoving. "I'll go get him for you, but it'll take him a few minutes. We're busy. It *is* Saturday, you know."

Mildly surprised at her sour disposition, Jack nodded as she walked away. "Yes, ma'am. Thank you." He had a hard time putting this woman with the kindly man he'd met a few days ago. In past years, he'd met a lot of families, and he'd seen his share of mismatched couples. People married for a variety of reasons, some reasons bearing a wiser and more lasting foundation than others.

He picked up a jar from an arrangement on the counter. His marriage had been short, and unexpectedly brief, but it had been a good one. Marriage was something in his past now, and he was at peace with that. He tilted the jar to read the label.

C.O. Bigelow Apothecaries of New York.

On a whim, he laid his hat on the counter and unscrewed the lid. He took a whiff, and his reaction surprised him. The scent painted a picture so vivid in his mind he doubted an artist could have done better. Prairie grasses, young and tender, bowing in the breeze beneath a simmering summer sun. He closed his eyes and he was there again, on the prairie—with land spanning out in all directions as far as he could see, wagon canvases gleaming so white in the early morning sun that it hurt his eyes to look overlong. And the excited chatter of families drifting over the plains as they pushed west to homes waiting to be built and dreams waiting to be discovered. A pang tightened his chest, knowing those days were past for him.

He opened his eyes and took a quick look around, making sure no one was watching him. Then he peered into the jar, feeling more than a little foolish that a silly concoction could evoke such emotion. He read the ingredients. *Lemon oil and extracts*—

"Are you planning on purchasing that?"

His head came up.

Mrs. Hochstetler had returned, and based on her scowl, her mood had further deteriorated—if that were possible.

He screwed the lid back into place, the tangy scent of the lotion lingering, like the power of the memory. He didn't need this. There was no good reason for him to buy it. "Yes, ma'am, I believe I will."

Though the woman's smile was an improvement, it wasn't enough to overcome the harshness of her features. "That just arrived from New York City, sir. I think it's going to be one of our most popular-selling items. That'll be a dollar, please."

A dollar! That would buy almost eight pounds of coffee, for pete's sake! Begrudgingly, Jack handed over the money, doubting the woman's prognostication one hundred percent.

"I'll go wrap this up for you, sir. And my husband will be right out."

Mrs. Hochstetler returned minutes later. Still brooding over his impulsive purchase, Jack was relieved to see her husband close on her heels.

"Brennan, it's good to see you again. I was in the back taking inventory of your supplies. They're all ready to go." Hochstetler motioned him off to the side, away from the crowd. "I've got a full load for your first trip, and I'm eager to get it sold."

Explaining his predicament was going to be harder than Jack imagined. "I . . . I'm afraid there's been a change in plans, Mr. Hochstetler. Something's happened, and I'm not going to be able to leave on Monday." Jack laid out the turn of events, without identifying the buyer of the wagon by name. Hochstetler's expression darkened by the second, telling Jack this might not turn out as he'd hoped.

"I hate that it happened too, Jack. I really do. But I've got to get those supplies up to Scoggins in Jenny's Draw. It's been almost a month since he's had a shipment. I've been carrying inventory on my books and I need to get it sold."

"I understand, sir. Mr. Sampson's agreed to build me another wagon, but . . . that will take some time." Jack looked at the hat in his hands.

"And time is a luxury I don't have. Neither does Scoggins, and neither do the other mining towns. If I don't deliver those goods soon, he's liable to seek a contract with a mercantile in another town, or hire his own freighter, and that hurts my business." Hochstetler rubbed his jaw. "You said somebody else bought your wagon. Any chance of renting it from them, even short term? Until Sampson gets the next one finished?"

Jack hesitated, then shook his head. "I've already been down that road. The owner's not willing to negotiate." Pressured by Hochstetler's obvious displeasure, he pictured Mademoiselle Girard, and the sweet innocence he'd attributed to her earlier faded a mite. "Would you be willing to give me a few days, sir? A week at the most. That'll give me time to check in Denver . . . to see if I can locate a wagon up there."

Hochstetler looked away, appearing to consider the request.

The hum of conversation filled the crowded store, but Jack's attention honed in on one voice in particular. He felt his blood rising. The closer the voice came, the harder his pulse pounded. When she stopped midsentence, he knew she'd seen him. He looked to his right. She stood only a few feet away.

"Monsieur Brennan!" Surprise heightened her brow.

"Mademoiselle Girard." With a nod, he acknowledged the girl standing close beside her. The girl looked vaguely familiar, but he couldn't place her.

Mademoiselle Girard's focus drifted to Mr. Hochstetler, then back again, and Jack couldn't help but wonder if she'd overheard their conversation.

"It is most surprising to see you again." She blinked as though remembering something. "May I introduce a friend of mine—"

"My apologies, mademoiselle, but . . . I'm in the middle of an important conversation." Jack indicated Hochstetler with a nod. "If you wouldn't mind excusing us, please."

"Ah . . ." Understanding slowly dawned in her eyes. "*Pardonnez-moi.* My apologies for having interrupted."

Hochstetler's deep sigh drew Jack's focus once again. With divided attention, Jack awaited the man's response while grateful to hear the retreat of footsteps behind him. If he was about to be fired, he'd prefer a certain little French coquette not be witness to it.

"I'm sorry to have to do this, Jack, but business is business. I've got to get those supplies up the mountain. If you can't do it . . . I'll have to find someone else who can."

Jack fought to think of another option. Even if he left for Denver immediately, the businesses would be closed for the day by the time he got there, and would remain closed on Sunday. He was grasping at straws. And from Hochstetler's dubious expression, he knew it too.

"Tell you what." Hochstetler looked Jack square in the eye. "I'll give you until Monday morning, like we agreed when we shook on the deal."

The reminder of their agreement felt like a hit below the belt. At their first meeting, he had made a point of telling Hochstetler there would be no need for a written contract between them, that his word was as binding as anything put on paper. "I appreciate that, sir. And again, I apologize for putting you in this situation." Jack felt a sudden flush and tugged at his shirt collar, wondering when the room had grown overly warm.

"I'm sorry too, Brennan. I was looking forward to working with you. Bertram Colby spoke highly of you." Regret weighted Hochstetler's tone, and knifed Jack's sense of obligation. "If you don't have anything worked out by Monday, I'll contact a local who bid for the job when you did. See if he's still interested."

Hochstetler's offer to wait until Monday—while generous—only fueled Jack's failed sense of duty. And the firmness of the man's parting handshake renewed his frustration with Mademoiselle Girard all over again.

Jack looked down at the wrapped package in his hand, wishing he could take it back. He could eat for a week on what he'd spent on the silly item, and his funds were becoming more limited by the minute.

He turned to leave and found himself boxed in by a crush of shoppers pressing toward the front counter. All aisles were blocked. The air around him grew stagnant and tired, as if it had been breathed and exhaled one too many times.

His vision blurred. He blinked to clear it. This couldn't be happening again. . . .

His breath caught at the base of his throat. His lungs rebelled at the lack of oxygen. He remembered again why he'd chosen a profession that kept him in wide open spaces. Seven aisles stood between him and the door. He spotted an opening in a side aisle and went for it, hoping to make it outside before the room closed in on him completely.

He rounded the corner, his focus intent on reaching the door. He was almost home free—when he collided with someone full force.

CHAPTER | TWELVE

WITH JACK BRENNAN'S ASSISTANCE, Véronique managed to steady herself. She could say one thing for him—the man was solidly built. If not for the table at her backside, he would have knocked her flat on the floor. She noticed his hat beside his feet and a package of some sort in his hand.

He quickly stepped back, his expression an odd mixture of anger and . . . panic.

"Monsieur?" she whispered. "Are you all right?"

The muscles in his jawline clenched tight, and she feared his teeth might shatter from the pressure. "I need . . . to get out of here."

His voice sounded husky and forced, and had a desperate *timbre* she recognized.

His breathing grew erratic. "Please, miss . . ."

Without a second thought, she bent, grabbed his hat and took hold of his hand. She cut a swath through the lines of patrons, pulling him with her. She skirted barrels full of dry goods and dodged bolts of fabric piled on edges of tables, never letting go of him. Not that she could have even if she'd wanted to. His grip was viselike, and growing painful.

When she reached the door, she glanced back. Monsieur Brennan's glazed stare was locked on their clasped hands as if that were his only lifeline.

She led the way to a wrought-iron bench on the boardwalk a few feet away and gestured for him to sit, then took a place beside him. For a moment, neither of them spoke. With his legs spread wide, he rested his forearms on his thighs. His breath came in short bursts. His hands trembled.

Véronique watched him, feeling the weight of responsibility, and guilt. She hadn't intended to stand around the corner and eavesdrop on his conversation. But what she had read in the mercantile owner's expression had been so ominous that her curiosity had gotten the best of her. Knowing she'd played a part in his being relieved of employment had rooted her to the spot as firmly as if her boots had been nailed there.

She stared at his hat in her lap. If only sins committed in secret were weighted less heavily by the Almighty than those acted out for all to see. . . . She knew she needed to apologize. But where to begin? Especially when he was unaware of her trespass.

What was it that Christophe had told her their last morning together at Cimetière de Montmartre? A lifetime ago now . . . That her honesty would get her in trouble if not balanced with good sense. But at the moment, honesty and good sense hardly seemed congruent. For every ounce of good sense within her screamed not to confess what she'd done. Yet the higher law to which she answered demanded it.

"Mademoiselle Girard . . ." Monsieur Brennan ran his hands over his face, his voice still shaky. He drew in a deep breath and held it, as though the act were a privilege. He let it out slowly. "I apologize for . . . for imposing myself on you like that."

She couldn't help but stare. What manner of man was this Monsieur Jack Brennan? Even with all she'd cost him, however unintentionally, he was willing to offer an apology to her?

"It was not an imposition, monsieur. You did not force your company or your attention upon me. Nor did you take unwarranted advantage. If I am correct in my memory, I took hold of your hand, and . . . it pleased me to be of assistance."

A faint smile crossed his face. "Do you always respond by using the definition of a word? Wait, please . . . don't answer that." He massaged his forehead. "I don't think my head can take it."

Smiling, she ran a forefinger over the crown of his hat. It was surprisingly soft and supple. "What is this material?"

"Beaver fur."

Beaver fur. "I did not know the fur of such an animal could be so soft." No doubt her father was accustomed to this texture. She stroked it again, memorizing the feel and the way it moved beneath her fingertips.

"What happened back there—" Jack Brennan motioned toward the mercantile—"it doesn't happen often. But that's twice today. Things just start closing in on me for some reason. I can't breathe, I can't think straight." He raked a hand through his hair, then rubbed the back of his neck.

"I recognized the crowded feeling in your voice. I too have experienced this, once. It was most unpleasant and something I do not wish to repeat."

"Where were you when it happened?"

"On the ship, coming from Italy to this country. I took passage with a family from Paris. Their four children were my charge during our months in Italy and then on the voyage. We stayed in a cabin together, the five of us. One evening there came a storm and the ship tossed and swayed all night. They cried, I cried," she said softly. "Come morning, it was not a pleasant sight in our quarters."

A faraway look moved into his eyes. "I've never been on a ship like that before."

"I am thinking you would not enjoy it. The chambers are very cramped, which did not bother me on the whole—just that night of the storm." She refrained from sharing that she'd never once ventured to peer over the side of the ship down into the murky waters. A cool shiver accompanied the mere thought of it.

She held up his hat. "I have seen many men wearing this fashion. I hope this is not offensive to you, but . . . I consider the style most odd."

He took the hat, a feigned look of hurt on his face. "This is the best hat I've ever owned. Keeps me warm in the winter, cool in the summer, and dry in the rain and snow." He worked the crease on the top into a more defined shape, treating the article of clothing as though it were a cherished item.

Véronique took a deep breath, wishing she had already delivered the words of apology forming in her mind. "About what occurred inside the shop, Monsieur Brennan, I need to tell you that—"

"Again, I'm sorry, mademoiselle." He shrugged, his soft laughter hinting at embarrassment.

Realizing he'd anticipated her remark incorrectly, she hesitated. Perhaps this was a sign she wasn't to proceed with her apology. Though the thought was tempting to believe, she knew it wasn't true. "Monsieur Brennan, there is something I must say to you, and I am having difficulty finding the words."

A spark lit his eyes, giving the impression he might say something. But seconds passed, and she decided she'd been mistaken.

His eyes were an unusual color, and Véronique found herself searching a mental *palette* for the precise combination of *bleu* and *noir* that would capture the richness of their depth—which only provided further diversion from her task at hand. "I fear that your staring at me is not assisting my effort, monsieur. In truth, I find it most distracting."

He slowly faced forward. "Does this work any better for you, ma'am?" No smile touched his face, yet one lingered around the edges of his voice.

Under different circumstances, she might have laughed. "*Oui*, that is much better for me. *Merci*."

"And just so you know, ma'am, I need to say something to you too. But . . . ladies first."

Her throat felt unusually parched. She swallowed but it provided no relief. "I do not know how to broach this, so I will say it without prelude."

He nodded, the corner of his mouth tipping. "That's usually the best way. Just get it right out in the open."

She took a deep breath. "I listened to your conversation with the gentleman inside the mercantile, and I know you have lost your employment."

The color in Jack Brennan's cheeks deepened.

"I sorely regret what I have done, Monsieur Brennan. And in addition to that, any trouble I have caused you. It is imperative that you know this."

All trace of humor drained from his expression. "Are you familiar with the word 'etiquette,' ma'am?"

The softness of his voice combined with the subtlety of his accusation sent an unpleasant shiver through her. "*Oui,*" she whispered, deciding it best not to look at him for the moment. "It is a French word."

"And do you know its meaning, Mademoiselle Girard?"

She nodded, feeling the heat of his stare. "The English have taken many of our pronunciations and claimed them for themselves. But the meanings are the same, if I am not mistaken."

He laughed, but the response lacked any warmth. "You sound as if what the English did displeases you."

She shrugged, unable to follow where he was leading.

"That's an interesting concept, isn't it, ma'am? To take something that doesn't belong to you and then claim it as your own."

Véronique looked back, now understanding. "I did not take the conveyance from you, Monsieur Brennan." She kept her voice low, aware of others standing nearby on the boardwalk. "I merely arrived at the livery first. And if you will remember, I kindly extended the offer that you may use my wagon whenever you like in exchange for—"

"Yes, in exchange for taking you to places you have no good reason to be heading off—" He paused. His eyes flitted to hers, then away again. "To places that are unsuitable for a lady to visit."

She started to reply but caught herself.

As she studied his profile, she somehow knew that the words she chose to speak next would either build a bridge, or carve a canyon. At one time in her life, her eagerness to have the last word, to make certain her opinions were stated and understood, would have blinded her to this awareness. Recognizing she had learned this tender truth bolstered her confidence and filled her with an unexpected calm.

She turned on the bench to face him fully. "Monsieur Brennan, I traveled far from my home in France to arrive at this place. During this time I witnessed many things and met a varied collection of people. Some of them have been most unpleasant, and I sincerely hope to never cross paths with them again. But I have also discovered kindness and gentility in this country in the most unexpected places." She waited for a reaction from him to gauge his thoughts, but his cloaked expression revealed nothing. "I have learned much in the past months, about others most certainly, but even more about myself. Regardless of what opinion you may hold of me, Monsieur Brennan,

I believe I have earned the right to make my own decisions about where I go and what I do."

Jack Brennan stared at the hat in his hands, unresponsive.

"I believe you tell me the truth when you say, as Monsieur Sampson does, that these mining towns to which I wish to travel are not suitable for a woman. I do not proceed arrogantly with my plans in light of your counsel, monsieur, I assure you. And I am convinced you have warned me in such a strong manner not in an effort to frighten me so you may claim this wagon as your own, but rather because you are an honorable man."

With unexplained certainty, she knew the man sitting beside her was the answer to her prayers. But how to convince him of that fact? "Yet I am equally determined to proceed," she said softly, "be it a wise choice or an imprudent one in your eyes, because what I stand to gain in traveling to those rough and crude places, as you describe them, is worth the cost of the hardship I will endure along the way."

She paused, watching for the slightest softening in him and detecting none. "You have not inquired as to my reason for wanting to visit these towns, and that is surprising given how adamant you are that I not. I am searching for my father, Monsieur Brennan. Willow Springs is the last place my mother—"

"I know about your father, ma'am." His voice was quiet, his expression a smooth mask. "Sampson told me, after you left the livery yesterday."

Véronique shifted her focus to the planked wood beneath her feet, the finality of her circumstances setting in. If his decision wasn't swayed by knowing her motivation, nothing would change his mind. And yet her calm remained.

She spotted Lilly inside the mercantile. They had agreed to meet outside once they were done, so the girl must still be shopping. The silence lengthened as the bustle of shoppers on the boardwalk thinned.

"Have you ever lost someone close to you, Monsieur Brennan?"

He didn't answer. But his fingers tensed around the rim of his hat.

"I have," she said, her throat tightening. "And one thing I have learned is that though death itself can be forever marked in a single moment of time, letting go of those you love can take a very long time. Perhaps years . . ." She watched an ant making its way across the scarred length of wood beneath her feet. The insect carried something on its back that equaled twice the size of its minuscule body, yet its progress remained steady and sure.

"Or sometimes it takes the better part of a life."

Hearing his soft whisper, she looked back, surprised not only at his response but also at what it revealed.

"Mademoiselle Girard, I know you've already hired a driver, so I realize this is too late in coming, but—"

"What has given you the impression that I have hired a driver?"

He sat up straighter. "I saw the notice posted outside the hotel."

She nodded, on the verge of telling him about the ad she'd foolishly placed and what Monsieur Baird had done. But the sense of calm inside her deepened and encouraged her silence.

"Ma'am, I realize you're new to this country and that you're young. You're probably not aware of this, but there are men who would offer to escort you to these places with the sole purpose of taking advantage of . . . the isolation along the way." His eyes grew earnest. "Do you understand what I'm saying to you?"

Véronique nodded but didn't speak, fearing she might interfere with what he would say next. And she sensed something else was coming. Could this quiet sense of discernment inside her be the "honesty coupled with good sense" to which Christophe had been referring? Simply knowing when to keep her mouth shut?

"As you well know, I need that wagon in order to keep my job, ma'am. What I'm proposing is that we—"

"The job is yours, Monsieur Brennan. If you want it."

His expression turned wary. "But we haven't even discussed terms yet."

"I will agree to whatever terms you set." She could hardly breathe, she was so grateful.

"What about the other guy who was hired?"

She worded her answer with care. "You were my first choice in drivers, Monsieur Brennan. I no longer require anyone else's services."

"Would you like me to speak to him? Tell him he doesn't have the job? Those situations can sometimes get sticky."

Véronique felt a tickle of humor inside her. "I have recently observed someone being relieved of employment . . . so I believe I can handle that task myself."

His gradual smile held surprise, and within his soft laughter lingered the sweet promise of retaliation.

She already knew this man liked to spar, but she noticed something else. When he smiled, the reaction reached his eyes a fraction of a second before it touched his mouth. And in that slight pause—in watching his lips curve, in seeing his dimples form, in anticipating the sound of his laughter—there existed a realm she found thoroughly unnerving and intoxicating. And altogether enjoyable.

"Now, Monsieur Brennan, we need to discuss our arrangement." She tried to focus—not an easy task when staring at that smile of his. "First, I believe we agree on the amount of remuneration per—" Seeing his look of question, she paused. "Is there something I have missed, monsieur?"

"I'd just appreciate you not staring at me, ma'am. I find it distracting when I'm trying to listen to you."

Hearing the teasing quality in his voice, she slowly faced forward. "Does this work any better for you, monsieur?"

"*Oui*, mademoiselle." Again, his soft laughter. "This is much better for me."

CHAPTER | THIRTEEN

THE INFORMAL NATURE of the church service was the first thing
Véronique noticed, and disliked. The informal dress of the
churchgoers was second. But what struck the deepest chord
within her—and that she found pleasantly unexpected—was what
Pastor Carlson said, and the manner in which he said it.

Lilly's father didn't come before his congregation with fancy
words or with attempts to impress by lengthy oration or memoriza-
tion of passage upon passage of Scripture—traditions with which she
was more accustomed. He came simply, humbly, and with sincerity
of heart that shone in every word.

"God gives talents to everyone as He sees fit. *He* decides who gets
what and how much they get. That's what this particular passage
says."

Hearing that, Véronique sat up a bit straighter, wishing she'd
thought to unpack her Bible and bring it with her. With a furtive
glance, she scanned Lilly's open text to see if that's what the verse truly
said, while wondering whether Jack Brennan was in the audience
somewhere.

She'd looked for him as she walked the short distance from the
hotel to the church, and then again before the service had started—
but there was no sign of him. Thinking again of their conversation
yesterday encouraged a smile. They would leave on their first trip to

a mining town tomorrow morning, and she could hardly wait!

"Now, how these talents are given may not seem fair to those of us who feel a mite less gifted in some respects. Or completely forgotten in others."

The pastor's comment—aided by his dry delivery—coaxed laughter from the parishioners. Véronique glimpsed Lilly's personality in the act and recognized the origin of the girl's dry wit. But Lilly also favored her mother too, in looks and coloring. Véronique snuck a glance at Hannah Carlson beside her, looking forward to becoming better acquainted with the woman over the noon meal in their home.

"But this distribution of talents, whatever the measure, is in exact accordance with God's eternal plan for each of us." Pastor Carlson moved from behind the orator's stand. His look grew surprisingly sheepish. "We must take care in how we esteem each other's talents, and be mindful to not elevate one gift over the other. I've often looked at people and coveted their talents. Or I've coveted the ease with which they seem to acquire and wield them. How God uses their talents—and blesses them—oftentimes far exceeds what He's done in my own life. And I've struggled with jealousy, and I've wondered"—his brow furrowed—"why them, and not me?"

Véronique could hardly believe he'd made such a public admittance. She pilfered a hasty look on either side of her to gauge Hannah and Lilly's reactions. But they didn't seem the least surprised or offended. Quite the contrary. Quiet pride shone in their expressions.

"At those times I try and remember that I haven't walked that person's road. It may well be that I haven't endured the crucible they've had to experience, and perhaps that's the reason they shine with such strength and luster. They've been through the fire, so to speak, where I've gone untouched by the flame. Something else to recall—and this is harder—is that I'm not competing with that person. God has simply gifted us for different purposes."

Véronique's thoughts went to the work of a fellow artist in Paris whom she greatly admired and with whom she'd attended the same studio. Berthe Morisot's talent was nothing short of brilliant, even if the more traditional instructors' opinions differed. Berthe's carefully composed, brightly hued canvases possessed a transcendent quality. Her delicate dabs of color and contrasting uses of light were techniques that Véronique hoped to incorporate more fully into her own painting some day, if that time ever came.

Pastor Carlson met her gaze, and Véronique wondered if he'd intended his last words for her. Surely not. They didn't even know one another.

Yet, hadn't she coveted Berthe's talent on more than one occasion? Hadn't she asked God why Berthe had been invited to join an esteemed group of painters, while she had not?

Pastor Carlson shook his head. "While I may desire another's gift-edness, I do not desire the shaping they've undergone from the Potter's hand. And I hardly envy the countless hours spent upon the Potter's wheel which is what may very well be what allows them to possess such giftedness in the first place."

He left the upper platform area and moved closer to the assembly. Véronique also considered this a bit odd.

"When we endure hardship and pain—when life doesn't turn out the way we thought it should—what do we do? Do we blame God? Think Him cruel and unfair?" He nodded, and Véronique saw others nodding in agreement with him. "I confess, that's exactly what I've thought on occasion."

He looked down briefly. When he raised his head, his expression had grown more thoughtful. "Recently, an individual crossed my path and I was stunned at how God has used some horrible things that happened in this person's life to shape him for the better and, in turn, to bless so many."

The pastor's gaze settled on someone a few rows behind Véronique, and it was all she could do not to turn around and attempt to locate the focus of his attention. But decorum demanded she not.

"He made a conscious decision to allow God to turn all that hurt into something good. Certain talents, perhaps nonexistent before the trial, or maybe waiting to be unearthed by it, now command respect from a huge number of people. This person has impacted no telling how many lives through the years. I so admire how he made a delib-erate choice to let God turn his losses into gain. First for others, and ultimately for him in the long run."

Véronique found herself caught off guard when Pastor Carlson asked the assembly to stand and sing. Sermons back home went on for at least an hour—most times twice that. Yet this one seemed hardly begun. She didn't know the words to the song, or the tune itself, so she listened, mulling over what she heard.

She couldn't help but wonder who it was sitting somewhere behind her who had endured such trials and had come through it with such strength and luster. She would like to know such a person.

Jack slowed the mare from its canter and reined in at the top of the ridge, unprepared for the scene spread before him. He'd followed the main road leading out of Willow Springs for a good half hour, and had begun to think he'd passed the turnoff to Casaroja, the ranch where he was buying his hitching team. Hochstetler had said he couldn't miss the place—and the man had been right.

Taking in the view, Jack briefly wondered why Jake Sampson hadn't directed him here to look for a wagon. Then he thought better of it. Jake Sampson had had an agenda, after all. Turns out, Sampson *could* be right persuasive when he set his mind to it.

Situated on a gently rising bluff, Casaroja's two-story red-brick residence was as grand as any Jack had ever seen. Massive white columns, glistening in the afternoon sun, supported a second-story porch that ran the length of the front of the house.

Cattle dotted the field to the north, and at a quick glance Jack estimated the herd to be at least three thousand head. Mares grazed at leisure in the field to the south, with a few foals bounding about, still testing their wobbly legs.

Jack nudged his mount down the fence-lined path leading to the main house. Ranch hands working in the fields acknowledged him as he passed, and he couldn't help but wonder what manner of gentleman had amassed this estate. *Imagine all the good a man could accomplish with this as his resource.*

He counted four structures with corrals off to the side and guided his mount to the one closest to the two-story house. The stable's construction and freshly painted wood lent it a considerably newer appearance than the others.

He dismounted and looped the reins around a post.

"Jack Brennan?"

Jack looked up to see a man approaching. "That's me . . . and you're Stewartson?"

The man extended his hand. "Yes, sir—Thomas Stewartson. Welcome to Casaroja. Glad you found your way out here."

Jack appreciated the man's firm grip. Taking in his surroundings, he blew out an exaggerated breath. "You've got yourself a nice little setup out here."

Stewartson chuckled, trailing Jack's gaze. "Yes, sir, we do. I've had the privilege of working here since the ranch started back in '60. You won't find any finer horseflesh in the territory."

Jack nodded toward the north fields. "And looks like your herd isn't too shabby either."

Quiet pride shone in the man's expression. "Miss Maudelaine Mahoney won't accept anything less than the best. From her employees or her animals."

Jack hesitated, thinking he'd misunderstood, but Stewartson's revealing grin said he hadn't. "You're telling me a . . . woman built all this?"

Stewartson indicated the main house. "Miss Mahoney runs Casaroja now. Has for the past three years. But everybody around here calls her Miss Maudie. It was her nephew, Donlyn MacGregor, who actually started the place. He's . . . not with us anymore."

Regret shadowed Stewartson's eyes, and Jack paused for a second, aware of the hesitancy in the man's tone and thinking he was going to say something more. "Well," Jack finally said, "Miss Mahoney is doing a fine job—with a little help from you, I'm sure."

"And many others, I assure you." Stewartson gestured toward the barn closest to them. "I've picked out two of our finest horses for you, Brennan. Percherons. We had eight of them delivered this past week, as a matter of fact. First of their breed to come to Casaroja, and to this part of the country. Finest workhorses I've ever seen. Originally from France, they tell me."

"From France, you say." The humor of this coincidence wasn't lost on Jack. *Won't Mademoiselle Girard love this. . . .*

Stewartson nodded. "Smart animals too—amenable, good tempered. And energetic to boot. The pair is well matched in height and size for pulling."

"I'm eager to see them. But first . . ." Jack had to ask the question, regardless of having already agreed to work for Mademoiselle Girard. "You don't happen to have any freight wagons available, do you?"

"We've got lots of freight wagons. But if by available you mean for sale, then I'm afraid you're out of luck." Stewartson frowned. "I was under the impression you already had a wagon, Brennan."

Jack smiled to himself. "I do. I was just checking."

Stewartson motioned for him to follow. "I'll show you these first, and then I'd encourage you to ride out and look at the rest of the herd too, if you're—"

"Thomas!"

Stewartson turned in the direction of the shrill voice, and Jack followed suit.

A woman rushed down the back stairs of the main house and ran toward them, the screen door slamming behind her. "Thomas, it's Miss Maudie. She's taken a fall!"

Stewartson immediately started for the house. "Brennan," he called back over his shoulder, "you go on ahead and—"

"If I can be of help, I'm willing."

At the man's nod, Jack shadowed his steps.

They climbed the back stairs and entered the house through the kitchen. The young woman gave Jack a brief nod, and then clutched at Stewartson's arm. "I found her at the base of the staircase, Thomas. I don't know how far she fell, but she says it hurts her to move." The woman cut a path around a large rectangular table and down an unusually wide hallway. "She tried to get up, stubborn woman, but I told her to stay put until I got you."

Jack followed after them, noticing the fine furniture perfectly arranged beneath painted canvases of distinguished-looking men and women.

"I've told her not to take the stairs alone, what with the dizzy spells she's had recently."

"It's all right, honey, we'll see to her. She's 'bout as tough as they come. Mr. Brennan—" Stewartson glanced behind him—"this is my wife, Claire. She manages the kitchen here at Casaroja."

Remembering his hat, Jack slipped it off. "Ma'am."

Claire looked back at him, tears filling her eyes. She offered a weak smile.

Jack rounded the corner behind the couple and spotted the elderly woman slumped at the base of the stairs. Her eyes were closed. His gaze quickly ascended the lofty staircase, and he prayed Claire

Stewartson was right in her hope that the woman hadn't fallen all the way down.

Claire knelt and arranged the woman's skirt over her lower legs. But not before Jack spotted the slight protrusion in Miss Maudie's right shin, just beneath the skin.

"Miss Maudie, Thomas is here." Claire tenderly brushed a shock of white hair from the older woman's forehead. "We're going to take care of you, so don't you fret."

Beads of perspiration glistened on the woman's brow. Her eyes fluttered open, then closed again. "Oh . . . I'm not frettin', dear. But I am—"she winced and drew in a quick breath—"hurtin' just a wee bit. If the room would cease its spinnin', I'd be the better for it."

"Where exactly does it hurt?" Claire asked.

"At this very moment . . . I'd have to say everywhere." Miss Maudie sighed, a shallow smile momentarily eclipsing her frown.

Jack kept his distance, not wanting to frighten the woman with a stranger's presence. Though, despite her frail appearance and delicate Irish lilt, he sensed that Miss Maudelaine Mahoney was not a woman easily alarmed—by anything.

Already kneeling over her, Stewartson leaned close to her face. "Miss Maudie, I need to check for broken bones, ma'am." Though he voiced it like a statement, the echo of a silent question lingered in his tone.

"That'll be fine by me, Thomas. As long as that pretty wife of yours won't be gettin' jealous over it."

With a subdued laugh, Claire pressed the older woman's hand between hers. "I've always known you had an eye for my husband, Miss Maudie."

Miss Maudie's gaze briefly connected with the younger woman's, and a look of endearment passed between them. Then Miss Maudie's focus shifted. She squinted as though not seeing clearly. "Who's that there?"

Stewartson motioned Jack forward. "This is Jack Brennan." He started a slow examination of the woman's arms and shoulders. "The gentleman who's buying the Percherons."

Miss Maudie lifted her head slightly. "Ah . . . the wagon master turned freighter."

Jack moved into her line of vision, smiling at how she'd

summarized his career so succinctly—reminded him of someone' else who'd done that in recent days. . . . "It's a pleasure to meet you, ma'am. I'm sorry about your accident."

She eased her head back onto the plush rug. "I am too, Mr. Brennan. That's a fine surname you bear. Would you be knowin' what area your people were from?"

"They hailed from Kilkenny, ma'am," he answered, slipping easily into the thick Irish brogue of his grandparents. "Me great-grandfather came over in 1789. Brought with him his beautiful bride and their three wee bairns. Triplets they were." He winked. "And holy terrors, the lot of them, if family tales hold true."

A smile bloomed across Miss Maudie's face. She chuckled. "What a blessin' to hear a bit of my homeland in the deep timbre of a man's voice. Where are your people livin' now?"

"My brothers and sisters live in Missouri, ma'am. The rest of the family is scattered back East."

"And your folks?"

Jack's smile grew more subdued. "I laid my folks to rest about ten years ago—God rest their souls."

Miss Maudie repeated the blessing in a whisper. "I remember passin' through Kilkenny when I was but a young lass." She raised her head again. "There was a—"

Stewartson held up a hand. "Okay, enough talking for now." Concern softened his expression. "I need you to lie still, ma'am, and save your breath. Doc Hadley's going to want an explanation once he finds out you've been climbing those stairs alone."

Miss Maudie frowned, but Jack caught her subtle wink seconds later and shook his head. Despite her present condition, he didn't have any trouble imagining this woman in charge of Casaroja, and would've welcomed her on any one of his caravans through the years.

As Stewartson started to gently run a hand over Miss Maudie's left leg, Jack knelt and pointed discreetly to her right shin, wanting to spare her the additional pain of having the injury touched.

With a quiet apology, Stewartson eased the woman's skirt to mid-calf to reveal the protrusion. He gently touched her right foot. "Miss Maudie, looks like you've got a break on this side, ma'am. Right near the middle of your shin."

"Well, that explains it." She sighed. "I heard somethin' like the crack of a whip when I went down. Flames shot up my leg good and hot."

Claire rose, looking at her husband. "I'll send for Doc Hadley."

"Oh, I wish we didn't have to be doin' that." As Claire left the room, a frown shadowed the elderly woman's pale complexion. "He'll use the opportunity to give me yet another tongue-lashin' about how I'm no longer a young lass."

Jack admired the woman's spunk. "It's not a clean break, ma'am, but I've seen this before. Hopefully it won't take too long to heal."

She smiled up at him. "And should we be addin' doctorin' to that list of your professions, Mr. Brennan?"

He briefly ducked his head, turning his hat in his hands. "Not hardly, ma'am. But when you're out in the middle of nowhere, sometimes doctors are scarce. I've managed to learn a few things along the way."

Her gaze held discernment. "I'm thinkin' you'd be a good man to have around, Mr. Brennan. You wouldn't be interested in settlin' down and workin' on a little ranch I know of, would you, now?"

"I appreciate the offer, Miss Mahoney. Looking at the setup you've got here, it's mighty tempting. But I've obligations to fulfill. And to be honest, I'm getting a mite restless for the trail again, and to see those mountains of yours up close."

He imagined accompanying Mademoiselle Véronique Girard through those mountains to the various mining towns—most of which were still uncharted territory for him—and while the image of her sitting beside him on the wagon seat wasn't altogether unpleasant, he couldn't help but wish she possessed a bit more of Miss Maudie's spunk, and a little less *fancy*. He had his doubts about how well she'd fare under such primitive conditions. Then again, she'd proven him wrong before, so it wouldn't be the first time.

He'd seen her at church earlier that morning, sitting between Hannah Carlson and the young girl he'd seen at the mercantile. Who turned out to be the Carlsons' daughter, Lilly. She was a younger version of her mother, and he wondered how he'd missed their physical resemblance the day before in the mercantile. Of course, his mind had been on other things that particular afternoon.

When Pastor Carlson secretly singled him out during the sermon, and said those kind things about him, the certainty of God's presence in Jack's life had moved over him to a degree he'd not remembered before. Or perhaps he'd just never experienced such a strong emotional reaction to the knowledge. Whichever, it had been both an uncomfortable experience for him and one that he welcomed to happen again.

As Jack helped Stewartson move Miss Maudie to the bedroom located around the corner, the reality of being responsible for someone else again began to weigh on him. The burden he'd carried in moving families west for thirteen years was one he'd gratefully laid aside last fall with his final trip to Oregon. Now it rested squarely on his shoulders again, and none too lightly this time. Especially when considering how disappointing Véronique Girard's search for her father could be. What if she never found the man? Or what if she found him and the man she discovered wasn't the father she expected?

Or worse still, what if Pierre Gustave Girard—like many of the foreign trappers he'd known or heard about—left his wife and daughter behind in Paris all those years ago with the intention of never being found?

CHAPTER FOURTEEN

For the third time, Véronique stopped on the boardwalk and set the tapestry bag down with a thud. Twilight hovered over the awakening town of Willow Springs, and her labored breathing sounded harsh against the quiet hush of early morning.

The leather strap of the *valise* wouldn't stay latched, which made the bag more difficult to carry, especially considering its weight. Monsieur Brennan had said this would be a day-trip, so she'd brought only the essentials.

By his calculations, they would reach the mining town of Jenny's Draw shortly after noon. If their journey went as discussed, they would sell their load of supplies to a storeowner by the name of Scoggins and would inquire of him about local miners with the purpose of gaining any information about her father. Then they would head back down the mountain to return to Willow Springs before nightfall. The way Monsieur Brennan had laid it out made it sound quite routine, but Véronique couldn't help but feel a rush of tempered excitement.

Finally, the real search for her father would begin.

Every step of her journey had brought her closer to this moment, and she found it exhilarating to finally be fulfilling her promise to her mother—and to herself.

She stretched her back and shoulders, and eyed the bag at her feet.

It had been on the tip of her tongue Saturday to ask Monsieur Brennan to pick her up at the hotel this morning, but he'd beat her to it and suggested she be at the livery at dawn. With things so recently smoothed over between them, she hadn't wanted to cause any further ripples.

But carrying her own *bagage* was not something to which she was accustomed. And she *was* paying him seven dollars a day.

Dawn's pale fingers spread a wash of *rouge* across the sky, snuffing out stars and telling her it was time to get moving again. She knelt and stuffed the contents of the bag farther down inside, then stretched the leather strap as far as it would go. But still it failed to reach the hook.

So she grasped the handles and hefted it against her chest, feeling less like a lady and more like a workhorse, despite the blue silk gown she wore.

It was an older ensemble—one that Francette Marchand had left behind upon her marriage years ago, and one well suited for travel. Véronique didn't mind if it became soiled. The gown was serviceable but not overly exquisite. It displayed slightly more décolletage than she was comfortable with so she'd stayed up last night adding a piece of ivory lace for modesty's sake. At the very least, she wanted to look presentable for the occasion. The mining town they would visit today might hold a clue about her father, or her father himself.

The boardwalk was quiet except for a few shopkeepers arriving to ready their stores. Across the street, a woman entered the dress shop and closed the door behind her. Farther down, a man unlocked the door to the land and titles office. Véronique had promised Monsieur Brennan she would arrive on time, so she plodded onward, satchel clutched against her chest.

Being delayed on their first trip together would not be the way to start this partnership.

One-handed, she gave her jacket a hasty tug and ran a hand over her hair. From necessity, she'd learned to fix her own hair months ago, but she still missed the elaborate *coiffures* of her former station in life. The way a woman presented herself in public spoke volumes about her character and self-worth, not to mention her social standing.

A thought flitted past, leaving a tickle in its wake.

She should open a second dress shop in Willow Springs—give the women of the town an alternative to the drab, monotonous selections she'd seen hanging in the store window down the street. She could design fashionable Parisian ensembles and hire seamstresses to sew the creations under her supervision. Though the idea wasn't without merit, it held more humor than practicality. Still, it lightened her step as she continued down the street.

She rounded the corner and all thoughts fled. Gasping, she came to an abrupt halt. She could scarcely believe what she saw.

Percherons!

Two of the enormous horses were harnessed to the wagon in front of the livery. Magnificent animals. Black as night and thickly built, all muscle and sinew and strength. She hadn't seen the breed since she'd departed Europe, but she easily recalled the first time she saw them as a young girl. It was her youngest memory of being with both of her parents, and of them as a family.

She had sat atop her father's shoulders, with her mother tucked close beside him, smiling up at her. Festive decorations and music floated overhead, and tempting aromas of fresh-baked bread and meaty sausages beckoned. She had something in her hand—a half-eaten *pâtisserie* perhaps. The memory of trumpet blasts and cheering embellished the recollection, as did that of uniformed soldiers riding past on horses that seemed fashioned for men at least twice their size. A parade in the streets of Paris, most likely. But for what occasion, she couldn't be certain.

Her father had adored horses—she did remember that much. While too poor to own Percherons himself, he had often taken jobs at liveries and stables, assisting with their care and training—this from her mother's shared memories.

Véronique slowly opened her eyes, unaware until that moment that she'd closed them. She focused on the horses harnessed to the wagon, the memory thick and vivid around her. One thought in particular loomed especially close, and she wondered why it hadn't occurred to her before.

When she was young, her mother had spoken constantly about her father, about his return, reading a letter or two to her at night, and telling tales about things the three of them had done together.

What Véronique couldn't pinpoint, what she couldn't remember, was when that had stopped. And why.

But stopped it had, and most abruptly if her memory served.

She blinked to clear her cobwebbed memory and noticed Monsieur Brennan by the wagon. He was securing stacks of boxes and crates in the back with ropes and netting. Jake Sampson assisted from the opposite side.

Where had Monsieur Brennan found such a pair of horses? Assuming he had arranged for them. And did he know they originated from France? If not, she could tell him the history.

Véronique knew the precise moment Monsieur Jack Brennan spotted her.

He halted from his task, rope in hand, and from the slight downward tilt of his chin, he was giving her a thorough perusal.

She couldn't see the exact details of his face in the pale light, yet a blush heated hers at his unexpected attention. But it pleased her to think he approved.

"*Bonjour, messieurs.*" She didn't dare attempt a curtsy with the *sachel* in her arms, but gratefully deposited the bag by the wagon.

Jake Sampson blew out a low whistle and gave his beard a good stroking. "Well, if you're not the prettiest thing I've seen yet today. What a way to start my week, ma'am." His brow rose. "If you don't mind me sayin' so."

"*Merci beaucoup*, Monsieur Sampson." She smiled, appreciating his reaction. But what drew her greater attention, and concern, was the dark look Jack Brennan gave the man right before he threw a scowl in her direction.

"Good morning, Mademoiselle Girard." For the first time, Jack Brennan's smile did not reach his eyes. "Are you ready for our journey today?"

His friendly tone belied his serious expression. And beneath his simple inquiry lurked another question, but its meaning remained hidden to her. "*Oui*, and I have great anticipation for it. Do you not as well, Monsieur Brennan?"

Wordless, he returned to his task of securing the ties.

Confused by his behavior, Véronique decided to try a different tactic. "Did you purchase the horses yourself, Monsieur Brennan? You may not be aware, but they are *Perch*—"

"I asked you to be here, ready to go, at dawn, mademoiselle." He glanced upward. "It's dawn." He looked back at her. "But you're not ready."

Véronique stared, not knowing how to respond. She felt as if she were addressing a different man, not the Jack Brennan with whom she had become acquainted, with whom she had planned this trip. Perhaps he'd had time to reflect on the transaction with the wagon or his employment being terminated in her presence. Maybe he was brooding. Christophe used to have a very similar expression when his plans had been thwarted. Regardless, she decided not to let Jack Brennan's ill temper rule the situation.

"*Oui*, it is dawn, Monsieur Brennan, and . . . *voilà*! I am here, as you can see. And I am on time as promised." No thanks to him for making her carry her own *bagage*.

Jack Brennan gave the rope in his hand a firm tug.

Véronique glanced at Jake Sampson for help, but the man kept his distance, saying nothing. She'd had such hopes for today. Why was Jack Brennan ruining it with a surly attitude?

She pointed to her *valise*. "Here is my *bagage*, Monsieur Brennan. Would you be so kind as to load it for me?"

"Why?" He didn't turn. "You won't be going."

Anger heated her instantly. She stepped closer. "*Excusez-moi?* Why will I not be going?" She waited for him to face her.

He didn't.

If a servant had spoken to her and treated her in such a manner in Paris, Lord Marchand would have dismissed the fool out of hand. However, under the circumstances, she didn't have that luxury. "I do not know the reason for your behavior, Monsieur Brennan. You are being most . . ." What was the word? She thought of the book in her *réticule*. Her brows rose. "Obtuse!"

He scoffed and shook his head. "If I'm being obtuse, ma'am, then you're being—" his gaze swept her from head to foot, then back again in a slow, appraising fashion—"ridiculous."

Véronique felt her mouth slip open.

"Mademoiselle Girard, I expressly asked you on Saturday to wear something suitable for where we're going. And this is what you choose?"

Véronique instantly put a hand to her bodice, pressing the lace to her chest. Her face burned with embarrassment. Then a second thought told her she had nothing of which to be ashamed—the lace she'd chosen was of a very fine weave. "My gown is completely modest, Monsieur Brennan. You have no right to—"

He moved within inches of her. "I'm not commenting on your gown's modesty, Mademoiselle Girard." His gaze dropped for the briefest of seconds. His voice lowered as he spoke. "Although that term could be open for discussion depending on how we're each using the word."

With their difference in heights, she had to tip her head back to see him properly. She kept her palm firmly planted over the piece of lace—which seemed as though it had shrunk by half. "My gown is modest, sir, in that it observes the proprieties of decency and good taste as are becoming of a lady in society."

He nodded. "I couldn't agree more. But we're not headed to society, ma'am. Where we're going, your dress will draw attention to you in a manner that will be most unwelcome. And that makes what you're wearing for this particular occasion . . . immodest, in my opinion. These mining towns—" He gave a sharp chuckle, then murmured something she couldn't hear. "We've already been through this. . . ." He raked a hand through his hair.

When he looked at her again, the harshness in his expression took her aback.

"The men in these towns won't have seen a real lady in months, ma'am. And their reaction at seeing a woman like you is not something I'm looking forward to dealing with. Do I need to make myself plainer than that, mademoiselle? I don't care to, but I will if it will help you understand the situation."

Véronique's defensiveness receded in light of his plainspoken concerns. She slowly lowered her hand. She didn't wholly agree, but thanks to what she'd learned from Christophe, she conceded that Jack Brennan was probably more knowledgeable about this than she. Yet her problem was not solved. "All of the dresses I own are"—she glanced down—"similar to this one. Except different colors."

A loud snort sounded from the other side of the wagon, and they both turned.

A grin plastered Jake Sampson's face. "I don't think changin' the color's gonna help you none, missy." He chuckled. "You agree, Brennan?"

A look passed between Monsieur Brennan and Jake Sampson which Véronique did not *comprend*. But from the censure in Monsieur Brennan's eyes, he clearly did not share the other man's humor.

Brennan glanced at the dusty blue sky overhead. "Mademoiselle Girard, we should already be gone by now."

"I will not be left behind, Monsieur Brennan!" She pulled a map from her *réticule*, resisting the urge to smack him in the chest with it. "There are forty-five mining towns in this area in which my father could be residing. I must visit these places before winter comes. And need I remind you . . ." She looked pointedly at the wagon, then back at him.

His eyes narrowed. "I didn't peg you as the threatening kind, ma'am."

Feeling only mildly guilty, she shrugged. "You have never backed me into a corner before, monsieur." At a loss to describe the emotion that moved in behind his eyes, she would have given much to know his thoughts at the moment.

"So what do you propose we do, mademoiselle? If I don't get this load of goods up that mountain today, I lose my job. And if that happens . . . you lose your driver."

Véronique tempered her smile. "Now who is doing the threatening, monsieur?"

He shrugged, returning the look she'd just given him. "I'll wait thirty minutes for you to find an appropriate dress, and then I'm leaving."

Believing he would do it, she hurried down the boardwalk without a backward glance.

Jack sat aboard the wagon, aware of Jake Sampson standing in the doorway of the livery watching him.

"You really gonna leave her behind, Brennan? You sounded serious, but I thought you were just kiddin'."

Jack checked his pocket watch. She'd been gone twenty-seven minutes and counting. He released the brake. "Do you have any idea what you've gotten me into, Sampson?"

"Actually, I think I do. You're where about every other man in this town would give his eyeteeth to be." The livery owner sauntered toward the wagon, making a show of looking down the boardwalk. "But if my memory serves, you said no to this deal the day I offered it to you . . . didn't you?"

Hearing levity in the man's voice, Jack heard truth in it too. "Have you started my wagon yet, sir?"

"It's at the top of my list, son. I'll have it done in no time."

Jack smiled but gave him a look that said he was serious.

Sampson finally nodded. Then he patted a crate in the wagon bed. "You think you'll sell all this stuff? Zimmerman sometimes came back from Jenny's Draw with half a wagonload."

"My goal is to come back empty. I paid Hochstetler outright for it all. He'd been carrying the inventory on his books, holding the job for me." Jack fingered the reins, considering what he'd done. "Call it an act of faith on my part."

Footsteps sounded behind them.

"Well, I'll be—" Jake Sampson chuckled.

Jack turned on the bench seat and couldn't decide whether what he saw coming toward him was an improvement or not.

When Mademoiselle Girard reached the wagon, her cheeks were flushed. Strands of hair fell loose around her face. She gripped the side of the cargo bed, her breath coming in short gasps. "I am . . . still on time . . . *oui?*"

He couldn't believe it. Draped in brown homespun from the top of her pretty little neck to the toe of her fancy pointy-heeled boots, Véronique Girard was still stunning.

And selling his load of cargo was suddenly the far lesser of his concerns.

Jack reset the brake and climbed down from the wagon. "Yes, ma'am, you're on time. Barely." The crinkle in her brow made him smile. "You did well, Mademoiselle Girard."

"The dress shop was not open yet, but when I knocked on her door . . . repeatedly"—she held up a hand as though signaling to catch her breath—"the shopkeeper granted me entrance . . . and was quite helpful once I explained to her the nature of our travels." She finished tucking her hair into place, minus a curl or two teasing her temples.

"I'll say you did well, ma'am," Sampson commented, tossing Jack an exaggerated wink over her head. "Mr. Brennan doesn't have a thing to worry about now."

Ignoring him, Jack offered her his hand. "If you're ready, mademoiselle, we need to get on the road." He assisted her up to the buckboard, then climbed up beside her. "Did you remember to bring a jacket? It gets cold up there."

"*Oui*, my *jaquette* is in my bag." She situated herself, then smoothed a hand over her bodice and her skirt. "Madame Dunston, the shopkeeper, invited me to return later this week. She said she would alter the shirtwaist and skirt to fit better."

Trying not to dwell on whether that was even possible, Jack chose not to comment and flicked the reins, hearing Sampson's laughter behind them.

CHAPTER FIFTEEN

GLANCING BESIDE HER, Véronique drew strength from watching Jack Brennan handle the wagon—his experienced hands holding the reins, the way he read the rocky path ahead and expertly maneuvered the team around potential pitfalls. Even the way he spoke to the horses—his deep voice soothing and instilled with confidence—had a calming effect on her.

Still, she kept a tight grip on the bench seat and concentrated on not looking at the sheer drop off to her right. Why she hadn't anticipated this part of the journey, she didn't know.

Jack pointed up the road. "According to the drawings, there's a place up ahead where the road gets pretty tight. I might need you to watch the wheels on your side for me, just to make sure we're okay."

She shivered at the thought, and her stomach went cold even as her body flushed hot. She managed a brief nod, thankful for the chill in the air.

"Are you cold, mademoiselle? Do you want your jacket?"

She shook her head and worked to keep her voice even. "*Non*, I am well, *merci*."

Despite this unforeseen portion of their trip, one thing had become clear in the three hours since they'd left Willow Springs—if God had chosen to linger over any portion of His creation during the seven days He formed the earth, she was quite certain He had devoted at least one leisurely afternoon to these mountains alone. There was a rawness to their beauty, but coupled with that splendor lingered an ever-present reminder of their power. And that awareness only grew more profound the higher the road twisted and climbed as it hugged the mountain.

Véronique chanced another look over the side of the wagon. The road ended a mere foot from the wheel before plunging into a canyon of churning water below. Fogginess crept in behind her eyes.

She closed them tight and concentrated on breathing—in and out, in and out, slow and deep—all the while wishing Monsieur Sampson had built this wagon with a roof and windows, and curtains she could pull closed around her.

"You all right, ma'am?"

Jack Brennan's voice drew her back. She opened her eyes and found him staring. "*Oui*, I am well, *merci*. . . ." She swallowed and forced a smile, then followed his attention to her white-knuckled grip on the bench seat between them.

"I know that look, ma'am. And I wouldn't call it 'well.'"

For some reason, she did not want to admit her fear. She already knew his, but that was different. Hers seemed so . . . silly in the face of all this man had likely encountered in his lifetime. She got the distinct impression that he viewed her as inexperienced and helpless, and that alone was enough to spur her to let go of the seat—almost.

She loosened her grip.

He maneuvered the wagon around a large rock in the road before looking back. "Heights."

She kept her focus ahead.

"You're afraid of heights. That's all right, ma'am." He paused, and she could feel him watching her. "That's nothin' to be ashamed of."

She winced slightly. "That is nothing of which to be ashamed."

"Pardon me?"

She ignored the glint of humor in his eyes. "I have noticed, monsieur, that on occasion you phrase your sentences in an incorrect manner, according to the rules of your language."

"You're kidding me, right?" His attention returned to the road.

"It is not an offensive thing." She shrugged, watching how easily he held the reins. "It matters not to me. I only point it out because I thought you might want to know it."

"You're big into the rules, huh?"

"*Pardonnez-moi?*"

"The rules." His eyes narrowed the slightest bit, still focused ahead. "You're big into doing things the way others say they should be done. I mean, I'm fine with that—it doesn't matter to me. I just thought I'd point it out, in case you wanted to know."

"Are you having fun with me, Monsieur Brennan?"

His laughter was instantaneous and full. "I think the phrase you're looking for, Mademoiselle Girard, is 'Are you making fun of me?'" He pulled back on the reins. "And no, ma'am . . . I'm not."

He motioned past her.

She turned and saw they were stopped alongside the road, at a place where the water from the bubbling creek she'd seen earlier had found haven in a protected cove. Not a whisper of wind moved through the trees. The surface of the water, tranquil and motionless, reflected the mountain reigning above it in amazing detail.

"*Très belle,*" she whispered, and for the first time in months she sensed the faintest nudge to reach for a pencil or brush to capture the beauty before her. She remembered the feel of each instrument in her hand, the way they fit into the curve of her fingers and palm, becoming an extension of who she was.

Then she remembered—the gift had been removed; she was certain. And as quickly as the urge had come, it faded.

Her gaze trailed the edge of the placid pool back in the direction they'd come, and suddenly her insides coiled tight. The section of road they'd just traveled seemed impossibly narrow for this size wagon.

"Monsieur Brennan, you were making fun of me just now, were you not? To tempt my thoughts away from the steepness of the ledge."

His answer registered first in his eyes. "You rescued me once, mademoiselle. I just figured I'd return the favor."

The thoughtfulness of his gesture touched her. "That was most generous of you." She smiled, unexpected mischief zesting her relief. "Although, I must say . . . I believe my *technique* of rescue was somewhat kinder than your own, *non?*"

"That may be, ma'am." His voice was surprisingly soft. "But since taking hold of your hand back there wasn't exactly an option, I think my way was safer . . . for many reasons."

She found herself staring at the delayed smile moving across his face. "Ah . . . much like the situation with my gown."

He held her gaze for a beat longer, then broke the connection. "Yes, ma'am, something like that." He jumped down and waited to assist her.

She liked the way he held her when he helped her down. Firmly, gently, yet his hands didn't linger overlong about her waist as other men's often did. She thought again of how he'd referred to her earlier that morning. ". . . *their reaction at seeing a woman like you . . .*" A woman like her. He hadn't said lady, or even young woman, but woman. Appreciation for his observance bloomed inside her.

"Would you be so kind as to retrieve my *bagage*, Monsieur Brennan?"

He lifted her satchel from the back and set it beside her. "What on earth do you have in there? Bricks?"

"You said to bring the essentials, Monsieur Brennan, and that is exactly what I did."

He nodded, but his expression communicated his doubt. "Another hour, ma'am, and we'll be to Jenny's Draw. I'll go see to the horses while you eat some lunch."

Lunch. She just now remembered that he'd told her to bring along something to eat. She'd been so intent on bringing extra items, her brushes and combs, her mirror and her books, that she'd forgotten about food.

"You *did* bring a lunch . . . mademoiselle?"

If there had been anything edible in her *valise*, be it the stalest bread crumb left over from the voyage across the Atlantic, she would have answered yes and fended off the ensuing guilt—anything to avoid looking foolish in this man's eyes.

She shook her head, expecting a labored sigh.

"That's all right. I asked Mrs. Baird to fix me a lunch last night, and I'm sure there's more than enough. That woman's idea of a meal is more like a buffet. Check the burlap sack beneath the seat."

Speechless, she watched him go, knowing again that God had delivered Jack Brennan into her life to help her at this point in her journey. She looked up ahead to where the road folded back into the mountain and thought about Jenny's Draw and the many mining camps dotting these mountains.

God had seen fit to answer her prayers pertaining to one man. Now if He would only see fit to answer her prayers concerning a second.

The acrid scent of burning coal reached them before Jenny's Draw came into view. Jack got an occasional whiff of something else, and finally decided it was either rotting garbage or human waste. He'd never been to Jenny's Draw, yet he'd been to enough mining towns in Idaho and California to know what to expect.

Mademoiselle Girard had grown unusually quiet beside him, and he was tempted to turn the wagon around and head back. But knowing he had a job to do, and that she wouldn't let him turn around if he tried, he guided the horses on around the curve. He'd made a mistake in bringing her, and didn't plan on letting her out of his sight.

Makeshift buildings, a scant arm's length from each other, lined the solitary thoroughfare that comprised the mining town. The road was muddy from melted snows, and layered in muck and manure. What few houses he saw were constructed of clapboard and odd pieces of lumber, and looked as though a stiff wind would seal their unquestionable fate. Tents squatted close behind the structures, one after the other, situated to take advantage of the scant shelter the buildings might provide from the north wind. He counted three saloons, and they weren't yet halfway down the street.

A blast sounded, ricocheting off the walls of the canyon.

Mademoiselle Girard jumped beside him.

Jack instinctively reached out and covered her hand on the seat between them. Realizing what he'd done, he started to pull back, surprised when she clutched his hand tighter.

Smoke rose over the buildings on the far side of town, and a piercing whistle split the afternoon.

Her grip tightened again. "What is that announcing?"

"Changing of the shifts." Which meant the street would soon be overrun with men. What timing . . . Best get their business conducted and be on their way.

He spotted a building that had steel bars fortressing the front windows. It was the largest establishment on the street, and he guessed it might belong to Scoggins. Guiding the wagon in that direction, his attention was drawn to a larger tent set off to the right. Women stood out front, all scantily clad and doing their best to entice would-be clients to join them inside. From the looks of things, their tactics were working.

Up ahead, groups of miners gathered in the road. In unison, they turned and spotted the wagon. Cheers went up and pistol shots rang out, echoing off the mountains and thundering back again. Jack would've liked to think their celebration was in response to his cargo and had nothing to do with the woman who sat beside him, but he had a feeling it might be both.

"You stay in the wagon, Mademoiselle Girard. And don't speak to any of the men, no matter what they say to you. I'll do the talking, like we agreed. And I'll inquire about your father. Do you understand?" When she didn't answer, he looked beside him to make sure she was listening. From personal experience, he knew how naïve she could be. Either that or thickheaded. His gut told him it was the former, but he wasn't quite ready to rule out the other.

Her brown eyes were wide and watchful. "I will do as we agreed." She turned to him, her expression earnest. "Do you have your weapon at the ready, monsieur?"

He couldn't help but smile. "Yes, ma'am, I do." He indicated the rifle loaded and resting against his thigh. "And I've got a Schofield tucked in my belt."

"If a Schofield is a gun, then that is good thing."

"I don't anticipate needing either, ma'am. But it's better to be—"

"Safe than sorry. *Oui*, I agree. I have learned this phrase. It means it is better to act cautiously beforehand than to suffer afterward."

She let go of his hand and squared her shoulders, lifting her chin in the process. Suddenly she looked more like royalty on an afternoon outing than a daughter searching for the father she'd never really known.

Jack pulled up alongside a building and set the brake.

Two dozen men quickly formed a circle around the wagon. Some simply stared at Mademoiselle Girard while others tried to gain her attention by speaking directly to her. Jack understood what most of the miners were saying, but there were a couple languages he didn't understand, Mademoiselle Girard's being among them.

She kept her focus ahead, her shoulders erect.

"Gentlemen." Jack stood, rifle in hand. "Would you tell me where I might find Wiley Scoggins?"

"You'll find him right here."

Jack hadn't pictured Wiley Scoggins beforehand but certainly would never have matched that name with the man filling the doorway of the building before him. Scoggins was about his height, but the man had him in spades when it came to girth. "I'm Jack Brennan, from Willow Springs. I've got your load of supplies."

"Is everything we see for sale?"

The voice came from behind him, so Jack couldn't single out its owner. Snickers skittered through the crowd.

"Is there any samplin' of the merchandise?"

"We got an openin' over at Lolly's tent."

More laughter, then shots rang out.

Jack scanned the faces in the crowd. The men ranged from youthful teens to aging codgers. Regardless of age, their collective expressions wore a flush of excitement that came only from seeing a beautiful woman. He'd felt it the first time he'd seen her that morning outside the washroom. But knowing they shared his reaction awakened a possessiveness inside him that went far beyond the need to simply protect her.

His grip tightened on his rifle. "The supplies in the back of the wagon are for sale. Scoggins, you get first dibs on everything, as agreed. Whatever you don't take becomes negotiable to the other men."

Scoggins stepped on a crate substituting for stairs beneath the doorway. The box creaked beneath his weight. "Sounds fair enough."

Jack met him beside the wagon, well aware of the man's lingering attention on Mademoiselle Girard—same as every other pair of eyes in the crowd. Jack motioned to the ropes securing the cargo, and Scoggins helped untie them. All Hochstetler from the mercantile had said about this man was that he liked to wheedle on the price, which was expected. But Wiley Scoggins had a quality about him that set Jack on edge.

Another blast sounded, similar to the one moments before.

But this time a low rumble followed. The earth trembled, and voices fell silent.

Jack studied the dirt under his boots, half expecting to see a fissure split the road. When he looked up, he discovered Mademoiselle Girard's eyes locked on his.

For several seconds, no one moved. No one spoke.

Then three shrill spurts of a high-pitched whistle sounded, and the men immediately fell back into conversation as though nothing had happened. Jack nodded to her, indicating everything was fine, and hoped that it truly was.

Miners huddled around the front of the wagon, getting as close as they could without actually touching anything. Jack kept an eye on Mademoiselle Girard, unable to see her face but noting that her posture was ramrod straight. He glimpsed a younger man's expression and could only describe it as smitten. But what he saw in the other faces made him glad, again, that he was armed.

Scoggins pulled a bowie knife from a sheath on his belt and pried open a crate containing bags of coffee. Then another filled with hammers and chisels. "I hope you plan on dealin' more fairly than Zimmerman did. That man was a crook. Never could count on what he'd be carrying or what his cost would be."

Jack met his stare straight on. "The price I quote won't change unless market prices go higher. I have to cover my costs, same as you. Give me a list of supplies you want, and when I'm up here next, I'll do my best to fill it."

Scoggins didn't answer but kept opening crates. He paused on occasion to give Jack a questioning look, then finally strode toward the building. "We need to talk, Brennan. Smithy, watch the wagon."

A man immediately stepped forward, thick-chested, belligerent-looking, and—in Jack's opinion—enough of a deterrent.

Jack tossed the netting back over the wagon bed, easily guessing what Scoggins wanted to discuss. Hochstetler had prepared him and said he would back Jack on his decision. Seems that Zimmerman, the previous freighter, had held some side agreements with Scoggins.

Jack stopped by the buckboard. Mademoiselle Girard's expression was a smooth mask of composure.

But when she slipped her hand in his after he helped her down, he found it to be ice-cold.

Jack tucked her hand into the crook of his arm and held her much closer than he normally would have. He guided her through the crowd, meeting every man's eye as he went. Murmurs of "Good day, ma'am" and "How'dya do, ma'am" echoed as they passed. Hats came off heads faster than he could count, sending puffs of dust into the air.

Jack assisted her onto the crate and was thankful to shut the door behind them. Until he saw the glare on Scoggins's face and knew he was responsible for putting it there.

CHAPTER SIXTEEN

WILEY SCOGGINS ADDRESSED Jack from behind a counter constructed of sawhorses and plank board. "Where's the whiskey, Brennan?"

Rifle in hand, Jack waited, letting the silence soak up the accusation. "I don't haul liquor, Mr. Scoggins."

The man laughed, then gradually sobered. "You're serious."

"Yes, sir, I am. But I've got plenty of other things that will interest the men."

"The men don't want schoolbooks and peppermint sticks, Mr. Brennan. They want liquor. Women and liquor. We've already got the one—we need the other."

Jack sensed Mademoiselle Girard's tension beside him but kept his focus on Scoggins. "Then you're going to have to arrange shipment for that through someone else. Liquor, the way it's consumed here, isn't something I condone. Among other things . . ."

"Teetotaler are you, Brennan?"

Ignoring the obvious taunt, Jack pulled the inventory list from his pocket. "Every other item you ordered is in the wagon. Just as you requested."

"Except the most important one!"

As though reconsidering his outburst, Scoggins smiled and spread his arms wide. "Listen, friend. The men around here like to enjoy a drink every now and then. There's no harm in that. After a hard day's work, they deserve it."

"From the looks of things here I'd hardly label the drinking these men do as 'every now and then.'"

The merchant's stare hardened. "I'll give you twice your normal profit."

"Not interested."

Scoggins moved from behind the counter. "Three times your profit, and that's my final offer."

Jack shook his head. "My answer stands."

An unexpected grin replaced the merchant's frown. "Don't tell me, Brennan . . . your father was a drunk and used to beat you senseless, so you've sworn off the stuff for good. Now you're on some kind of"—his voice deepened, and he jabbed his forefinger in the air like some sort of hellfire-and-brimstone preacher—"holy rampage to rid the world of the evil brew."

Jack was only mildly amused. "You have the phrasing down, Scoggins. I'll give you that. But you couldn't be further from the truth. My father was the kindest man I've ever known, but I've seen what liquor can do to a man. I won't be party to it, and there's nothing you can say or do that will convince me otherwise."

The blood vessels in Scoggins's forehead became more pronounced. "What if I tell you I'm not interested in anything you've got today, Mr. Brennan?"

Jack carefully let out his breath, knowing he had yet to inquire about Mademoiselle Girard's father—and knowing Scoggins would likely be of little help to them now, even if he did know something. "Then I'd say I'm sorry we can't reach an agreement. And like I told you earlier, I'll sell whatever you don't want to the miners outside, if they're interested."

Mademoiselle Girard stepped forward, but Jack caught her arm.

Scoggins's attention shifted. "I haven't had the pleasure, Brennan. Is this your wife?"

Jack hesitated. "The lady is with me."

"The lady . . ." Scoggins nodded slowly. "Well . . . that answers that, now, doesn't it."

She scoffed. "Monsieur Scoggins, you are being most unreas—"

"Mademoiselle, please." Jack pulled her close and leaned down. "You gave me your word."

"But he is being unfair to you," she whispered, their faces nearly touching.

Scoggins snickered. "She's a feisty one. Aren't you, mademoiselle? *Est-ce que les choses vous rendent toujours si passionnée? Si oui, je voudrais discuter autres choses qui vous intéresse.*"

Jack felt her arm tense beneath his hold.

She slowly faced Scoggins again. *"Voire l'injustice, c'est ça qui me rend passionnée . . . ça et les imbéciles qui ont été donné l'autorité."*

The man's laughter filled the room.

Jack stared between them. He'd not seen this steely look in her eyes before, though the high-and-mighty tone sounded vaguely familiar. "What did you just say to him? And what did he say to you?"

Scoggins stepped forward. *"Et si j'achète tout ce qu'il a, ma chérie, que vaut-il à vous? Il y a certaines choses qui je suis toujours prêt à marchander."*

Jack didn't understand the words, but from the tone of Scoggins's voice—and the outraged disbelief on Mademoiselle Girard's face—he didn't need to. Her honor had been insulted.

Knowing he had only one chance on a guy this size, Jack sank the butt of his rifle into the man's midsection, then came up hard with his elbow and caught the man in the mouth.

Scoggins staggered back a few steps, a string of profanities punctuating his groans.

Jack quickly laid aside his rifle and braced himself, reminded again of what a bad idea it had been to accept Mademoiselle Girard's offer.

Regaining his balance, Scoggins tensed for a charge. Then he froze. His eyes went wide.

Confused, Jack followed the man's gaze. And the same numb shock that lined Scoggins's expression coursed through him.

Mademoiselle Girard had the butt of the rifle pressed flush against her shoulder, her chin tucked and the barrel pointed—from best Jack could tell—somewhere within a six-foot proximity of where Scoggins stood. Though her aim needed work, the effect was intimidating—more so if you couldn't see that the safety was still on. Which Scoggins couldn't from his vantage point.

"Mademoiselle . . ." Jack spoke softly, moving to place his hand over hers on the barrel. "I don't believe it will come to that today." He took the rifle from her and felt her trembling. "I'd appreciate you waiting by the door for me, please."

"But this man! His behavior! I fail to *comprendre*—"

Jack pressed his fingers to her lips, apparently surprising her by the gesture as much as he surprised himself. "*Please*, Mademoiselle Girard," he whispered, finding the softness of her mouth distracting. "Trust me in this."

She studied him, struggle evident in her expression.

Jack stared at her pert little pout. She possessed such fire, such presence, for one so young. To his relief, she did as he asked and went to wait by the door.

But her look told him she was none too happy about it.

Jack turned. "Scoggins, be assured that I'll never—"

"I'll buy the whole load—everything but the books and candy." Scoggins rubbed his jaw, smiling. "There hasn't been this much excitement around here in a long time." He looked at Mademoiselle Girard. "*Je suis désolé, mademoiselle. Je viens de faire le sot, et dans le très mauvais goût.*"

Jack turned to her, seeking translation.

"Monsieur Scoggins offered an apology to me . . . which I accept." Her smile only hinted at warmth. "And an apology to you, Monsieur Brennan. And as a token of faith in future dealings, he offers to pay an additional . . . ten percent on the total amount of his receipt." Her eyes narrowed. "Is that not correct, Mr. Scoggins?"

The man stared, then shook his head. "Yes, ma'am. That's correct."

Not believing for a second that Scoggins had made that offer, Jack accepted. And his respect for the diminutive woman beside him increased tenfold.

As they finalized the transaction, Scoggins ordered the supplies be unloaded and Jack inquired about Pierre Gustave Girard, briefly explaining the situation. "He originally came over in the early fifties and—"

Mademoiselle Girard laid a hand on his arm. "*Pardonnez-moi*, but that is not correct." Her voice dropped to a whisper. "My *papa* left Paris in 1846, when I was but five years old."

Jack let that sink in. "But that would mean you're thir—" Seeing the subtle rise of her brow, he caught himself. He curbed his smile, both at her reaction and at realizing they were much closer in age than he'd imagined. "I stand corrected, Scoggins. Her father came over in '46."

Scoggins finished counting out the bills according to Jack's itemized receipt. And he shot Mademoiselle Girard a begrudging look as he tacked on the extra ten percent. "I've never heard of the man, and I've been here since the first blast nineteen years ago. Most of the Frenchmen who came through here in the beginning moved on to prospecting when gold showed up in the streams. Either that or they went to camps that were mining more gold than Jenny's at the time."

Jack's interest piqued. "Which mines were those?"

"Let's see, of the mines that are still operating . . . that would've been Duke's Run, Sluice Box, Deception, and the Peerless. Oh, and Quandry too." Scoggins pushed the money forward, hesitated, and stretched out his hand.

Jack shook it. "I appreciate your business."

"I'm sure you do." Scoggins shook his head, but Jack sensed humor in the sarcasm. "Good luck in your search, to you both." Scoggins included Mademoiselle Girard in his nod. "*Au revoir, mademoiselle.*"

"*Au revoir, et merci.*" She offered a passable smile, lowering her gaze.

Eager to get her out of the place, Jack opened the door to leave and quickly realized that would not be easily done.

Four times the original number of men now gathered in the street outside the supply building, surrounding the wagon and clogging the narrow roadway.

Holding her close to him, Jack carved a path to the wagon and helped her up. Despite the catcalls and whistles, she searched the crowd, face by face. Jack didn't try to dissuade her. He knew who she was looking for. He prayed that one day she would find him—and that Pierre Gustave Girard would be a man worthy of her search.

He flicked the reins and the wagon lurched forward.

The crowd parted, but the miners kept calling out to her. He wanted to defend her against the inappropriate remarks, but he couldn't fight a hundred men. And he'd warned her about this. Perhaps now she would listen to him.

But seeing the determined set of her chin—probably not.

They were nearly out of town when she laid a hand on his arm. "*Merci*, Monsieur Brennan, for defending my honor. And for inquiring about my *papa*."

Seeing the restrained emotion in her face, Jack knew two things. However long it took and however many towns they had to visit, he would do his best to help her find her father. And furthermore, he was bone weary of having to address this woman as Mademoiselle Girard. Especially when she had such a beautiful first name. "It was my pleasure . . . Véronique. Thank you for making this such a profitable trip for me."

Warmth slipped into her eyes. She threaded her hand through the crook of his arm. "The pleasure was most assuredly mine . . . Jack."

They drove in silence for a ways. Part of his motivation for taking this job had been based on how young he'd thought she was. He shook his head to himself.

"What is the reason behind that look, Jack?"

He hesitated. "I'm not altogether sure I should tell you."

"Which is the reason that you must."

Hearing the playfulness in her voice, he looked at her. "Part of why I took this job was because I thought you were much younger. You certainly don't look your years, Véronique. And that's meant as a compliment."

She softly sighed. "So my mother was right after all . . ."

"Right about what?"

"Many times in recent years *Maman* told me that a day would come when I would be thankful to look so young. I did not believe her. Always, I have wanted to look like a woman and not a little girl."

Jack took care with his next words. "If you'd allow me to be so bold, ma'am . . . Looking like a little girl isn't something you have to worry about anymore."

"*Merci beaucoup* again . . . Jack," she whispered.

He didn't understand it, but somehow this woman stole his breath away. All while making him feel as if he'd finally come home again—after so many years of wandering.

CHAPTER SEVENTEEN

Véronique STRETCHED AND pushed herself to a sitting position in the freshly ticked hotel bed. The sun streamed in the dust-streaked windows as she combed her hair back with her hands and leaned to look at her watch on the night table. Half past eight. She threw back the quilt. She hadn't planned to sleep so late.

Thoughts of the trip to Jenny's Draw yesterday and of Jack Brennan, *Jack*—she smiled, remembering—had kept sleep at bay until the wee hours of the night, despite her being exhausted and sore from the journey along the furrowed roads.

Upon returning to town last evening, Jack had dropped her off at the hotel before heading to the livery to board the horses. Watching him drive away, it occurred to her that she had no definite way of contacting him in case she needed something. Unless, of course, he was still staying at this hotel. Possible, even though she'd not seen him in the hallways. A quiet query to Lilly could settle that issue. But he hadn't mentioned anything about when their next trip was scheduled either. A question she planned on having answered the next time she saw him.

Several tasks awaited her that day, so she gathered her personal items and visited the washroom down the hall. The most important errand on her list was to pay Monsieur Sampson for the freight wagon. In all her dealings with him, she'd never presented him with payment. Nor had he requested it. She'd remembered her oversight late yesterday afternoon when Jack had told her he'd commissioned Monsieur Sampson to build a wagon for him, identical to hers. The news shouldn't have surprised her. She'd known all along he wanted his own wagon.

But the way he'd said it reminded her of his initial reservations regarding the formation of their partnership, and that the current arrangement was quite temporary. In his mind at least.

As she washed her face, the journey to Jenny's Draw flitted through her memory in color-washed *vignettes*. But one scene stood out above all others.

Never had a man come so boldly to her defense. Jack could not have understood Monsieur Scoggins's vulgar suggestion. Yet somehow he had known, and his retribution had been swift and deserving. The exhilaration of gripping Jack's rifle in her hands also remained vivid with her.

She chuckled as she reached for the towel, recalling the look on Jack's face when he'd seen her. The poor man had been stunned. But no more than she. Never would she have attempted something like that before coming to this country. She would have considered the action unbecoming of a lady. But now . . .

Now she not only wanted to hold the gun again, she had aspirations of learning how to shoot it!

She ran a brush through her hair. Much had changed in the months since leaving Paris. *She* had changed.

One by one, she slipped the combs into her hair and gathered it atop her head, arranging the curls. Pausing, she closed her eyes.

She imagined herself standing in the grand front foyer of the Marchands' home once again—fresco-painted ceilings soaring overhead, polished marble beneath her feet—surrounded by opulent furnishings bequeathed from generation to generation within the Marchand *famille*. Breathing deeply, she recalled the sweet fragrance of fresh-cut white roses—her mother's favorite—that had always graced the front foyer table. And she could still hear the crescendo of the grand piano as Lord Marchand played in the ballroom late at night.

The rumble of wagons and the smell of livestock from the street below helped dispel the cherished memory. Her eyelids fluttered open. The webbed crack in the upper portion of the mirror suddenly seemed more pronounced, as did the peeling wallpaper and the dust-laden cobweb draping the top of the window sash. The wooden floorboards creaked as she returned to her room.

This journey had taken her not only far from her home, but also far from whom she used to be. Yet somehow she felt more alive and free in this uncivilized territory than she'd ever felt before. How could that be when Paris was still so dear? As was the refined existence of her previous life.

As she slipped into the matching jacket to her ensemble and tucked Monsieur Sampson's money inside her *réticule*, a single question replayed in her mind. She might be enjoying these newly discovered changes in herself, but were they for the better? Or was she succumbing to the lure of this untamed land?

And what of Jack Brennan? Here in these United States, the distinction between social classes often blurred until it was impossible to distinguish where one group ceased and another began—so different from France.

Jack was a man of integrity, honorable and kind, and he was proving to be an excellent driver and defender, but he fell far behind her in terms of rank and standing. And she knew that—despite how much they would be traveling together, and the relaxed norms of this infant country—it would be best to keep a certain distance between them.

And she determined to do just that.

Outside, Véronique followed her customary path to the livery. Her pace slowed when she saw a crowd gathered at the corner, with more people flocking around by the minute. She considered taking another route, but a man standing atop an upturned barrel drew her attention. He waved and pointed to something beside him, and excited murmurs rippled through the crowd.

Her curiosity eventually won out.

When she got close enough to glimpse the object of everyone's scrutiny, disappointment set in.

It was only a *vélocipède*.

"Step right up, folks!" The salesman's voice escalated in enthusiasm. "It's the latest thing from Europe. The conveyance of kings and queens! It's called a bicycle, and it's going to change life as we know it!"

Véronique lingered a moment, delighting in the crowd's reaction at seeing the man riding the bicycle up and down the street, though his comment about royalty was absurd. Never had Emperor Napoleon pedaled the streets of Paris on a *vélocipède*. Preposterous!

She remembered her own response upon first seeing the odd-looking contraption. Christophe had purchased one for himself some years ago when they'd been all the rage in Paris. Late one evening, he finally convinced her to try it, assuring her that no one was watching. But two turns around the back courtyard, trying to balance on the tiny seat while also managing her dress, proved far more trouble than the effort was worth. Not to mention the solid rubber tires over the cobblestones nearly jarred her teeth from her head.

Véronique heard her name and climbed the boardwalk to get a better view. She scanned the crowd, finally spotting Lilly waving to her from the other side of the avenue.

Lilly motioned for her to wait, then lifted her skirts and dodged the potholes and horse dung to cross the street.

Véronique noticed a group of boys and girls, about Lilly's age, she guessed, behind Lilly on the boardwalk, paying special attention to the girl's progress. One of the boys—blond, tall, and slender—began lurching about, holding his right pant leg in his grip. At the stifled giggles of the others, his actions became more exaggerated.

Véronique suddenly realized what he was doing, and indignation churned inside her. She sent the scoundrel a scathing look, which he apparently did not see.

"*Bonjour*, Mademoiselle Girard." Lilly climbed the stairs to the boardwalk, one at a time, her face flush with pleasure. "*Comment allez-vous?*"

Véronique smiled and worked to mask her anger, impressed with Lilly's skill at learning and her near perfect accent. "Good day, Miss Carlson. I am doing well, thank you. You have been studying the phrases I penned for you, *non*?" She motioned down the boardwalk. "I am on errands. Would you like to join me?"

No doubt Lilly had dealt with her share of teasing in her life, but Véronique wanted to protect her from dealing with more today. Certain children possessed a skill for such cruelty—be it about an impediment, or the lack of a father in the life of a *petite fille.*

Lilly's long dark curls bobbed as she nodded. They started down the boardwalk. "I have the phrases all memorized, Mademoiselle Girard. Would you write down a few more, please? When you have time?"

"You have committed the entire list to memory?"

"*Oui,* mademoiselle." Lilly's eyes sparkled.

Véronique decided a test was in order. She cleared her throat in an exaggerated manner. "Good evening, Mrs. Carlson."

"*Bonsoir,* Madame Carlson." Lilly rolled her eyes as if to say "give me something harder."

Véronique raised a brow. "Let me introduce myself. I am Miss Lilly Carlson."

"*Je m'appelle* Mademoiselle Lilly Carlson."

Trying not to smile, but secretly proud of her young pupil, Véronique tried one more. And she was certain Lilly would remember the evening this had happened to her. "I closed the door to my room and left the key inside."

Grinning, Lilly lifted her chin in an air of superiority. "*J'ai fermé la porte de ma chambre et j'ai laissé la clé à l'intérieur.*"

Véronique paused at the corner and clapped softly. "*Magnifique!* I am most impressed with you, Lilly. You are an astute learner. And yes, I will be pleased to pen more phrases for you. I will do it tonight . . . immediately following our first lesson in curtsying." She winked. "You thought I had forgotten, *non*?"

Lilly's grin communicated suspicion of just that. "Thank you! I can hardly wait!"

Hoping the lesson would not end in frustration for the girl, Véronique motioned in the direction of the livery down the street. "But for the moment . . . I have an appointment with Monsieur Sampson, so I must be on my way."

"That's okay. I have an appointment too, and then I have to get to work." Lilly gave her a quick hug. "Let's meet in the hotel dining room tonight, following dinner. And one more thing . . . I'm going out to see a friend of our family the Sunday after next. She lives a ways from town, and I wondered if you might want to come along." Her dark brows arched. "Mama's going to make her oatmeal muffins with homemade strawberry jam, and I'm sure Miss Maudie will share with us."

After yesterday's trip to Jenny's Draw, the idea of riding any distance in a wagon wasn't at all appealing, but spending time with Lilly was. They agreed on a time and place to meet.

Véronique reached the livery only to find the place overrun with customers. Since that meant the shop was full of men, she decided to wait outside.

A bright summer sun shone from its cloudless azure perch, reminding her she'd forgotten to bring along her *parasol*. But she didn't wish for it. She tipped her head back, relishing the warmth of the sun's rays on her face and feeling a trifle rebellious in the act. Such a short time in this country, and already she was suffering beneath its influence. Madame Marchand had always scolded her when she forgot her *parasol*, saying it was a *faux pas* tantamount to forgetting one's gloves. Véronique glanced down at her bare hands and wriggled her fingers, feeling positively scandalous. None of the women she'd seen in Willow Springs ever—

"You best be coverin' up that pretty face of yours, ma'am. Those pretty little hands too. 'Fore they get all freckled."

Véronique saw the old man and backed up a step, clutching her *réticule* to her body.

He pulled a two-wheeled cart behind him, reminding her of the paupers who lined the streets outside the opera house in Paris. After a performance, many would call out as the finely dressed men and women returned to their carriages. But others would stand silent, hands outstretched, dark eyes hollow. These always frightened her most—their faces gaunt and void of emotion, as though death had already visited them unaware. Yet on those evenings, Lord Marchand had never failed to have pocketfuls of coins. And he hadn't tossed the coins out like so many did before rushing back to their lives. He'd distributed each personally, looking every man, woman, or child in the eye.

But the very thought of having to touch this man caused Véronique to shudder. His teeth, what few remained, were yellowed. His shirt, stained and dirty, hung on frail shoulders, and if not for the suspenders he wore, his trousers would have puddled about his ankles. A strong odor wafted toward her, and she swallowed convulsively, thankful she'd chosen to go without breakfast that morning.

The stab to her conscience was swift and well aimed.

A knot formed in her throat. Wishing she could turn and leave, she found it impossible to look away.

"That's a mighty pretty dress you got on there, ma'am. Not sure I've ever seen one quite like it." The aging pauper grinned and made a show of peering around behind her to look pointedly at the bustle of her dress. "Kinda reminds me of a little caboose, if you don't mind me sayin'." His laughter came out high-pitched and wheezy, and ended in a fit of coughing.

Véronique backed up another step, fairly convinced the man meant her no real harm. Perhaps if she gave him a coin or two, he would leave her alone. Still holding tightly to her réticule, she rummaged for her change purse.

"Care to look at my wares? I've got some mighty fine things here." He began pawing through the contents of his cart. "I've got some nice picture books, or maybe jewelry would be more to your likin'." He held up a pair of earrings, holes where the jewels had once been. "These aren't nearly as pretty as yours, but you'd brighten 'em right up, for sure."

Wishing she'd worn her gloves, Véronique held two nickels out between her fingertips.

He looked at the money, then at her. A frown shadowed his sun-furrowed face. "But you haven't picked out anything. Besides . . ." He glanced from left to right as though perilous spies lingered near. His voice lowered. "You need to ask me if I'll take any less." He winked. "I always do."

Wanting him to leave, Véronique nodded to the coins between her fingertips. If he would only take them, her obligation would be fulfilled. "I am not in need of anything today, monsieur. But I am offering these to you." She thrust it forward. "You may have them."

Bushy brows shot up. "You're not from around here, are you?"

"Please, monsieur. If you will but accept my charity and depart from my—"

"Why, Mr. Callum Roberts. Good morning to you, sir."

Hearing Jack's voice, Véronique felt a rush of relief. She readied her thanks, only to discover Jack wasn't looking at her at all. His attention was fixed on the beggar.

The old man's face split into a grin, revealing fewer teeth than she had originally attributed to him. "Why, Jack Brennan, how are you today?"

Jack shook Monsieur Roberts's hand. "I'm very well, thank you, sir. I saw you both out here and thought I'd come join you."

Wondering how Jack knew this man, Véronique caught the subtle look Jack tossed her, and returned one of her own that said she appreciated his rescue. *Again.*

Jack peered into the man's cart. "You got anything new since Friday? I sure am enjoying that rolling pin I got from you."

A rolling pin? She tried to catch his eye but couldn't.

"Well, let's see what other treasures I've got. . . ." Monsieur Roberts dug around for a moment.

Véronique watched Jack as he watched Mr. Roberts. Genuine concern shone in Jack's expression, as well as attentiveness. Strange, but his ease with the beggar only served to deepen her discomfort.

"Here we are. This might be somethin' that'll work for you." Mr. Roberts straightened with effort and presented Jack with a rust-covered iron.

Véronique waited, eager for Jack's reaction. An iron was the last thing she could imagine a man like him needing.

A slow smile crossed Jack's face. "This is perfect."

Monsieur Roberts shook his head as Jack took the item from his frail hands. "Now, don't you be buyin' it if it's not somethin' you can use. There's nothing worse than throwin' your money away on an iron you won't use or don't need."

Véronique found herself smiling at the old gentleman's concern. And at Jack's *gentil* way with him.

"I wouldn't buy it if I couldn't use it, sir. I give you my word. Matter of fact, I'm heading out of town on Friday and my . . . traveling partner can be mighty particular about things. Likes everything just so, and I'm thinking sh—my partner—will put this to good use."

It took her a moment, but Véronique realized he was referring to her. And that he was telling her they were leaving on another trip in three days! Another chance to search for her father—and anticipating time in Jack's company wasn't altogether unpleasant either. In fact, it gave her far more pleasure than it should have.

Aware of his watchful glances, she took care not to show her excitement at the news—while already picturing how she might use that iron the next time he got flippant with her.

Jack placed a gentle hand beneath her arm. "Mr. Callum Roberts"—his voice took on a more formal tone—"have you had the pleasure of meeting Mademoiselle Véronique Girard? She's new to Willow Springs and hails from Paris, France."

Gripping the side of his cart, Monsieur Roberts bent briefly at the waist. "Mademoiselle Girard, it's a real pleasure to be makin' your acquaintance, ma'am."

Surprised at his bowing to her, she hoped the man didn't also know that etiquette demanded she proffer her hand for a kiss. But she knew, and from the look on Jack's face, so did he. She couldn't imagine the pauper's mouth actually touching her skin. No matter what she told herself, her arm would not move from her side—until she looked at Jack.

He gave her an almost imperceptible nod, his eyes telling her it would be all right.

Embarrassed, not wanting to, her stomach in knots, she curtsied and extended her hand. "The pleasure is mine, Monsieur Roberts." She tried not to wince as he took her hand and kissed it. When she lifted her gaze, her throat closed tight.

The man's rheumy eyes were swimming, and despite the undeniable chasm in their social classes, Véronique felt strangely unworthy of his obvious adoration and esteem.

"Now, ma'am, you need to pick something out." He waved an arthritic hand over his cart. "No charge today. Anything you want."

She shook her head. "*Merci beaucoup*, but I am not in need of anything today, monsieur." The man's chin lowered ever so slightly, and the subtle shake of Jack's head told her she'd made a mistake. "However, thinking better of it now"—already Jack's smile returned—"I might be able to find something if . . . I were to look more closely."

"You bet you can." The man pulled a cloth from his back pocket and started wiping off the discarded trinkets as he presented them to her, one after the other.

Véronique finally decided on a china cup regrettably relieved of its handle, though no matter what Jack said or did, she would never use it for its original purpose. She did have her limits. "*Merci*, Monsieur Roberts. And I insist that you have this." She held out the coins, sensing Jack's approval. "There is nothing better than finding treasure in unexpected places, *non*?"

VÉRONIQUE RIPPED THE piece of parchment in half and wadded it up into a ball. The pencil would not obey her mind's instruction. For an instant, she almost gave in to the desire to break the drawing implement, but then remembered a fellow painter who had injured his fingers in just such a foolish gesture.

She rose from the desk in her hotel room and paced the brief length of floor unoccupied by trunks.

She could see his hands; the picture was vivid in her mind, as clear as if the old beggar were standing there before her, frail arms outstretched, palms facing downward.

She closed her eyes, concentrating.

Ever since she'd bid farewell to Monsieur Roberts earlier that day, her thoughts, of their own bothersome accord, kept returning to his hands. Their arthritic-swollen joints, the parchment-thin skin, mottled with markings of years and age, draped over gnarled fingers. What living those hands had done, and what pain they had endured, if the scars covering them were evidence.

She had drawn countless pairs of hands, feet, arms, and legs, as well as other parts of the body—the soft curvature of a woman's bare back, the well-defined, muscled shoulders of a man—in the art studio where she had studied in Paris. Nude models were often the subject of their lessons and, though capturing the nuance of the human body was, without question, more intriguing than sketching a vase of sun-flowers or a field of poppies, it was also far more difficult. Showing movement, conveying *life*, in a still rendering of the subject was an art she'd studied for years—and was something with which she still struggled.

Véronique walked to the desk and from faraway corners deep within herself, summoned every scrap of confidence she'd ever possessed and every last compliment someone had paid her work. Focusing that energy on the fresh piece of parchment before her, she began again.

The pencil moved over the paper with a rhythm that was at once second nature, and at the same time was distant and disturbingly foreign.

Jack came to mind, and with every painstaking stroke she made on the page, she wondered what he would think if he were to see her paintings and drawings. Would his expression fill with a look of politeness tinged with discomfort over what to say?

If only she possessed the talent of Berthe Morisot and the others. Then Jack might come to think more highly of her than he did now. He had not indicated that he thought ill of her at present, but he might see her as more capable, more deserving if she possessed that level of talent.

Véronique lifted the instrument from the parchment and surveyed her work, finding little worth in it. The lines of the beggar's hands were awkward, forced, void of movement and life. She crumpled the page and threw it into the corner along with the previous failure.

It suddenly seemed a great offense for God to give someone a talent, only to take it away at His slightest whim. It would have been better had He never gifted her at all, rather than to leave her empty and wanting of the pleasure she had once experienced when the art poured through her hands, through her body, as though issuing from His very heart.

Would she ever become skilled enough to command paint on canvas as did Berthe? Chances of that happening in the tiny town of Willow Springs seemed nil at best. Students needed instruction to better themselves, *non*? And who in this place possessed the necessary skills to tutor and challenge her, to broaden her knowledge of the arts?

As she stared at the crumpled balls of paper in the corner, she recalled Pastor Carlson's recent sermon. Never before had she considered God to be cruel, even in her mother's untimely death. Death was part of life. A ceasing of it, to be certain, but nonetheless the natural order of things. She knew this, for since a young age she had rousted about on death's threshing floor, in the shadow of its grasp, at Cimetière de Montmartre.

But the removal of her ability to draw, to paint, felt like a removal of God's very presence. And in light of everything else that His grace—however bent with human will by His own design—had allowed to be taken from her life, that filching seemed especially cruel.

"*Très bien*, Mademoiselle Carlson!" Véronique clapped as she rose from her chair, imbuing her voice with enthusiasm based not on the girl's correctness of form but on her effort and dedication.

Lilly straightened from the attempted curtsy, her brow glistening from the past hour's lesson. The hotel dining room was vacant, the dinner hour long ended. "You're very kind, Mademoiselle Girard . . . and generous with your praise. I'm *not* doing well. But I can do better. I know I can."

As Véronique had anticipated, the brace on Lilly's right leg greatly encumbered the bowing gesture, and not even the luminescent quality of Lilly's eyes could mask the dull of pain in them. Whether it stemmed from the girl's overexertion during the day or from the repeated attempts to master this act of etiquette, Véronique couldn't be certain.

But she desired to put an end to it. "You continually surprise me with your dedication to learning, *ma chérie*. But I believe we have had more than enough practice for one evening. You must rest now."

Lilly took a deep breath. Her slender jawline went rigid. "No, ma'am! I'm going to continue until I get it right!"

Véronique raised a brow at the harshness in the girl's voice, full well knowing the tone wasn't meant for her. She recognized the obstinacy behind Lilly's attitude, and her frustration—because she shared it. Had she not experienced the same roil of emotion earlier that day with the pencil and parchment as her formidable foes?

With a determined look, Lilly placed her left foot forward again and attempted to sweep her right leg behind her in a graceful gesture, all while bending at the knee and holding her skirt out from her body. Either her knee buckled or she lost her balance, but if not for grabbing hold of the chair beside her, she would have fallen altogether.

Véronique hurried to help, but Lilly waved her away. Tears rose in Véronique's eyes, and fell from Lilly's.

"This is so . . . *stupid!*" Lilly regained her balance and shoved the chair away. "I'll never be able to do this! Not like you can!"

"And who says you must do this the way I do, *ma chérie*? Is there some unwritten rule of which I need to be made aware?"

At the sudden quickening in her conscience, Véronique stilled. How dare she dole out such appeasing words to this precious young girl, when she—a grown woman—still struggled with the same thing?

"But you're so graceful, and so pretty, Mademoiselle Girard. And I'll never even—" The sentence caught in Lilly's throat. She shook her head.

Véronique moved closer and gently lifted the girl's chin. Despite the wide span in their ages, she and Lilly were eye level with one another. Though with Lilly's youth, the girl would easily surpass her in height in the coming months.

Véronique fingered a dark curl at Lilly's temple. "Already you are such a beautiful girl. This silly gesture we practice here tonight is incapable of enhancing what is already an immutable fact. Is something else of bother to you, *ma chérie*?"

Sighing, Lilly bit her lower lip. "We met with Doc Hadley today—my parents and I. About a kind of surgery."

At the mention of *la chirurgie*, Véronique's concern escalated. "For your leg?" she whispered.

"Yes, ma'am. I was born with one leg shorter than the other, and my right one's never grown straight like it should. My father always padded the bottom of my right boot and it was enough. But, in the last year . . ."

Véronique thought she understood. "As your body has been growing from that of a child into that of a young woman . . ."

Lilly nodded. "It's gotten a lot worse. About a month ago, Doc Hadley told us about an operation he read about that's being done by a surgeon in Boston. My parents said they were interested in finding out more, so Doc Hadley wrote the surgeon about me. Today we went back to Doc Hadley's clinic, and he measured my legs and knees and hip joints, took all sorts of notes on my posture and how my legs move. He's sending all that to the surgeon back East. It'll take a couple of months to find out what the surgeon says about my leg, and if he thinks the surgery will help me or not." She looked at the floor, fingering her calico skirt. "Doc Hadley told us more about the operation today too."

Véronique read ill news in Lilly's expression. She encouraged the girl to sit and then claimed a chair beside her. "This *procédure*, it is a dangerous one?"

"It comes with risks, the doc said. And it's more expensive than we thought." Lilly gave a humorless laugh. "I've been saving, working at the hotel as much as I can. My folks have been working extra too. Mama's taking in more mending and washing. Papa's taking odd jobs at ranches and in town—whatever he can find." She firmed her lips together. "But it'll take years to earn enough."

"Dr. Hadley is favorable that the *chirurgien* in Boston will agree to perform this *procédure* for you?"

"The surgeon told Doc Hadley that he typically does this on younger children, not someone as old as me. But as I see it, it's a good sign that he's willing to look at my charts, right?"

Véronique nodded, wanting to give the girl hope. "And what does Dr. Hadley make of all this?"

"He says that, with how quick my body is growing and the way my joints are positioned, he thinks the operation—*if* the surgeon says yes—will need to be done by year's end at the latest. Else my leg will be too far gone." Lilly lifted the hem of her skirt, revealing the brace extending the full length of her right leg. "My left leg will continue to grow like normal, he says." Her voice softened. "My right one won't. But the real problem isn't with my legs. It's with my spine."

Lilly sat up straighter as she said it, though Véronique doubted the girl was even conscious of the gesture.

Lilly placed her hand on her lower back. "My lower spine is curved to one side, and it's pressing on a nerve."

Véronique frowned. "This causes you much pain, *non*?"

"Only some days. For the past few months Doc Hadley's given me medicine for it—a powder I mix in my tea—but it's not working like it used to. There're exercises he taught me to do too, but those aren't working anymore either." She glanced down at her hands clasped tightly in her lap. "The pain's not really that bad though. I've learned to make do pretty well."

The maturity in Lilly's tone, the finality and acceptance of her circumstances, only deepened Véronique's hurt. Someone so young ought not to have to be so strong.

Véronique worded her next question with care. "Did Dr. Hadley say what other options would be available if you and your parents elect not to have the *chirurgie*?"

A shadow passed across Lilly's face. "Based on the notes about me that Doc Hadley sent to Boston last month, the surgeon said that without the operation . . ." Her voice fell away. Her chest rose and fell, yet she didn't make a sound. "He said that within a year"—tears welled in her violet eyes—"I won't be able to walk anymore."

The knot in Véronique's throat cinched taut. She tried to say something, but couldn't.

"I'll be twelve years old this summer, Mademoiselle Girard." A sad smile ghosted Lilly's mouth. "And I've never even danced with a boy. I've danced with my papa." All courage fled, and the mask of bravery slipped. "But he doesn't count!"

Véronique pulled Lilly to her, whispering words of comfort. Suddenly her frustration over the inability to sketch or paint any longer seemed unimportant by comparison, and selfish at heart.

She drew back, pulled the kerchief from her sleeve, and handed it to Lilly. Surprised at the girl's youthfulness—she was even younger than Véronique had imagined—her mind raced, processing all that Lilly had told her. Véronique kept her voice hushed. "There is one more thing Dr. Hadley shared with you, *non*? The risks of the *procédure*? Are they great?"

Lilly's expression turned guarded. "The surgeon told Doc Hadley that he's operated on forty-eight children so far who've had the same problem as me, or similar. Thirty-nine of them got better and were able to walk normal. Four of them didn't, and they went crippled anyway."

Véronique frowned. "But what happened to the oth—" Seeing the look on Lilly's face, she stopped midsentence, and wished she'd reasoned her thought through before giving it voice. She nodded. "So . . .

have you and your parents made a decision, *ma chérie*? If the *chirurgien* says yes to your request."

"My folks aren't in accord yet. They talk about it a lot. I hear them at night, when they think I'm asleep. Even if we had the money, I'm not sure what their decision would be. Doc Hadley told Papa that if people in town knew, they would want to help by giving, after all the good my folks have done here."

"I am believing the words of this doctor. Though I have been in Willow Springs for only a brief time, I know that your *papa* and *mère* are well esteemed in this community."

A fragile smile touched Lilly's lips. "*Merci beaucoup*, Mademoiselle Girard. But lots of people suffer from maladies and don't come asking for special help. They just get through it as best they can with God's help."

As swiftly as the idea entered her mind, Véronique couldn't believe she hadn't thought of it sooner. Her first order of business tomorrow morning would be to seek out the Willow Springs physician and discuss the situation with him. Then she would pay Monsieur Gunter a visit at the bank.

———

Jack nodded to the young woman approaching him on the boardwalk, hoping her destination was the land and deed office. He'd been waiting a good twenty minutes for the office to open, and precious moments of daylight were slipping away with each tick of his pocket watch.

She coerced a key into the lock and jiggled the handle. "Have you been waiting long, sir? My apologies if you have. I'm running a bit . . . late this morning."

Jack shook his head. "Not too long. I'm just eager to get on the road. I've got a load to haul up the mountain today."

"I can see that." Smiling, she glanced past him to the wagon. "And it looks like a heavy one." She opened the door and motioned for him to follow. "You must be Mr. Brennan, Mr. Hochstetler's new freighter."

With the size of Willow Springs, her comment wasn't surprising. Jack nodded and stepped inside. "Yes, ma'am, I'm Jack Brennan." He removed his hat.

"I'm Miss Duncan . . . Aida Duncan, if you'd like. Pleasure to meet you." She hung her shawl and bonnet over a hook on the wall. "I think I saw you at church on Sunday." Her brows arched.

"Yes, ma'am. I snuck in a bit late. Sat in the back."

She stared for a second, her smile softening. "A friend told me about you, Mr. Brennan. Said you came from up around Oregon?"

"That's right. But I'm afraid you have the advantage over me, ma'am. I didn't realize the position of freighter held such status among the townsfolk. I'm deeply honored." He punctuated the tease with a smile.

She dipped her head and shrugged, fussing with the ties on her skirt. When she looked back her cheeks had gained a rosy hue and her eyes held a sparkle.

A bit too much of a sparkle for Jack's ease. He got the sneaking suspicion that this woman—while friendly, and right pretty, he admitted—was fishing for something. And he'd been single long enough to guess what it might be.

He also knew he wasn't interested. Not that anything might be deficient with Miss Duncan's character or person. He'd simply put thoughts of this ilk behind him a long time ago.

For the past fifteen years, he'd good-naturedly put up with matrimonial-seeking mothers who tried every day of the months-long cross-country trek to pair him with their available daughters. Stopping by his tent in the evenings with a slice of dried-apple pie or a pan of warm biscuits had been a favorite "coincidence" of those kindly women. And though he'd eaten like a king much of the time, he'd acted with utmost care to gently discourage their endeavors.

After losing Mary and Aaron, he'd gradually grown accustomed to the rhythm of his solitary life, to its ebb and flow within the boundaries of cherished memories. Life was simpler, easier, with only him. And it was enough.

He cleared his throat and gave the faintest of smiles. "I stopped by this morning to check on a piece of property west of town. I came across it yesterday afternoon, and I'd like to know if it's for sale."

Flirtation faded from the woman's expression, leaving kindness in its place. "And where is this land located, sir?" She walked to a desk situated against the wall and opened a drawer.

"It starts about a two-hour ride west by mount, along the banks of Fountain Creek. I didn't spot any homesteads or ranches, but I didn't go up into the hills. Just scouted the perimeter. I'm curious as to whether any of that land might still be available and, if so, who I need to speak with about it."

She flipped through the files jamming the length of the drawer. "You're thinking of settling down here, then?"

"I might, yes, ma'am. If all goes well."

She looked up, and while her smile said she wished things would go well for him, it also conveyed that she harbored no ill will. "Willow Springs is a very nice town, Mr. Brennan. I've been out here for a couple of years, and I don't think you'll find better people." She pulled a folder from the drawer. "Mr. Clayton, the gentleman who handles all property sales in the area, won't be in for a while. He usually arrives later on Wednesday mornings due to township meetings. But I should be able to determine whether land in that area is available for purchase or not." She raised a brow. "Not an inch of land is sold in these parts without the deeds coming across our desks. And Mr. Clayton is a stickler for maintaining accurate records."

"Well then, I've come to the right place, Miss Duncan."

"Let's see . . ." She opened the file flat atop her desk and ran a forefinger down the top page. "Depending on which area we're talking about, and looking at this plat . . ." She turned the mapped grid around so he could see it too. "There are several quadrants in the vicinity. Which of these are of interest to you?"

Jack leaned closer to read the markings. "This should be the area right here." He marked the spot with his forefinger.

Nodding, she returned her attention to the open file. "The majority of that section was purchased back in '60. By a sole buyer, it says, and proprietary rights for Fountain Creek were issued with that original deed." She read on, her head moving slightly from side to side. Her brows rose. "Then it was sold in an auction in the fall of '68, at the courthouse in Denver." She tapped the file with her index finger. "Let's see if we have a record of who purchased . . ." She turned the page and immediately fell silent. She frowned, picked up the file from her desk, and tilted it toward herself.

Jack got the distinct impression she thought he'd been trying to read it.

Miss Duncan flipped to the next page. And the next. "Odd. It doesn't list who purchased that land at the auction, Mr. Brennan. But it does show a portion of it being sold again. Only days after it was purchased in Denver, in fact."

"But only a portion of it was sold?"

Her expression skeptical, she nodded.

"So that means that some land might still be available for sale in that area?"

"That's my understanding from reading the file. I'm certain Mr. Clayton will have a record of the transactions and will be able to answer your questions." She closed the file and slipped it back into her desk. "I'll inform him that you're interested, and that you'll be in touch when you return from your trip."

"I'm much obliged for your help, Miss Duncan. And for your warm welcome." As Jack closed the office door behind him, he couldn't deny the vein of excitement shooting through him.

That property was exactly what he'd dreamed about—land cradled in a cleft of the Rocky Mountains, with an abundance of aspens and willows, and nourished by the bubbling waters of Fountain Creek. With little effort he envisioned the cabin he might build there one day.

He climbed into the wagon, released the brake, and guided the team of Percherons down the main street. He intended to thank Stewartson at Casaroja again for his assistance in choosing this pair. He'd never had such superb draft horses—so well matched in height and strength, standing eighteen hands high, and with a smooth stride—not as choppy as that of other heavy horses. All of these attributes made heads turn when the horses passed. Black as a starless night, they were magnificent animals.

The hour was still early, so only a few folks braved the morning's chill. Jack glanced at the empty place beside him on the bench seat. Funny, even though they'd only been on one trip together, it felt sort of odd not having her—

"Monsieur Brennan!"

He pulled back on the reins, wondering if he was imagining her voice.

But when he spotted Véronique striding toward him, her cheeks flushed, a scowl darkening her pretty face, and the fancy little feathered hat atop her head bobbing up and down, he knew he hadn't imagined it. And he also knew that she was *très* unhappy about something.

CHAPTER NINETEEN

MONSIEUR BRENNAN, may I ask why you are departing town at this hour?"

Holding the reins in check, Jack couldn't help but grin at the smartness of her tone and the way her tiny hands were knotted on her slender hips. Her frown deepened, and he guessed that humor was apparently not the reaction she'd hoped for.

"Good morning, Véronique. How are you today?"

Momentary shyness replaced her frown, as though she only now realized what a serious breach of etiquette she'd committed by addressing him so curtly. This woman was indeed a handful.

Jack eyed her fancy getup, the rich purple skirt and matching jacket. Her sleeves had little flowers sewn on the edges, same as graced the front of her jacket. What exactly had this woman done, or been, back in Paris? If Sampson at the livery knew, he'd never let on. Whatever her occupation before Willow Springs, her budget on clothing had been exorbitant. But he had to admit, the garments suited her.

"Good morning . . . Jack. I am well, *merci*." She offered a cursory smile—just enough to satisfy the merest guideline of etiquette—then indulged her previous frown. "I will ask you again, *s'il vous plaît*. Why are you departing with *my* wagon at this early hour?"

"I'd think it would be obvious, ma'am. I'm heading out of town on a supply run."

She stepped closer. Her brown eyes flashed. "And to what destination are you . . . *headed*?"

Her strident voice sliced a portion of Jack's humor. "To Duke's Run, Véronique. One of the mining towns Scoggins mentioned to us the other day."

She nodded. "And why, may I ask, was I not informed of this trip? Only yesterday you said our next journey would be on Friday of this week. And yet, here you are"—she made a sweeping gesture with her arm, her voice growing louder—"supplies loaded and secured, and not a word to me about this premeditated and deliberate expedition!"

"Actually, ma'am," Jack said, working to keep his tone light, aware of the attention of curious onlookers, "the use of premeditated and deliberate in the same sentence is redundant. Since the word *premeditated* actually means to think, consider, or deliberate beforehand." He winked and nodded at the reticule hanging on her arm, hoping to ease her ill temper. "You can check your little book on that one, if you'd like. Now if you'll please get into the—"

"Ah!" Her mouth dropped open. Her face turned three shades of crimson. "Why you did not inform me of this trip?"

At the undainty stomp of her foot, Jack's own face heated. He kept his voice low. "Véronique, please get into the wagon and we'll—"

"Please provide an answer to my question, monsieur!"

His patience went paper-thin as two shop owners appeared on the boardwalk, evidently enjoying the scene before them, their grins amused. He looked back at her. "We had an agreement on the front end, mademoiselle, that the trips involving an—"

"*Oui!* And you have apparently set aside our agreement with no concern for our discussed terms. I demand that you—"

He set the brake and jumped down. Managing a stiff smile at the men on the boardwalk, he gently took hold of Véronique's arm and leaned close. "I'm asking that you please get into the wagon, mademoiselle. I'll gladly discuss this with you *again*, at great length, but only in a more private setting."

She glanced about, then raised her chin in an imperious fashion. "I will go with you, but only because I consider it prudent to do so.".

Jack took a calming breath and aided her ascent into the wagon. "And we both know you're nothing if not prudent."

She spun on the seat. "What was that you said?"

He climbed up beside her and released the brake. "I said such prudence becomes you, ma'am."

Jack guided the wagon down a lesser-used side street and reined in. She was staring straight ahead, jaw tense, her posture straight as a board, and with an aura about as welcoming.

"Mademoiselle, we clearly have had a misunderstanding."

"*Oui*, and I am thinking you believe it is *my* fault."

Sighing, Jack removed his hat and scratched the back of his head. "I honestly haven't gotten that far in my thinking. You give me too much credit if you think I have. I'm just trying to figure out what's got you so all-fired angry." Seeing her pert little mouth drop open, he held up a hand. "I offer you my apology if I misrepresented anything about our travels to these towns together. But I thought I made it perfectly clear, Véronique, that you would *not* be accompanying me on the overnight trips."

That pert little mouth clamped shut. But only briefly. "I remember our discussion quite well, Jack. I also remember voicing my concern regarding my personal interests being properly managed in my absence." She turned toward him on the seat. "I have given more thought to the subject at hand. With you being in my employ, and understanding that we are both two mature adults, I desire to broach the subject again."

Jack stared, not following. "You desire to broach what subject again?"

She huffed softly. "The subject of the overnight trips. I am certain I could manage to find an appropriate *chaperon*, and therefore would be able to confirm for myself whether my father has been in that particu—"

"That subject is not open for discussion, mademoiselle."

A single manicured brow arched in determination. "Let us not forget who is the employee here, monsieur, and who is the *patronne*."

"I'm hardly forgetting that, ma'am. But let's also not forget who's the man, and who's the woman." As he had anticipated, her eyes widened. "I realize, more than I care to distinguish in conversation, what differences there are in our genders. Suffice it to say—" he paused and looked at her pointedly—"*please*, let it suffice to say . . . that while I consider traveling with you to be a pleasure, it also presents a . . . challenge, from time to time."

She stared at him, unflinching. "I am aware of these ... challenges. Christophe has told me of such things. But I was also under the impression that a gentleman possesses the ability to not act on such challenges, even though he may be tempted to do so."

Jack looked away. He suddenly felt like a schoolboy attempting to explain why he'd been caught cheating on a test. Why was nothing ever easy with this woman? And how could he explain this to her without embarrassing them both? *And who on earth is Christophe?!*

Then it hit him. "Have you ever walked by a dress shop, Véronique, and had something catch your eye? Say a dress or a bonnet?"

She shook her head, laughing. "Certainly not here in Willow Springs."

Jack bit the inside of his cheek. "In Paris, then. Use your imagination, please."

She gave him a curt look. "*Oui*, I have experienced this. What woman has not?"

"Very good, we're getting somewhere. Say that when you left the house that morning you had no intention of shopping for a dress or a bonnet. You were on your way to the mercantile to do your shopping." Anticipating the shake of her head, he quickly added, "Or on your way to see a friend. You *did* visit friends on occasion in Paris, did you not?"

Again, the look. "*Oui*, I visited friends. On occasion." She mimicked his tone.

"Wonderful." He ignored it. "You're passing by this dress shop, and a bonnet in the window draws your attention." He shrugged. "You don't need a bonnet, you weren't thinking about bonnets. But nevertheless, there it is, and you're thinking about it now. In fact, you find you can think of nothing else but that bonnet."

She looked at him as though he had sprouted another head. "There is nothing wrong with thinking about a bonnet."

Jack slowly exhaled through his teeth. "Mademoiselle, you do realize this is an analogy. Correct?"

Her expression clouded. She reached for her reticule and pulled the tiny book from within. As she turned the pages with enthusiasm, Jack rested his forehead in his hands.

She whispered under her breath as she read. "Ah ..." She looked up again, her expression brightening. "The story you are telling bears resemblance to the subject at hand, *non*? I will be able to draw a comparison between the two when you have reached the conclusion."

Jack didn't dare blink. "That is my sincerest hope, mademoiselle."

She looked at him through squinted eyes. "Continue with your . . . analogy, *s'il vous plaît*."

"Okay, where were we . . . ?"

"I have seen the bonnet," she supplied in a none-too-serious tone. "I do not need a bonnet, but I find I can think of nothing else but that bonnet."

Jack quelled the urge to throttle her, quite a challenge in itself. He cleared his throat. "You go into the dress shop to inqui—"

"Millinery, you mean."

"What?"

"I would see a bonnet in a millinery, Jack. A hat store. Not a dress shop."

He ran a hand over his face. "Fine. As I was saying . . . you go into the *hat store* and inquire about the bonnet. But as it turns out, you don't have the means to buy it. Nor do you have the right to—"

"But what if I do possess the means to buy it?"

He sighed. "For the sake of the analogy, Véronique, let's say that you do not."

Frowning, she nodded.

"So not only do you not have the money to purchase the bonnet, you also realize that you don't have the right to buy it. Because the bonnet is being held for someone else."

"For whom is it being held?"

"It doesn't matter *for whom*. The point is—"

"Because in the most prestigious shops in Paris, you may only hold a bonnet for one day. If you do not return with payment within that time, then—"

"It's being held in the interest of someone who is the rightful owner of that bonnet." He silenced further interruption with a raised forefinger. "Though this person has not yet purchased the bonnet, though she has never seen it, she is the rightful owner. Because when the seamstress created this special bonnet, she had that particular customer in mind. She uniquely fashioned it for that person. And for no one else." He waited, frustrated, fearing he'd made a mess of things in trying to paint a more vivid picture for her. He wondered why he'd even attempted to explain it in the first place. "For you to demand ownership of that bonnet just because you saw it and wanted it, though it seemed like the perfect fit and selection for you at that particular moment, would be wrong." He held her gaze. "Are you following this story at all?"

She stared at him for a moment, giving a faint nod. A light slowly dawned in her eyes, then flickered and died. "*Non*, I am afraid I do not. I understand wanting the bonnet, and . . . almost I can imagine not having the means to purchase it, but that is where my understanding parts most abruptly with your story." She reached out and patted his hand. "I am sorry, Jack."

Jack closed his eyes, unable to look at her as he spoke next. "If you and I were to travel together on these overnight trips, Véronique, the temptation for me to want to be closer to you could present itself . . . from time to time." *Would* present itself, and often, if his unexpected reaction to her now was any indication. How could he so desire silence from a woman while also wanting to kiss her . . . thoroughly. He blinked to clear his imagination. "I do not want to put myself—or you—in that circumstance. I *will* not put us in that circumstance, mademoiselle. And I humbly ask that you *please* not pursue this subject further. Now, or in the future."

When he finally lifted his head, she had turned away.

All at once, he felt clumsy and boorish. "It was not my intention to offend you, Véronique. I was trying to do just the opposite, in fact. I'm sorry."

When she looked back, unshed tears filled her eyes. "*Au contraire* . . . You have not offended me, Jack. You have made me want for home, and for my conversations with Christophe." She nodded, her smile fragile. "I understand your story now and will abide by your wish. I give you my word not to broach this subject again."

Jack let out a held breath. "And I give you my word, Véronique, that I will be your mouthpiece in these towns when you are not with me. I'll seek information on your father, I'll follow every lead." He caught her eye and smiled. "As though you were standing right beside me, with my rifle aimed and at the ready."

She chuckled and tears slipped down her cheeks.

But Jack resisted the urge to catch them, recalling in vivid detail what it had been like to be with Mary as her husband, and how she had responded to him when he had comforted her at times like this, when her emotions were tender and raw. His body responded to the memory, and to the woman sitting beside him, and he hungered for the intimacies shared between a husband and his wife.

Desire fed imagination, and imagination needed no prompting.

He made himself look away from Véronique, knowing full well that for him to console her now would be like him opening the door to the millinery . . . ever so slightly.

B E MINDFUL OF THE PASS on your way up to the Peerless today, Brennan." Monsieur Hochstetler paused from his task, and Véronique read warning in his expression. "Remember, right around Maynor's Gulch is where Zimmerman went—"

"Will do, Mr. Hochstetler. Thank you!" Jack's quick response seemed a bit overly sincere, even for him. "I appreciate your advice."

Jack strode from the mercantile and Véronique hurried to catch up with him. "Be mindful of what pass, Jack? To what was Mr. Hochstetler referring?"

"It's nothing to worry about, Véronique."

She quickened her steps. "Who is this Zimmerman Mr. Hochstetler mentioned?"

Jack hefted a box and situated it in the wagon. "Can you hand me that other one right there, please?" He pointed. "The small one?"

She did as he asked. "And what are you supposed to remember?"

From the opposite side of the wagon, he peered at her across the cargo, then tossed over one end of a rope. "Can you pull this taut?"

She gave the rope an anemic tug, knowing what he was trying to do. "What was Mr. Hochstetler's meaning, Jack? He said Zimmerman went somewhere. Who is Zimmerman and where did he go?"

Sighing, Jack came around and tied the rope himself. "It's all right, Véronique. I've got everything under control. You've given me a job to do—now let me do it. I'll be ready to go in a minute, so why don't you go ahead and climb up? Mrs. Baird sent some muffins this morning. Cinnamon, I think. They're beneath the seat." He turned back to his work.

She stared after him. It felt as though he'd just patted her on the head and sent her off to play. *She* was the employer in this situation. It was *her* wagon! She was paying *him*! How dare he try to dismiss her as though she were some—"Jack, you will cease your duties this instant and give heed to my question."

Gradually he turned to face her.

The furrow in his brow, coupled with the way his eyes narrowed, made her wish she'd taken more care in phrasing her request. "Please," she added more softly, "I would appreciate your attention for a moment. I am asking you a simple question and yet you continue to avoid giving response."

"In our culture, ma'am"—he jerked the rope tight—"that could be seen as me trying to give you a polite hint." He secured the knot and offered a stiff smile. "Maybe you should consider taking it."

"I do not care for these . . . *hints*, Jack. I have never done so. I prefer for thoughts to be expressed explicitly and in clear order. So that everything can be understood."

"Why doesn't that surprise me . . . ?" He blew out a breath as he walked around the corner of the wagon.

Faced with his stony silence, she climbed up onto the bench seat and waited. Maynor's Gulch was a pass they crossed on their way to the Peerless, if her map reading from the previous evening was without error. Five hours up and five hours down. Jack couldn't avoid her forever.

This morning hadn't come soon enough for her. She was eager to renew the search for her father and—at least up until now—to be in Jack's company again. He'd already summarized his supply trip to Duke's Run. His overnight venture had yielded success in sales, but not in discovering anything about her father. Yet no doubt existed in her mind that he had 'overturned every stone' in his search, as went the recently learned saying.

Eyeing Jack as he finished securing the wagon, Véronique found her thoughts returning to Lilly Carlson. The visit with Dr. Hadley early Wednesday—prior to her altercation with Jack in the middle of

Main Street, for which she had promptly apologized to him this morning—had proven informative, but also distressing.

Dr. Hadley had painted a far less hopeful picture of the surgery's likelihood of success than had Lilly. "I appreciated your note requesting a meeting with me about Lilly Carlson," the doctor had stated. "Your desire to help the Carlson family is most noble, Mademoiselle Girard, and I took the liberty of meeting with Pastor Carlson—though I did not reveal your specific intent to him, as you requested in your note. I learned from him that you and Lilly have become good friends. You've been a guest in their home. The girl esteems you most highly, mademoiselle, and gives weight to your counsel. With Pastor Carlson's permission, and in consideration of the generous offer you present on the family's behalf, I'll discuss the details of the surgery with you.

"Lilly's bones have been so long in their current growth pattern, Mademoiselle Girard, that I'm not at all convinced her body will respond to this procedure in a positive way. The anesthesia has certain risks as well, as does the length of the operation."

"But Lilly Carlson is young, Doctor. And she is strong, *non*?"

"Yes, mademoiselle, she is. But successful surgeries of this kind have consistently occurred with much younger patients—not those Lilly's age." Concern weighted his sigh. "Doctors take an oath to first do no harm. Not to knowingly take steps that will leave a patient in a worsened condition than when they first inclined themselves to our services." The earnestness in his voice matched that in his expression. "Since the day the Carlsons moved to Willow Springs, I've cared for their family and have watched Lilly grow into a beautiful girl who has such promise ahead of her. I have no desire to bury that child sooner than her Maker wills."

That possibility gave Véronique pause, again. "But the surgeon in Boston believes there is hope for the success of the *procédure* with Lilly."

"He's cautiously hopeful, yes, and he's considering her case right now. But what he deems an acceptable risk, and my definition of that term, are not necessarily in harmony with one another, mademoiselle." Removing his glasses, Dr. Hadley had massaged the bridge of his nose. "Granted, my personal involvement with the patient and her family could well be clouding my judgment." His focus was direct. "But I've seen many a patient live out a full life from the confines of a wheelchair, Mademoiselle Girard. I have never witnessed such from the confines of a coffin."

As she waited on the wagon's mercilessly hard bench seat, remembering the conversation with Dr. Hadley stirred up a jumble of emotions. The estimated price for the surgery was greater than she had anticipated, but if the established pattern of Lord Marchand's deposits continued—and she had no reason to believe they would not—she would have ample money to cover the *procédure.*

Dr. Hadley had graciously offered to confirm the costs with the *chirurgien* in Boston, and if the man agreed to perform the operation on Lilly, then Dr. Hadley agreed to go with Véronique to present the idea to Pastor and Mrs. Carlson.

When Jack finally joined her in the wagon, the firm set of his jaw told her not to push the subject of Zimmerman. Which, saints help her, made her want to know all the more.

When they reached the edge of town and he'd still said nothing, she laid a hand on his arm. "Please, Jack. I must know. What was Monsieur Hochstetler referring to?"

His smile was unexpected. "Don't you mean . . . to *what* was Monsieur Hochstetler referring?"

Realizing her mistake, she tried to think of an excuse—and couldn't. Other than the fact that listening to the constant diatribe of butchered English since she'd arrived in this country had finally left its tainted mark. Though tempted to share that thought, she decided against it.

"Véronique . . ."

The tender way he spoke her name drew her attention.

"If you want me to tell you what Mr. Hochstetler was referring to, I will." The steady plod of horses' hooves pounded out the seconds. "But, for what it's worth, it has nothing to do with what we're doing today, and I think it would be better if you didn't know. I wish you'd trust me in this."

Sincerity tendered his voice, echoing what shone in his eyes.

Everything within her said to trust him. She knew she could. She nodded slowly, smiling, appreciating his desire to protect her. "I still want you to tell me."

Instantly Jack's expression sobered. He turned back to the road.

"Zimmerman is the man who held this job before me. On his last trip up to the Peerless, he tried to haul too heavy a load over the pass at Maynor's Gulch. His wagon clipped the edge and went over."

"Went . . . over?" She shuddered. "Went over . . . where?"

"The side of the mountain."

Her head swam and oxygen grew scarce as she pictured the scene. Putting her head between her knees would have helped, but the thought of how unladylike that would appear kept her from it. "Did he . . . Is this Zimmerman . . . deceased?"

"No, ma'am. But he busted up his leg pretty good and spent a couple of cold miserable nights out there before somebody came along and found him." Jack glanced at her, his eyes dark. "So . . . are you happy? Now that you know?" The look on his face told her he certainly wasn't.

She trusted Jack's skill in maneuvering the wagon, yet could not dissuade the knots twisting her stomach, or the ache in her knuckles from clutching the bench seat so tightly.

The higher the wagon climbed the ribboned path that morning, the cooler the air became, and the thinner. Véronique worked to catch her breath.

Three hours later they continued to climb. The narrow, rutted ledge carved into the side of the mountain clung like a frantic child to its mother. It was a wonder these roads even existed. And then it struck her that perhaps they were not naturally occurring.

Jack laughed when she posed the question. "No, these roads aren't here by chance. They had help. Striking a vein of gold or silver is one thing, but it's not worth much just holed up in the side of a mountain. You have to mine it, of course, but there's also the problem of getting your equipment up to camp, and the gold and silver down to town." He indicated the snaking road before them. "They use dynamite nowadays but used to have to dig it by hand."

Since the sheer drop-off was on Jack's side this time, she didn't have to stare at the thin line where land abruptly ended and plunged into the chasm below. The discovery earlier this morning that Jack was on that side of the wagon had been comforting, at first.

Until she realized that the opposite would be true on their way back down the mountain. And no matter what side the cliff was on, if the wagon went over, they went over with it.

A sudden jolt brought Véronique back to the moment. A wave of nausea hit her. The image of her and Jack lying at the bottom of the canyon was all she could see, their bruised bodies broken and bloodied.

"Can we . . . pull over, Jack, *s'il vous plaît?*"

Silence. "Where exactly would you like me to pull over?"

The narrow thread of steep incline blurred in her vision. She had to get out. If only for a moment.

"Véronique, what are you—" His arm came around her waist and pulled her firmly back down beside him.

Her stomach roiled. The back of her throat burned. "I think, I am going to be . . . unwell, Jack." She put a hand over her mouth. Her eyes watered.

His grip lessened, but he still held her secure. "Do what you have to do, but I can't stop the wagon on this incline, and there's no pulling over right now."

Feeling it build inside her, she tried to distance herself from him. She could not do what she was about to do while sitting next to him.

"You cannot stand up, Véronique! It's not safe." He crushed her back against him.

The pressure in her temples became excruciating. She tried to scoot to her side of the wagon, but Jack insisted on pulling her close, as though trying to comfort her.

"It'll be all right, Véronique. Just hang on. We'll be over this rise in about ten minutes."

Ten minutes was an eternity. Every bump, every jostle on the rutted road reminded her of the yawning cavern to her left and churned the upset inside her.

Until she could hold it in no longer.

"Jack, I am so sor—"

She emptied the contents of her stomach on the floor of the wagon. Her breath wouldn't come. She gulped for air. And then it happened a second time.

Jack let her go and recoiled beside her, bracing his legs against the footrest.

Tears choked her throat. Her eyes burned. Hot and cold flushes ransacked her body, resulting from her nausea, most certainly. But also from mortal embarrassment.

Head cradled in her hands, she snuck a look at his splattered pant legs and wished she could crawl into a hole in the side of the mountain and never come out. It was not fitting for a *patronne* to . . . become sick all over her employee. She had a strong sense that this would do little for her goal of maintaining a respectful boundary between them.

A burst of cool breeze felt like heaven against her face and neck, and helped dispel the stench. The pounding in her temples gradually eased, her head cleared. She put a hand to her hair and found it in complete disarray. Funny how little that mattered now, comparatively.

After a moment, she chanced another look beside her.

Jack was concentrating on the road, and yet she knew he was aware she was looking at him. One corner of his mouth twitched. "Feeling better?"

His question—so innocent, so lacking in judgment—didn't help her embarrassment, and Véronique covered her face with her hands.

"It's okay, Véronique, really. First place I can, I'll pull over and we'll wash up. Okay? Shouldn't be too long."

She nodded, keeping her face averted.

Moments passed, and she felt something on her back—a most tentative touch. It startled her at first. Her throat tightened with emotion.

Jack combed his fingers gently through the hair now falling loose down her back. He encouraged her to move closer. "Come here," he whispered. He moved his hand in slow circles, urging her over beside him.

Surprised by the forwardness of his actions, she resisted.

But when she felt the pressure on her back increase and heard the hushed whisper of his deep voice, she acquiesced. As she scooted close against him, she felt a shiver and looked up. Something flashed in his dark blue eyes. He didn't seem to be frustrated with her, and yet the intensity of his expression made her wonder.

She laid her head on his shoulder and peered down, then winced at the condition of his clothes, not knowing whether to laugh or cry. But she did know everything was not all right.

"Jack?" Her voice came out a broken whisper. He didn't respond, and she repeated his name.

"Yes?" His chin brushed against the crown of her head.

"The next time . . . I will trust you."

A chuckle rumbled from deep inside him. His arm tightened around her shoulders. He cradled her head against his chest. "Then this was worth it."

CHAPTER TWENTY-ONE

T HE PEERLESS MINING CAMP was a good distance higher in the mountains than Jenny's Draw, and though it was April, a fall-like coolness braced the air. They'd arrived later than Jack had estimated, a little past noon, with having to stop and clean up from Véronique's . . . incident.

A fine sleet filtered down from the ashen clouds shrouding the highest peaks, cloaking the stands of blue spruce and towering pines until their needles shimmered in the gray light.

Jack stood just inside the open doorway of the supply building and listened as the merchant counted the payment. The old man's gnarled fingers moved slower than Jack would have liked.

Véronique remained in the wagon, swathed in a blanket she kept tucked close beneath her chin.

They'd stopped shortly after her illness so she could rinse her skirt in the creek and freshen up. The floor of the wagon had borne the brunt of it and he'd easily set that to right with a bucket of water. He only wished he could say the same for her ransacked pride. A quick pilfer through the supplies in the wagon bed afforded him what he needed. Miners' shirts and dungarees were standard freighting items.

Unfortunately, women's skirts and shirtwaists were not.

He knew she had to be chilled with that damp skirt on but she'd insisted on wearing it. And the look she'd given him when he offered her a pair of miners' dungarees was something he wouldn't soon forget.

Miners continued to flock toward the building and were forming a lengthy queue that managed to wrap itself closely around the wagon.

So far most of the men were only looking at Véronique. One would occasionally gain the nerve to call out to her. But despite that and their obvious ogling, she somehow managed to appear at ease and in complete control. Though Jack knew quite the opposite to be true.

That morning, as they'd passed over Maynor's Gulch, he'd spotted splintered boards and debris from what he assumed was Zimmerman's wagon far below at the base of the canyon's throat. Not wanting to risk Véronique's seeing the wreckage, he had persuaded her to move closer to him in order to divert her attention. It had taken some doing, and at first she had resisted, as he'd expected. But when she'd finally moved closer and tucked herself against him, the memory of what it had been like to be a husband in the intimate sense had returned again with such force that his response to Véronique's nearness almost made him regret his action.

Almost.

Many years had passed since he'd felt Mary's soft female form curved into him. But that was one memory time could not erase.

The feel of Véronique pressed against him had been more stirring than he'd imagined, and he'd already spent too much time trying not to imagine it in too great of detail. The brief encounter wasn't helping that struggle, which was why it couldn't happen again.

Not out here, not alone like they were.

Jack took in a deep breath, held it, then slowly let it out, trying hard to think about something else.

A miner approached the wagon, his focus on Véronique, his intent on speaking to her obvious. Jack stepped through the threshold and onto the boardwalk, making his presence known. The man spotted him and slowed. The fella's gaze went from the rifle in Jack's hand, to Véronique, and back again. Apparently changing his mind, he wandered back through the crowd.

Jack sensed her stare and looked up, but she quickly averted her eyes.

He'd tried his best to coax her into talking when they stopped at the creek earlier. He'd even joked about what had happened. But the more he'd attempted to draw her out, the more reticent she'd become. Her responses had been polite, brief, and void of their customary sparkle.

He thought back to the morning they'd met in the washroom of the hotel. His first glance had told him she was feminine through and through. That was impossible to miss. Since then, he'd witnessed her confidence, her ability to take charge of situations and communicate her desires—she had no problem with that last one.

But what he hadn't realized until this morning was just how much of Véronique Girard's confidence was rooted in her maintaining that carefully manicured appearance and textbook ladylike behavior.

It was a fragile façade at best, and one destined to be shattered and reshaped if she was going to survive this territory. He had a feeling she'd give fate a fair fight at it too.

"You're most welcome to count it yourself, Mr. Brennan." The merchant laid the final dollar on the stack and tapped it with his forefinger, or what was left of his forefinger. "To make sure it's all there."

Even before learning the merchant's name, Jack had detected the trace of an accent in the man's voice. His gut instinct nudged him to trust Bernard Rousseau, so he took the bills, folded them, and shoved them deep into his pants pocket. "I appreciate your business, Monsieur Rousseau." He pulled the inventory list from his pocket. "These are all the items available. Might see if there's anything else you want added for next time. Mark it and I'll make sure it's delivered."

As Rousseau reviewed the list, Jack stole a glance at Véronique.

Her gaze was on him, the look on her face expectant. Since the Peerless was one of the mines that had attracted Frenchmen in the early days, according to Scoggins, anyway, Jack knew she had great hopes for discovering something about her father here.

Jack cleared his throat, knowing she was watching—and waiting for some sign of recognition from the merchant. "Could I bother you with a question, sir?" He waited for Rousseau's attention. "How many years did you mine the Peerless before you decided to move into supplying?"

Rousseau smiled, revealing a surprising number of straight, albeit yellowed, teeth. "I mined her for my first twenty years over here, until I lost the hearing in one ear . . . along with a few other things." He wriggled his right hand. Not only was the tip of his right forefinger missing, but his ring finger and pinkie were absent as well. "Blasting powder. Funny thing is, I still feel an ache in those fingers every once in a while." He shrugged. "Running the supply store is easier on an old man's body, not to mention safer. I've been doing this since '63."

Jack quickly did the math. This man came over two years before Pierre Gustave Girard. "Have you ever returned home, sir?"

A wistful look moved over the man's face. "Only every night, in my dreams. I would give much to see the light reflecting off the river Seine one more time. Or to visit the Sainte-Chapelle at sunset"—the look in his eyes went vague as though reliving a memory—"and watch *rouge* settle across the city as evening falls."

For Véronique's sake, Jack prayed this man would at least have heard of her father. He briefly described the circumstances of their search for Pierre Gustave Girard. "Does he sound familiar at all, Mr. Rousseau?"

The man sighed, shaking his head. "I'm afraid that can describe a number of men I've known in the past, and still do. We all came with such dreams. . . ." He indicated for Jack to precede him out the door to the muddied street. "The name is common enough among my countrymen, but I can't say I know the man you're asking about. Many of us have passed through the Peerless. Quite a few have stayed." Rousseau's brow crinkled. "You're welcome to ask around just down the road there." He motioned. "Just past the last saloon on the right. You'll come across a row of bunkhouses. We call it Ma Petite France. Some of the men have been here since the first blast, like I have. We came over together. But they still work the mines. If this . . . Pierre Girard is here, or if he has been through here in recent years, they'll know it." He glanced from Jack to the wagon. "*Très belle*," he whispered. "You've got a fine-looking wife, Brennan, and it's an honorable thing you're doing in searching for her father. Especially after all this time."

Jack followed the man's admiring stare, pleased when Véronique met his gaze and offered the tiniest smile. "Actually, we're n—"

"You're wise not to let her out of your sight, and if I may be so bold, I'd suggest you rethink bringing her along with you in the future. Marriage isn't necessarily a respected union in places like this. Not by some, anyway." His expression sobered. "If anything happened to you up here, Brennan, she'd be left on her lonesome. And that wouldn't be a desirable thing."

Jack nodded. "I understand."

Rousseau opened his mouth as if to say more, then firmed his lips. "I wish you both safe journey."

Jack tilted his head slightly. "Is there . . . something else you wanted to say, Mr. Rousseau?"

His eyes narrowed as he surveyed the wagons and miners cramming the street. "Only that you ought not delay getting back down the mountain." The older man took off his hat and ran a hand through his thinning hair. "There've been some . . . accidents of late." His gaze settled on the dirt beneath his worn leather boots. "You seem like an honest man to me, Brennan, but your predecessor"—his voice lowered—"was not. Nor the fella before him. They dealt unfairly and earned a lot of enemies in this town, and others nearby."

Jack thought of Zimmerman and of the scene he'd viewed earlier that day—plank boards and wagon wheels splintered at the bottom of the canyon. Something about the scene had bothered him then, and it struck him now what it was.

He didn't remember seeing any remnants of supplies scattered among the debris. Perhaps some of the miners had scavenged them. Rescuing Zimmerman from his ledge had to have been difficult, but that canyon wall was a sheer drop-off of at least three hundred feet on all sides. It would have been near impossible for anyone to retrieve the supplies after the fact.

Jack shifted his weight. "Why would someone hold a grudge against me for something Zimmerman did?"

Rousseau looked at him pointedly. "Sometimes the only thing revenge needs is a target, Mr. Brennan. It doesn't care who's to blame. Now the two of you had best be on—" A sudden cough hit him. The spasm seemed to deepen, and Rousseau clutched his chest until he regained his breath.

Jack recognized the phlegmy sound. Lung congestion was familiar among old-timers in the mining camps. "I appreciate your advice, sir." He extended his hand. "We'll stop by Ma Petite France, then promptly be on our way."

Jack returned to the wagon, aware of Véronique's keen attention every step of the way. He climbed to the bench seat beside her.

"We're going to head on down the road a ways. Rousseau said that—"

"Rousseau?" She looked from him to the man standing in the doorway.

"He came over a couple of years before your father did. I'm guessing, but I think he's probably about your father's age."

"But, he looks so . . . old."

Jack nodded, having thought the same thing. "Mining's hard work. It tends to age a man before his time." *If it doesn't kill him first.*

He guided the wagon through the hordes of men lined up for supplies—and no doubt a look at Véronique—then followed Rousseau's directions down the street to the cluster of bunkhouses.

One hour and countless inquiries later, Ma Petite France had offered up no clue to Pierre Gustave Girard's whereabouts. If the old-timers' testimonies were accurate—and for some reason, Jack believed they were—Pierre Girard had never worked at the Peerless. But Jack had watched, stunned, as Véronique was transformed.

She conversed with the miners in their native tongue, laughing and speaking to them of Paris and their homeland—at least that's the gist he got from the few familiar words he caught. She listened attentively to their stories and occasionally translated for him, telling him they shared with her about their families left behind, or family members buried shortly after their arrival in this new country.

Most of the miners seemed respectful enough, but Jack stayed close by her side, allowing his presence to stake his claim. From the distance the miners maintained, they got his meaning, even if Véronique was oblivious to it.

Back in the wagon, he and Véronique headed toward the main thoroughfare. She was quiet beside him, but he sensed a renewal within her, and a lightness that hadn't been present before.

Then he remembered.

He guided the team in the direction of the supply building. "I forgot to collect the inventory list from Rousseau." After angling the wagon adjacent to the building, he reined in and set the brake. "I won't be but a minute." He hopped down, tempted to remind her again about not speaking to anyone in his absence. But being aware of her sensitivity to his being in *her* employ, and not wanting to alter her current mood, he quelled that impulse. He'd had enough theatrics for one day.

Véronique watched Jack disappear inside the building. She'd wanted to accompany him, but he hadn't asked. So neither had she. She took in the dismal view of the town from where she sat in the wagon.

How could anyone live in such a place? Why would they choose to? Something caught her attention—a rundown shack across the street. Constructed of gray clapboard and leaning slightly to one side, it squatted in the mud and muck and held no appeal whatsoever— save for the sign tacked above its door.

It read simply *Crêperie.*

She wasn't so much hungry in her stomach as she was hungry in her heart. For a taste of home. The miners in Ma Petite France had proven to be a gentlemanly group, putting her at ease. More so than she'd ever thought she would be in such a place.

Hesitating, she glanced at the supply building and saw Jack inside speaking to Monsieur Rousseau. She looked back at the shack. It would only take her a moment, and she could keep Jack in her view the entire time.

She climbed down from the wagon, ignoring with a practiced air the looks and comments from miners as she crossed the street. The inside of the rudimentary *crêperie* looked no better than its outer shell. But the aromas wafting from a back room enticed her with memories of Paris, and warm crepes she and her mother had often purchased from a street *vendeur* near the Musée du Louvre.

The front room of the shack was empty. Véronique peered down a narrow hallway to the right, then decided to see if Jack had completed his transaction. A glance through the grimy front window confirmed he was still engaged in conversation with Monsieur Rousseau.

She peered around the corner, down the hallway. *"Bonjour!"*

No answer.

"Monsieur? Madame? Are you open for business?" Taking a step into the hallway, she was certain she heard a voice coming from the back. Never would she have considered consuming anything from a place like this before coming to this country, much less crossing the threshold of such an establishment. This newfound bravado of hers was exhilarating. And frightening. Knowing Jack was close at hand bolstered her shifting courage.

"Is anyone there?" She glanced down the hallway behind her, no longer able to see Jack, but still able to see the wagon. "I am interested in purchasing something, *s'il vous plaît.*"

"Exactly what is it you're interested in purchasing, *mon amie?*"

Véronique spun to find a man standing in the hallway, close to her. She stepped back—then calmed when she got a better look. He resembled some of the gentlemen she'd just visited at Ma Petite France and could well have been one of them. "*Bonjour*, monsieur. I saw your sign out front and was tempted to see what your establishment might offer." She shrugged. "It has been a long while since I have enjoyed the tastes of home."

He bowed briefly at the waist. "I am honored that you would visit my humble establishment." His accent thickened, and grew playful. "I have warm *crêpes* in the back and was just about to bring them out. Would you like to help me?"

She gave a brief curtsy. "*Oui*, monsieur. I would be happy to assist a fellow countryman in such an honored task."

She followed him down the hallway, her shoulders nearly brushing the walls, the passage was so narrow. This man looked to be about the age of her father, and she found herself imagining, as she had when she was much younger, what her father looked like. And if the years of adulthood had granted her any outer resemblance to him at all.

According to her mother, she was Arianne Girard's daughter on the outside but was Pierre Girard's on the inside. *"When we peer into the mirror, my dear daughter, we see identical faces,"* her mother had said more than once, gently caressing her cheek. *"We are so alike. But within your eyes and within your heart's cadence, Véronique, lingers your father, always. His passion, and his life."*

In latter years, her mother became less willing to speak of her father, and when she did, she became withdrawn and reticent afterward. Which was understandable, given what he had done. To them both.

The room at the back of the shack was small, but true to the man's word, fresh crepes were spread out on a board, with more stacked in a skillet perched on a black stove in the corner.

He glanced back over his shoulder. "We need only to butter them, *mon amie*. The butter is there, on the shelf."

Véronique glanced behind her, then reached for the metal container. "The *crêpes* smell *délicieuses*. How long have you been—"

The man pressed close from behind, pinning her against the cupboard and holding her there with his body. "*Mon amie*, indeed." His breath was hot against the side of her face. "I'd like to taste something from home too."

Véronique screamed and clawed his bare forearms. Then grabbed his hands to still their progress.

He tried to turn her toward him, and at first she resisted. Then she remembered something Christophe had taught her after a boy had attempted to take liberties. Loathing this man's hands on her body, Véronique allowed him to turn her to face him.

Then she did exactly as Christophe had demonstrated.

The man loosened his hold and staggered back a step. He bent at the waist, his expression one of shocked fury, and pain. "Why you little—"

Not looking back, Véronique ran down the hallway to the front room, certain she heard the door open. "Jack!"

But the man standing in the doorway wasn't Jack. And she skidded to a halt, breathless.

CHAPTER | TWENTY-TWO ✦

T HE MAN STANDING IN the doorway was broad-shouldered and
        thick through the chest, giving the appearance of being as wide
        as he was tall. His bald head gave him a menacing look that was
offset by the kindness in his eyes.

But she'd trusted appearances before. . . .

His gaze flickered past her, his expression wary. "Somethin' wrong
here, miss?"

Trembling, Véronique nodded, hoping she wasn't going to be sick
again. "The man in the back . . . he tried to—"

"Véronique!" Jack burst through the open doorway, pistol drawn.
He took stock of the man beside him and moved to stand close to
her. He stared down hard, his breath heavy. "Are you all right? What
are you doing in here?"

The rush of courage that had emboldened her only moments
before evaporated at the concern in his voice. Cradling her midsection, she slowly nodded. "I am all right."

Footsteps sounded in the hallway behind them—then hastened in
the opposite direction.

"Miss . . ."

Véronique looked back at the stranger.

"You said the man *tried* to do something. . . ."

Understanding his unspoken question, Véronique shook her

head. "*Non*, he did not hurt me." She watched understanding flood Jack's face, followed by fury. "I managed to escape him," she added quickly, hoping to allay his fears.

Relief diluted Jack's anger, but only briefly.

"You get her on outta here, friend. And keep her safe." The stranger tipped his head toward the hallway. "I'll take care of him, with pleasure."

Jack hesitated, then took hold of her hand.

"I'm sorry for what happened to you, Miss ... ah ..." The man obviously struggled to remember her name. "Vernie. But decent women have no business going around here unaccompanied." He threw Jack a look that said he should've known better.

Jack's grip tightened around her hand.

Knowing their situation wasn't Jack's fault, Véronique expected him to set the stranger aright of that fact. Regardless of Jack's being in her employ, she knew she deserved the public correction.

Jack tucked the revolver inside his belt. "We'll be on our way, then. I'm obliged to you for taking care of things here." He tucked her hand into the crook of his arm and escorted her outside.

The action felt stiff, formal, and she sensed a different anger building inside him as he drew her with him across the street.

A shrill whistle blew, and in no time the thoroughfare was again flooded with miners. Jack lifted her by the waist up into the wagon, then climbed over her and sat down, not bothering to walk around to the other side as he customarily did.

When they reached the outskirts of town, she could no longer bear his silence. Or her guilt. "I am sorry, Jack. My actions were impulsive and foolish and—"

"Yes, ma'am, they were." He stared ahead, jaw set.

Véronique smarted at his tone, then thought again of what might have happened to her had she not managed to get away from that man. Sickly chills inched up her legs and pooled in the pit of her stomach. She wrapped her arms tightly around herself.

They rode in silence. Jack glanced behind them on occasion, as though expecting to see someone following them. It only added to her unsettled feeling.

It was later in the day than she had realized, and from reading the sun's position in the blue overhead, she wondered whether they

would arrive back in Willow Springs before dark, as Jack had predicted earlier that morning.

"You said you escaped him." His deep voice came out flat and
thin, telling her he was still angry. "How did you manage that?"

She confined her gaze to her lap. "When I was younger, Christophe
gave me instruction on how a woman can defend herself against a
man."

"Christophe, huh?" He scoffed softly. "And what did he teach you
exactly?"

She didn't care for his patronizing tone. "I hardly think I need to
spell it out for you, Jack."

"And I hardly thought I needed to spell out to you that you were
supposed to stay in the wagon while I went inside. But apparently I
was mistaken."

Véronique didn't like this side of Jack Brennan, yet she felt
responsible for its manifestation. "I have apologized to you, Jack. And
I have well imagined what could have happened to me, if perhaps
you are thinking I have not." Her voice caught. "It was impulsive on
my part. I know this. But I saw the sign on the building and—"

"What did the sign say?"

She hesitated. *"Crêperie."* Her neck heated, knowing how foolish
that would sound to him. "In your language, it means . . . crepe shop.
Much like a bakery, to you."

He shook his head but said nothing.

With every bump and jolt of the wagon, she felt his censure. Seeing a sharp bend in the path ahead, where trail and chasm met with
little introduction, she closed her eyes tight, determined not to look
over the edge. Once they traversed the curve, she opened them again.

"I only wanted a taste of home, Jack. Of something familiar. And
my desire for that outweighed the logic of my actions. It will not
occur again. I give you my word."

After a long moment, he looked over at her. "See to it that it
doesn't." His expression softened a fraction. *"S'il vous plaît."*

Jack's senses remained on alert as they wound their way down the
mountain. After an hour, his pulse had returned to normal. Once
they'd crossed Maynor's Gulch, he began to relax. When they were
little more than two hours from Willow Springs, the trail they were

on joined up with the route they'd taken from Jenny's Draw. And once he'd traveled a route, it remained etched in his memory.

"Jack?" Her voice sounded overly small.

He looked beside him. Her brown eyes appeared luminous in the half-light of approaching evening. Seeing her arms wrapped around herself, he wondered if she was chilly. "Would you like your coat?"

"*Oui*, please. It is in the top of my *bagage*."

Jack stopped the wagon. He reached behind him and located her satchel, unlatched it, then felt around for her coat. Unsuccessful, he finally stood and leaned over the seat. He couldn't believe the assortment of items she'd stuffed inside the bag—mirrors, powders, a bottle of perfume, books, and undergarments galore. But not a coat to be seen. He finally came across something and held up a tiny nothing of a jacket. "This is the coat you brought along with you to stay warm?"

A nod, far less confident than usual.

He stuffed it back into her bag and reached beneath the bench seat for a miners' jacket he kept stored there. "Put this on."

She did so without question. It dwarfed her small frame.

Between the events of the day and the earlier drizzle of sleet, her blond hair had long since evaded her efforts to keep it situated atop her head. It fell in a thick swoop over one shoulder. With her customary defenses reduced to shambles, she looked more than a bit defeated—and far too alluring.

He found himself thanking God again that nothing worse had happened to her back at the Peerless. When he'd returned to the wagon to find it empty, he'd panicked. He knew enough to realize that the deeper root of his anger was tethered back fifteen years ago. But the emotions of that day, and of the days following Mary's and Aaron's death, had returned with a vengeance when he'd seen the empty wagon.

Véronique was in his care, and he hadn't been there to protect her.

"I would like to speak with you about something, Jack, if I may."

Her formality struck him as odd, in light of all they'd been through. "You may speak with me about anything you wish, Véronique."

She gave him a tiny smile. "I realize that the likelihood of finding my *papa* in this Colorado Territory is ..." She paused as though searching for the right word.

"Slim?" Jack supplied, his voice soft.

She shot him an unexpected look. "It was my intention to say 'not as promising as I once considered it to be,' but ... I suppose the idea of my hopes becoming more slender also fits the description."

The serious tone of her voice kept Jack from smiling at her mild correction. "Twenty years is a long time to go with no word from a man."

"*Oui*, it is." She slowly inhaled, then let her breath out quickly. "Something I have not told you ... and I do not know why I tell you now, other than I want you to better understand this search I am on. I was sent on this journey. I came not of my own choosing but at someone else's behest—that of my *maman*, God rest her soul."

A rush of cool air hit them as they rounded a corner, and she tugged the miners' jacket tighter around her chin. Jack wanted to offer his condolences on her mother's passing, but somehow the timing of it didn't feel right. Hearing her intake of breath, he remained silent.

"I do not want you to think that I am brave, Jack. That I decided to come all this way on my own. I would never have gotten on that ship if given a choice. Yet over the past months, my reasons for continuing this journey have changed. It has somehow become my own journey now. That is influenced, I am sure, by the last request of my *maman*, as well as my desire to know the man who won, and somehow managed to keep, the heart of my *maman*"—her tone bordered on skepticism—"despite his broken promises to her. To us both."

Jack trained his focus on the road, hearing her pain and not wanting to add to it. "My main fear, Véronique, is that you'll get your hopes set on something and then get hurt in the process. There's great potential for that to happen in this situation."

"I understand what you are saying to me, and I appreciate the heart with which you say it. But you must know that I have not let my hopes run away with me like some winsome child. I know what 'odds I am up against,' as your people phrase it, and I will be fine."

He wondered where on earth she'd picked up that phrase, and knew how much the advice he was about to give her also applied to himself. "Just remember that sometimes it's the one thing we've never had, but have wanted for so long, that has the power to disappoint us the most."

She sat quietly for a moment, as though letting that wash over her. "What kind of disappointment have you suffered that has taught you such discernment?" Admiration and curiosity threaded her soft question.

Jack knew that whatever he shared couldn't be taken back. He trusted her with knowing about Mary and Aaron—it wasn't that. But something told him that telling her about them at that moment wouldn't help her find the answers she sought. "I guess it comes with age, and with having wrestled against my own desires from time to time. Having expectations can be a good thing, unless they take over. Then they can rob you of the happiness you might've had, had you been more content from the start."

She didn't answer immediately. "I am at peace with whatever my journey reveals."

He detected tenuous confidence in her tone.

"I have never really known my father, and have only the vaguest of memories of him. So if I do not find him"—she shrugged—"I will have lost nothing, *oui*?"

But deep inside, Jack knew that wasn't true. And from her guarded expression, he thought she knew it too.

Night had fallen by the time he pulled up in front of the hotel in Willow Springs. Véronique was asleep beside him, her head on his shoulder, her body tucked warm against his. With that combination, he'd been tempted to keep on driving into the night. His back and shoulder muscles ached from the miles of rutted roads, and from not having changed positions in the past hour. He hadn't wanted to waken her.

The still of night settled around them like a cocoon. It wasn't much past nine o'clock, but the town was unusually quiet. With the faint murmur of Fountain Creek hovering over the stillness, Jack remembered what Jonathan McCutchens had told him about this town last summer. He would never have come to this place without McCutchens's recommendation. He owed that man a debt of gratitude, and he determined, at his first opportunity, to visit the banks of Fountain Creek and pay it.

Véronique sighed against him. Jack lightly brushed the top of her head, and then let his hand linger there. If anything had happened to this woman that day—any of the myriad of horrible things that had repeatedly come to mind as they'd traveled down the mountain—he wasn't sure how he would've dealt with it.

She did not belong in mining camps. She attracted too much attention. She was naïve in ways that could easily get her—and him—into trouble. It wasn't safe. It wasn't wise. He shouldn't allow her to accompany him again. But he knew he would.

Because if he didn't let her go with him, she was just stubborn enough to find someone else to take her. And Jack was certain that the average male in this territory wouldn't have her best interests in mind. Far from it.

Staring at her without fear of being caught, he found his focus drawn to her mouth. Even in sleep, her lips hinted at a smile. How could lips that looked so soft, so delicate, fire back with such deadly accuracy? That thought made him smile. He allowed himself to imagine what it might be like to kiss those lips, often, and what they might taste like. But doing so only encouraged desires he knew were best left unstirred, for both their sakes.

He gently nudged her awake.

She moved beside him. "Are we home, Jack?" She stretched and opened her eyes. They suddenly widened, and her expression went shy. While busying herself with smoothing the edges of the miners' jacket, she demurely put distance between them on the seat.

Her reaction didn't surprise him. "Yes, we're home . . . Vernie."

He grinned when she sat up a bit straighter. Her brows arched in question. He'd had plenty of time to relive the scene from the ramshackle hut that afternoon and recalled how the stranger had addressed her.

She cocked her head to one side as though to say she remembered the name's origin. "I prefer my given name, monsieur."

Jack's smile deepened as he assisted her from the wagon. "I'll try and remember that, ma'am."

She shrugged out of the jacket and handed it to him. "*Merci* for the *jaquette*," she whispered, covering a yawn with her hand.

He opened the front door to the hotel and waited to see her safely inside, then set her satchel by the front desk. He heard Mr. Baird's voice coming from the back office.

Pausing at the staircase, Véronique glanced back, her hand poised on the rail. "Try hard to remember . . . Jack." She said his name with emphasis. "For I have never been partial to nicknames." Sleep enwrapped her voice, but her tone was all seriousness.

Jack gave her a mock salute. "Which, as you well know, makes me want to use it all the more . . . Vernie." He closed the door before she could respond.

CHAPTER | TWENTY-THREE ❖

I 'M AFRAID THAT LAND isn't for sale, Mr. Brennan. At least not through the normal course of land trade." Mr. Clayton rose from his desk chair and walked to the large-paned window overlooking a busy thoroughfare of Willow Springs.

Seated on the opposite side of the desk, Jack eyed him, both disappointed and confused. He'd had such hopes for this working out. "What does that mean, sir? The land is either for sale or it isn't. That shouldn't be difficult to determine."

Clayton turned, smiling. "I would completely agree with you, under normal circumstances." He struck a match and held it to the pipe clenched between his teeth. He puffed in and out on the stem until a steady rise of smoke issued from the bowl. "The portion of acreage you're inquiring about is part of a larger holding of property in that area."

"And does this larger holding of property have an owner?"

"Indeed it does, sir."

"And is this owner open to selling any of his land?" There was other property for sale in the area, but none that Jack desired as much as this piece. He'd already checked out everything available. Nothing matched the quality and location of his chosen plot. In his mind, he'd already started constructing the two-story cabin and knew exactly where he'd situate it.

"That's where the difficulty comes in, Mr. Brennan. The current owner purchased the land from an auction in—"

"In Denver. Yes, sir, I realize that. Miss Duncan shared that with me the other day." Jack didn't want to give the mistaken impression that this was news to him.

"Very good." The leather chair creaked as Clayton eased his weight into it. "As is customary in auctions, the highest bidder is awarded the prize. And this auction was no different. The only part of the proceedings that was out of the norm was the desire of the purchaser to remain anonymous on public record."

Jack looked at him more closely. "I thought public record was just that—public."

"Yes, as did I. And indeed, the name of the buyer is listed in the county records should anyone have cause to go looking. Or should I more aptly say, it's buried there, in case anyone goes looking."

"I don't see what this has to do with me."

Clayton nodded, indicating there was more forthcoming. "When the auctions for that period were listed in the local paper, that specific buyer's name happened to be excluded from the accounts. Apparently no one noticed, or cared enough to follow up."

Jack sifted through the details, wondering why Clayton was telling him all this, when he happened upon a nugget of possibility. He looked squarely across the desk at the land and title officer. "Are you intimating that sections of this land are still available for sale . . . but that I cannot know, and will not know, the seller?"

"That is precisely what I'm telling you, Mr. Brennan. At least in part. . . ." Clayton steepled his hands beneath his chin. "There is one more factor involved. The owner won't sell to just anyone. We've had many offers on that property in the past couple of years. Could have sold it all five times over by now."

"So money's obviously not a factor for this person."

Clayton remained silent, his expression unrevealing.

"So what's the owner waiting for?"

"The better question is who. *Who* is the owner waiting for? And I wish I could tell you that with accuracy. Personally, I haven't figured it out yet. All I know is that this person likes to interview the potential buyer before agreeing to a contract."

Jack laughed softly. "Tell me where and when, and I'll be there. If my offer is within an acceptable range of the asking price."

"Oh, your offer is within acceptable limits. That's not an issue. The question that remains, Mr. Brennan, is . . . will *you* be acceptable to the owner?"

Véronique seated herself at a vacant table in the dining room, away from the other hotel guests and near the front window, where she could watch the goings-on outside as the evening hour approached. Evenings in this territory were her favorite time of day. Especially with May's hasty approach and the days growing warmer. The cool nights issued a standing invitation to come and take the air.

But she wished Christophe were there to stroll with her. Or perhaps Jack Brennan.

"Good evening, Mademoiselle Girard, would you like to try the special for the evening?"

Véronique smiled up at Lilly, recalling the conversation with Doc Hadley. "*Oui*, Mademoiselle Carlson. I have heard a *rumeur* that the fried chicken is especially *délicieuse* tonight."

"*Oui*, mademoiselle." Lilly dipped her head. "*Très délicieuse*."

Watching Lilly walk away, noticing the exaggerated limp, Véronique hoped the *chirurgien* in Boston wouldn't delay in responding to the town's doctor.

A family's laughter coming from a table in the corner drew her attention. A *petite fille*, no more than four or five years old, sat atop a block of painted wood situated on a chair between the two adults. The father reached over and tweaked the little girl on her nose. She cupped her hands over her face amidst a fountain of giggles, trying to hide as her father reached for it again.

Véronique looked on. What would it be like to be loved like that by one's *papa*? To be shown such earnest, playful adoration? She wished she'd asked her *maman* more questions about him before her passing. They'd had numerous discussions about Véronique's father when she was young, but as the years passed, and they accepted their lot, the conversations about 'him' became fewer and more distanced with time.

Véronique angled her chair so the family was no longer in her direct line of vision.

The past week had kept her busy accompanying Jack on three shorter supply runs, and all without any of the challenges of their journey to the Peerless. These mining towns—Beaver Run, Spitfire, and Bonanza—were smaller communities, closer to Willow Springs, and nearer the foothills, so even the heights hadn't proven too hard for her.

But one thing *had* proven difficult—no one had heard of her *papa*. It was as though he had never existed, at least not in this area.

She thought of her mother's bundle of letters buried deep in a trunk in her hotel room two stories above. At the bidding of her *maman*, she'd read them aloud, one by one, in the weeks preceding her mother's death. She remembered her attempt late one night to make one of the letters briefer by skipping parts, as she was exhausted and wanting for bed. But apparently her *maman* knew the missives by heart. "You have left out a part, Véronique. Please read more carefully, *ma chérie.*"

Perhaps reading the missives again might offer insight Véronique had overlooked before, while also fulfilling another last request of her *maman*.

"*Pardonnez-moi*, mademoiselle. Might I join you for dinner?"

Véronique firmed her lips to quench the impulsive smile. "Though it saddens my heart to say it, monsieur, I must answer *non*. For I am waiting for a most important guest to join me. I must ask you to kindly dispose of yourself at another table, *merci.*"

Jack pulled the chair out beside hers and sat down, his large frame dwarfing the poor chair, and filling a portion of the emptiness she'd been feeling.

"I think I'll just dispose of myself right here, seeing as you have room to spare, ma'am." He gave an exaggerated sigh.

"How are you this evening, Jack? Did your supply run to Briar Rose go well?" She'd last seen him two days prior, before he left on the overnight trip.

"It did, thank you. A bit quieter than usual, but nice."

She gave him a droll look, secretly wondering if he enjoyed the time without her. Or maybe, if he missed her company. She waited, knowing he would volunteer the information without her having to prompt him.

"I checked with the supply merchant, and I also stopped by the livery." His expression sobered. He shook his head. "I'm sorry. No one had heard of him."

The familiar news hit her strangely this evening, and Véronique had to look away. "Thank you, Jack . . . anyhow," she whispered, using a new word she'd learned that week. One that wasn't in her little book.

When Lilly brought her meal, she also brought one for Jack. And as the two of them ate, Véronique marveled at the ease with which they spoke and laughed together. It was as if she'd found another Christophe. Except that she'd never thought about Christophe Charvet the way she did about Jack Brennan.

She looked up and caught him staring.

He tucked his napkin beside his plate and stood. "Would you care to take the air with me tonight, Vernie?"

She cringed at the nickname, knowing that the more she opposed it the more he would insist on using it. The past week had proven that. "I would love to, monsieur. *Merci.*" He would forget in time. Or until she discovered something of equal irritation to use against him. She accepted the silent challenge with enthusiasm.

As they strolled the boardwalks, Véronique was surprised at how many people she recognized, and at how many greeted her by name.

"Want to check on the Percherons with me?"

She glanced up and saw the livery ahead in their path. "*Oui,* I would enjoy that. But does Monsieur Sampson not do this for you? You pay him to board the horses. I have seen commerce change hands between you, *non?*"

"Sure, he does it, but I like to do it too." The front doors to the livery were closed, but Jack led her around to the back entrance. "Watch your step." He briefly took hold of her hand, and let go too quickly. "Sampson might still be here, I'm not sure."

But the place was empty, save for the animals.

She followed Jack to a stall near the back and immediately spotted his team. The Percherons stood taller than any of the other horses, and more stately. "You do realize that these horses issue from my beloved home country."

He nodded. "But I bought them anyway."

She nudged him in the side, then paused at the look in his eyes. For a moment, neither of them spoke.

Surprisingly, she didn't find the silence awkward. Nor did he, by his contented expression. The sudden turn of her thoughts as she stared at him took her by surprise. Until she realized that, in truth, her thoughts had been approaching that gradual turn all evening.

She'd come to know this man, how he reacted when challenged, how he conducted himself under adverse conditions, how he accepted blame for something that was not his fault. And she also knew what it felt like for him to touch her—to touch her hand, help her from the wagon, put his arm around her as they navigated a crowd of miners—but what occupied her mind at the moment was something far more intimate, and that went beyond mere touching.

She blinked at the fullness of her imagination and knew she needed to veer her thoughts from their present course. Posthaste! "Are you aware that this breed originated near Normandy in the Le Perche region, not a great distance from Paris, and that they're prized most highly in my country, serving as army mounts, among—" She drew a needed breath, watching as the contentedness on Jack's face deepened. Which didn't help the adjustment of her own thoughts. "Among other . . . highly important duties assigned to them."

He stared, not answering for the longest time. "Is that so? I wasn't aware of that, but it's nice to know. Thank you."

Feeling overly warm, she backed up a step. "It's quite true. The lineage can be traced back to a single horse that was foaled at Le Pin in 1823." She stroked the muzzle of one of the horses.

"You're just a wealth of information tonight, aren't you?"

From the gleam in his eyes, she got the impression he had read her previous vein of thought. Which made her grow even warmer. "What are their names?"

"Names?" He shrugged. "I've never been big on the name-calling thing."

She tilted her head to one side. "From personal experience, I happen to know the extent of that falsity, Monsieur Brennan." If not mistaken, she thought his face deepened in color.

He feigned pulling something out of his chest, near the spot covering his heart. "If you'd like to name them, I'd not be opposed to it."

Looking back at the first Percheron, she remembered when, as a *petite fille*, she'd first seen the breed. She'd been riding atop her father's shoulders at the time.

Jack leaned against the stall, listening, watching her as she shared the memory with him. "What else do you remember about your father?"

Closing her eyes, Véronique reached back as far as she could into her memory. "The way his large hand curved around my smaller one as he showed me how to hold a pencil." She breathed in. "And his scent. He smelled of pipe smoke and sunshine when he kissed me good-night. And I remember what I felt like when I was with him." *Cherished, chosen, loved.*

Overcome by sudden emotion, she slowly lifted her face. "The rest of my memories are as real to my inner eye, but were told to me by my *maman.*"

"Do you think your mother would have been untruthful about such things?"

"*Non, non,* not untruthful. But . . . she had a way of seeing things that differed from mine. For instance, in the retelling of a situation I had also witnessed, she would give it a different hue from what I remembered. So I am not certain about how reliable these borrowed memories are—if that makes sense."

"It does." His eyes narrowed slightly. "I bet you have one vivid imagination."

Her thoughts circled back to what had originally prompted their conversation. "Too vivid for my own good, at times."

He pushed away from the wall. "So, what do you think we should do about it?"

Her eyes widened.

"Naming the horses, I mean."

"Ah . . ." She let out a breath, then sized up the first animal. "I think . . . Napoleon Bonaparte for him." She moved to the next stall. "And for this majestic creature . . . what other name could we bestow but Charlemagne."

Jack's laughter echoed through the livery. "I think I should've made some rules at the outset."

"Too late, I am afraid. As you can clearly see that Napoleon and Charlemagne are quite pleased with the outcome."

When they arrived back at the hotel, Jack accompanied her up the stairs. At the second-floor landing, she paused. "You are still a guest here at this hotel as well, *non*?"

"Yes, ma'am. I am."

She nodded and continued her climb.

Jack followed, gaining far too much pleasure from the view than he should have. But those little bustled dresses she wore, fitting snug in the waist and then fanning out, were like waving a red flag in front of him. He'd figured she knew he was still staying at the hotel but was relatively certain she wasn't aware that his room was directly across the hall from hers.

Unless she'd asked Lilly—something he wouldn't put past her. Those two seemed like sisters separated at birth.

"Thank you for seeing me to my room, Jack, and for a lovely evening. It was most unexpected, and welcome."

"I enjoyed it too, as did Napoleon and Charlemagne." He did his best to say their names like she did, enjoying her reaction. He briefly studied the rug beneath his boots, knowing this was as good a time as any to bring up what he needed to discuss. "In the next couple of weeks, I'll be returning to some of the mining towns we've already visited."

"Business is good for you, *non*? Congratulations is the correct word, I believe."

He nodded. "Business is very good. A bit too good, as it's going to be keeping me busier than I'd planned on being."

"I believe the wagon you are using is a great contributor to this success, would you not agree?"

Hearing the tease in her voice, he laughed softly. "Yes, ma'am. I'd say that was real accurate." How could he phrase this? He'd already given this a lot of thought before their evening together, but after what had nearly happened in the livery a few minutes ago . . . He'd almost taken her in his arms and done what he'd been thinking about since dinner. Truth be told, since having met the woman. And if not for her sudden diatribe on Percherons, he would have. "In considering the day-trips to places we've already visited, Véronique, I think it would be best if you didn't accompany me on those particular runs again."

The light faded from her eyes. A tiny frown creased the bridge of her nose as she looked away. "Why do you consider this best?"

"I enjoy having you along, so don't take this as commentary on that." He bent down a mite until he'd secured her attention again. "I want you to hear me on that count, all right? I enjoy having you with me. This is not about that."

She nodded. "And for the purpose of being clear, that enjoyment is reciprocated on my part as well."

He reacted to the vulnerability in her voice, to the innocence in her brown eyes, which made him even more determined to get this agreement settled. "As we've discussed before, it's always dangerous having you along. Since we've already visited these places, it doesn't make sense for you to go again. The risk outweighs the benefit in those cases. Do you see the logic in that?"

"I see it. I do not like it, but I see it."

He smiled at the unexpected response. "Always such honesty. That could get you in trouble one of these days, you know."

Her mouth slipped open. "That is what Christophe used to tell me. In almost the same words."

All sense of playful banter left Jack at the name. "Christophe?"

"*Oui*," she whispered. "A dear friend from whom I have not heard in some time."

"You've been writing him?"

"*Oui*, and I am awaiting his response. You would like him very much, I think."

Doubtful. "I'm sure I would. Well . . ." Jack slipped her key from her hand and unlocked the door. "I hope you rest well this evening."

"Thank you, Jack. I wish you the—"

He spotted it just after she did.

She bent down to retrieve an envelope that had been shoved beneath her door. She stood, excitement lighting her face. "It's a letter from—"

"Christophe," Jack softly supplied. "How timely. I'll leave you to it, then. Good night, Véronique."

"Good night, Jack, and thank you again." She closed the door before he'd even turned to go.

CHAPTER TWENTY-FOUR

VÉRONIQUE WAVED TO Monsieur and Madame Carlson as she and Lilly pulled away in the wagon. Having spent time with Lilly's parents two Sundays previous and then at lunch again today following the church service, Véronique didn't have to look far to see why Lilly was so special. And her younger brother, Bobby, was *adorable*, even if Véronique had grown somewhat self-conscious beneath his constant staring during mealtime.

She wished Jack would have accepted Hannah Carlson's invitation to lunch as well. But he had begged her pardon, saying he needed to take care of some business. She'd only seen him once, in the mercantile, since their dinner together last weekend, and he'd seemed more distant, aloof. She would have given much to know the cause.

Lilly maneuvered the wagon down the road from her house and onto a main thoroughfare in town. Véronique studied the girl's every move, noting the confident manner in which she gripped the reins, how she braced her feet against the footrest, and how every so often—Véronique hadn't figured out the pattern yet—Lilly would glance back over her shoulder.

"Mademoiselle Girard, would you like a lesson in driving the wagon this afternoon?"

Knowing she'd been caught, Véronique tried to match the teasing quality in Lilly's voice. "And to think I considered myself furtive in my close observation of your talent."

"If by furtive you mean staring at me from the corner of your eye and being obvious as the day is long, then you were." Lilly flashed a grin at her before returning her attention to the road. "Just let me get us on the road leading out to Miss Maudie's, then I'll pull over and let you drive."

Véronique felt a tingle of anticipation and was glad she'd agreed to come with Lilly on this outing. Being with young Lilly always boosted her spirits, which was a welcome antidote since she'd wrestled with lingering melancholy in recent days.

Christophe's letter discovered beneath her door had been brief, and hastily penned if the uneven markings of his script were any indication. The Marchand *famille* was once again situated in their home in Paris, Christophe along with them. But all was not well. Lord Marchand had fallen ill in Brussels, and even the practiced care of his personal physician provided no ease to the sickness. Christophe's description of the return journey to Paris and of their discovered fallen city had read quite grueling. Beneath his words, Véronique sensed a gravity to the situation that even Christophe's positive spirit could not fully conceal.

She had authored a response missive immediately, filled mostly with questions as to Lord Marchand's health, the political climate in Paris, their safety, and Christophe's current situation.

The woman at the post office had informed her it could take two months or more for a missive to travel from the Colorado Territory to Paris. The Paris hand stamp on Christophe's envelope read February eleventh—over two and a half months earlier. What had transpired in all that time? The Denver newspaper was the only publication she'd found that carried news of Europe, and even that was weeks old at the time of printing.

As Véronique had departed the post office after mailing the letter, she'd paused and stared at her hand on the latch. Had her father stood in this very same place many years ago, mailing his letters to her and her mother? She had brushed off the unexpected sense of connection, attributing it to her imagination.

But still, she wondered.

After visiting several of the mining towns with Jack, it dawned on her how far she'd come in her journey. But it also struck her as she recalled searching the faces of the miners—specifically the scores of older men who lived in Ma Petite France at the Peerless—how far she had yet to go. And how many mining towns she and Jack had yet to visit—thirty-nine remained—before winter set in again.

The dawning of that discovery thinned her tenuous hope of ever finding her father, until she remembered whose desire had birthed this journey.

Bittersweet memories of her *maman* pressed close, and she wished for the remembered touch of her mother's hand on her younger brow. The coolness of her mother's fingers, the feather-soft love in them. Or to watch her mother stirring the cream into her coffee, until it matched the warm color of her eyes.

Véronique tilted her head back and searched the yawning blue canopy overhead, the breeze stirring tendrils of her hair. Could *Maman* see her right now? Could she see Véronique's father? And if so, per chance would God allow a moment's reprieve so that her mother could give direction to her search? But perhaps her *maman* already knew the whereabouts of her *papa* because she was already reunited with him, up there somewhere, the two of them, without her.

The likelihood of that thought brought a sudden pang.

Lilly chose that moment to pull the wagon off to the side of the road, adjacent to the church where her father delivered his sermons.

Unsettled inside, Véronique studied the white-steepled structure perched proudly on the edge of town, thankful for the excuse to abandon such melancholy thoughts.

Though far from ornate, the church building possessed a welcoming quality with its colorful confetti of flowers dotting the front walkway leading to the stairs. Her focus moved past the church to the cemetery some yards beyond. Pale shadows of gray hovered over the hallowed ground, and she pictured the slab of polished marble marking her mother's resting place half a world away.

It seemed an almost frivolous thought in light of everything else, but she hoped someone—Christophe, possibly?—was tending that patch of earth, since she could not. It hurt to think of her mother's grave being covered by weeds and thorny briars.

She squinted, able to distinguish the shadowed outline of headstones beneath the bowers of trees bordering Fountain Creek. Its churning waters issued from the heart of the great Rocky Mountains and cascaded down the narrow canyon off to her right. On their way back into town one evening Jack had explained that, years ago, the French traders had dubbed the creek *Fontaine qui Bouille* or Boiling Fountain.

Her father had been in this town—that much she knew from the postmark of his last letter to her mother. But had he walked the shores of Fountain Creek? Had he heard the ancient melody of its icy waters crashing down and tumbling over smooth rock?

Movement in the cemetery drew her eye.

She spotted someone walking through the headstones in the distance. A grown man, she guessed from his height and long gait. He paused as if searching for something, then walked to a grave and knelt down.

"You're going to love doing this!"

At Lilly's exclamation, Véronique redirected her attention, reluctant to look away from the man's private vigil.

Lilly held out the reins. "It's only fair that I teach you something in exchange for all the French lessons you're giving me."

"Ah . . . but we shall soon see if I am the astute learner you have proven to be. Perhaps I will disappoint you, *non?* Prove to be less than you have considered me to be." Véronique took hold of the leather straps, struck by the harnessed power now in her control.

Feeling a touch on her arm, she looked back.

Lilly's eyes sparkled, but with tears instead of her customary smile. Her delicate chin shook. "You are so much more astute . . . and beautiful . . . and cultured than I'll ever hope to be. I'm so glad we're friends, Mademoiselle Girard. And I'm so glad you came to Willow Springs."

Taken aback at first, Véronique reached out and touched the girl's cheek. "Ah, *ma chérie*, but you already are those things—every one of them." She tipped Lilly's chin and smiled. "But I am wondering . . . how can you not be aware of this?"

Lilly shook her head. "I stopped by the mercantile yesterday and there was this—" She hiccupped and sniffed.

Véronique pulled a handkerchief that had belonged to her mother from her *réticule*. An embroidered corner of the soft cloth bore the cursive initials A.E.G. She nudged it into Lilly's hand. "Here, take this and tell me what has upset you so."

Lilly nodded and dabbed her tears. "It's not like this hasn't happened before—it has." She hesitated. "There's this boy I've sort of . . . liked since I was nine. Sometimes I thought he liked me back, but I was never sure. Then yesterday morning, he was standing outside with some of his friends, and—" she winced, pressing her lips together—"I tripped as I was leaving the mercantile, and I dropped Mrs. Baird's groceries all over the boardwalk. That's when his friend called me . . . a name and—" Her breath caught. "Jeremy laughed. He didn't help me. He just . . . laughed."

A maternal instinct rose so swift and livid within Véronique that she was glad the boy was not within her reach. She pulled Lilly into a hug and stroked the back of her head. Strange how the gesture encouraged her own tears as she remembered her mother doing the same with her when she had faced similar disappointments. And how Jack had comforted her the day she'd made such a fool of herself by becoming so nervous she made herself sick.

Véronique drew back and brushed a stray lock from Lilly's face. "I am sorry this happened to you, *ma chérie*. And as sure as I am looking into the eyes of a beautiful young woman mature beyond her years and lovely beyond words, there is a young man out there whom God is preparing only for you. This boy will love you for who you are, instead of who you are not. But you are young yet. It could be some time before this boy comes into your life."

Lilly frowned.

"Because . . ." Véronique arched a brow. "Whomever God has chosen for you will be special, Lilly. This boy must be the equal to your traits of kindness and generosity, intellect and honor. And, in my experience, these qualities are not often found in abundance, and certainly not coupled together." She pictured Jack, and silently ticked off the characteristics again in her mind, finding he possessed each one. How was it that no woman had ever claimed him as her own?

A tear trailed Lilly's cheek.

But Véronique warmed at the sparkle slowly returning to her young friend's eyes, and she recalled what her mother had said to her when she'd had a similar altercation with a member of the opposite sex. "That moment outside the mercantile, when those boys laughed at you, does not define the young woman you are, Lilly. Who you are is defined by what you will do with this experience, and how you will act toward those boys the next time your paths cross."

Lilly nodded, looking mildly convinced. "*Merci beaucoup*, Mademoiselle Girard."

"*De rien*, Lilly." She patted the girl's back, wanting to inquire about the surgery but hesitant to bring up the subject. Especially now. She gave Lilly one last hug, then gripped the reins and squared her shoulders. "And now . . . I am ready for my first driving lesson, *non*?"

Lilly giggled and released a lever on the side of the wagon. "That may be, but as my papa might say, are the streets of Willow Springs ready for you?"

The patch of earth where Jack knelt was damp, and gradually the moisture sank through his pants to his knees. He remained bowed beside Jonathan McCutchens's grave, lingering, relishing the peacefulness that embraced this hallowed spot.

He had awakened long before sunrise that morning, his room dark and still, and stretched out an arm, the space in the bed beside him feeling empty and wanting. After so many years of accepted solitude, the discovery caught him unaware. He'd finally risen and reached for his Bible, taking advantage of a few moments of unclaimed time and hoping to fill the void within him—if not the one beside him.

As the sun had risen through his open window, and the bubbling echo of Fountain Creek serenaded the dawn, he found himself praying for Véronique as she slept just across the hall from him. For her to find peace in her journey, and that her father would be a man worthy of such a daughter—if Pierre Gustave Girard was even alive after all these years.

Pulling his thoughts back to the moment, Jack reached down to the grave and scooped a fistful of dirt. He held it in his hand, then let it sift back to the earth. "'One short sleep past, we wake eternally.'" He kept his voice hushed, as seemed right. "'And death shall be no more; death, thou shalt die.'"

Weeks after Mary's passing, he had finally worked up the courage to go through her things. As he'd sorted through the books in her trunk, he'd run across a collection of sonnets tucked amid the treasured volumes she'd used in her teaching. The particular sonnet containing this verse had been underscored and the page dog-eared. In the margins of the text, she'd penned a Scripture, one he'd since written on his heart.

"Death is swallowed up in victory. O death, where is thy sting? O grave, where is thy victory?"

It had taken years, but the sting of Mary's and Aaron's deaths had lessened for him. Though death had taken them, it did not hold them in its grip. It never had. Christ had seen to that.

Looking around, Jack could understand why Jonathan McCutchens had wanted to be laid to rest in this spot. Thinking about Jonathan and Annabelle McCutchens—the couple he'd met last spring on his final caravan—his appreciation for what they had endured grew. Upon Jonathan's untimely death on the trail, Annabelle had traveled from the plains north of Denver all the way back to Willow Springs, by herself, to fulfill her husband's wish of being buried on the banks of Fountain Creek.

In all of Jack's travels, no other place equaled the beauty he'd discovered in these mountains nor possessed the welcome feel of this community nestled at the base of Pikes Peak. He rubbed his jaw, smiling as he thought of what else he'd found in this town, and in recalling what Jonathan McCutchens had said to him the last time they'd spoken.

"I didn't find what I came looking for in that little town, but I discovered what I'd been missin' all my life."

Jack let his attention wander the jagged mountain peaks to the west. "I'm not quite sure yet, Jonathan, and I certainly didn't come to this town looking for it, but . . . I'm thinking I just might've found what's been missing for so long in my life too."

When Hannah Carlson had extended an invitation for Sunday lunch a while earlier, he'd been tempted to accept. Especially once learning that Véronique would be there. His gaze dropped to the cross at his feet—but this particular visit had been long overdue.

For several minutes, he kept his head bowed and laid his thoughts before his Maker, who already knew every one of them even before they were on his tongue.

Sighing, he stood and headed to the mercantile to load the shipment. Hochstetler had come by the hotel before church to tell him that Miss Maudie from Casaroja wanted her supplies delivered first thing Monday morning. But Jack figured he'd use the afternoon to get a jump on a busy week, and Hochstetler said he'd leave the back entry open. Besides, he would enjoy the trip to Casaroja and looked forward to seeing how that lively little Irish lady was faring since her fall.

→ C H A P T E R | T W E N T Y - F I V E

VÉRONIQUE PAUSED MIDSTEP in the doorway of the bedroom, her attention fixed on the frail woman in the bed. She hoped Lilly was right and that their hostess wouldn't mind a stranger visiting as she recuperated.

Lilly leaned down and kissed the woman's cheek. "Mama sent along something for you, Miss Maudie. And I'll give you one guess as to what it is."

"There'll be no need for guessin', Lilly dear. Your mother knows my favorites and never disappoints." The older woman tilted her head, squinting. "Now, who did you bring with you there? A new friend, I hope?"

As Lilly made the introductions, Véronique approached the bed.

The woman's subtle air of regality, coupled with the way her face lit when she smiled, brought back memories of her mother, right before the illness had claimed firmer hold. An unwelcome wave of *déjà vu* swept through her.

She curtsied at the appropriate time and was about to respond when, from a corner window, she glimpsed a wagon heading up the road toward the house. A rush of excitement accompanied her when she recognized the driver.

"Well, if that's not a tellin' expression, Miss Girard, my Irish eyes are failin' me for sure."

Véronique's face heated at the older woman's comment and at having been caught not paying respectful attention. She curtsied a second time, cautious in meeting the woman's discerning gaze. "My sincerest apologies, Miss Maudie. I fear I was—"

"Momentarily distracted? Yes, I can see that." Miss Maudie's smile deepened. She craned her neck to peer out the window, and her brow slowly furrowed. "And I can easily see why, my dear. I've met that gentleman, and if I were thirty years younger, I'd not let you have him without a fight. Though with the pretty French package I see before me . . ." She made a tsking noise with her tongue. "I would've hardly stood a chance even then."

Véronique laughed softly, feeling an instant bond with the woman.

"Véronique, it's a pleasure indeed." Miss Maudie reached for the bell on the night table and rang it twice. "I've known my share of Frenchmen, to be sure. But it's a rare treasure to meet a lass of your heritage."

The woman who had allowed them entrance when they arrived appeared in the doorway. "Are you and your guests ready for tea, ma'am?"

"Yes, indeed we are, Claire. Thank you. We'll take it in here, dear."

"Tea and Lilly's mother's oatmeal muffins coming right up!"

"Now, to the both of you"—Miss Maudie patted the bed—"sit down here and tell an old woman what's happenin' in the world outside these walls. That ol' Doc Hadley trussed my leg up so good and tight I can hardly be movin' it." Her covert wink said she was only half serious. "I feel like a hen ready for the oven, and I'm as bored as a spud in the mud."

"Mademoiselle Girard is the one with all the interesting stories." Lilly nodded her way. "So she should go first. She just arrived from Paris, after all. And she's been visiting some mining towns in the mountains." She widened her eyes, encouraging Véronique to tell more.

"I would hardly label most of my stories as interesting. But a few of them have been rather exciting. . . ." Véronique looked pointedly out the window. "And they involve a certain gentleman who just arrived."

Miss Maudie tried to push herself up, and more from reflex than forethought, Véronique adjusted the pillows behind her back.

"Why, thank you, dear. Now ... do tell me everything." Miss Maudie's countenance brightened with anticipation. "And don't leave out any details, startin' with when you left your homeland, to when you first set foot in Willow Springs, and then to those mountain treks of yours." A wistful expression swept her face. "It's been ever so long since I've seen our mountains up close. I miss them so. And"—she raised a forefinger and offered a look befitting the most venerable teacher—"lest you be forgettin', I want a full account of your time with your gentleman friend too. And not to worry, dear. Whatever you say, Lilly and I will keep locked up tighter than a drum!"

Jack finished unloading the supplies and sat down on the back steps to enjoy a glass of water and a slice of warm blueberry pie, courtesy of Claire Stewartson. From the wagon parked out front, and the occasional laughter he heard coming from inside, he figured Miss Maudie was entertaining guests.

"Well, that disappeared in a hurry." Mrs. Stewartson pushed open the screen door. "How about seconds?"

Standing, Jack hesitated, not wanting to appear greedy.

"Okay, hand over that plate, Mr. Brennan." She reached out. "We don't allow shy eaters here at Casaroja. One of Miss Maudie's rules."

"Thank you, ma'am." Jack held onto his fork.

The young woman returned minutes later with an even larger slice than the first.

"My thanks again, ma'am." He loaded a bite onto his fork. "How's Miss Maudie doing since the accident?"

It was Claire's turn to hesitate. "Doc Hadley said her leg should heal up just fine, as long as she doesn't try to do too much, too soon. But she's still having those dizzy spells. Doc doesn't know what's causing them either."

"I'd imagine keeping a woman like Miss Maudie down would take some doing."

"You're telling me!" Claire glanced in the direction of the nearest barn. "Thomas stopped by earlier to let me know that one of our mares is expected to drop her first foal in the next couple of days. When Miss Maudie heard about it, she could hardly wait. Said she wanted to be there, that she hadn't missed a first birth in years. Then Thomas reminded her that it was against Doc's strict orders for her to be up and walking about. . . ." She shook her head. "You'd have thought he'd told her Christmas was cancelled."

A cackle of feminine laughter floated toward them through the open door.

Claire smiled. "She's entertaining guests right now. I haven't heard her laugh this much in a long time, even before the accident." Her expression softened. "Does my heart good after all that sweet woman has been through."

Claire's comment, similar to one her husband had made, caused Jack to wonder just what Miss Maudie's story was, and what had happened to her nephew.

Footsteps echoed in the kitchen, accompanied by voices—one of them unmistakable.

Jack peered over Claire's shoulder just in time to notice Véronique's face brighten when she saw him. It didn't necessarily reflect the surprise he'd expected, but then she had a way of hiding things when she wanted to. He'd learned that early on.

He held open the door for them and enjoyed the way Véronique lightly touched his arm as she passed.

"*Bonjour*, Monsieur Brennan. What brings you to Casaroja?" Her accent gave the name of the ranch a pleasing sound.

"*Bonjour*, Mademoiselle Girard." Jack winked when only she was watching. "Mr. Hochstetler asked me to deliver an order from the mercantile. So I loaded up and came on out." Wondering at Lilly Carlson's coy smile, Jack greeted her before returning his attention to Véronique. "I didn't know you knew Miss Maudie."

"I did not have that pleasure before Lilly invited me on this outing." Véronique slipped an arm about the girl's shoulders and gave Claire Stewartson a sheepish look. "We had a most enjoyable time, but I think our laughter exhausted the dear woman. She was asleep before we left the room."

"It wasn't our laughter that put her to sleep." Lilly nudged her in the side, and Jack sensed a deepening friendship between the two. "Véronique rubbed her shoulders and back, and Miss Maudie said she hadn't felt that good in years."

"Speaking of which . . ." Claire took a step back toward the house.

"I think I'll run and check on her." She reached for Jack's empty plate. "Thank you again for delivering those supplies so quickly, Mr. Brennan. And Lilly, feel free to show Miss Girard around the place if you'd like. The wild flowers just over the hill are in full bloom, and they're a sight to behold!" Claire grinned as she let the door close behind her.

"Oh, let's go see!" Lilly exclaimed, urging Véronique to follow her.

Véronique turned to go, then paused. "Would you like to accompany us, Monsieur Brennan? Or are you not a fan of wild flowers?"

"I appreciate flowers as much as the next man, and the wilder the better." He wriggled his brow. "But I've got some things I need to see to in town. Thank you for the invitation though."

"Perhaps some other time, then?"

That sparked an idea within him. "Perhaps some other time . . . like tonight?"

Her expression turned sweetly suspect.

"For dinner, I mean, with me. Not to look at flowers." To say he was rusty at this would have been an understatement. The other night had been easier, when he'd discovered her already seated in the dining room. Jack could feel Lilly's stare from where she stood a few feet away. Clearing his throat, he decided to start over again. "If you're not otherwise engaged, Mademoiselle Girard, I would like to take you to dinner tonight."

Seeing the sparkle in her eyes, he discovered he could hardly wait to get back on the trail with this woman. Who would have ever thought . . . ?

"*Oui*, I would like that very much, Jack. And for the record . . . I am not otherwise engaged."

Standing nearly a foot taller than she did, Jack noticed how she tipped her head back in order to look up at him. She'd worn another one of her fancy gowns, and though it wasn't too revealing, it still invited the eye. He tried not to linger overlong on the inviting curve of her neck or the soft hollow at the base of her throat, or at the slow rise and fall of her bodice as she—

Realizing he was failing miserably at not lingering, Jack cleared his throat again and forced his attention elsewhere.

Véronique leaned slightly to one side as though to catch his eye again. If she only knew how effortlessly she did that already. "So I will see you tonight, Jack?"

"Yes, ma'am. I'll come by and pick you up at seven o'clock."

"And I will be waiting for you."

As he watched Véronique walk away, he couldn't help but think of Mary, and how different a man he'd been with her. And how different a woman she'd been from Véronique Girard.

He walked toward his wagon—wait, *Véronique's* wagon, he corrected—and tried to recall what he'd been like with Mary. Tentative and shy at first, unsure of himself. Everything about their relationship had been so new, for them both. And that time of discovery, of learning together, had been exciting.

But things were different now.

When he looked at Véronique, it wasn't through the eyes of some wide-eyed schoolboy. It was through the seasoned perspective of a man who knew what it was like to be married, to have an intimate relationship with a woman. In the same breath, Jack reminded himself that Véronique did not have that same perspective. At least he didn't think she did.

She'd obviously never been married—the title of mademoiselle told him that much. He didn't know much about her background other than what Sampson had told him, but he would bet she'd had plenty of beaus lined up on her doorstep. It struck him then that he probably ought to tell her about Mary and Aaron. The timing just hadn't seemed right yet. Not that he thought it would matter to her, but it was part of his past, part of who he was. And he would forever carry a part of Mary and Aaron with him.

He guided the wagon down the front road of Casaroja, admiring again the beauty of the ranch. For so many years he'd never stayed in one place more than a few days, and that's how he'd liked it. But not anymore. He looked forward to settling down and—

He yanked back on the reins and cocked his head, certain he'd heard something.

Once the horses came to a standstill and the squeak of the wagon quieted, he heard his name being called. He stood in the wagon and peered over the fields. After a minute, he saw a man waving.

Jack secured the wagon and jumped down.

When he reached the lower field, he recognized Thomas

Stewartson kneeling in a sea of blue and white columbine. Beside him, a mare lay on her side, breathing heavily. Thomas was rubbing the horse's distended belly in slow arching circles.

Jack was winded when he reached them. Taking a minute to catch his breath, he quickly read the situation. "Has her water broken?"

"About ten minutes ago, but nothing's happening yet. She keeps trying to roll and raise up."

The mare let out a sudden high-pitched whinny and did just as Stewartson said. Pressing his weight against the horse, Stewartson managed to keep her down.

"It's all right, girl," Jack cooed, running a hand over her belly and feeling the foal move inside. "Her first?"

"Yes, and she wasn't showing signs of dropping this soon. We normally bring them into the barn for their first deliveries. Make them as comfortable as possible. One of Miss Maudie's rules."

With a laugh, Jack rolled up his sleeves. "That woman seems to have a lot of those."

"You have no idea, Brennan. But there's a heart of gold behind each one."

"I don't doubt that." Jack bent to inspect the mare's progress. "The foal looks to be presenting fine."

Stewartson nodded. "I rode out this morning looking for her. Couldn't find her, and that's when I knew."

The mare reared her head. Her body shuddered. Bathed in sweat, her tan coat glistened in the afternoon sun.

Jack rubbed his hand over her haunches in smooth, firm strokes, whispering to her.

"Thanks for stopping." Thomas pulled a handkerchief from his pocket and wiped his forehead. "No matter how many times I see this, it never gets old."

Jack understood. "It's like assisting God in a miracle."

"Claire and me . . ." Stewartson paused. "We've been trying to have children for a while now. I keep thinking it's gonna happen for us. But so far, it hasn't."

"It will. Sometimes it just takes some trying." Jack thought back to the night Aaron was born, and how happy he and Mary had been. He'd been so thankful for her brief labor and for a healthy son.

"Don't get me wrong—I don't mind the tryin' part." Stewartson caught his eye and they both smiled. "But it's seeing Claire get her hopes up and then it not comin' about that makes it hard. You married, Jack?"

"I was, many years ago. I lost my wife and son in an accident on our way out west."

For a moment, Stewartson said nothing. "I . . . I'm so sorry for your loss."

"I appreciate that." Jack slowly swept a hand across the tops of the wild flowers growing beside him. "Aaron, our son, would have been sixteen this year." He laughed softly. "Hard to think of me having a sixteen-year-old son. Come to think of it, that's not far from the age I was when I got married." He shot Stewartson a look. "Thanks for makin' me feel so old."

Stewartson shrugged as if to say it wasn't his fault.

A thought crept up on Jack, one he hadn't entertained in a long, long time. Did God take Aaron at such a young age because he knew Jack wouldn't be a good enough father to the boy? Even as the punishing question tried to take root, Jack refused it. Again.

For years he'd struggled to search out the *why* behind Mary's and Aaron's deaths. And gradually he'd been led to accept that he might never know. Odd, the older he got—though he thought he still had some good years left in him—the less of a hold this life had on him. Maybe age did that to a man. Or maybe it was God that did it, preparing him for all that waited on the other side.

Death marked another beginning for him, not an end. He'd come to see it as part of his journey to God.

"You know, Jack, if you're ever—"

The mare whinnied, and followed it with a low moan.

Jack knelt for another look, then exhaled aloud. "Stewartson, looks like we're in business."

CHAPTER TWENTY-SIX

ONE MORE HILL?" Lilly's eyes danced.

"I am willing if you are." Véronique breathed deeply, relishing the scents of spring. "But I do not want you to strain yourself."

Lilly paused at the crest of the hill. "I'm okay. It doesn't hurt too badly today." She motioned off to the right. "Let's take this way. It leads around the lower pasture and brings us up in front of Casaroja. There's a whole bed of columbine blooming there. I saw it when we drove by. Which reminds me—you did very well on your first driving lesson, Mademoiselle Girard."

Véronique offered a brief curtsy. "*Merci beaucoup*, Mademoiselle Carlson. I had a very good teacher, *non?*" She was careful to watch where she stepped, as Lilly had warned earlier. She and Christophe had often walked through the pasture behind the Marchand stables in the evenings, so she was accustomed to this. But as fine as Lord Marchand's stables and horses were, they could not compare to the boastings of Casaroja.

"May I ask you a question, Mademoiselle Girard?"

She glanced beside her to find Lilly watching. "Of course, *ma chérie*."

Lilly looked away. "It's personal."

"It is good that it is personal, since you and I are friends of that nature." Véronique wondered if this had anything to do with the boy Lilly had told her about earlier. That Jeremy, the *racaille.*

Lilly looped her arm through Véronique's. "How did you get Mr. Brennan to like you so quickly?"

Véronique stopped short. *"Pardonnez-moi?"* Her face heated. She thought back to how they'd kidded together in Miss Maudie's bedroom. "Mr. Brennan and I are friends, Lilly. If I have led you to believe there is more between us, I have misspoken. I admit again, as I did with you and Miss Maudie, that I like him . . . very much. But he has given me no indication of anything beyond friendship on his part." Though there were moments when she'd questioned it.

Lilly curled her tongue between her teeth, and slowly nodded. "He just asked you out to dinner. I saw the way he looked at you."

Véronique liked the way Jack Brennan looked at her, but that certainly wasn't an indicator for a man's true feelings. She'd seen many men—married gentlemen—take second and third looks at a woman, when a first glance should have more than sufficed. *"Oui,* he asked me to dinner, and I will enjoy Mr. Brennan's company."

Lilly's expression said she wasn't convinced.

Véronique took the girl's arm and drew her forward toward the flowers. "Jack Brennan is the type of man who is kind to everyone, Lilly. I have observed this about him. It is his nature to be cordial and caring." How did she explain their relationship when she wasn't quite sure of it herself? "I have hired Mr. Brennan as my driver, and that affords us a . . . closer relationship of sorts because we spend more time together, but it is not what I believe you are thinking."

Lilly made the same tsking noise with her tongue as Miss Maudie had done earlier. "He stammered, for heaven's sake. Didn't you notice that?"

She had noticed that. But she'd witnessed that kind of thing before when a lesser servant was addressing their superior. "Perhaps he was nervous because I am his employer. There is a . . . respect that runs between us."

"Well, there's something running between you, but I don't know that I'd call it respect." They walked a few steps farther. "So you're not going to tell me what you did to get him to like you?"

"The young man meant for you, Lilly, will not require any tricks or ploys to be played upon him. He will see you, he will grow to know who you are—both the good and the bad—and he will realize he does not wish to live another day of his life without you."

Lilly sighed and rolled her eyes. "I knew you'd say something like that. I was looking for something more practical. Maybe something that happened between you and Mr. Brennan."

The trip Véronique had made with Jack to the Peerless came to mind, and she was reminded of what she'd done along the way. An accounting of that mortifying event would hardly help the girl in winning a boy's heart, and Véronique dared not share that story. It was embarrassing enough that Jack harbored that memory of her.

Lilly stopped and took hold of her arm. "Whatever you're thinking right now, you have to share it. Your face is positively on fire."

Véronique put a hand over her mouth, and shook her head. "I cannot. It is too compromising."

Lilly's shoulders fell. Her expression darkened. "Did Mr. Brennan . . . try to take advantage of—"

"*Non!* It was nothing like that. Jack Brennan would never do such a thing. It was . . . something else that happened." Suspicion lingered in Lilly's eyes, and Véronique knew of only one way to dispel it. Though she regretted having to do so. "You remember, Lilly, that I am afraid of heights."

The girl's expression clouded.

"On one of my trips with Jack, the mountain gave way into a ravine. It was very steep, and frightening. I became nervous, and my stomach became . . ." She wanted to phrase this as delicately as possible.

"Unsettled?"

"*Oui,* unsettled. And then I . . ." She put a hand over her stomach at the memory.

Lilly bit her lower lip but couldn't hide her smile. "You didn't."

Véronique closed her eyes. "I did."

"In the wagon?" Lilly waited. Then her dark brows shot up. "On *him*?"

Véronique nodded as embarrassment swept through her. Hearing Lilly's giggles didn't help. "Please, Lilly, you must promise not to tell anyone. It was a very . . . humbling experience for me."

Lilly's laughter eventually quieted. "You know what my father would say to that, don't you? God had to humble you before He could raise you up. So get ready to be raised!" She rolled her pretty eyes again. "I've heard that all my life."

"I like your father's way of thinking."

Lilly took a deep breath. "So, you've answered my question. I just need to find a boy that I like"—she ticked the items off on one hand—"get him to take me on a wagon ride, and then regurgitate all over him."

"Ah! What a rude thing to say!" Véronique gave her a shove.

"Rude to *say*? What a rude thing to *do*!" They both dissolved into giggles, until Lilly suddenly went quiet. "Wait!" She held up a hand. "Listen."

Véronique heard it too. A strange cry, primal sounding.

"Come on!" Lilly hurried toward the sound.

Véronique followed, wondering if this was the wisest course of action. She rounded the copse of trees behind Lilly and skidded to a halt, breathless. Her eyes went wide.

"The foal's not coming out right, Jack. Either that, or he's a really big one."

Concern hardened Thomas Stewartson's voice as he knelt by a laboring mare, and Véronique saw the same concern reflected in Jack's strained expression.

She'd met Monsieur Stewartson upon arriving at Casaroja. Lilly had introduced them. He seemed quite amiable, and a capable foreman, though right now a scowl darkened his features.

Jack shifted his weight from one knee to the other and examined the mare more closely. "I think the shoulders are caught."

Lilly was already beside the young mother, stroking her neck and speaking in hushed tones. She waved for Véronique to join her, but Véronique stayed right where she was. As young girls, she and Francette had once snuck into the stables to watch a birthing, curious as to the way of things. But when Monsieur Laurent spotted them, he had scolded them both, saying that proper young ladies should not witness such a thing.

And yet Véronique could not look away.

The horse suddenly writhed and tried to regain her footing, then fell back. Lilly immediately moved out of the way, then crept close again once the mare calmed.

"Mademoiselle Girard." Lilly gestured to her a second time. "Come here. It's all right."

Véronique stepped closer, both curious and unsure. She knelt beside Lilly, careful to stay away from the mare's mouthful of enormous teeth. She'd been bitten as a little girl, and her right shoulder still bore a tiny scar.

Thomas peered up. "You think you gals can keep her down?"

Lilly nodded. "We'll try, Mr. Stewartson."

"Well, do more than try. If she manages to get up, we could lose both her and the foal."

As if accepting the challenge, the mare pushed with her forelegs and tried to roll, then struggled to rise a second time.

Véronique immediately shrank back.

But Lilly pushed against the mare, managing to slow her efforts. In an instant, Thomas was there. He settled his full weight against the horse and urged her back to the ground. Once she was lying on her side again, Thomas blew out a breath.

Véronique stepped forward, but he stopped her with a look.

"Ma'am, why don't you just wait over yonder. I've got enough to handle without worrying about you too."

Unaccustomed to being spoken to in such a manner, and from a man of Stewartson's position, Véronique backed away, her chest tightening. She glanced at Lilly, who offered a weak smile.

"Véronique, you want to give me a hand down here?" Despite his grimace, Jack's voice was surprisingly calm. "Can you grab me that rag?"

Keeping her eyes down so as to avoid looking at Stewartson again, she did as Jack asked, and he wiped off his hands and arms before laying the rag aside.

She bent down beside him and saw a head and a pair of legs protruding from the back end of the mare, wrapped in a kind of milky white sack. The foal wriggled, the mare writhed, and Véronique felt the air squeeze from her lungs.

Jack glanced at her, then looked more closely. "You've never seen this before?"

She shook her head. "But I promise, I will not get sick."

He gave her a brief smile, then returned his attention to the mare. "The shoulders are stuck in the birthing canal." He pointed. "The foal's still wrapped in the birth sack, but can you see how the forelegs are even with each other right now?"

She leaned closer.

"Typically one leg will advance before the other, letting the shoulders pass through one at a time. But this young mother needs some help. We only pull when she's pushing. Otherwise she might stop, and we don't want her to do that."

The mare whinnied. The muscles in her great underside rippled.

Jack lifted his head. "You ready, Stewartson?"

"Ready."

Jack gripped the foal just above the fetlocks and pulled downward.

As Véronique watched, she couldn't help but reflect back on all those times Lord Marchand and his *famille* had been presented with a showing of newborn foals. To think—all of this had occurred beforehand, a short distance from where she lived every day, and she'd never experienced it. She felt strangely cheated.

Jack let up and caught his breath. "One more should do it, Stewartson."

The foal wriggled, and Véronique spotted a tiny slit beginning in the sack by the foal's head. The foal must have sensed it too because he squirmed even more vigorously.

Jack began pulling again, and the foal slid out a few more inches. Just as he started to pull a third time, the mare whinnied and pushed the foal out the rest of the way.

Véronique knelt watching, wordless. Tears choked her throat.

She'd never been so close to the beginning of a life before. She thought of her mother and wondered what Arianne Elizabeth Girard would say if heaven's veil were lifted for the briefest second and she could see her only daughter kneeling in a stained silk gown, in a pasture in the middle of the Colorado Territory, witnessing the birth of a foal.

Thomas and Lilly joined them, and at Thomas's instruction, they all stood and moved back, watching as the newborn worked its way from the birth sack.

After a moment, Thomas approached her. "Miss Girard, I'm sorry for how I spoke to you, ma'am. But when the life of one of my mares is on the line, I can get a mite worked up."

"You have no reason to apologize, Monsieur Stewartson. I was the novice in this situation and did not understand. I offer you my gratitude for letting me witness this."

His expression softened even more. "It's something, isn't it?"

"*Oui.*" Her throat closed. "It certainly is."

After a while, Thomas and Jack moved the mare and her newborn to a stall in the barn. With admiration, Véronique observed Thomas, Jack, and Lilly as they worked together to get the new mother and baby situated. Then Thomas headed up to the main house to tell Claire and Miss Maudie the news.

"Well, ladies," Jack said as he grabbed a cloth from the workbench, "if you'll excuse me for a few minutes, I'm going to go out back and wash up."

Véronique watched as he walked away.

Lilly sighed and leaned closer. "You were absolutely right, Mademoiselle Girard. Nothing but respect between you two."

Véronique ignored the comment but couldn't keep from smiling.

She and Lilly watched the new mother and baby get acquainted and laughed at the way the foal tried to balance on its spindly legs.

Finally, Lilly turned to go. "I'm going to run up and see if Miss Maudie is awake. You want to come? Or would you rather wait here." Lilly's tone said she already knew the answer.

"I believe I will choose to wait here, *merci.*"

Véronique was standing on tiptoe peering over the stall wall when she heard a sound behind her. She looked over her shoulder.

Jack approached, wearing his undershirt and carrying the other soiled shirt in his hand. The hair at his temples was still damp, his hands and arms freshly scrubbed and clean. He took a place by the stall beside her and made no pretense of watching either the mare or the foal, as she did.

He simply watched her.

She tried hard not to act self-conscious, but the pressure got to be more than she could stand. She finally smiled. "What are you doing, Monsieur Brennan?"

"I'm looking at you, Mademoiselle Girard. Is that within the accepted boundaries of our employee-employer relationship?"

She shrugged, hearing the teasing in his voice and feeling as though there was a more serious question beneath his obvious one. And it was a question she was not ready to answer. "This is a free country, *non*?" She loved the sound of his laughter.

"You did well out there, Vernie. I'm proud of you."

She chose to ignore his use of the dreadful nickname. "I did not do anything. It is you who was the hero. But I am thankful I was there to watch it all."

He gave her a slow smile, and his focus moved from her eyes, to her mouth. He slipped an arm around her waist, and Véronique angled herself toward him.

"Hey, you two . . ." Thomas's voice sounded from the front of the barn. "Claire's cooking supper for everyone up at the main house. Miss Maudie's asked everyone to stay."

The pressure of Jack's hand on her waist increased just before he moved away, and she got the unmistakable impression that he would have kissed her right then had Thomas not interrupted. Then Jack flashed that boyish grin as though having been caught, and she was certain of it.

As they walked to the main house, he gave her a look that could best be described as one of promise. Véronique only hoped he was serious. Because regardless of rank or standing or expectations or otherwise, this was one promise she planned on making sure Jack Brennan kept.

ACK SO SOON, Mr. Brennan? It's not been a week yet since you were last here." Miss Maudie waved at him from her perch on the oversized sofa in the front room. Or perhaps it was Miss Maudie's petite size that made the sofa look overlarge.

Her foot was propped up on a cushion on a low-standing table, and a blanket draped her lap, covering her injured leg. A book rested on the sofa beside her, and color laced her cheeks with a healthy glow.

"Yes, ma'am, I'm back." He held his hat in his hands, careful not to knock any of the road dust loose. "Seems Hochstetler can't get his shipments to arrive in sequence from Denver, so I'm delivering the rest of that new stove you ordered."

She nodded. "You've had to make several runs to Casaroja of late."

"I never mind the extra trips, ma'am."

"Be givin' you time to think, now doesn't it? Bein' on the road, I mean. You've a likin' for it."

"I think I'm made for it, actually," he agreed. "But not like I used to be. I'd like to be able to come home at night now, to a familiar place. I'm looking forward to settling down here, if things work out." He nodded to the book. "What are you reading?"

"Oh, these eyes of mine aren't readin' much of anything these days. Claire was reading to me earlier. She's sweet to be doin' it but much too busy to be bothered." Miss Maudie smiled and patted the cushion beside her. "I've heard a rumor, Mr. Brennan, that you'll soon be buyin' yourself some land. Would there be any truth to that at all?"

He sat down, careful to lay his hat on the floor. "Now, where on earth would you be hearin' that from? And what broodin' fool has been spillin' his mouth about my personal business, I have to ask ya?"

Hand to her mouth, she giggled. "I love it when you speak with the brogue, Mr. Brennan. Takes me back some years. If I close my eyes," and she did, "I'd for sure be thinkin' my younger brother Danny was in the room with us." She peered at Jack again, her gaze thoughtful. "You remind me of him, you know—very much. He was a handsome man. Tall and strappin', like you, and with a heart as good as ever could be had by a mortal. I've a notion the same heart beats within your chest, Mr. Brennan."

"I appreciate your kindness, ma'am. Is . . . your brother gone now?"

"Oh, my yes." She nodded. "He left the family first, God bless his soul. Only twenty-six years he walked this earth. My parents never did get over his passin', but I didn't hold that against them. Some people we love have a way of workin' themselves into us so much that even after they're gone, they're still here in so many ways."

The manner in which she looked at him made Jack feel as though she already knew his story. "Yes, ma'am, I believe that's true. We carry bits and pieces of them inside us."

Her eyes sparkled. "Like precious little jewels." With a soft laugh, she pointed to a silver tea service on the table. "If you've time to spare, would you do the honors of pourin' us each a cup, Mr. Brennan? And then let's return the conversation to the subject of land."

Jack poured as she directed and handed her a cup, not at all comfortable with the procedure but not making too big of a mess. He wiped up the few stray drops with a towel lying beside the tray.

"Tell me about this land of yours, now. And I have my sources, Mr. Brennan, to be sure. They're reliable too, so don't you be tryin' to pass any falsehoods along to me."

"I'd never try that, ma'am. I fear you'd find me out, and then I'd be in for it." He smiled and took a sip. "You heard rightly, Miss Maudie. I've got a bid in for a piece of land west of town, about a two hour ride out. Runs along the border of Fountain Creek on up the mountain a ways."

"Along Fountain Creek, you say." Her voice grew soft.

"Runs adjacent to it. Someone else already owns the land abutting the section I'm interested in. So I'd have some ready made neighbors when I start to build."

Her features softened with question. "And have you met these neighbors yet, Mr. Brennan?"

"Oh no, ma'am. I'm still waiting to find out from Mr. Clayton at the title office if the owner's accepted my offer." He leaned close, lowering his voice. "Seems I have to be interviewed by the owner first. I'm still waiting for Clayton to set up the meeting. Guess they won't sell to just anyone, according to Clayton."

Miss Maudie lowered her cup and cradled it in her lap. "Yes, I'd be knowin' that's the owner's preference, from personal experience, you might say."

Jack went stock-still, his china cup poised in midair. And then it hit him. Miss Maudelaine Mahoney could be the owner of that property. He placed his cup on the table, sorting back through their conversation for anything contrary he might have said. "Miss Maudie, if I've spoken out of turn in any way, ma'am, I beg your pardon. I didn't mean to—"

She reached over and squeezed his arm. "I tried my hand at buyin' some of that land a coupl'a years back. Oh, I didn't need it for myself, of course. I had in mind to give it as a gift, to some friends."

Jack exhaled. "That's an awfully nice gift."

She lifted her brow. "They're awfully nice friends." She held out her cup, and Jack refilled it. "But the owner wouldn't sell to me. Guess I didn't pass muster in their opinion. But no mind, it's all part of God's great design. I wasn't meant to have it, but perhaps that's because . . . you were."

Jack let this new information sink in and wasn't encouraged by it. If the owner wouldn't sell to Miss Maudie, as fine a woman as she was and with her good reputation known throughout Willow Springs, his chances seemed slim at best.

Claire Stewartson appeared in the doorway. "Is there anything I can get for either of you? I need to head out to the smokehouse for something. I won't be long."

"No, my dear, we're fine. You go on ahead. I wish I could be followin' you out there, though. The day looks so grand."

After Claire left, Jack moved his cup from the table to the tray and stood. "Miss Maudie, would you do me the honor of allowing me to . . . escort you around the grounds of Casaroja?"

She peered up at him, confused. Then a pleasant expression moved across her features. "Are you proposin' what I think you are, Mr. Brennan? If so, I'm not sure my old ticker will be able to stand it. But if not, I'll die one happy woman, truth be told!"

Laughing, he leaned down and gathered her in his arms. Her weight was less than he'd anticipated, and even through her clothes, he sensed the frailness in her bones. He pushed the screen door open with his shoulder, careful that it didn't bump her leg.

"Please let me know if I'm hurting you. I don't want Doc Hadley after me."

Miss Maudie slipped her arms around his shoulders. "That old coot! I wish he'd drive up in that buggy of his right now and see us traipsin' across the yard. That would bust every one of his buttons." She closed her eyes and tilted her head back. "Oh, the sun feels so good on my skin. Let's go sit, just over there." She pointed to a grassy area beneath a large cottonwood, by a cottage set off to the side.

Jack eased her down and joined her on the grass. "I sure do admire all you've accomplished here, Miss Maudie."

"Oh, it wasn't me who did this." Her gaze traveled over the pastures, the main house, and the barn before resting on the cottage. "It was my nephew, Donlyn, who built all this. I only inherited it, by default you might say, and have simply tried to keep things goin'."

"You've done more than keep things going, ma'am. You've made it thrive."

"God has done that, Mr. Brennan. I've only been as good a steward of His gift as I could be."

The warble of birds in the tree overhead drew their attention, and Jack's thoughts went to the land he hoped to purchase. Silently, but certain heaven was listening, he made a pledge. *If given that land, Father, I'll be as good a steward of it as I know how to be. And even better, with you beside me.*

When he looked at Miss Maudie again, sadness had settled over her features. Before he could speak, she turned to him.

"My nephew is in jail, Mr. Brennan." Tears filled her eyes. "For tryin' to kill a man over the very land you're seekin' to purchase."

Stunned, Jack couldn't have spoken if he'd wanted to. But the comments that Thomas and Claire Stewartson had made about Miss Maudie's past struggles suddenly became clearer. And more tragic.

"I don't even know where my nephew is now. Only that he's somewhere back East. He wants nothing to do with me, and they say that's his right to be left alone." Miss Maudie worried the hem of her dress sleeve. "I've written to him, care of the Denver judge who sentenced him, but I haven't heard from Donlyn except once. And I won't be repeatin' what he wrote in that letter." She bowed her head. "But neither will I be forgettin' it anytime soon," she whispered.

Unable to think of anything worthy of being spoken in light of what she'd shared, Jack reached over and covered the older woman's hand.

She sighed. "You've a kindness about you, Jack Brennan. I saw it in your eyes that day I fell, and when you helped Thomas carry me back to my room. In my experience that depth of kindness doesn't come without a refining of some sort."

Early on, Jack had sensed something special about this woman. She had a strength about her, a determination in her spirit, that he admired, and he knew exactly what she was asking. "In April of '56, my wife and I decided to head west. We had a son, Aaron." Jack remembered the morning they'd loaded up. He even recalled the last thing he'd packed into that wagon—Mary's trunk of books. She'd wanted to keep them close so she could read them as they journeyed. Strange how some memories faded with time, while others, seemingly less important, remained clear. "Aaron was only a year old. He didn't really understand what was going on, but he was so excited."

Miss Maudie was attentive as he told her about his past. She shared more about her nephew, how she'd raised Donlyn MacGregor, and about their coming to the Colorado Territory and starting Casaroja. Jack got the impression that no matter how long they went on, the dear woman would have been pleased to sit there and talk all day. But he had shipments to make to other vendors in town, and he needed to get to them.

He rose and scooped her into his arms.

"Thank you, Mr. Brennan, for takin' the time to visit with an old woman. It always amazes me to see how God will work in a person's life, if they'll only let Him."

Jack carried her inside and, at her request, situated her in her bed. "And I thank you for sharing with me about your nephew, Miss Maudie. And for the delicious tea and the enjoyable company."

She caught hold of his hand as he turned, her expression earnest. "So many times I've wondered what I might have done differently with my Donlyn. What I could have changed in my raisin' him that would've prevented his heart from turnin' so hard. You see, he lost his wife and child just like you did. And for the longest time I thought that was the turnin' point for him. That if only God hadn't allowed that to happen to him, things would've been different." She sighed. "But I see now how wrong I was. The same thing happened to you, but you chose a different path, Mr. Brennan. You chose the better one."

Jack cradled her frail hand between his. "I honestly don't remember choosing any path, Miss Maudie." He hesitated, and swallowed against the tightening in his throat. "I just remember being so lost at the time I didn't know where else to turn, other than to Him. He was the only solid thing in my life. He still is."

Tears fell from her eyes. Her grip tightened. "For us both, Jack. For us both."

Véronique packed quickly for another day-trip to a mining camp, wishing she'd done it the night before. But she and Lilly had stayed up late comparing life in France to life in America, talking about boys in both countries, and anything else that had entered their minds. Surprisingly, Lilly hadn't broached the subject of her *chirurgie*, so Véronique hadn't either.

Nearly a month had passed since she'd visited with Dr. Hadley about her desire to cover the expenses for Lilly's *procédure*. He'd said the *chirurgien* in Boston could take up to two months to give his response, but she hoped it would be sooner than that, and that the word received from him would be positive. Then at least Pastor and Mrs. Carlson would have the option to elect for their daughter to have the operation, or not.

Véronique limited the number of items she was taking with her.

Past experience told her she packed far too many things she never used. Only the essentials this time, especially since she'd grown weary of lugging her *valise* all the way to the livery.

She really should have insisted upon Jack picking her up in front of the hotel. A wicked enjoyment skittered through her, imagining the feigned scowl on his face if she did.

Over the past couple of weeks, they'd visited eight new mining towns, all with the same result. Each time, Jack returned with an empty wagon. And she returned with an empty dream. But there were another thirty mining towns yet to visit, so hope still existed. However thinning.

The *valise* latched this time without the least struggle. Closing the door behind her, Véronique caught it the second before it latched. She stepped back inside and crossed to the trunk standing open in the corner. Laying aside her bag, she rummaged through the clothing until her hand finally brushed against something. She withdrew the bundle and fingered the ribbon still tied tight by her mother's hand.

Véronique stared at her father's letters. *I will read them again* Maman. *Every one. For you.*

A draft moved through the room, causing a chill up her back. Véronique turned to close the window but discovered it already closed, with the latch securely fastened.

Then she felt it again.

A brush of air. This time not on her skin as before. But within. Like a flutter in her chest, a whispered breath. She closed her eyes, heart pounding, and stood silent, listening. For what, she didn't know. A sweet scent layered the air, and tears rose to her eyes. She drew in breath after breath, waiting for the heady aroma to disappear to prove she was imagining it . . . and yet praying that it didn't.

. She knew when she opened her eyes there would be no white roses filling every corner of the room as her sense of smell told her there were. So she lingered in the moment, treasuring it, picturing her mother's face, feeling the flutter inside her chest, and the faint beating of a heart in rhythm with hers.

"Oh, *Maman*. I miss you so. . . ."

A knock on the door jarred Véronique back to the moment.

She blinked, wiped her cheeks, and surveyed the room. Just as she had predicted, no white roses. Nothing seemed out of the ordinary. And yet it had been so real.

She cleared her throat. "Who is there?" The door was closed but not latched. Whoever it was could have walked right in.

"It's Jack. I've got the wagon out front, if you're ready. Thought I'd surprise you." A pause. "But don't get used to it."

She smiled at his humor, and at the thought of traveling with him again. "*Merci*, and it is a pleasant surprise, Jack. I will be right there, and I will be expecting this courtesy henceforth."

Two hours into the trip, Véronique was already rubbing her lower back, wishing she could rub even lower than that.

"Having some problems over there?"

She glanced beside her and squinted at the grin on Jack's face. "I do not *comprends* why these seats are not made with cushions. It would be far more comfortable for everyone."

Jack laughed. "I'll be sure and ask Sampson to make that change the next go round. I'm sure he'll appreciate the suggestion."

While the trail they traveled was new to her, Jack had traveled it on one of the overnight trips he'd made without her. The road carved into the mountain was wide, with room to spare, and gently sloped down on the open side to a creek not far below. Even the mountainous slope angled upward at a friendly ascent, with dense growths of pine and aspen clustered together.

Véronique was proud of her ability to identify most of the trees now, aided by the book she'd borrowed from the library in Willow Springs entitled *Mountainous Nature and Wildlife*. The section of the book dedicated to wildlife was rather lacking, however, and the drawings of the animals were annoyingly childlike.

The mid-May sun burned bright overhead, and she shielded her eyes from the glare. A canopy would also be a considerate addition to a wagon like this, but she kept that suggestion to herself. "I much prefer these trips that do not take us as high into the mountains. But I do miss the cooler air."

Jack motioned. "Those clouds layering the north promise some afternoon shade. Maybe even rain. I've noticed you don't carry that umbrella around with you anymore. Would come in handy today though, wouldn't it?"

"Umbrella?" She tried to mimic the way he said it. "Do you refer to my *parasol*?"

"You know exactly what I'm referring to, Vernie. Whatever name you want to give it."

She smiled despite his use of that horrid nickname. It was still her theory that if she ignored it, he would cease using it. "I am thinking that if I had it with me now you would demand that I—"

The sudden pop beneath the wagon sounded like a firecracker going off. Another crack followed.

Jack immediately pulled back on the reins. Napoleon and Charlemagne responded but snorted and stomped at the sudden command.

Holding onto the seat, Véronique leaned over her side of the wagon and briefly peered beneath. "Nothing is broken with *your* wagon . . . that I can see."

Jack sent her a look that said he'd caught her inflection. "Oh sure, it's *my* wagon when it breaks."

"I believe that would be a good rule for us to make."

He got out and came around to her side. "With a noise like that, it doesn't sound promising." He ran a hand along the front wheel, stooping as he went. Then he stopped and blew out a breath. "Cracked felly."

Véronique didn't know what a felly was, but she knew from the tone of his voice that the repair would not be an easy one. "Was there something wrong with the wheel Monsieur Sampson made you?"

"No." He sighed. "This just happens over time when you're hauling heavy loads over rough terrain."

"We will need a new wheel?"

He stood, took off his hat, and wiped his brow with his sleeve. "Yes, ma'am, we will. Thankfully we've got one attached to the underside of the wagon bed. But . . . this means I've got to unload everything."

Véronique looked at the boxes and crates stacked high and filling every inch of space. "The entire shipment must be removed?"

"Everything." He began loosening the ties of the netting. "The wagon is heavy enough on its own. I can barely manage it empty."

Véronique stretched her back and shoulder muscles, then turned on the seat to see him better. "You have done this before, *non*?"

His hands stilled. He tipped back his hat. "Just what is it you think I've done for the past thirteen years, Véronique?"

She shrugged, then seeing his expression darken, wished she hadn't. "You were a driver of wagons. You . . . 'guided folks.' That is what Monsieur Sampson told me."

Jack shook his head and went back to his task. "This'll take me about an hour to unload, about that much more to change the wheel, and then another hour to pack everything back in. So you might want to get comfortable."

Véronique climbed down from the wagon, wishing she hadn't sounded so flippant about his former occupation. That hadn't been her intention. And she sensed she'd hurt him. "I will help you do this, and then I must take a . . . brief respite."

"I can get this. You go ahead and take care of business. But don't go far." Without looking at her, he took off his hat and tossed it up on the bench seat.

Véronique scanned the slope leading down to the creek but saw no opportunity for privacy there. She looked above to where the mountain angled upward and chose that option instead. Trees were plentiful and boulders large enough to stand behind dotted the wooded landscape.

Needing some therapeutic papers, she turned to retrieve her *valise* and found Jack already holding the papers out to her.

Unable to look him in the eye, she took the bundle from him. "*Merci beaucoup,*" she whispered, then quickly crossed the narrow gulley and began her climb.

The aspens were just beginning to leaf, and as she forged a path upward through the trees, she looked behind her on occasion, setting that perspective to memory as Jack had taught her on a previous trip. But she had little worry of getting lost on such a short climb.

The pungent scent of musk mingled with the sweetness of the pines, and she was reminded again of how much she enjoyed spring. A ways uphill, she located a large boulder companioned by an ever-green that provided sufficient privacy. She knelt behind it.

The sound of Jack rearranging the crates and boxes in the wagon on the road below drifted up to her, and she was thankful for the ambient noise. This was one aspect of traveling with him that she hadn't grown comfortable with, and doubted whether she would anytime soon. He, on the other hand, didn't seem bothered by it in the least.

"You all right?" he yelled.

She smiled. If ever she'd been gone for any length of time, he'd always called out to her. "*Oui*, I am fine. . . . *Merci beaucoup*."

After a moment, she stood and adjusted her skirt, then used the extra papers to wipe her hands. She looked at the name printed on each one of the sheets. *Joseph Gayetty*. What kind of man would print his name on a piece of paper created for such use? She shook her head. *Americans . . .*

She bent down to retie her boot and spotted a furry black-and-white nose edging its way through the low-growing brush.

Véronique crept back a step, resisting the urge to run or scream. She had read about the animal in the book from the library and had also seen them on her journey to Willow Springs with Bertram Colby. Though the ones they had seen then had been quite dead at the time—just as she wished this one to be.

She slowly backed away, feeling behind her for anything in her path.

The animal crawled out from beneath the shrub, completely black except for the white strip on its forehead that extended into a V down its back.

It made a path straight for her.

"Jack," she called, increasing her backward momentum.

Bertram Colby had said these animals, similar to those in France, came out only at night. But apparently he had been mistaken. He'd also said they were naturally afraid of humans. Again, a fact not proving true in this instance.

Perhaps Monsieur Colby's knowledge didn't extend to the animals living in this part of the—

The skunk darted for her, sending Véronique's heart to her throat. Then he stopped and walked stiff-legged for a few paces.

Or perhaps Monsieur Colby had been right but there was something wrong with this particular animal.

Véronique met with a tree at her back and quickly maneuvered around it. "Jack!" She raised her voice only slightly, remembering that the book recommended "not to cry out when confronted by a skunk, as this mammal could become easily agitated."

The animal's head went low, and came up sharply. He stamped his front feet and ran full out straight for her.

Véronique started to run downhill, but a rise of boulders blocked her path. So she ran on the slope, finding it hard to keep her footing amid the rocks and low-growing branches.

From the scurry of the skunk behind her, it was clear he was not having the same difficulty.

"Jack!" She screamed as loudly as she could, figuring the animal had already reached an agitated state. She glanced behind her.

The skunk was at least six or eight feet behind but was covering the ground more quickly.

Véronique turned back and spotted the pine branch just as it caught her in the face. Her right cheek felt like someone had struck a match against it.

"Véronique!" Jack's voice sounded muted, far away.

"Jack!" She pushed limbs from her path as she ran. Just ahead, she spotted what looked to be a more level path to her right, and she took it.

Then quickly realized what a poor choice that had been.

CHAPTER TWENTY-EIGHT

T HE CAVE LOOMED AHEAD, the skunk loomed behind. And Véronique found neither choice appealing.

Breathless from her run, she paused and braced her arms on her thighs. She drew in air and swallowed, trying to ease the burning in her lungs. From the tall earthen walls on either side, she guessed the entrance to the cave had been carved out by hand rather than by nature.

The skunk crested the hill, took a few steps, and stopped.

Véronique eyed him. Perhaps the wicked little creature was as tired as she was and had finally decided to—

The fur on its back went stiff. The skunk turned, and raised its tail.

Véronique put her hand over her nose and mouth and ran.

She ducked into the cave, stopping within a few feet of the opening. Everything beyond that point was darkness.

The pungent spray filtered in. Her eyes began to burn. Her throat tightened with the same stinging. She squeezed her eyes shut, hoping to ease the pain and adjust to the lesser light.

Using the wall of the cave as a guide, she took measured steps deeper into the cavern, aware of the fading light behind her. She swallowed, and the saliva caught in her throat. Coughing, she tried to catch her breath as the fog of skunk spray grew thicker.

She took more steps. Darkness closed around her.

Her eyes watered, and she was unable to keep them open but for one or two seconds at a time. Her hand ran across something wet on the cave wall and she cringed. Then just as quickly, she got excited thinking it might be water. She blinked but could see nothing. She brought her hand to her face with the intention of wiping her eyes, but . . . what if it wasn't water?

Véronique lifted her palm to her nose but could smell nothing but skunk. With her eyes already watering, she didn't realize she was crying until her hiccupped sobs echoed back to her.

She took a few more steps inside the cave then leaned down to rub her eyes with her skirt. But that only worsened the sting.

She grew disoriented. "Jack!!" Her voice echoed back to her, Jack's name spilling over itself in decreasing waves, one atop the other. Where was he?! And why hadn't he come to help her?

Even that far back the stench was nauseating. Then slowly, Véronique realized it wasn't the lingering musk in the air. It was *her*! Her clothes reeked, her hair reeked—everything about her reeked. Which only encouraged her tears. Which should have helped her eyes. But it didn't.

"Véronique!" Pistol at the ready, Jack quickly discovered the scattered therapeutic papers and followed the trail of strewn leaves and broken branches to the first crest in the mountain.

That's when he smelled it.

He pulled the kerchief from his back pocket and tied it over his mouth and nose.

"Véronique!"

If she'd somehow met up with this skunk, Véronique might be scared, she might be smelling something awful, but chances of anything worse were remote. He'd seen rabid animals, but they weren't nearly as plentiful as myth led people to believe.

Jack ran along the slope, careful with his footing, then slowed when Véronique's trail abruptly ended. He spotted the cave just as he heard something rustle in the brush behind him.

The skunk crawled out, stiff-legged, and began to stamp its feet. It darted forward, veered, and stopped. Then lowered its head as though about to charge.

That's all Jack needed. He aimed his pistol, gauging his sight as far away from the dangerous tail end of the varmint as he could, and fired.

The animal dropped, and Jack quickly put distance between them in case the skunk had gotten off another spray. The gunshot reverberated against the mountain walls, weakening with each returning echo.

Sure the skunk was dead, Jack turned back to the cave and approached the entrance. "Véronique!"

"Jack?"

At the sound of her voice, the first thing he felt was relief. The second thing was a cold sweat. Jack peered inside the cave and was seven years old again, standing beside Billy Blakely, staring into the dark yawn of that deserted miners' dig. *Billy Blakely* . . .

Jack tried to shake off the memory, but it hung close. "Are you all right?"

Nothing, and then a faint whimper. "I will be."

He had no choice, and he knew it. He clicked the lock on his pistol and shoved it into the waistband at his back, all the while staring at the entrance of the cave. The skin on his back and neck crawled. "I'm coming, just stay where you are."

As he took the first step, it struck him that those were the same words his father had yelled down that abandoned miner's shaft to him, thirty-one years ago. Jack wondered if Véronique drew as much comfort from hearing his voice as he had his father's. He doubted it, because she didn't sound nearly as scared as he remembered being.

He entered the cave and paused, letting his eyes adjust. The smell of skunk was strong, and his eyes watered, his throat burned. But he didn't dare pull the kerchief any tighter. He could barely breathe as it was.

"Véronique . . ." He waited for the echo to pass, and for his pulse, hopefully, to slow. "Can you clap your hands?"

Seconds passed. "*Oui.*"

He waited. "Would you do it, please . . . one time."

A single clap sounded.

"Good. Do that . . . every few seconds."

A clap . . . Silence . . . Another clap . . . A slow pattern developed.

Jack followed the sound, and with each step the rush in his ears grew louder. He forced the air in and out of his lungs—evenly spaced breaths—ignoring the pace fear wanted to set for him. He would've sworn he could feel the walls of the cave closing in. He stretched his arms out in front of him—then to the sides just to make sure the walls hadn't moved.

The clapping grew closer, and the stench grew stronger.

A conversation he'd had with his father returned to him. It had been years after the incident, when his father had confessed to him how frightened he'd been to learn that his son had fallen down that hole. But to Jack's young ears, when his father had called down to him that day, his father's voice hadn't sounded frightened at all. It had sounded of courage, and bravery, and certainty.

The claps stopped. "Jack?"

The echo of his name faded. "Yes, Véronique?"

Time hung like a stilled pendulum. "Are you scared?"

Jack stopped in his tracks, heart knocking against his ribs, barely able to breathe. And he laughed. He couldn't help it. Scared as he was, his hands shaking as he held his arms out in front of him, he laughed. "A bit . . . are you?"

"Not since I . . . can hear your voice."

Her voice was close. She was within a few feet of him now, and the smell was overwhelming. He untied his handkerchief, since it was of little worth, and shoved it into his pocket.

She started humming. It wasn't a tune Jack recognized, but it was beautiful. The hum didn't echo as much as their voices had, and the way the cave turned the music back upon itself was . . . comforting.

Jack's hand came into contact with something that was most definitely Véronique Girard. The humming stopped. Her hands touched his chest, then fisted his shirt. Her arms came around him.

Jack held her tight, telling himself it was more for her benefit than his. But he had a feeling they both knew better. Fuzziness crowded his head, and he knew he needed to get out. "Ready?" he whispered. He slid his hand down her arm and laced his fingers through hers.

"*Oui*, but can I do something first?"

About to say no, Jack heard her intake of breath.

"Véronique," she called out. When the echo had ceased, she called her name again, then spoke something in French that he didn't understand. But the language foreign to him floated back toward them just the same.

When the last echo had faded, she squeezed his hand. "*Merci.* I am ready now."

"What were you doing?"

She laughed softly. "Hearing my mother's voice." She sniffed. "I am sorry about the smell, Jack."

"Not a problem." He started to move, then suddenly didn't know which way to turn. Yet he knew enough to know not to move without being certain. "Véronique?"

Her hand tightened around his. "I am here."

Shame poured through him. He'd led hundreds of families across this country, yet he couldn't find his way out of this cave.

He felt the tug of her hand. She moved past him, and he didn't need a source of light to know which part of her body had accidentally brushed against him.

He followed, careful not to step on her heels but close enough to where there was no chance of her losing him. When the light at the mouth of the cave appeared, Jack's breath left him in a rush. Emotion tightened his chest as he recalled the feel of his father's arm around his boyish shoulders as they walked out of the abandoned mine together.

But what had haunted him for the past thirty-one years, and what he would remember forever, was the sight of Billy Blakely's father kneeling on the snow-covered ground, weeping.

CHAPTER TWENTY-NINE

J ACK HELD HER HAND as they trekked down the slope to the wagon. Véronique stared at his back as he led the way, so proud of him, so thankful he'd come for her. Yet she wondered what lay beneath the tears he'd quickly wiped away when they'd stepped from the cave moments ago. Whatever their cause, she had felt needed inside that dark cavern. And that was something she hadn't felt in a long time.

They reached the wagon and she loosened her grip first. Jack let go of her hand. She blinked, still adjusting to the sun's brightness, but even more, trying to rid her eyes of the foul musk. Her throat was raw from coughing, and she was certain her eyes were swollen from the rubbing.

Yet what she'd experienced in that cave had felt like a gift.

For so long she'd wanted to hear her mother's voice again. Just one more time. And she had, in the most unexpected place. But she still wished she'd been the one to shoot that confounded skunk. Which reminded her . . .

"Jack, I would appreciate learning how to shoot your gun."

He set down the crate of supplies he'd retrieved from the wagon. "Right now?" He handed her the canteen.

She drank liberally and handed it back, matching his smile. "Not at this precise moment, but soon. Will you teach me?"

"It'd be my pleasure, ma'am."

She looked down at her clothes, then down at the creek. "I do not think I can ride all day like this."

He shook his head. "No need for you to. I've still got to unload everything and fix the wheel. You'll have plenty of time to bathe ... if you'd like."

She nodded, and glanced again at the creek. He seemed to follow her gaze as it followed the shoreline for a good distance in either direction, the view of the creek unobstructed and unhindered—and completely lacking in privacy. She met his stare and a slow grin tipped one side of his mouth. The *racaille* ... Surely he could read her thoughts, as easily as she read his.

"I'll create a shelter for you with this." He grabbed a blanket from beneath the bench seat. "That way you'll have privacy from the road-side. But if any squirrels or prairie dogs sneak up from the opposite bank, I can't be held responsible."

"*Merci*, Jack. I appreciate this." She reached for her satchel, then hesitated, realizing what she'd done. Or rather, hadn't done.

"What's wrong?"

On previous trips she'd at least brought along extra under-garments. The one day she'd decided to try and pack lighter ... "I do not have a change of clothes."

He considered this. "Then I'm afraid you don't have much of a choice." He grabbed the crowbar, pried open two of the crates in the back, and pulled out a miners' shirt, followed by a pair of dungarees.

She took a backward step. "You cannot be serious."

"I am, unless you want to stay wrapped in this all day." He held the blanket up in his other hand.

She grabbed the shirt and dungarees, making a silent vow never to travel anywhere again without a full change of clothes. And she was removing "packing light" from her vocabulary. "I have soap in my *valise*. And perfume."

Jack set her bag on the ground and opened it for her. Then wrinkled his nose when she got closer, and winked. "I hope you have lots of both."

Véronique stepped behind the makeshift shelter and wished there wasn't such a steady breeze blowing down through the canyon. Not only for the comfort of bathing—she'd already checked, and the water was icy cold from the melting snows—but for the dependability of her shelter. She feared one healthy breeze would lay waste her bathing screen, along with her last shred of decency.

She unbuttoned her shirtwaist and laid it aside. Then shed her skirt. The breeze whipped the blanket, and she was afraid she was ruined. But Jack's stakes and ties held, and she continued disrobing, watching the opposite bank of the creek for any sign of movement.

She knew with certainty that Jack Brennan would not peek. But she had a strong feeling that he would very much like to. When he'd accidentally touched her in the cave earlier she'd been startled but not offended. It had been dark, after all, and he hadn't done it with intention.

With her clothes lying in a pile beside her, Véronique took her soap and the towel Jack had given her from the supplies and walked the brief three steps to the creek. Jack had situated the blanket around a place in the creek that ran deeper than the rest. But still the water was no more than two-feet deep, and the space was not wide enough to submerge her body. She shivered just imagining the thought of that cold water covering her entirely.

She lathered her body and scrubbed. Then smelled her hands and arms, and lathered again, letting the soap rest on her skin. She washed her hair, twice, until her fingers ached from the cold. Using a drinking tin from Jack's inventory, she poured clean water over her shoulders, arms, and legs.

Bent over by the creek, she was in the sunshine, but when she stepped back to the shelter to dress, the air held a chill. She dried off quickly and reached for the miners' shirt. It was enormous, and she had nothing to wear beneath it . . . or the trousers. She bent and picked up her chemise, then immediately let it fall again. Out of the question.

She slipped the shirt on, finding immediate warmth in its folds. It came well past her knees and was thicker than she'd expected. The dungarees were another matter entirely. The material was comfortable enough, but even with the drawstring cinched tight, the trousers puddled at her ankles. She pulled them up and held them there and began her ascent back to the wagon.

Jack was removing the broken wheel from the wagon when he saw her. He went absolutely still.

Véronique kept her gaze averted and carried herself with some measure of comportment until she stepped on a rock and nearly dropped her pants.

Jack turned back to his task, but she heard his laughter.

It was midafternoon by the time he got the wheel fixed, the cargo loaded back into the wagon, and the horses harnessed again.

"Thought I'd bathe real quick before we go," he told her. "You mind?"

Véronique raised a brow. "Actually, I would prefer it. And I promise, I will not peek." He had already taken down the blanket.

"Good. And I ate lunch while you were bathing. Yours is beneath the seat when you want it."

She watched him go, wondering how men did that. Just traipsed off to the stream and removed their clothes without a single thought of who might be watching. He returned a while later dressed in garb identical to hers. Except his clothes fit, and rather nicely.

They reached the mining town by late afternoon, and Jack quickly worked his transaction with the store owner. Véronique had thought that perhaps her variation in clothes would draw less interest from the miners this trip. But her attire only seemed to invite more comments, along with jokes about why she was wearing them and other coarse remarks.

By the time they returned to Willow Springs, the sun had set, bringing a welcome cloak of night.

Jack stopped outside the hotel and helped her down, then caught hold of her hand. "Thank you . . . for what you did for me in the cave this morning."

She waited, half hoping he would share the reason behind his reaction in the cave, which was similar to his reaction in the mercantile when they'd first met. When he didn't, she decided to take the hint. "And thank you," she whispered, securing the dungarees at her waist, "for coming in after me. I can imagine how much that cost you, Jack."

Acting on impulse, she stood on tiptoe and kissed his left cheek first, then his right, then repeated both again. She stepped back, pleased with the look on his face. "That is how we do it in France."

He reached up and gently touched the curve of her cheek, then fingered a strand of her hair. His smile started in his eyes first. "Plenty of responses come to mind at present, ma'am"—he gave her hair a gentle tug—"but I think I'd do best just to say good-night."

"But do you realize how expensive those are, Miss Girard? The price listed in the catalog is by the bottle." Madame Hochstetler's voice rose in volume as she spoke, as though it took a great effort to help Véronique understand.

It was all Véronique could do to hold her tongue and contain her temper. Especially with the mercantile as crowded as it was, and her hands full of packages from her shopping that morning.

Jack had left over a week ago on consecutive trips to mining towns that demanded overnight stays, and Véronique hadn't seen him since. Time spread out before her like an empty canvas, and she had nothing with which to fill it. Even Lilly was busy with her duties at the hotel. The hotel had no piano, and Willow Springs had no art galleries or tulip gardens through which to stroll. So she found herself bored, irritable, and growing more so by the hour.

She spent some of her evenings rereading her father's letters, and their contents were proving of no use in her search for him, nor were they improving her demeanor. Her father mentioned no specific mining towns, but he often went into great detail about his attitude toward his new country and how certain he was that both she and her mother would cherish it. And always, at the end of every letter, the same closure: *My deepest love always, until we are joined again.*

Madame Hochstetler leaned a beefy arm on the counter. "And these are very expensive since they'll be coming all the way from New York City. My counsel would be for you to start out by orderin' a smaller amount, and then—"

"*Merci beaucoup*, Madame Hochstetler, for your . . . *counseil*. But I am quite aware that the price is per bottle, and I would like you to order every color I have indicated on the page . . . *s'il vous plaît*." Véronique forced a stiff smile, not appreciating the mercantile owner's patronizing tone nor the way the woman looked her up and down as she quoted prices from the *catalogue*. Nor the way she tucked that double chin and peered over those spectacles as she started filling out the order form! *Infuriating woman!*

Though Véronique had grown to like many things about this infant country, there were days when she longed for the simple response of *"My pleasure, Mademoiselle Girard"* from the lesser-ranking servants, instead of their questioning her at every turn.

Véronique shifted her weight, certain that Madame Hochstetler could write faster than she was at the moment. "I am in a hurry this morning, madame. Is it possible for you to pen the order in a more hasty fashion?"

Madame Hochstetler ceased her writing and slowly straightened from her crouch over the counter. "Do you want me to order these things for you or not?"

Sorely wishing that dismissing this woman was within her realm of authority, Véronique nodded. "You may continue your task."

Time moved slowly as the woman wrote, and Véronique's thoughts turned to her search. Once Jack returned—*if* he ever returned—the number of mining towns they would have visited, either together or him alone, would be twenty-five. That meant only twenty mining camps remained where her father might be, if he'd stayed in the area. Véronique worked hard to ignore the foreboding feeling, but she was beginning to believe she would never find him. And more, that God had never intended it in the first place.

After what seemed like enough time to construct another Arc de Triomphe, Madame Hochstetler straightened. She turned the order form around and shoved it in Véronique's direction. "Sign at the bottom."

Véronique lingered over the document, confirming that everything was correct before signing, and making sure Madame Hochstetler knew who the servant was in this situation. "Please see that my order is executed promptly, madame. I would like the paints delivered as soon as possible."

The woman offered a tight smile. "Takes three weeks minimum for the order to be processed in New York and shipped by train to Denver. Then another week, maybe more, for our normal freighter to get them here, depending on his schedule. If you want to pay extra for the stage, that'll save you a few days, but will cost you an extra two dollars. I don't think that's worth—"

"I will pay most happily. It is important for me to get them here swiftly." Véronique retrieved a bank draft from her *réticule*. As Madame Hochstetler tallied the order, Véronique followed along to make sure she added properly.

"Here's your receipt for what you paid today . . . Miss Girard." Madame Hochstetler peered over her spectacles. "The other half is due when the shipment comes in." The woman stuck the pencil back into the mass of gray curls framing her round face and stared at the bank draft. "Just so we're clear . . . This is a special order, so you can't return the items unless there's something wrong with them."

"*Oui*, you have already stated this to me."

"We always make sure folks new to town understand because they tend to think they can just decide later whether—"

"I understand what you have explained to me, Madame Hochstetler. I would appreciate prompt notification at the hotel the moment my order arrives." Véronique gave the slightest curtsy demanded by etiquette and then hurried from the mercantile.

Her boots pounded the boardwalk as she cut a path to the dress shop. She clutched the numerous packages and cloth sacks, finding them growing heavier by the minute. She couldn't pinpoint why, but from the moment she'd met Madame Hochstetler, the woman had worn a ridge in her nerves. What was the word Lilly had used the other day to describe a demanding hotel guest . . . ?

Véronique could visualize the definition in her mind—*difficult or irritating to deal with*. The word was odd sounding in itself, and actually resembled its meaning. What was it . . . ?

Cantankerous! That was it!

As Véronique crossed the street, she worked to form sentences in her mind using the word. The customary practice helped newly learned words take firmer root and—at least for today—it also gave vent to her frustration.

Madame Hochstetler is one of the most cantankerous *women I have ever met.*

Madame Hochstetler's behavior ranks among the most cantankerous *I have ever experienced.*

Cantankerous *best describes the wife of poor, unfortunate Monsieur Hochstetler.*

Véronique's hand was on the latch of the dress-shop door when it occurred to her that the face foremost in her mind at the moment wasn't Madame Hochstetler's at all—it was Madame Marchand's.

The realization was jarring. And it made her wish she'd been a bit more lenient with Madame Hochstetler.

It had been months since she'd experienced even a fleeting thought of Madame Marchand, yet Véronique could easily see the similarities between the two women. Part of leaving Paris had meant leaving Madame Marchand behind, and Véronique had not wasted a single moment lamenting the woman's absence. How could such a vindictive woman have been mother to a man as generous and kind as Lord Marchand? It was not a logical progression from matriarch to son.

The latch suddenly moved in her hand. The door opened from the inside.

"Véronique!" Surprise lit Jack's expression. "What are you doing here?"

Stunned, Véronique checked the shingle over the door to make sure she was in the right place. "Jack, you have returned!"

"Yes, ma'am. Just got back into town a little while ago. I stopped by the hotel, but you weren't there."

Véronique held up a bag. "I'm enlisting Madame Dunston to alter a dress I purchased." She smiled at the odd look on his face, and decided not to tell him she was also there to commission Madame Dunston to sew her several new dresses—ones better suited for their travels. Homespun, but made with more flattering colors and, hopefully, a Parisian flair of her own influence. "What are *you* doing here, Jack?"

He glanced back over his shoulder. "I was . . . making a delivery."

She looked past him to where Madame Dunston was busy wrapping something behind the counter. "I did not know you delivered items for Madame Dunston."

He shrugged. "I'm a freighter. I deliver goods to the people who need them. And speaking of—I've got some business to attend to." After glancing over his shoulder, he opened the door wide. He bowed at the waist and made a sweeping motion with his arm. "I grant you entrance, mademoiselle."

Smiling at his antics, she stepped inside, wishing he wouldn't leave so soon. She suddenly pictured him dressed in a formal tailcoat and trousers, complete with a silk *cravate*, and quickly decided she much preferred his white button-up shirt, worn leather vest, and dungarees. His clothes suited the untamed masculine quality she'd come to appreciate about him.

He moved past her. "Are you ready for another trip?"

"I am more than ready. I am bored silly in this town. When do we leave?" Something flashed across his face. An emotion she couldn't identify but was quite sure she didn't like.

"You're . . . *bored*?"

"*Oui*. You have been away and Lilly has been occupied. There is little else for me to do, other than to shop." She gave the street outside a cursory glance. "And there is only so much shopping one can do in a place like this."

He glanced at the stringed boxes and cloth sacks filling her hands. "But it looks like you've given it a brave effort."

"It took some time, but I located the items I needed—and two specific items that I believe Lilly will enjoy." She smiled, imagining Lilly's reaction at seeing them. "Things every young girl should have."

"Depending on what those things are, you might consider asking permission of her parents before you give them to her."

Véronique scoffed. "Nonsense. She will enjoy them, and I am content in the belief that her parents will be pleased."

With his current mood, she decided not to tell him about her order at the mercantile. It was an expensive purchase, to be certain, but necessary. In the past week, she'd discovered that all of her paints had dried or turned grainy in the combined months of travel. She had yet to draw anything of worth recently but trusted that holding a palette full of colors in one hand and a fresh brush in the other would be inspiring. Not to mention the canvases she'd ordered as well.

Jack glanced down, then back at her. "Véronique . . . have you given any consideration to looking for employment here in Willow Springs?"

He said it so quietly, so matter-of-factly, and with such affection, that Véronique couldn't take offense. But she sorely wanted to. "For what purpose would I seek a position of employment, Jack? My financial requirements are met, and my first responsibility is to search for my father." She shifted the packages in her hand and added, "When you'll allow me to accompany you."

His expression drained of warmth. "I just made an observation and thought I would offer a suggestion."

"Exactly what observation have you made?"

Jack glanced over her shoulder, and she turned to see Mrs. Dunston having stilled from her task.

The woman's gaze darted between the two of them. "If you'll excuse me for a moment." She walked into the back room.

"My observation is simply that . . ." Jack lowered his voice. "Perhaps you would find greater contentment in giving of yourself instead of"—he glanced at the packages again, not offering to take any of them from her—"attempting to fill your time with other things."

His closely targeted observation stung, and her defenses rose. "I am still in the process of becoming acquainted with Willow Springs. Once I am settled, I will seek out opportunities as time—" She couldn't continue. The sincerity in his eyes, and the loneliness inside her, wouldn't permit it.

"This is just an idea, Véronique, but I've been out to Casaroja several times in recent weeks, and I've spoken with Miss Maudie on occasion. I think the two of you would be very good for each other. I haven't presumed to speak with her about any sort of arrangement like this, but I know she'd enjoy your company." Jack lightly touched her right cheek, reminding Véronique of the nearly healed scratch she'd received days ago, running through the trees from that rabid skunk. "Will you at least consider the idea?"

She finally nodded, remembering how much she had enjoyed Miss Maudie's company. "Yes, Jack, I will." She managed a brief smile. "You asked if I was ready for another trip. Do you have another planned?"

"Day after tomorrow. We'll leave at—"

"Dawn. *Oui*, of the departure time I am always certain."

She watched through the front window of the dress shop as he crossed the street and rounded the corner. Then it occurred to her that she hadn't asked about his trips of the past week, and neither had he volunteered any information. Which meant he hadn't discovered anything new about her father.

Again the recurring thought—perhaps finding Pierre Girard was not part of God's master plan. But if that proved to be true, then why had God brought her to this place.

CHAPTER THIRTY

J ACK TOOK ACCOUNT of the stack of bills in Véronique's hand, hesitant to accept the money. She'd been at him to take it ever since she'd arrived at the livery that morning. "Why don't you keep it for now, Vernie, and we'll settle up later."

In the dim light of dawn, he ignored the familiar challenge in her stance and adjusted the harness straps on Charlemagne and Napoleon. He shook his head at the names she'd insisted on giving his horses. But oddly, the names fit.

Hearing a snicker, Jack spotted Jake Sampson sitting just outside the open livery doors, well within earshot. A telling grin curved Sampson's mouth as he wriggled his bushy brows.

Jack pretended he hadn't seen.

Véronique nudged the money forward again. "This is as we agreed, *non*? You have earned this money for services rendered."

That only encouraged Jack's hesitance. He walked to the wagon bed and double-checked the tie-downs. "Véronique, I don't—"

"It is yours, Jack. You have earned it. Please take it from me now."

He recognized the resoluteness in her tone and knew she wouldn't let it drop. What he didn't know was where this woman got her continual supply of money. He'd watched her pay Sampson cash for the wagon a while back—a sum that had taken him months to earn. And save the trips they'd made together last week, so far she'd paid him seven dollars for every trip they'd made—*services rendered*, as she'd phrased it. He hoped no one else had heard that comment. Didn't sound too respectable.

Then there were all the packages she'd had with her at the dress shop. But what topped it off was overhearing Mrs. Hochstetler rave to her husband that same afternoon about how "that snooty little Frenchwoman" had waltzed in and placed an order equal to nearly two weeks' worth of profit for the store, and then how Miss Girard had "demanded" it be shipped via stage for the fastest delivery. He didn't know what the order was for and didn't consider it his business. He only hoped Véronique knew what she was doing in her spending.

But the real truth was . . . he felt guilty about taking her money. He'd brought her no closer to finding her father than when they'd first started out, and Jack had a feeling little was going to change in that regard.

And yet *much* was changing in regard to his feelings for her— which also stiffened his resistance to taking the stack of bills in her hand.

Véronique huffed a breath. "You leave me no choice." Using the spoke of a wheel for leverage, she situated a dainty boot and hoisted herself up. "I will leave the money here, on the seat, for you. You may do with it . . . as you wish."

If that were truly the case, he'd stuff those bills right back inside that fancy little drawstring bag of hers.

She climbed back down and brushed off her skirt and shirtwaist, a routine he'd come to expect from her, whether her clothes needed it or not. And looking at her clothes, Mrs. Dunston had apparently gotten her hands on them again because they accentuated every inviting curve Véronique Girard had been blessed with.

Jack gave an already taut rope another firm tug, wishing—right now, anyway—that Véronique hadn't been quite so blessed.

"Ah! I forgot something!"

He turned to see her wide-eyed expression. In answer, he merely looked up at the sun cresting the eastern horizon. She was well aware they had two deliveries to make. Granted, the towns didn't look far apart on the map, but he didn't know how long it would take with the twisting mountain trails.

She held up a hand. "I will hurry, *non*? I give you my word."

Watching her race back down the street in the direction of the hotel, Jack couldn't hold back a grin. She hadn't even waited for his response. The little scamp knew he wouldn't leave without her.

Véronique topped the third-floor landing of the hotel, winded from the brisk walk back but not daring to run for fear of someone seeing her—even so early in the morning. Yet she knew Jack would be counting the minutes, and though she felt with relative certainty he would wait for her, she wouldn't have bet her life on it.

When she neared her room at the end of the hallway, her steps slowed.

The door to her room stood open.

She peered around the corner and saw Lilly standing just inside, perfectly still. The girl's arms were laden with soiled linens and she appeared to be staring at something on the far wall.

Véronique stepped forward. The floorboard creaked beneath her boot.

Lilly spun. "Oh, Mademoiselle Girard!" Her cheeks took on a deeper tint of *rouge*. "I'm sorry, I didn't mean to—I mean, I was just—" The girl's stare returned to its former focus. "Where did you get these?"

Véronique followed Lilly's line of vision, and felt her own cheeks heating with embarrassment. Her paintings were lined up on the floor opposite the window, just where she'd left them the previous evening.

After reading a few more of her father's letters last night, she'd felt a twinge of homesickness and had retrieved her paintings from the trunk. Those of the grassy expanse along the Champs-Elysées and its *jardins*, the Château de Versailles, the Place de la Concorde, the Arc de Triomphe, the Cimetière de Montmartre, and several of a bridge that crossed the river Seine. No matter how many times she'd tried, Véronique had never managed to capture the emotion she'd experienced every time she visited that special bridge. Still, surrounding herself with scenes of Paris had provided comfort and made her feel not quite so far from everything familiar. From her mother. From home.

But in her haste to leave this morning, she hadn't had time to return the paintings to the trunk.

Véronique crossed the room and quickly gathered what canvases she could in her arms, then began turning the rest to face the wall. Once discovering who had painted them, dear Lilly would feel compelled to offer compliments Véronique knew were undeserving. "*Pardonnes-moi*, Lilly. I am sorry to have left these out."

"Mademoiselle Girard, I hope you'll abide me asking again. . . . Where did you get these paintings?"

Something in her young friend's voice made Véronique go still inside. She ceased her efforts and lowered her face. The rhythmic ticking from the clock on the mantel filled the silence. "I brought them with me, from home."

Hearing Lilly's quick intake of breath, Véronique knew what was coming.

A pain tightened her chest, remembering with detailed clarity a particular instructor's unflattering critique of her work, her style. She'd heard all the criticisms before—that her work was unconventional, not worthy of distinction, that her talent was lacking. But the criticisms had never come from someone—and this struck to her vanity, she knew—who had grown to admire her so much in such a short time.

"These came all the way from Paris?" Lilly laid aside the linens and moved closer. "They're simply . . ." Her laughter came out breathy and halting. "*Magnifique!*"

Véronique didn't know how to respond.

Lilly leaned forward, squinting. "It's funny, when I look at them up close, I only see tiny little splotches of paint. But when I back up, it's like I'm looking out a window to some magical place I could only dream of visiting. They're so real. How could you ever choose to leave such a place?"

Words failed to describe Véronique's emotions at what she saw in Lilly's face. Though young and lacking training in the arts, the girl thought her paintings had merit. "*Oui*, Paris is quite beautiful." She glanced past Lilly out the window to the pale outline of the Rockies. "But this place is as well."

Lilly laughed again. "Willow Springs is nice, but it's certainly nothing like this." She picked up the painting of the Château de Versailles, one of Véronique's favorites—as was the memory of the last day she had spent there with her mother. "What is this place called?"

Véronique told her, and gave a brief history of the palace and how it was built. "Versailles is at its most beautiful in early morning. The sun's rays bathe the marble courtyard and send shards of light reflecting into the pools below the gardens. That is the best time to capture the color of the water and the flowers."

The interest in Lilly's expression underwent a subtle shift. A question slipped into her eyes. Lilly looked from Véronique to the paintings and then back. "Did *you* paint these, Mademoiselle Girard?"

Véronique felt her lips tremble. She slowly nodded.

Tears welled in Lilly's eyes. "As my papa would say, you have been given a gift from the Giver, Mademoiselle Girard."

Véronique tried to stop the hiccupped sob before it worked its way up her throat and escaped, but she could not.

"From where I'm sittin', things look like they're shapin' up pretty well for you, Mr. Brennan."

Humor laced Jake Sampson's tone, and though Jack was tempted to react to it, he curbed his smile so as not to give the man any satisfaction.

"Things are going all right, I guess." Jack glanced in the direction where Véronique had just run off down the street, then he knelt to check the underside of the wagon. A portion of his cargo was unusually heavy this time, and costly, and he searched for any signs of bowing due to the excessive weight.

Hochstetler had assured him that the printing press was well crated and would fare the journey. Not a single cloud dotted the dusky blue overhead, but Jack had already confirmed that the oiled tarpaulins were stowed beneath the bench seat as usual just in case.

"That wagon'll hold your goods. Don't you worry none."

Jack rose and gripped the side of the cargo bed. "So far, she's made it over every pass without a hitch." With the exception of the cracked felly days earlier, but that wasn't a reflection on his workmanship. More a hazard of hauling the loads over mountain passes. "You built her strong, Sampson. And you built her well. I appreciate that."

Sampson's boots sounded behind him on the gravel-packed road. "It was your design done that, Brennan. I only followed the steps you laid out for me."

The reply prompted something within Jack. "You're always so

quick to ward off praise, sir. It's all right to accept thanks for something every now and then. Especially when it's a good deed you've done for someone else. The craftsmanship in this wagon is worthy of credit. You should take it, sir. You've earned it." He clapped Sampson on the shoulder. "By the way, I've been meaning to get your thoughts on something."

When the older man didn't respond, Jack looked back.

The grin on Sampson's face slowly faded, and shades of regret crept into place. Sampson laughed softly, but there was no humor in it. "Most of what I've done in my life isn't worthy of much credit." His brow furrowed. "You ever wish you could go back and do some things over in your life, Brennan? And I mean the things that matter, in the long run."

Jack held his stare, surprised at this turn in conversation. And at the turn in this man.

"Every man has regrets, Sampson—if he's honest enough to admit it. And, yes, sir, I've got some of my own." Though nearly fifteen years had passed, it felt as if he were standing on that Idaho prairie again. He had looked away—for the briefest of moments—to help another family, when he'd heard the snap of a rope. He'd turned back to help the men lowering the wagon, but it had been too late. Despite his grip, the other ropes slipped, then snapped beneath the sudden weight, sending the wagon careening downhill. He could still picture the scene. The splintered wreckage of the wagon, beneath which lay his wife and son.

Jack looked down at his hands, and at the faint scars the ropes had burned into his palms that day. "Some of the bad in this life, a man brings on himself. Other times, it seems to seek him out. But either way, I've chosen to trust that God will bring good out of it all. He already has for me."

Sampson gave a nod. "I believe that way too. But sometimes I wonder . . . will the good ever outweigh the bad?"

Though Jack had answered that question within himself years ago, he understood the days of doubt. They still visited him on a far too frequent basis. "In the long run . . . yes, sir, I trust that good will win out. But some days, it doesn't feel like that."

If Jack wasn't mistaken, the older man's eyes misted as he looked away.

After a minute, Sampson cleared his throat. "You take care of her out there. And you do your best to help her find what she came lookin' for."

"You mean *who* she came looking for."

"I mean, as you help her in her search, Brennan. She may never find her father, and God help her not to find him, if he's a man unworthy of such a one."

Jack felt a quickening in his spirit. Hadn't he said the same thing to the Almighty more than once since getting to know Véronique?

"That young lady didn't come all this way just to find her father." Sampson shook his head. "She came here firstly because her mama asked it of her. And second, she came lookin' to find out who she is." Sampson's crooked smile slowly slid back into place. "Then at just the right time you arrived in town, and the Almighty saw fit to pair the two of you together."

Jack shot him a look. "From what I remember, seems that was less the Almighty's doing and more yours."

"Either way, I'm trustin' He'll bring some good out of it all," Sampson said with a shrug.

Jack laughed and shook his head.

"Well, I'm glad we had us this little talk, son. Now, was there something else you were gonna ask me?"

Jack had nearly forgotten. "I'm considering buying some land and wondered if you might be willing to speak on my behalf, if the situation calls for it. Being new to Willow Springs I don't have an established reputation here yet."

"Sure, I'll put in a good word for you, son. You can mention Bertram Colby too. Clayton over at the title office has known both of us forever. Use our names if that'll win you some points."

"Thank you, sir." Jack stretched out his hand, and was quickly reminded that Sampson had a grip worthy of the hours the man spent pounding the anvil. "And one more thing. How's my wagon coming along? I didn't see any sign of it inside." Jack waited, expecting Sampson to have a good excuse.

Sampson glanced away. "Business has been right busy lately, but I guarantee you, I'll have it ready for you soon. Don't you be givin' me that look now. I'm not joshin' you. I've got enough work for two men at least."

"Why don't you hire someone, then? Cut down on your load. I'm sure there're men in this town who could use a job."

Disgust darkened Sampson's expression. "I've already tried three locals. Slack hands, every one of 'em. I reckon I could try again, but it's easier just to do a job right the first time than to come behind somebody and fix their foolishness." Sampson's brow shot up. "You wouldn't be interested in a second job now, would you, Brennan?"

Jacked waved him off. "My hands are full enough already, thanks mainly to you."

Sampson peered over Jack's shoulder. A grin puffed his bearded cheeks. "Well, you'd better get ready.... I think those hands o' yours are about to get a mite fuller."

Seeing Sampson's wink, Jack knew without turning around what he was referring to. Finally, he looked back.

Véronique scurried down the street toward them—another satchel in hand. If that woman didn't beat all.... She already had one loaded in the back. How many bags did she need for a day-trip? Then he thought about the incident with the skunk and was surprised she wasn't pulling a trunk behind her.

He started to give her a hard time about it, but when she drew closer, he guessed from the puffiness around her eyes that she'd been crying.

He hopped down and relieved her of the bag. "Is something wrong?"

"*Non*, I am quite well. *Merci*." Her smile appeared genuine, despite the obvious signs to the contrary. Looking around, she lifted her shoulders slightly and let them fall. "Are you ready to leave?"

Jack took the hint and stowed her second bag, which weighed next to nothing, beneath the bench seat, then helped her up. Whatever had upset her apparently wasn't open for discussion. And he knew better than to push.

When a woman didn't want to talk about something, it was best to let it rest until she did. He hadn't thought of it in ages, but he remembered the handful of times his Mary had been upset, and how it had served him best to let her cool down.

Three hours into the trip and still hardly a word out of her. Jack kept watch on the gray skies overhead, wary of the scent of moisture in the air. He snuck another glance beside him. She certainly didn't appear to be sad.

On the contrary, her eyes were bright and attentive to everything they passed. She seemed to be taking it all in—every bird flying overhead, every chipmunk scampering into the brush as the wagon approached. Even the increasing altitude didn't seem to bother her. Of course, the portion of road they were traveling was lined with clusters of aspens and willows, so the steep ledge was relatively obscured.

But if he read the terrain right, that would be changing soon enough.

"We'll stop in a few minutes to let the horses rest, and we'll eat some lunch. Sound good?"

She cut her eyes in his direction. "The . . . *horses?*"

Hearing the teasing lilt in her voice, he decided this was the break he'd been waiting for. "That's right. The horses. What else do you want me to call them?"

She had the droll look down to perfection. "These animals have been bestowed grand names worthy of—"

"Emperors, yes, I know. So you've said. Your Charlemagne I've read about, but who was this Napoleon Bonaparte?" He loved the way her jaw dropped in disbelief as she took the bait.

The library in Willow Springs was limited and claimed no books on French history. But he'd recalled seeing a history text among Mary's collection, and sure enough, it contained a brief chapter on European history. He'd reread that one a couple of nights earlier.

"Napoleon Bonaparte"—Véronique repeated the name, accentuating the French pronunciation—"was a great French leader. He expanded the empire through western Europe and accomplished many great things for our country."

"So he's your favorite leader in French history?" Anticipating her positive response, Jack readied his facts on a little incident he'd read about called Waterloo.

"*Non* . . ." She gave a shy chuckle. "I do not have a favorite leader, as you say it, but . . . there is one king in our history who I know better than others due to visiting his home, on many occasions. That would be Louis the Sixteenth."

The name was familiar to him, but Jack scrambled to remember that particular leader's distinction. "Wasn't he married to a Marie . . ."

"Marie Antoinette, *oui*. Very good, Jack. You are familiar with my country's history?"

He decided to come clean. "I only know a little. I've been reading up on you."

Her laughter trickled over him. "I am most impressed, and honored that you would do such a thing."

A tight switchback called for his undivided attention, and he turned his focus to the road ahead.

He felt Véronique tense beside him as the canyon to their right, on her side, opened wide into a yawning chasm that scooped deep into the mountain's belly. The beauty took his breath away, and apparently hers too—telling by the ashen color of her face.

CHAPTER | THIRTY-ONE

J ACK WATCHED HER knuckles go white as she gripped the seat between them. Her breath went shallow. Perhaps he should have warned her, but he doubted whether that would have made any difference.

In the interest of keeping her dignity intact—and his pants clean—he attempted to renew the conversation. "So what is it about this Louis the Sixteenth that makes him stand out in your memory?"

She didn't answer.

He turned and found her staring off into the chasm, her pallor dangerously pale.

"Véronique, look at me."

Slowly, she did as he asked. Fear was imbedded in her eyes.

Another curve loomed ahead. He had plenty of room to negotiate it, but he couldn't do that and see to her too—not if she reacted as she had the last time they'd faced a drop this sheer. The incline on the road was steep, and stopping wasn't his first preference—not with the extra heavy load in the back. The horses were straining enough as it was.

The pending curve demanded his attention. Maybe if she were closer to him she wouldn't be as frightened. He remembered that about his son. When Aaron had been scared of something and Jack had held him, it seemed all his tiny son's fears had evaporated. What a feeling it had been to have that power to comfort.

"Vernie, I want you to move over beside me." He thought for sure the nickname would get her.

But she didn't budge. She started to look back to her right.

Jack sharpened his voice. "Véronique!"

She jumped.

"Move over beside me *now*."

She scooted an inch or two, never letting go of the seat.

The road narrowed. "Closer."

She moved another inch at best. And glanced *again* at the chasm.

Jack hadn't had a problem with cursing in years, but a few insolent choices sprang to mind. He grabbed the reins with one hand and grabbed her with the other. If she were any closer now, he'd have to marry her.

"Hold on to me and close your eyes."

Wordless, she looped one arm through his and gripped his vest with her other hand.

"Are your eyes closed?"

She nodded against his shoulder.

"Now tell me why Louis the Sixteenth is your favorite."

She lifted her head.

"But tell me with your eyes closed." He intentionally softened his voice. "And no peeking."

The horses slowed, straining to negotiate the wagon around the curve. Jack knew they were tired and needed to rest. But first they had to get around this bend and over the ridge. He whipped the reins.

Véronique pressed her forehead into his shoulder, and he could feel the quick rise and fall of her chest.

After safely navigating the corner, he gently nudged her. "Louis the Sixteenth is your favorite because . . ."

"I did not say he was my favorite. He and his wife came to rather sad ends, in fact. Yet I admire their home . . . the Château de Versailles."

"And what is . . . the Château de Versailles?"

He heard a small gasp and wasn't sure if she was amused at his pronunciation, or if she was about to be sick. He braced himself just in case.

"The Château de Versailles was the residence of Louis the

Sixteenth and Marie Antoinette. It is quite simply . . . *magnifique.*"

"You've seen this place. . . ."

"*Ah oui.* My *maman* and I accompanied Lord Marchand, our employer, to parliamentary gatherings there on a number of occasions." Her death grip on his arm lessened a fraction. "I wandered the grounds with Christophe. He knew the palace well, as he had been there many times before me. He showed me all of the—"

"Tell me again who this Christophe fella is?" The question was out before Jack had thought it through.

"Christophe is . . ." She hesitated. "Christophe is a dear friend . . . back in Paris. We grew up together, he and I."

The pressure on Jack's arm increased, and he sensed that Christophe, and whatever the man represented in Véronique's life, wasn't a place to go at the moment. "What did you like best about the chateau?"

She gave a sigh. "Where to begin? When first the carriage pulls up, you see gardens spreading out in all directions. They are exquisite. The Versailles gardeners are elite artists of their trade. Always before, the gardens I had seen were planted in rows, but not so here. The shrubberies are arranged in patterns, to create a design, of sorts. And the flowers . . ." She blew out a breath. "They are everywhere, in every color on the palette. My mother used to say it was a feast for the eyes, God's way of nurturing the weary soul."

She quieted, and Jack felt compelled to speak, remembering the day at the livery when Sampson had confided in him about her history. "I've wanted to say something before now but . . . I'm sorry you lost your mother. Was it long ago?" He felt the shake of her head.

"She died shortly before I left Paris." Moments passed. "I remember our last visit to Versailles, not long before she grew ill. *Maman* finished with her duties for Lord Marchand and sought me out. Hand in hand, we walked the great expanse of the gardens"—her voice faltered—"all the way down to the Grand Canal."

Jack nodded. "Is that where the ships come in?"

She giggled. "*Non,* not the kind of ships you are picturing, I would imagine. It is where Louis the Fourteenth hosted his boating parties. But these were small boats. My mother and I picnicked there by the canal that afternoon, the two of us. We feasted on fresh bread, wine, and cheese. I still remember the taste on my tongue. I only wish

I'd known it would be our last time there. Perhaps I would have treasured it more."

From the tenderness in her voice, Jack doubted that was possible. He wondered if she was aware of the way she caressed his arm as she spoke. He figured she wasn't, but he could concentrate on little else.

He shifted in the seat, and her hand went still on his arm. "So is the house nice too?" He'd worded the question intentionally.

She swatted his arm. "The *palace* is also beyond compare. It is over two hundred years old. And yet it is more beautiful than ever. But the pinnacle, to me, is the long hallway lined with mirrors. I will never forget the first time I saw it. Lord Marchand instructed my mother and me to follow him. I remember because when we reached the closed doors, he bent down and told me to shut my eyes, that he had a surprise for me. And when I opened them, all that was before me was brilliance and sparkles."

That didn't sound like the actions of an employer to Jack, but more like those of a father. He spotted a place in the trail ahead where they could stop and rest Charlemagne and Napoleon. He guided the wagon over and set the brake.

Véronique gently disengaged herself from his arm and moved away. A shy smile turned her mouth. "Thank you once again, Jack, for the skill you have of removing my mind from what is at hand. Do not think I am blind to it."

He smiled at her phrasing. "My pleasure, Vernie."

She shook her head. "You insist on using that name."

"I like it. It suits your personality, in a way."

"We both know that using that name suits your personality far more than mine."

He laughed. "I'll concede to that." He held her waist as he lifted her down, and found himself none too eager to let go. She didn't move either. "But know that when I use it, it's meant in a kindly way. Endearing, if you will."

She considered this for a moment, fingering the buttons on his chest. "If that is true, then use it as often as you desire."

Over a lunch of corn bread and ham—courtesy of Mrs. Baird—Jack carefully broached the question lingering in his mind. "You've mentioned Lord Marchand before, along with a Francette. They were special people in your life?"

"*Oui*, Lord Marchand was my mother's employer, and mine. Francette is his daughter to whom I was a companion since the age of five."

As she described growing up in the Marchand household, things shifted into place for him. Véronique was far from the spoiled, rich daughter he'd first imagined, though it did sound as though all the privileges of that life and what it afforded had been hers. Which also explained the air she had about her at times. No wonder this territory seemed primitive to her. It was, by comparison.

He smiled as he watched her. He enjoyed the way she used her hands when she spoke, and if ever he wanted to quiet her down, he knew exactly what to do. Glancing at the position of the sun overhead and knowing the horses were well rested, he decided he needed to test that theory.

"But Francette and I were never close, not like you might think. Growing up, I had always wanted a sister. It did not matter to me whether she was older or younger. I simply—"

She stopped midsentence and stared at his hands covering hers. She lifted her eyes. "I am talking too much, *non*?"

"No, not at all. We just need to continue this conversation in the wagon."

Two hours later they approached Sluice Box, a tiny mining town literally perched on the side of a mountain. As Jack stole a look at Véronique beside him in the wagon, he sensed he knew more about the inner workings of her thoughts than anyone he'd known besides Mary. He'd felt comfortable to comment or not, and she'd apparently felt the same. The comfortable silences with her had been as enjoyable as the conversation, and even a tad more restful.

He tipped his head back to take in the view. He'd never understood the draw of mining, but he certainly saw why a man would want to stake his roots in this area of the country. God had worked overtime on this part of creation.

The grayish-white mist ghosting the highest peaks in early morning had finally relinquished to the sun's persistence, and its absence revealed the brilliant jagged heights of the uppermost summit. Jack wondered what it would be like to traverse those mountains in the full grip of winter. He thought of an article he'd read several years back about a party of travelers who had crossed the Sierra Nevadas in the winter. He shuddered remembering what they'd resorted to when they had become trapped by the weather and their food had run out.

Families traveling in his care had sometimes complained about the daily progress he demanded, but they had always appreciated reaching their destination before first snowfall. He'd never been one to take chances with the lives of others.

Nothing was that important.

Sluice Box was the tiniest town Jack had delivered to, but from the looks of the men spilling from tents pitched along the creek and from the saloon they'd just passed, Jack figured this was the roughest bunch they'd encountered so far. He reached for his rifle on the floor of the wagon and situated it against his thigh.

Picking out which of the three structures was the supply building was easy. The word *SUPLIES* had been painted in bold red letters over the doorway of the last building on the street. Whoever had written it apparently didn't hold to the use of a proper shingle, or with learning how to spell.

Jack kept an eye on the road and the growing number of miners flocking to the street. They called out to Véronique, some making crude gestures he hoped she didn't see. He unlocked the safety on his rifle. "We're going to do this as fast as possible. I'll unload the supplies and—"

"I will say nothing, I promise. But please, do not leave me, Jack. If you go inside the building, take me with you."

He gritted his teeth at the fear in her voice, and for allowing this situation in the first place. He held himself responsible. "You're not leaving this wagon, and I'm not going anywhere. Behind the seat is a blanket. Grab it and cover yourself with it."

Without question, she did as he asked.

"Here, take this." He slipped his Schofield revolver into her lap. "It's loaded, and the safety is off."

She stared at the gun nesting in the folds of the blanket as though it were a snake. "But you have not yet taught me how to shoot it."

"I know, and chances are you won't have to today. All you have to know for now is to point and pull the trigger. But don't do *anything* without my signal. You understand?"

She nodded.

"Now take hold of the handle and let it rest in your lap where they can see it." It would've been safer for him to leave her outside of town than to bring her into this.

He couldn't believe his next thought—he saw no signs of a brothel anywhere. And for once, he found that discovery disturbing.

The single street running through town was unusually narrow. The left side boasted what little commerce Sluice Box offered, its few buildings crammed against the wall of the mountain. Tents and makeshift shelters dotted the other side, which was the bank of a creek running high with winter melt-off. There was no way to head the wagon in the opposite direction in a single turn. It would take a series of maneuvers, which meant he couldn't do it quickly.

As they neared the supply building, a man stepped out. He was shorter than Jack, but his upper body was twice as thick. He looked like a tree trunk with legs.

He peered up. "Jack Brennan?"

Jack nodded, pulling back on the reins. He set the brake and kept his rifle in clear view. "Sol Leevy?"

Intended or not, the fella gave off an air of indifference. According to Hochstetler's records, Leevy ran both the mine and the supply store. And none too well from the looks of things.

Leevy's focus shifted to Véronique, and he arranged himself right in front of her.

She lowered her eyes, but showed no other reaction Jack could discern.

Jack's finger rested on the trigger of his rifle. "I've got your supplies. Let's get them unloaded. I've got another delivery up the mountain this afternoon and they're expecting me." He purposefully spoke only of himself, not wanting to draw any more attention to Véronique than her presence did already.

Leevy's stare encompassed the men gathered. "Well, if they're just expectin' you, Brennan, then maybe you can leave the woman with us. You can pick her up on your way back through in a couple weeks."

Laughter rang out, followed by several vulgar suggestions of what Véronique could do if she were to stay.

"Take off the blanket, missy. We want to see what you're hidin'."

Another man standing by the wagon just below Véronique cursed. "Blanket, ha! Go ahead and take off everything, honey." Then he named exactly what he wanted to see.

Jack didn't dare look at Véronique, but he could feel the heat of her humiliation. Anger built white-hot inside him. He cocked the rifle, and the raucous laughter died. He aimed the gun square at the man's chest. Despite the cool air, beads of sweat trickled down his back. "I don't appreciate you speaking that way about my wife. An apology is in order."

The majority of smiles dissolved. Seconds ticked by in tense silence.

The fella stared back hard. "Come on, we were just havin' some fun. Can't blame us for wantin' to—"

Jack lowered his aim to something he figured the man might consider more valuable.

The man backed up a step. His face reddened. "I'm sorry, missus." His jaw went rigid. "I shouldn't have said what I did."

Jack held the man in his sights for a few seconds more, then lowered the gun.

The miner turned and elbowed his way through the crowd. The others shoved him back, snickering as he passed.

Jack sized up the rest of men pressing close around the wagon. Young and old, foul best described them, both in manner and in their unbathed state. The responsibility he felt for Véronique rested like an anvil on his chest.

Leevy gestured to the cargo in the wagon bed. "So that's not all for me, then."

Jack took a steadying breath. "Half belongs to you. Your order's loaded in the back."

"I might be persuaded to take more."

Jack heard the unspoken question. "More's not available this time, Leevy. If you want additional supplies, I'll bring them back through when I come next."

Murmurs rippled through the crowd, and all attention shifted to Leevy.

Jack quickly gathered that their boss wasn't accustomed to being told no.

Leevy barked an order, and two men stepped up and began

untying the roped netting. "Why don't you come inside, Brennan, and we'll negotiate a sum."

"The total is listed at the bottom of your order. It's nonnegotiable. Pricing won't change on a whim like it has in the past. I'll treat you fairly . . . and I expect the same in return." Jack held out the order slip, then finally let it drop. It drifted and settled near Leevy's boots. "Pay me and we'll be on our way." Being the only supplier currently operating this route, Jack felt relatively confident in his bargaining position.

Where that confidence ended was in the possibility of any harm coming to Véronique.

Leevy's glare went steely before he strode back into the building.

Jack kept an eye on the men unloading the supplies and signaled when they reached the large crate at the middle. "That's as far as yours goes." Law and order was fluid in such a place, and men with the most power were commonly the ones who controlled the tide. In Sluice Box, that appeared to be Leevy.

Jack reached down and lightly touched Véronique on the shoulder. She didn't look up. With one hand she gripped the Schofield, with the other she clutched the blanket to her chest.

Both hands trembled.

Leevy returned, money in hand. He approached Jack's side of the wagon and handed up the cash. His focus went to the remaining cargo in the back, then briefly settled on Véronique. "I'm still interested in what you've got in your bed, Brennan."

Jack stared, unblinking.

Leevy finally let out a laugh. "You really need to work on your sense of humor, Brennan—you know that?"

Jack counted the cash and pocketed it. "You really need to work on your sense of decency, Leevy." His gaze swept the town. "And from the looks of it, how you run things around here too."

Leevy's expression darkened. He nodded toward the supplies. "Last chance, Brennan. Everything you've got left—cash on the table. You willin' to deal?"

Jack remembered the warning Rousseau had given him a while back at the Peerless. He could flatly refuse Leevy's offer, and chances were slim the man would do anything in front of all these witnesses. But on the road, maybe not this time, or even the next, but somewhere down the line, he might retaliate. And what if Véronique was with him when that happened? It was one thing for him to take the risk, but for her . . . If anything happened to her because of this, he wouldn't be able to move past it. He wasn't strong enough to go through that again.

Yet Jack knew that if he gave in, there would be no limit to Leevy's future demands. He quickly weighed his options. If Leevy's issue was only about supplies, he'd dump the load of them in the center of town himself. But it wasn't. It was about integrity. And honor. And truth. And doing what was right, no matter the cost.

There was only one option Jack could live with.

"No deal. These supplies are spoken for, and they're headed up the mountain." He reached for the reins in order to maneuver the wagon around.

Leevy's face went stony. "Well, it's good to know where we stand, Brennan. I'll look forward to our future dealings." He touched the rim of his hat. "You two have a safe journey." Challenge tainted his smirk. "Especially you . . . Mrs. Brennan."

CHAPTER THIRTY-TWO

THE TENSION AND FURY emanating from Jack was enough to keep Véronique silent for a good ten minutes after they'd passed the outskirts of Sluice Box. Then she couldn't stand it any longer.

She moved closer to him on the seat. "Jack, may I ask why you told them I was—"

"Véronique, not yet."

She promptly closed her mouth, and let her eyes roam the line of pine trees nestling her side of the road.

Jack's rifle rested between his thighs, and the revolver he'd originally given to her was tucked back in his trousers. She noticed his grip on the reins. He was holding them so tightly his hands were shaking. Or were his hands shaking for some other reason?

She had an inkling as to why he had introduced her as his wife but wanted to hear it from him. Not that it had offended her. Surprised her, yes, but not offended. Perhaps if she approached it from a different angle. "Would you have truly shot that man?"

"Véronique, please . . ." His voice was intense but soft, not the least harsh, and that's when she knew.

She slowly faced forward. The pounding of Charlemagne's and Napoleon's massive hooves scattered what silence there might have been. She'd never seen Jack Brennan truly frightened before. Nervous in closed spaces, yes, but this was different. Truth be told, she hadn't imagined it was possible for him to be so scared.

As soon as she had processed the thought, she realized how silly it was. Everyone was afraid of something.

What Christophe had once told her, was true. Sometimes there wasn't the space for words. Or the need. There were other ways to communicate. She looked at Jack and clearly read fear in his stern expression and tense jaw. Words weren't needed. Not yet.

She scooted closer and slid her hand between his as he gripped the reins.

Jack held onto her hand as tightly as he held the leather straps. But she didn't mind. She liked the feel of his hands on hers. She was content to ride like this all the way to the next town, then back down the mountain to Willow—

Jack exhaled an audible breath, brought the wagon to a stop, and set the brake. He lifted her hand to his lips and kissed it once, and then again. Then he circled her waist and pulled her against him. He kissed her forehead. His hands moved over her arms, her back, then to her shoulders and her arms again. They seemed to have taken on a mind of their own.

Then he went absolutely still. He couldn't seem to catch his breath.

Véronique knew the feeling.

With her head tucked beneath his chin, she reached up and touched his cheek, wanting to comfort him, wanting to relieve him of whatever burden he carried. And she wished she could find the words to tell him how proud she was of how he'd conducted himself back in that town.

The upper part of his cheek was smooth against her fingertips, and at the same time the lower half was rough against her palm. "Everything is all right now." She kept her voice soft. "I am not afraid anymore."

A noise rose from within his throat. Not a sigh really. Something more. With one hand, he cradled the nape of her neck. With the other, he caressed her lower back.

"Jack?"

"Yes?" he finally whispered.

"May I say something else?"

He gave a soft laugh. "Will I be able to stop you?"

She pulled back slightly in order to see him. And at the look in his eyes, she forgot everything except the unspoken promise he'd made to her at Casaroja, after the birth of the foal. But was she ready for him to keep that promise? No, she wasn't ready! She'd never done this. Well, that wasn't quite true. . . .

Jack brushed a strand of hair from her face. With his finger, starting at her brow, he traced an achingly slow path down her temple and across the curve of her cheek. "What was it you wanted to say?"

She swallowed. With him this close, doing what he was doing, it was hard enough for her to breathe, much less hold a thought in her head. "I was wanting to say . . . how proud I . . ."

He placed soft kisses on her forehead, lingering between each one.

Christophe had kissed her once, but it hadn't been anything like this. And then Véronique realized—both with pleasure and panic—that Jack hadn't really kissed her yet. Not on the lips like Christophe had done.

"If you're going to say something, Véronique, I sure wish you'd do it soon."

She nodded, struggling to remember both what she had wanted to say, and how a kiss was supposed to work. "I think . . . I was saying . . . how proud . . ."

He kissed her cheek, then the edge of her mouth, and his warm breath against her skin chased away the last fleeting hope of capturing any thought.

"Jack?"

"Yes?"

"I cannot remember."

"In that case"—he pulled back slightly—"may I say something?"

Knowing what he was asking, she reached up and touched his mouth. "Oh, I wish you would. . . ."

She tasted like fine wine, sweet and rich. Jack kissed her mouth, her cheek, her mouth again, and in his mind, he covered the soft hollow at the base of her throat.

He didn't realize how much he'd been anticipating this until she'd taken his hand a mile or so back. His relief at having gotten out of Sluice Box unscathed poured through him again. He would not bring her with him anymore. His heart nearly failed him every time he thought about what could have happened back there. What could happen in any one of the towns they had visited.

Her hands stayed on his shoulders, and with no small effort, he kept his from wandering. Their kiss grew more heated, and Jack knew they needed to stop.

He was just about to pull away, when *she* deepened the kiss.

He didn't know what to do at first, and then quickly knew exactly what he needed to do. And fast! He gently broke the kiss and untwined his fingers from her hair.

Her eyes remained closed, her lips parted and slightly swollen.

Any question he'd had about her feelings for him had been answered. And then some. And no doubt she knew how he felt.

"Vernie?"

She couldn't seem to catch her breath. *"Oui?"*

Heaven help him, he wanted to kiss her again. He put distance between them on the seat, wishing he could get out and walk . . . for about three days.

Either sensing or feeling his retreat, she opened her eyes. And blinked.

He released the wagon brake and gathered the reins. "We need to be on our way."

She lightly touched the corners of her mouth and nodded. Her expression clouded, and she reached for his arm. "Jack, did I . . ."

He waited, having no idea what she was going to ask him.

The blush on her cheeks deepened. "Did I do something wrong?"

He stared, not understanding. But when he saw the doubt reflected in her eyes, her question became clear. He gave a soft laugh, filled more with irony than humor. "No, you didn't do anything wrong, believe me."

"But you stopped when I"—uncertainty lined her brow—"kissed you back."

Is that what she called it? Jack rubbed the muscles in his neck. For one so stuck on etiquette and staying within the lines, she was approaching a boundary best left unexplored between them.

And then it hit him—she had no idea what effect she had on him. No idea how easily moved he was by her.

"Véronique . . ." Jack glanced at the reins in his hands and cleared his throat. He didn't want to embarrass either of them, but he also didn't want her thinking she was inadequate, in any way. "The reason I . . . stopped just now is because if we'd kept on, I—" He found he couldn't do it. Not even as husband and wife had he and Mary spoken so plainly about such things. "The reason I stopped is that we need to be getting back on the road. We've got a schedule to keep, and I'm afraid we might run out of daylight before we get back to Willow Springs." Flimsy excuse, but she seemed to be buying it.

Relief slowly replaced the concern in her expression. "I only inquire because . . . What I am intending to say is . . ." She lifted a shoulder and looked down at her lap. "I have only done this once before. And the kiss with Christophe—" she slowly raised her chin— "did not have the effect on me the way yours did now."

Jack suddenly had trouble breathing. He didn't know how to respond to such honesty. Then he found he had to curb a grin when thinking about Christophe. *Poor fella.*

He'd forgotten how powerful the touch and taste of a woman could be. After Mary's death, he'd asked God to take away that physical yearning, and for the most part, God had answered those prayers—up until now. Now it felt like God had stopped listening and had opened the floodgates.

Jack took the opportunity to look at Véronique, her head bowed again, her hands folded in her lap, and a tender passion threaded through him. Mary was gone, and he was a different man now—but the fact that he was experiencing this depth of feeling for another woman, after having been so blessed with Mary, just didn't feel right somehow. He didn't feel deserving, and he struggled with a sense of unfaithfulness. Guilt tugged him at that silent confession, no matter how illogical.

Véronique lifted her face.

Seeing the fragile look in her eyes, the trusting innocence, Jack knew he was going to have to tread carefully where this woman was concerned. He reached over and covered her hand on the seat between them. "About what I did back in that town, Véronique. I figured they might be a bit more respectful if they thought you were my wife. It wasn't planned on my part, it just kind of came out. I'm sorry if that offended you."

Her eyes narrowed playfully. "Offended—to cause difficulty,

discomfort, or injury." She gently fingered her chin. "*Non*, monsieur. I do not believe 'offended' describes the emotion I was feeling when you referred to me as your wife." Her gaze went to his mouth, and she smiled.

Knowing he'd better get this wagon moving, Jack gave the reins a flick. Charlemagne and Napoleon surged forward, apparently eager to get back on task. Jack was mentally counting the hours back to Willow Springs when he remembered they still had another drop to make. It was later in the day and they were behind schedule. It would be well past dark, again, before they made it back down the mountain. He noticed an unhealthy pattern developing in that regard.

Sol Leevy's parting comment returned to him, and he weighed the option of heading back to Willow Springs immediately. But with his schedule it would be two weeks or more before he could make another run to this area, and the town was overdue on getting supplies. He stopped the wagon again and retrieved his map.

"Do we not know where we are, Jack?"

He laughed at the unexpected question, and at how she'd phrased it. "Losing faith in me so soon?" He shook his head at the bland look she gave him. "I'm just checking the distance to the next town. The turnoff doesn't look too far ahead. A couple of miles up the trail, maybe three." This close, it made sense to go ahead and make the run.

She rubbed her arms.

"You cold?"

"A little."

This was the opportunity he'd been waiting for. He set the brake and reached behind him for the package he'd tucked there earlier that morning. "Here you go." He set the brown wrapped box on the seat between them.

"What is this?"

"Open it and find out."

Her eyes gained a sparkle, and she ripped into the paper like a child on Christmas morning. She lifted the box lid. "Oh, Jack . . ." She glanced up at him, tears in her eyes. "It is beautiful." She pulled the coat from the box and stood, holding it up against her. "And the color . . ."

"I tried to get a color that would match your eyes. Mrs. Dunston was wrapping it that day I ran into you at the dress shop." He pointed to the sleeves. "She did some altering on it too, since she's familiar with your size." He stood and helped her put it on. The coat fell just below midcalf, right where Mrs. Dunston said it would.

Véronique ran her hands down along the sides. "How can I thank you, Jack? Your gift is so thoughtful of me. *You* are so thoughtful." She put a hand to his chest and reached up to kiss his cheek. She lingered after, and Jack knew what she was lingering for.

He was going to need to speak with the Almighty about those floodgates. "I'm glad you like it. Listen, we need to be—"

"Getting back on the road?" she whispered.

He smiled at her humor. "Yes, ma'am, we do."

She nodded, then paused. "What is this?" Her hand rummaged inside the right pocket of the coat. She pulled out the jar and read the label. "'C.O. Bigelow Apothecaries of New York. Lemon Lotion.'" A brow rose.

"I bought it at the mercantile a while back, on a whim." Jack shrugged. "I liked the way it smelled. . . . It reminded me of the prairie and the years I spent guiding wagons. But I've never used it, and I figured you might."

She unscrewed the lid and sniffed. A most peculiar expression came over her face. Her eyes glistened. "This scent resembles a lotion I brought with me from Paris. My favorite, and that of my *maman*. I used the last of it shortly after arriving in this country." She stared at him for a long moment. "*Merci beaucoup*, Jack."

Longing to take her up on the offer in her eyes and the softness in her voice, Jack wrestled his attention back to the trail.

The wind had picked up a notch, and the sun ducked behind the clouds, before reappearing momentarily. He was debating whether to put the tarpaulin over the cargo bed when the first raindrop hit his arm.

By the time he had climbed back in the wagon minutes later, not another drop of rain had fallen. The gray skies were probably harmless enough, but at least the supplies were protected if the weather changed.

"Would you desire for me to drive for a while, monsieur?"

He tried not to laugh too hard. But with the reins in her hands and her tiny feet braced on the footrest, she almost looked like she knew what she was doing. "Sure, *mademoiselle*, I could use a rest."

She gave the reins a hard flick and he was jolted hard against the seatback.

"I didn't know you were serious!" He sat close, ready to grab the reins, but she was actually doing pretty well. And she seemed to be enjoying it, so he let her be.

Véronique giggled, keeping her focus on the road. "I tell you this now. . . . As soon as the trees leave us, I do not think it would be wise for me to continue."

He knew exactly what she was saying. This part of the trail was shielded on both sides by thick stands of towering pine and aspen, with the occasional willow challenging their ranks. Their bowers met far above the trail to form a natural canopy that would be welcome if it rained. The view of the canyon, Jack's favorite part of these trips, wasn't visible yet.

The afternoon sun drifted behind some clouds, leaving the trail draped in shadows. They'd gone well over a mile when a tingling sensation crept up the back of Jack's neck. The air seemed to thin, and he took a few extra breaths to clear his head.

He sat up a bit straighter and scanned both sides of the road, searching the shadows hiding behind the trees and crouching between the rocks and boulders. He watched for movement of any kind.

Nothing.

Perhaps it was only his imagination causing his heart to race, or maybe it was the weight of responsibility he felt for the woman beside him. Véronique didn't appear to sense anything out of the ordinary, but he couldn't shake the foreboding feeling.

Leaning forward, he rolled his shoulders and stretched, and as he sat back, he casually picked up his rifle from the floor of the wagon, not wanting to alarm her.

"You are tired, *non*?"

"No, not really." He drew the gun up beside his left leg, pretty sure she hadn't noticed. He blinked, not certain if his vision had hazed or if the shadows on the trail were playing tricks on him. He wondered if the closeness of the trail was bothering him, but he didn't feel like he had back in the cave.

He spotted the turnoff ahead, leading up to the right. "Why don't you let me take over here?"

She brought the wagon to a stop. "I have done well, *non*?"

"You've done very well." He kept his voice lowered, and in the brief seconds following, he examined the silence and heard only the wind in the trees and the cry of a hawk he couldn't see.

"Lilly taught me how to drive. I am only capable of going forward for now, but she and I have another lesson planned for later this week."

"That's real good. I appreciate you giving me a break." He smiled and figured it came across as genuine by the looks of the one she returned. He took the reins and guided the wagon up the turnoff, glancing behind them as they went. It felt good to be driving again, and as the wagon ascended the path, his nerves eased considerably.

It was a steeper incline than he'd expected from the map's notations, and Jack made a mental note to jot that on the drawing later. Looking ahead, he breathed easier when his side of the road opened to the canyon below. The slope angled down about ten feet to the first shelf, then dropped sheer off to the bottom of the ravine. "You can move closer, if you'd like."

She came without hesitation, and looped her hand through the crook of his arm.

After going a ways farther, he finally attributed his earlier sense of foreboding to a case of nerves. Nothing more.

"You did very well in the tunnel of trees, Jack."

He glanced down. "You knew?"

She smiled and squeezed his arm. "Mmm . . . at first, not so much. But then in your posture and the way you breathed, I knew something was not right."

The woman was more observant that he'd given her credit for being.

Rounding the first curve in the switchback road, Jack saw the felled tree just before Charlemagne and Napoleon did. The horses reared, and the wagon jolted forward, then slid back until the horses regained their footing.

"Whoa!" Jack held the reins taut and searched the upper ridge. Sol Leevy was the first to come to mind, but there was no way Leevy and his men could've gotten ahead of them to do this without being seen. Unless he'd planned it beforehand, which didn't seem likely under the circums—

A single raindrop hit Jack's hand. Then another. He peered up into the steely skies.

CHAPTER THIRTY-THREE

THE SKIES OPENED UP and, within minutes, reduced the road to mud. Véronique wrapped her new coat around her upper body, thankful for the warmth and for how the water cascaded off the resilient material.

Holding her hand at her brow, she strained to see Jack's face as he strode back toward the wagon. She needed to read his expression in order to know whether she should be alarmed, but the angle of his hat blocked her view. He approached her side of the wagon.

When he lifted his head, her stomach went cold.

"You need to get out."

She could barely hear him above the rain. She began to climb down and had her boot situated on the edge of the buckboard when he lifted her in his arms and carried her to the side of the road. He set her down and she tipped her head back to see him. But when she did, the rain in her eyes made the effort useless, so she kept her head down. "Can the tree be moved?"

"Not without a saw and a good half day's work." He strode back to the wagon and pulled something from beneath the seat, then returned and draped the blanket over their heads. Surprisingly the cloth repelled the moisture, and the water ran in rivulets off the blanket's edge.

"Do we not have a saw?"

"I've got one in the back, but I'll need to unload some of the supplies in order to get to it."

She looked up, able to see him now. Droplets of water clung to his stubbled jaw. "I will help you do this."

A smile briefly touched his mouth, and disappeared. "I appreciate that, but I can handle that part. It's cutting the tree and moving it out that's going to take some doing. I can barely see two feet in front of me, and that's a steep drop."

"Charlemagne and Napoleon are able to help with this work, *non*?"

He took a moment to answer. "Charlemagne looks fine but Napoleon's foreleg caught part of the tree when he reared up. It's not bleeding too badly, but I won't know for sure until I can see it better." With one arm he held the blanket over their heads, and with the other he gently urged her to follow him. "I'll get you situated, then come back and brace the wagon and see to the horses."

She stopped. "I do not need to be situated, Jack. I told you I will help you do this."

"Véronique, I'm not of the mind to argue with you right now. If the rain doesn't stop, we're going to be stuck out here most of the night just clearing that tree."

While she could think of worse things than spending a few hours alone with Jack Brennan, being stuck on the side of a mountain in a rainstorm wasn't at all appealing—not with the wind blowing as it was. "Neither am I *of the mind*"—she mimicked him as best she could—"to argue with you at this moment. I am simply offering you my services."

He stared down, conflicting emotions warring on his face. "The temperature's going to drop. It's going to get cold. We're going to be wet, Véronique. Please, just let me do my job."

"*Oui*, that is what I am trying to do. Now how do we brace the wagon?"

His jaw muscles clenched. He shook his head and sighed. "With rocks. Same as what's in that pretty little hea—" He made for the wagon, taking the blanket with him.

"*Pardonnes-moi?* I did not hear all of what you said."

Véronique could see where to walk well enough, but the rain-slicked trail combined with the steep incline made the ground slippery beneath her boots. She picked her way, taking one step for every three of Jack's. Apparently his boots were better suited for this terrain than were hers.

Spotting him ahead, she went and knelt beside him and picked up a rock, then traced his path to the wagon. She could only manage a stone a third the size of his but planned to make up for it in quantity.

"Place yours there." He pointed to the wheel. "Behind and around that bigger one. The rain's going to wash out the dirt so we'll need to pack them in there good and tight."

She did exactly as he said, and by the time they'd gathered enough rocks for the front two wheels, she was exhausted.

Jack, however, didn't even appear to be winded.

Véronique flexed her fingers. The palms of her hands had begun to sting.

Kneeling by the wagon, they had just started packing the fourth wheel when a deep rumble rolled toward them from overhead. It picked up momentum as it roared over the mountains. Véronique covered her ears as Jack's arm came around her shoulders. From the corner of her eye, she saw a jagged burst of light shoot down from the clouds. An explosion sounded nearby, followed by a plume of flame that the rain swiftly extinguished.

"What was that?" she shouted.

He leaned close. "Don't you have lightning in France?"

"*Oui*, of course we have it. But it is not like that."

He pointed to the sky. "It's because we're up so high." He studied the wagon wheel, then the storm. "That'll have to do for now. I'll grab some food from the back and we'll take shelter."

Famished, she nodded, thankful the rock work was done.

By the time Jack had retrieved the food and saw, and secured the cover over the wagon again, the last hint of daylight had disappeared behind the tallest peaks, and the darkness of night had begun to descend. Despite her coat, Véronique shivered, the rain having somehow sleuthed its way past the protection of the outer garment. Her shirtwaist was wet, as was her chemise beneath.

Jack handed her a sack of food and resituated the blanket over her head and shoulders. Rain trickled off the wide brim of his hat.

She reached up and flicked the edge of it with her finger. "It keeps you dry in the rain?"

"It does. My head anyway." He cinched the blanket closer beneath her chin. "Stay here ... please. I'll see to the horses and come right back. If you hear thunder again, get next to the cliff wall and huddle close to the ground."

He hadn't taken six steps before the darkness and sheets of rain enveloped him.

Véronique stared at the spot where he'd disappeared and found herself thanking God again for this man and for what he was helping her do. If someone had asked her one year ago what she would be doing today, never would she have imagined being in such place, under such circumstances. Yet looking back, she could see the faintest shadow of a line connecting events in her life leading up to this moment. Though she had not seen it then, God had seen, and perhaps her mother too, and they'd been preparing her for this journey.

Something cracked on the ridge above her head.

She peered up. With the rain, she could make out only the edge of the overhang and roots protruding from rocky crevices.

Seconds later it sounded again, farther down. Perhaps Jack had found a passage to the top and they would have shelter for the night. With relief, she spotted him walking toward her. She squinted as he drew closer.

Only it wasn't Jack.

And the man had a gun.

JACK HEARD VÉRONIQUE SCREAM his name.

He dropped the harness and grabbed his rifle. Panic gripped his chest. The wind whipped the rain sideways, and runnels of water channeled downhill. Twice he nearly lost his footing.

He spotted her, backed up against the cliff, and then made out the blurred outline of a man only a few feet away.

He raised his gun and took aim. "Come no closer!"

The man went stock-still, his rifle lowered at his side. He raised his other hand in a sign of truce. "I mean you no harm. I saw your wagon from above and came to see if I could help."

Jack slowly approached him. "What are you doing out here, on a night like this?"

"I live just over the ridge. Shot a buck earlier and was on my way home."

Both answers raised suspicion. Jack hadn't seen any dwellings in this area since they'd left Sluice Box. "Where's the deer?"

The man gestured behind him, never turning his head. "I left it up on the ridge before I came down."

Likely answer. Jack wished he could see the man closer up, gain a glimpse of his face, get a better sense of whether he was telling the truth. But the storm had brought night on early and the man had his coat pulled up around his neck.

"Listen, friend . . ." The stranger slowly lowered his hand. "My family and I would welcome you and your wife in our home for the night, if you need a place to stay. I can stable your horses too. There's a path on down the road a piece where we can lead them over the ridge. But if you'd rather stay here, I'll walk back out just like I walked in. It's your call."

It didn't add up to Jack that this fella just happened to be out wandering the forest. Not with the threats, both those spoken and otherwise, they'd had in their visits to the mining towns. But one thing was certain—Sol Leevy and his men wouldn't walk in like this man had done, rifle lowered, offering a truce.

A quick glance at Véronique confirmed she was soaked clean through. If this guy was telling the truth, he offered a much better alternative to spending the night outside.

Relying on instinct, and hoping it was accurate, Jack slowly lowered his gun. "We're much obliged. Let me unhitch the horses and get a few things from the wagon."

His attention never leaving the man, Jack walked to where Véronique stood. She laid a hand to his chest, and he quickly covered it.

"Can we trust him?" Her voice was low, and he could feel her shivering. "And what of all your supplies?"

"My gut tells me we can trust him. And if it comes to it, everything in that wagon can be replaced, Vernie. Get what you need for the night. We'll leave the wagon and come back for it in the morning." He squeezed her hand before letting it go.

The stranger fell into step beside them as they walked to the wagon. "From up top it looked like you've got a pretty full load."

Something about the man's voice rekindled Jack's suspicion. "We do. I run supplies to the mining towns. We were on our way up to Quandry but ran into some trouble."

The man nodded, looking past the wagon. "I saw the tree. I'll come back with you in the morning and we'll get it cleared."

"That's kind of you, sir. I'm Jack Brennan"—he shook the man's hand—"and this is Véronique . . . my wife."

"Pleasure to meet you both." Looking at Véronique, the man touched the rim of his hat. "I'm Larson Jennings. And my wife, Kathryn, will be more excited about me bringing you home, ma'am, than that buck up on the hill. She'll enjoy the chance to visit with another lady."

"We are grateful for your generosity, Monsieur Jennings, and I am most eager to meet your wife."

A woman met them at the door of the rustic cabin and welcomed them inside. The first thing Véronique noticed about Kathryn Jennings was the way she greeted her husband. She kissed him full on the mouth and hugged him tight, despite his being soaked.

The next thing she noticed, as he turned toward her, was Larson Jennings's eyes—and his face.

His eyes were a startling, piercing blue. But his face and neck were covered with scars. She made an effort not to wince when she first looked at him. Then she realized she'd been looking at him for the past half hour as they'd followed him home, only the darkness and his coat pulled high about his neck had masked the disfigurement.

It shamed her to admit, even to herself, that had she first met Larson Jennings in the daylight, she would not have been receptive to him.

Larson took off his coat and made the introductions, and Véronique accepted Kathryn's outstretched hands. She glanced at Jack, expecting him to jump in and explain that they weren't truly husband and wife, but he seemed oblivious.

"It's such a pleasure to have you in our home." Kathryn seemed as gracious as she was beautiful. "And your timing is perfect. I've been holding dinner for Larson, so we can all eat together."

"Papa!"

A little boy ran from a side room, his arms outstretched. Larson grabbed him up and nuzzled the boy's neck.

The boy squealed in delight, pushing against his father's stubbled chin. "That tickles, Papa!"

Véronique laughed along with them until she caught Jack's wistful expression. Beneath his smile lingered . . . longing. She recognized it only because it so closely resembled her own. His attention drifted, and she followed it to see a little girl toddling toward them in stocking feet. Her steps were new and unsteady, and too late, Véronique tried to reach out and catch the child before she fell.

The toddler's sweet face crumpled when her knees hit the wooden floor.

Kathryn scooped her up and dusted her off. "Oh, sweetie, it's all right. Look who's home!" She moved closer to her husband, glancing back over her shoulder. "May I present our children—William and Katie."

Larson set his son down and gave his dark hair a tousle, then reached for his daughter. Véronique noticed he wasn't nearly so boisterous with her. He cradled the side of her little blond head and kissed her nose, whispering her name over and over.

The tiny angel tucked her head beneath her father's chin, looked at Véronique, and smiled.

Véronique returned it, and felt her throat starting to ache. "How old is she?"

Larson pressed a kiss to the crown of Katie's head. "She'll be a year old in a couple of months."

Véronique couldn't stop the tears from welling. What would it be like to hear her father whisper her name with such tender affection? To be treated in such a cherished manner? "*Très belle.* She is beautiful," she whispered, hoping her tears would pass for adoration.

She thought they had, until Jack slipped an arm around her waist.

"Are we ready to eat?" Larson pulled a chair back from the table.

Running a hand through her wet hair, Véronique saw the look Kathryn gave her husband.

"Men . . ." Kathryn rolled her eyes and took Véronique by the hand. "Larson, you and Jack help yourself to some corn bread. I'll put a batch of biscuits in the stove in a minute. But first . . ." She gestured toward a room off to the side. "I'm going to help Véronique into some other clothes so hers can dry. Mr. Brennan, my husband can help you with whatever you need."

After dinner, Kathryn excused herself to get the children ready for bed. "Would you like to help me, Véronique?"

Surprised at the invitation, Jack waited to see how Véronique would respond.

"*Oui,* I would like that very much." Véronique reached out and made a pinching motion at William, who giggled and promptly ran into the next room.

"We'll be back shortly." Kathryn scooped up Katie and glanced at her husband. "Then we'll have some pie."

Larson pushed back from the table. "I need to see to that buck I shot back on the ridge first. That'll take a while."

"I'd be happy to help." Jack stood and reached for his coat. "The work'll go faster with two of us."

"That'd be much appreciated, Jack."

Thunder rumbled overhead as they walked out to the barn. Rain fell in thick sheets, and if the temperature dropped much lower, they'd awaken to snow. Jack winced just thinking about it. Snow would only further hinder their trip to Quandry—and anywhere else.

He helped Larson hoist the carcass of the deer so that it hung head up from a rafter. Jennings made a circular cut around the throat, connecting it with the cut made in the stomach during the field dressing. His movements were smooth and expert—surprising with the apparent injuries he'd suffered. The scars covering his face, neck, and hands bespoke an acquaintance with physical pain that Jack could not imagine.

They worked in silence as if they'd done this together a thousand times before. They removed the hide and cut the meat into slabs, then stored it in readied barrels, covering it with brine. They walked a short distance to the creek to wash up, and Jack's hands were nearly numb when they finished. He figured Larson's were too.

Arriving back at the cabin, they found the main room empty. A sliver of pale orange still glowed beneath the children's bedroom door, and he caught soft murmurs of conversation.

Larson reached for the coffee pot still warming on the stove. "Kathryn doesn't get the chance to visit with women much, so we might not see them for a while."

Seating himself at the table, Jack wrapped his hands around his cup, noticing that Jennings did the same. "I sure appreciate you coming along when you did today, Larson. It would've been a miserable night out there for the two of us."

"I remember a similar night years ago, when Kat and I were first married. We got stuck out in a storm like this, maybe not quite so cold. But I tell you, Jack, it wasn't half bad." Giving Jack a look, he smiled and sipped his coffee. "I wasn't too sure then how Kathryn would do out here. But she's done well. Better than I have in some ways. So don't you worry."

Jack caught Jennings's meaning, and what he was inferring about Véronique. He also realized that Jennings and his wife still thought the two of them were married. "About that, I—"

The door to the side room opened and the women appeared, no children in tow. Véronique wore an odd expression on her face, and Jack got the feeling she wanted to speak with him privately.

"Katie's asleep, but William woke up after dozing for a bit," Kathryn said. "Larson, he said you promised him a story about a . . . wolf cat?"

Larson's expression turned sheepish. "Something he came up with, Kat. I don't know where he got it from."

"Uh-huh." Kathryn nodded, her brow raised. "Well, just see to it that the story's not so scary he can't fall asleep again." She turned to Jack. "I was just telling Véronique that Larson and I will sleep in with the children tonight, and the two of you can have our bedroom. We just need to get a few things out of there first."

Jack saw Véronique's eyes go wide. "That won't be necessary, Mrs. Jennings, I—"

"I'm afraid we insist on it, friend." Larson slipped an arm around Kathryn's waist and pulled her close. "You and your wife need a good night's rest if you're traveling up to Quandry tomorrow."

Jack actually felt himself blush. First, for not having said something sooner. And second, because for a moment he'd imagined himself sharing that bedroom with Véronique. "I need to clear up something. Something that's completely of my doing, I admit. But it was done with the best of intentions." He caught Véronique's eye. "Véronique and I are not . . . husband and wife." He looked at Larson. "I introduced us that way at the outset because I wasn't sure about who you were, Jennings. And because I figure it's safer her traveling under the guise of being my wife, instead of as a single woman."

A smile ghosted Kathryn's expression. "I must admit, Mr. Brennan, I wondered at dinner when I heard you ask *your wife* if she'd ever cooked on a stove in this country before. Most husbands and wives get that settled early on."

They all laughed, and Jack didn't miss the intimate look Véronique gave him.

"In that case"—Kathryn pulled his attention back—"we'll make you a pallet in here, Mr. Brennan, and Véronique, you can have our room."

"*Non, non,* I would not feel comfortable taking your personal *chambre.* I would be pleased to be installed in the children's room, if that is acceptable to you both."

Jack couldn't help but watch Véronique as she and Kathryn worked out the details. She'd come so far in such a short time. From palaces in Paris to a rustic cabin in the wilds of America.

"But I must take the opportunity to inform you, Monsieur Jennings"—a sparkle lit Véronique's eye—"that if a wolf cat happens to come creeping along during the night, I am holding *you* responsible."

Jack caught her subtle wink meant for him, and he knew without a doubt she would do well in the Colorado Territory. Whether she ever found her father or not, she would find her way.

Jack stared at Véronique across the breakfast table the next morning. She looked pretty in her freshly ironed shirtwaist and skirt. She looked refreshed too, and he gathered she'd slept better than he had. The four adults had stayed up into the wee hours of the morning talking, and discovering they had similar connections in Willow Springs and Casaroja. The other couple even knew Matthew and Annabelle Taylor and Sadie. But what had robbed Jack most of sleep was the memory of Véronique's expression when she had watched Larson with little Katie the night before.

Jack couldn't understand how a father could abandon his wife and child. Just leave them behind to start a new life.

The more mining towns he and Véronique visited—the more acquainted he became with the way the miners lived—the greater his fear that finding Pierre Gustave Girard might not be the answer to Véronique's prayers.

Or to his prayers for her.

Jack thought of men like Sol Leevy and Wiley Scoggins, and the question that had haunted him during the night returned. If he happened upon Pierre Gustave Girard in one of these mining towns and this was the type of man Girard had become, would it be best for

Véronique to know the truth? Or would it be better for her to gradually let the hope of finding her father die and allow her to move on with her life?

If given a choice, which would *he* prefer?

Véronique shifted in her seat, and Jack blinked. She'd caught him staring.

"More coffee, Mr. Brennan?"

Jack held a hand over his cup. "No thank you, Mrs. Jennings. After that second serving of biscuits and gravy, I can barely finish what I've got here. Everything was delicious, thank you."

"Brennan, that foreleg on your horse is going to be fine." With a nod, Larson excused little William from the table, and the boy ran to the hearth and pulled a train out of a box. "I rubbed some salve into it again this morning and wrapped it up. I've got some bandages for you to take with you so you can keep it fresh. Should be fine."

"I appreciate that."

Larson stood. "We'd better get a move on. You said you're heading up to the Quandry today. That's a good four- to five-mile trek on up the mountain."

Jack frowned. "Are you sure about that? My map indicated it wasn't that far from the turnoff."

"Oh, I'm positive." Larson lifted Katie from her high chair. "I make that trip on a regular basis. The miners up there buy cattle from us."

Jack thought of the fallen tree they had yet to cut and move this morning. Then pictured what might have happened if he and Véronique had traveled higher on that road last night and gotten stuck on a narrow passageway somewhere. He drank the last of his coffee, considering how quickly his outlook on things could change with a slight shift in perspective.

Véronique rose from the table. "*Merci beaucoup*, Kathryn, Monsieur Jennings. The meals were *délicieux*, and spending time in your home has been most enjoyable."

Kathryn reached to clear the dishes. "The pleasure has been ours, Véronique, I assure you."

"Brennan, any time you need a place to stay while you're up in this area"—with a look, Larson included Véronique—"you're both welcome."

To Jack's surprise, Véronique didn't offer to help clear the dishes but walked back into the bedroom she'd shared with the children. He shot a look at Kathryn to see if she'd taken offense, but none showed in her expression. Working to mask his embarrassment, he helped stack the dishes and take them to the sideboard.

Kathryn waved him off. "Oh, Mr. Brennan, you don't need to do that."

"I don't mind it one bit." He glanced at the bedroom door and saw it close behind Véronique. He reached for the dirty cups. "You're kind to make us feel so welcome."

Kathryn glanced at him over her shoulder. "It's not often we get guests up here, Mr. Brennan. And I've missed a woman's company something fierce."

"If I were a lesser man I might take offense at that." Larson's soft laughter conveyed his humor.

Kathryn's hands stilled from washing. "Reminiscing about Matthew and Annabelle and their family last night brought back so many memories." Her voice grew soft. "Made me miss Annabelle and that sweet little Sadie all over again. I'm glad you were able to visit them on your way back here, Mr. Brennan."

"I am too." Jack deposited the cups by the wash bucket, wondering what Véronique was doing in the next room. "Like I said last night, when Annabelle shared her story . . . Well, it was quite a shock. And then to learn about Sadie . . ."

Larson nodded, his expression mirroring the pain Jack had felt upon hearing about it. "We got a letter not long ago from Matthew and Annabelle." Larson situated Katie by her older brother and enticed her with a rattle. "Matthew wrote that Sadie's pretty much taken over the care of his father now. She takes Mr. Taylor for walks on the ranch and reads to him every night. Matthew said she's become partial to the book of John."

Kathryn dried her hands on a towel. "What also touched me was when he described coming upon Sadie and his father one afternoon as they sat on the front porch. He overheard Sadie telling Mr. Taylor a story about her past—one Sadie wouldn't share with most anyone else. Matthew knew she'd shared the story with his father before, but with the disease Mr. Taylor has, he doesn't remember things from day to day. Sometimes from moment to moment." Her eyes misted.

"Matthew said he stood in the doorway and watched as his father cried right along with Sadie, like he'd never heard the story before. Then the next minute he was asking if they could make his favorite cookies again."

Larson moved in close beside his wife. "We're thankful to know Sadie's doing so well, that she's finding some peace. She deserves a slice of happiness in this life, after all she's been through."

Kathryn covered her husband's hand on her waist and looked up at him. "God's healing will come. I'm certain of that. It'll just take some time."

The creak of a door drew their attention.

Jack turned to see Véronique standing there, a satchel in her hand. He recognized it as the one she'd gone back to her room to retrieve yesterday morning, the one that hardly weighed anything.

From its folds she pulled out a piece of parchment. "Kathryn, Monsieur Jennings, I have something to give you." Her expression was both eager and unsure. "Last night, Kathryn, you shared a desire to see Miss Maudie from Casaroja." She stepped forward, her gaze flitting to the paper in her hand, then back to Kathryn. "I offer this as a gift, an expression of my gratitude to you and your husband."

Kathryn took it from her and turned it around. "Oh . . ." Her breath left in a rush. She covered her mouth with her hand.

Jack stared at the penciled sketch of Miss Maudie set against a backdrop of Casaroja. The main house, the stables—everything was captured in intricate detail. His eye was drawn to a horse in the lower pasture. And close beside it, a newborn foal. Véronique had done this? He looked up and saw tears pooling in her eyes.

Kathryn's fingers trembled as she touched the drawing. "This is so beautiful. Véronique, you're truly gifted. This is just like looking at Miss Maudie." She held it so Larson could see. "But how can we accept this? It's too much. Surely Miss Maudie will want to keep this. What did she say when she saw it?"

Jack read the answer in Véronique's face before she spoke.

"I drew this for you last night. Miss Maudie has not seen it."

Kathryn's smile faded. "But how did you—"

Véronique shrugged, uncertainty shadowing her smile. "From the time I was a little girl, I have seen things and remember them. All of these images collect inside me, tucked away." She lifted her shoulders again, and let them fall. Her attention shifted to Jack. "It has always been this way for me."

"Look here, Kat." Larson pointed to something on the sketch. "She got the little cottage where . . ."

As Larson and Kathryn examined the drawing more closely, Jack crossed the room. He took hold of Véronique's hand, pride welling up within him. "I had no idea you could draw like that."

She laughed softly. "I did not know whether I could either. It has been such a long time since I have felt the prompting. But recently, I have experienced a stirring within me."

Jack could relate. He touched a curl lying on her shoulder.

"I thought God had removed it from me, the ability to draw, to paint. But now, it is awakening again, and the loneliness I have held so long inside me, is lessening . . . every day." A sparkle lit her eyes. "Of course"—her voice dropped low—"the company I have been keeping of late can be blamed for that as well."

Wanting to kiss her good and long, he settled for a peck on her forehead, and caught the faintest scent of lemon. *The lotion* . . . "You smell real nice today."

"*Merci*, monsieur. But are you implying that I smell like a prairie?"

He enjoyed the way she dipped her chin and playfully peered at him beneath a furrowed brow.

"Véronique?" Kathryn's voice drew them both around. "I don't know if there's time, but . . . could I persuade you to sketch William and Katie for Miss Maudie? She hasn't seen them in so long."

Véronique smiled. "I would like nothing better. But may I include you and your husband as well?"

Larson bounced little Katie in his arms. "That'd be fine with me. As long as you promise to get my good side."

"Let me grab my saw and we'll be on our way." Jennings headed toward the barn, walking with a bit of a limp.

Jack had noticed it last night, but it seemed more pronounced this morning. He walked to where Charlemagne and Napoleon were tethered and knelt to inspect Napoleon's leg, appreciating Jennings's handiwork with the bandage.

Jack stood and looked around at the cabin, the barn and corrals, and imagined having a place like that one day. He'd lain awake by the fire last night, and when he hadn't been thinking of Véronique being in the next room, he'd admired Jennings's craftsmanship. The wind and rain had continued throughout the night—thankfully not giving way to snow—but the cabin had stayed cozy warm and sealed tight.

The skies overhead were as blue as he could remember seeing. And not a cloud in them. This stretch of land had to come near to backing up to the land he'd put a bid on with Clayton. It was definitely in the same area anyway. He'd noticed that on their way up the mountain yesterday.

"Okay, we're ready to go." Jennings returned with a two-man saw in his grip. "With the two of us working we should be able to get this done in a couple of hours, tops."

Jack untethered the horses. "I sure appreciate this, Jennings." They walked a few paces. "And if you don't mind, I'd like to ask you about your land and how you—"

Something caught Jack's eye. Beneath a tall spruce growing near the cabin. When he realized what it was, he took a closer look. Seeing the name and the epitaph etched across the top of the tombstone, he slowed. Reading the dates below, he came to a full stop.

Jennings looked between him and the grave marker, and laughed softly. "That has a story behind it."

Jack nodded. "I would hope so. And I bet it's a good one."

"Good *and* long." Jennings motioned him on down the trail. "How about we talk as we saw."

I CAN'T TELL YOU what a nice surprise this will be for her, Miss Girard." Claire Stewartson indicated for Véronique to follow her down the hallway. Miss Maudie's bedroom door was closed, and Claire lightly knocked, whispering over her shoulder. "Sometimes she takes a nap about this hour of the afternoon."

Claire opened the door a few inches, then stepped to one side.

Miss Maudie was in bed, her eyes closed. "Perhaps I should come back another time," she whispered, but Claire shook her head and left the door ajar. Véronique followed her back to the foyer.

"If you don't mind waiting, she'll be awake soon—I'm sure. If I tell her you came and went, she'll put me on the same list as Doc Hadley. And I don't want that!" She winked. "You can wait in the parlor, if you like. It shouldn't be long. Would you care for something to drink?"

"*Non*, I am fine. *Merci*, madame."

Claire returned to the kitchen, and Véronique stood by the sofa, knowing she should make herself comfortable and yet unable to. It had taken her well over a week to work up the courage to come to see Miss Maudie, and still her insides were knotted tight. Why, she didn't know.

Jack had offered to accompany her, but she felt this was something she needed to do on her own. She'd even managed to drive the wagon by herself, and had enjoyed every mile of Napoleon's and Charlemagne's companionship. Though it occurred to her once out of town that if she'd had a "broken felly" she wouldn't have known what to do.

Remembering that day with Jack, and thinking of that wretched-and-now-thankfully-dead skunk, made her smile. She brought her hand to her nose and sniffed. Sometimes she could still smell the foul musky odor, but Jack said it was her imagination.

A shiver replaced the lighthearted memory as she considered the danger they'd faced on the trip to Sluice Box—both from Sol Leevy and his men, and from the elements of the Colorado wilderness. On the way down the mountain, after staying the night with the Jennings family and traveling to Quandry, Jack had grown quiet beside her in the wagon.

Even before he'd spoken, she'd known what he was going to say.

"I don't think you should travel with me anymore, Véronique. If Leevy and those men had decided to—" His jaw clenched tight. "If they had decided to hurt you, I couldn't have stopped them. I could've taken three or four of them, maybe, but . . . there're just too many men in these towns. I can't protect you."

The question rose quickly in her mind, yet it wasn't new. It had lurked beneath the surface since the day they'd emerged from the cave and she'd seen his tears. The day in the mercantile, the dread of being in closed spaces—it all fit. "Like you could not prevent whatever happened in the cave so long ago, Jack?"

"Yes, like that," he finally whispered. The raw truth in his expression caused an ache in her chest. "I knew what Billy and I were doing was dangerous. Billy didn't. He'd never been around mines before. He thought it was an adventure. I knew better, but I thought we'd be okay. I'd take care of him. We'd stay near the entrance."

"But Billy did not listen to your warnings."

"Billy should never have been there in the first place—that was my fault. He didn't see the boards. They were rotten, and he fell through . . . into an old mining shaft. The tunnel sloped down a few feet before dropping off. He managed to grab hold of a root tangle and hung on. He wasn't that far from me—only a couple of feet. He kept screaming my name, begging me to get him out." Desperation permeated his tone. "I went in after him. I was bigger than he was and my legs were longer, so I wedged them against the walls for leverage. I had hold of his hand, but we were both slick from the mud." His voice faltered.

He stared ahead, but Véronique knew he was in that mining shaft again, cloistered in the darkness.

A long moment passed. "I couldn't hang on to him. He slid the rest of the way down the shaft to where the tunnel angled straight down, and then he disappeared into the dark."

Véronique's stomach went cold imagining what terror that young boy must have felt—and what guilt and pain the man beside her must have lived with for so many years.

"I couldn't climb out by then. I was too far down." He gave a humorless laugh. "So I just hung on and cried for help, and listened to Billy call my name, over and over, from far away. By the time help got there, he'd gone quiet. They told me he died from the fall."

"*Oui*, the fall killed him, Jack." She touched his arm. "You did not."

He turned to her, his expression fierce. "You try losing someone in your care, who you're responsible for, and then you tell me that."

Standing in the pristine surroundings of Miss Maudie's home, Véronique still felt the sting from that moment and could see the glistening in his eyes. When the time came for their next trip, she had shown up early at the livery, and when he arrived, Jack had stood for the longest moment, staring at her. Then he'd walked toward her and handed her his gun. "We'll have a lesson before we leave, and we'll see how you do."

And that's all that had been said since.

Had he made peace with what had happened to young Billy? Or just realized that he couldn't protect everyone, all the time? Véronique didn't know. But she did wonder . . . If Arianne Girard had known what risks this search would mean for her daughter, would she still have asked it of her?

A stirring came from within Miss Maudie's room. Véronique tiptoed across the polished hardwood floor and peeked inside. The woman was still asleep.

An oversized hallway extended down the length of the home on her left, and Véronique walked a few paces, admiring the paintings adorning the walls. She guessed them to be the patriarchs and matriarchs of Miss Maudie's *famille.*

The portraits were stately in appearance, the frames exquisite, and the subjects possessed a certain realness about them. But whoever painted them had failed to capture the individual qualities of each person. All of the eyes gazing back at her—while unique in details of size, shape, and color—held the same emotion. Or lack of it. In Véronique's opinion, the painter had been so concerned with capturing the person's exact likeness that he or she had missed the essence of who the person was.

"Donlyn . . ." A faint crying. "Donlyn . . ."

Véronique turned at the frail whisper, realizing it had come from Miss Maudie's room. She stepped inside and saw Miss Maudie still sleeping, but her face was twisted in pain.

Véronique laid aside her *réticule* and *valise,* and knelt over the bed. "Shhh. . . ." She stroked Miss Maudie's forehead as a mother might a child's, until gradually the lines of the older woman's face smoothed into tranquil sleep again.

She claimed the chair in the corner of the spacious room and sank down into the cushions. A warm June breeze wafted through the open window, sending the lace curtains billowing. Her thoughts went to her *valise* and the family sketch she'd drawn of Larson and Kathryn Jennings and their children. She was both eager and anxious to see the woman's reaction.

Reaching for her *réticule,* Véronique spotted a wheelchair in the corner. Perhaps Miss Maudie would feel well enough to take a turn about the grounds later. Véronique opened the drawstring and withdrew a thin stack of letters. She was nearly finished rereading her father's missives and had begun to recognize a pattern in them that had gone unnoticed before.

Not in what he wrote but in how he wrote it—the indentation of the pen on the page, the slant of the individual letters, the way the pen had paused until it left an ink-soaked blotch on the page, as though her father had taken care in contemplating his next thought.

"Miss Girard . . ."

Véronique looked up from the open letter in her hand to see Miss Maudie's eyelids fluttering.

"What a pleasant awakenin' to find you here, dear."

Véronique rose and went to the bedside. "*Bonjour,* Miss Maudie."

She smiled down. "I offer you my humblest apologies at the outset. For I disregarded the first rule of etiquette and stopped by un-announced, but Claire encouraged me to wait." She lightly touched the woman's brow. "How are you feeling today?"

"That Claire's a wise woman." Miss Maudie sighed. Her eyes closed briefly. "Your hands, they feel so good, my dear."

"Are you overly warm?" Véronique felt the woman's cheeks. No fever.

"No, I'm fine, lass. But there's nothin' like a kind touch to soothe a bit of the loneliness in us all."

"Hmmm . . ." Véronique recalled the conversation with Jack that had prompted today's visit. "*Oui*, I think we all possess a portion of that within us. Some more than others." She'd recognized a loneliness in the tone of her father's letters this time that had gone unnoticed before. And she found her disappointment in him and the hurt she felt over his broken promises weakening in the face of it.

Miss Maudie pushed herself up, and Véronique situated the pillows behind her back. "What were you readin' there, Miss Girard?" Miss Maudie smoothed the sides of her coiffed silver-white hair, and then motioned for Véronique to sit on the edge of the bed. "Don't let me be interruptin' you, child."

Véronique reached for the letters. "These are missives my father wrote to my mother many years ago. They are penned to her, but on occasion he included a note to my attention." She fingered the three remaining envelopes. "Before she passed, my mother asked me to read them again."

"Again?" Curiosity colored Miss Maudie's expression.

"*Oui*, my mother read them to me when I was little girl, and I've read them again, many times, through the years." She turned the opened letter in her hand. "But it seems that no matter how many times I read them, they always say the same thing."

"And you were hopin' to find a hint, a bit of somethin' new that might aid in your search."

"*Oui*, that was my hope, mademoiselle."

"'Mademoiselle . . .'" Miss Maudie repeated the word in a mock-ing tone. "That's a mighty fancy way of callin' me an old maid, Miss Girard."

Véronique frowned, not understanding. If only she'd brought her dictionary along, she could have looked up the phrase *old maid*.

Maudie laughed softly. "I'm just playin' with you, my dear. I love the language of your people. I don't understand it, mind you, but I could listen to it all day."

Relieved, that gave Véronique an idea. "Would it please you for me to read aloud, Miss Maudie? Or perhaps recite poetry. Are you familiar with the English-born poet John Donne?"

"Never heard of him. Is he a nice fellow?"

Véronique laughed. "Master Donne was born in 1572, so I fear he is quite deceased now. However, his words live on, and with good reason. Perhaps you would like to hear one of his Holy Sonnets? I could recite it for you, if you wish."

"My dear, you are a treasure. But might I be so bold as to request a readin' of somethin' else?" Miss Maudie glanced at the letter lying unfolded in Véronique's lap. "At the oddest times I've found myself thinkin' of your father, Miss Girard. Wonderin' what ever became of him. If you're willin', I'd like to hear something from his hand."

"I am most willing, Miss Maudie. But you must promise to tell me if you grow bored. While the letters are precious to me, for obvious reasons, I realize they might not hold the same appeal for others."

Miss Maudie waved the comment away as if it were absurd.

Véronique smoothed the deeply creased letter on her lap. "'My dearest Arianne,'" she began, translating the sentences as she went along. "'This letter will be brief, as our company departs this morning for an expedition farther into the mountains where there will be few towns, and no opportunities to post. The streams and creeks we've trapped for the past four months are thinned of prey, so we must move on to meet our quotas. I am eager to receive word from you, telling me of your current state and that of our darling daughter.

"'I fear your letters are not finding me, as I have not heard from you in some time. In their absence, I reread the ones in my possession and pray you and Véronique are well. Please tell her that her drawing of the Rocky Mountains was quite good and that I am eager to show her their beauty. The mountains are larger and even more fierce than your imagination will allow, Arianne. I have seen magnificent sights, and have tried to capture the power of this land on the page in my letters, but I know my descriptions have failed.'"

Miss Maudie shifted on the bed. "Do you remember drawin' that picture, dear?"

"*Oui*, a bit. I remember more the act of drawing it with him in my mind, more than I do the drawing itself."

Miss Maudie nodded, and smiled for her to continue.

Véronique readied to turn the page. "'I pray you are both in good health. In my dreams, I imagine Véronique grows to favor you more with each day, my dearest. Dwelling on that thought pleases me, as I have your beautiful face forever captured in my heart. I will write in greater length in coming weeks, saving my daily entries and sending them as one. My deepest love always, until we are joined again.'"

The initials PGG, tastefully larger than the scripted body of the letter, slanted across the bottom of the page below the closing in an elegant manner.

"Beggin' your pardon, Miss Girard, but that doesn't sound like a man eager to be castin' off his wife and child."

Véronique felt a measure of shame. She remembered their first conversation weeks ago, in this very room, and knew that she'd given Miss Maudie that impression of her father. "No, ma'am, it does not. And yet, in the end, my father did not fulfill his promises, did he."

"Oh, I'm not belaborin' that point, my dear. Time has proven that out, I'm afraid. My meanin' is that sometimes people have the best of intentions, and yet somethin' draws them off the path." Earnestness sharpened Miss Maudie's eyes. "It's not that they're bad people at heart, lass. They just lose their way." She held out her hand. "May I?"

"*Oui*, but of course." Véronique handed her the letter.

Maudie held it close to her face. "Your father has beautiful penmanship, especially for a man. Even if I can't read the language." She threw Véronique a grin. "Most men I've known do not hold that ability in high regard. Would you read another?"

"Certainly, but first, would you care for something to drink? Or perhaps to eat?" Waiting for Miss Maudie to answer, Véronique suddenly realized she hadn't given her the drawing of the Jennings family yet. She bent down for her *valise* and withdrew the parchment.

"Miss Maudie, I nearly forgot—I have something for you, a gift. I drew this at the request of some dear friends, to us both." She turned the page.

Miss Maudie held the drawing close. "Oh, my dear William! And my Katie! Look at how they've grown." Her hand trembled over her mouth. "And their dear parents . . . But tell me, how did you come to be meetin' them?"

Véronique explained the events of that stormy evening, and of the family's hospitality.

Miss Maudie listened, focus glued to the parchment. "Is there no end to your talents, my dear? How can I thank you enough?"

Véronique beamed, not only at Miss Maudie's reaction but at how comfortable she felt, how quickly she'd slipped back into the familiar role of companion, and how much she enjoyed Miss Maudie's company. Jack had been right about her coming here—but no need for him to know that.

A soft smile tipped her mouth knowing she would thank him at her first opportunity. "And now, Miss Maudie, would you care for something to eat? Or to drink?"

"I'd love it, Miss Girard, but I'll be wantin' to go along for the ride, if you don't mind." Maudie motioned to the wheelchair.

With less effort than Véronique expected, she got the woman situated, and a blanket tucked around her legs.

Miss Maudie caught her hand. A mischievous look filled the woman's eyes. "I had myself a visitor a while back, and we took ourselves a walk outside. But I didn't have need of this chair at all when he was here, I'm tellin' you. He just scooped me up and carried me in his arms. And talked we did, for a long while. It was a pleasure." With a deep sigh, Miss Maudie made a show of fanning herself. "Handsomest man he was, and with a heart as gracious as ever beat in a man's chest." She pulled Véronique closer, failing to stifle her giggle. "And that chest was a mite broad, and well-muscled too, if I might add."

"Miss Maudie!" Véronique playfully patted her hand, having quickly caught on to the woman's antics, and to whom she was referring. "Might I ask what you and . . . this gentleman discussed during your walk?"

"Of course you can, my dear. I won't be tellin' you, but you can surely ask."

A while later, situated beside Miss Maudie in her wheelchair, and beneath the welcome shade of a cottonwood, Véronique finished reading the next letter and tucked it back inside the envelope.

"That was delightful, Miss Girard. The way your father describes what he's seen on his journeys . . . It's like I'm there alongside him, seein' it all for myself. And how he described that avalanche." She rubbed her arms in a mock shiver. "I was for certain the snow would be comin' down upon me any minute."

Miss Maudie's tinkling laughter reminded Véronique of the clustered bells that adorned the harnesses of Lord Marchand's Percherons in winter. Thinking of her former employer, she quickly prayed for his health, and just as swiftly sifted her prayer free of the selfishness underlying it. Yet she couldn't help but wonder—if anything happened to him, what would happen to her?

"What a treasure these letters must have been to your mother, child. And to you. Do you have time to read another?"

Véronique stared at the last envelope in her lap. "*Oui*, this is the final letter my father wrote, so it will be our last . . . for today." She hesitated, wanting to phrase her next sentence with as carefree an air as possible. "I can bring the earlier ones when I come again, if that would be pleasing to you."

Miss Maudie's eyes softened. "I can't be tellin' you how pleasin' that would be for me, child." Her gaze wandered over their surroundings. She sighed deeply. "It's been lonely for me in recent years. I find myself with time to brood . . . and think about the past. Not a good thing, my dear." She started to speak, then stopped. "I never married, Miss Girard. I had the opportunity . . . once, but my father didn't consider the man worthy of my hand. And truth be told, I didn't either."

Véronique heard the loneliness in Miss Maudie's voice, and wished it hadn't taken her so long to make the trip to Casaroja.

Maudie smiled and shook her head. "He was a rougher sort, ya know—didn't have the smooth manners and way of conversin' that was accepted in my circle." She lowered her eyes. "I don't know why I tell you all this now, Miss Girard. I guess what I'm tryin' to say is that I find it easy to be in your company. I enjoy our conversations and would welcome them anytime." She raised a stately brow. "If you can abide an old woman's ramblin's."

Véronique smiled, knowing Jack would be pleased beyond words.

"I would do more than abide them, Miss Maudie. I would cherish them."

"You do my heart good, Miss Girard. Now . . ." She resituated herself in the wheelchair. "How about that last letter."

Véronique untucked the flap of the envelope and pulled out the familiar white pages. But another piece of paper fell into her lap. She picked it up, recognizing the soft *lavande* of the stationery. It was from her mother's desk.

She turned it in her hand, her heart beating faster.

"Take them. Read them, ma chérie." The words came back with such clarity and force that her mother's request suddenly sounded more like a warning instead of a whispered plea.

Véronique opened her mother's letter and read the first sentence.

Her chest tightened. Her hands shook. Her mother's handwriting wasn't the artistic swirls and loops she remembered from younger days, but neither was it the arthritic scrawl that had accompanied the last days of her life.

Her mother had penned this before the final stages of her illness. Yet she had said nothing.

"My dear, what is it?" Miss Maudie leaned forward in her wheelchair.

Véronique swallowed. "It is a letter from my mother." She read the first paragraph, and the next, and suddenly felt ill. The air squeezed from her lungs.

"Miss Girard! Are you all right? Should I be callin' for Claire or Thomas?"

Véronique waved a hand, declining the offer. *"Non, merci."* But it would help if she could breathe. She pulled in air and let it out slowly. Then repeated the act. It felt as though the world had shifted on its axis.

And it had, for her.

CHAPTER THIRTY-SIX

M R. CLAYTON GREETED Jack at the door of the title and deed office, his hand outstretched. "Congratulations, Mr. Brennan. I had a feeling things would work out favorably for you."

As the man pumped Jack's hand, Jack eyed him, confused. "There must be some mistake, sir. I'm just stopping by to check on my bid. To see if you've heard anything back yet."

"Your bid has been accepted, Mr. Brennan. The land is yours." Clayton stopped abruptly. His mouth fell open. "I thought my secretary sent word to you."

"No, sir." Jack glanced at her vacant desk. "I received a note at the hotel saying you wanted to see me." Then it hit him. "I haven't had my interview with the owner yet."

A smile crept over Mr. Clayton's face. "Actually, Mr. Brennan, you have." He waved Jack into his office. "We need to talk." Clayton closed the door and sat down behind his desk.

Jack claimed the chair on the opposite side. "Are you telling me I had my interview with the owner and didn't know it?"

"What I'm saying, Mr. Brennan, is that the owner had a conversation with you in recent weeks and has approved your offer." Clayton leaned forward. "There's not much more I can tell you, I'm afraid."

Jack scoured his memory for conversations he'd had in the past few weeks, trying to pinpoint people he had spoken with who could be the owner of the property. He'd met every vendor in Willow Springs during that time, plus people in town, at church, guests at the hotel. Not to mention people in nearly every mining town in the area. There was no way to narrow it down.

"Mr. Brennan, I'd encourage you to simply accept your good fortune and move on. Don't try to piece it together. Put your efforts toward getting that cabin built before winter."

Jack let it sink in. He could hardly believe it. After so many years he was finally going to build his own home on his own land, and it would be exactly as he'd dreamed in younger years. Thoughts of Mary and Aaron rose in his memory. Well, not exactly as he'd dreamed.

He stood and stretched out his hand. "Thank you, Mr. Clayton. When would you like the money?"

"No time like the present, Mr. Brennan. As soon as you return, we can sign the papers and make if official."

Jack smiled, already at the door. "I'll be back within the hour."

That evening, Jack took the hotel stairs by twos up to the third floor. He reached the landing, heart pounding, and headed toward Véronique's door. Everything was right with the world. He'd signed the contract with Mr. Clayton and paid the money. The land was his. He'd visited the mercantile earlier that afternoon and ordered the tools he needed to get started on his cabin. He'd start cutting trees and preparing the logs as soon as possible.

And he already had a neighbor to help him. As Jack had suspected that day while at the Jennings's home, their land shared a property line with his. Once Larson Jennings learned that Jack had put a bid down, he had offered to help him build. Jack couldn't think of better neighbors.

He also couldn't stop thinking of Véronique, and couldn't wait to tell her about the land.

Throughout the day his thoughts had returned to her. He hoped her visit with Miss Maudie went well. When she'd told him she was headed out there, he'd sensed she was nervous about it. But he knew both of those women and was certain they would get along grandly, as his grandmother used to say.

He knocked on her door. And knocked again.

A shuffling noise sounded from within, and the door slowly opened. "I just stopped by to—" He stepped closer. "Vernie, what's wrong?"

She shook her head and started crying. Or crying *again*, from the looks of things. "*J'ai trouvé une lettre.*" The words tumbled out. "*C'est de ma maman. Elle l'a écrit avant qu'elle est morte et—*"

"Slow down, honey." He cradled the side of her face and wiped her tears. "I don't understand. I'm sorry."

Véronique took a deep breath and let it out. "I found a letter . . . from my *maman*. She wrote it before she died." She shuddered as her eyes slipped closed. "It wasn't my *papa*, Jack. It was her," she whispered. "It was *her* decision. Not his."

Emotion tightened Jack's throat as the possibility of what she was saying took hold. He pulled her to him. She slipped her arms around his waist and pressed close. The dampness of her tears soaked through his shirt.

He kissed the crown of her head and smoothed her hair. "What does the letter say?"

She walked to the bed and returned with the letter in her hand.

Jack took it from her, then smiled softly. "Vernie, I can't read this. Are you able to read it to me?"

She looked at the letter, then at him. "*Oui.* Do you have time?"

Jack stepped close and tipped her chin. He kissed her forehead, aware of how she moved toward him. "I have as long as you'd like, Vernie."

She sat down on the bed and indicated for him to take the chair by the desk. Rethinking the situation, he walked back to the bedroom door and drew it fully open, then claimed the chair beside her.

She massaged her forehead and briefly squinted. "I may need to stop, on occasion."

He covered her hand, wishing he could do or say something to take away her pain. "Take your time."

"'My dearest Véronique, I have always lacked courage, and I fear that even now I fail to possess the quality of strength to speak these words to you before—'" Her voice caught. She cleared her throat. "'Before I depart. If it lends the least comfort, and if it aids you in finding mercy to forgive me, please know that what I did—'"

Vernie pressed her lips together. "'I did with the conviction that it was best for you, however misplaced my intentions.

"'Your father is a good man, and if one weakness were to be assigned to him, it would be in his believing that I possessed a strength I never did.'"

Jack watched her face as she read. From what she'd told him about her mother, he could picture a woman, an older version of the one before him, sitting at an ornate desk, penning this letter.

"'When I was by your father's side, I was the woman I always wanted to be. Not the woman I truly am.'" Véronique paused. "'Your father and I dreamed of having a different life, far away from Paris and the conflicts here, in a place where greater opportunity would abound for our family, and for you. Your father paved the way for that dream, and my deepest regret will always be not taking you and leaving with him when he left.

"'But I convinced him that it would be best if he went ahead and prepared a place for us, and then we would join him. Looking back on that decision now . . . and on myself with the clarity of passing years, I realize it was fear that bartered that negotiation. Fear of uncertainty, fear of taking a step into the unknown when what I had here was firm and safe and familiar. Which leads me to the purpose of this letter.'"

Véronique's eyes skimmed across the page, and her tears renewed. Jack bowed his head and prayed for her, for her mother, though she was gone, and for her father—wherever he was. Jack hadn't realized it until then, but as his feelings for Véronique had deepened, so had his resentment toward Pierre Gustave Girard.

Now he felt a kinship with the man—they'd both lost a wife and child.

The stationery crinkled in her hand. "'Lord Marchand is acting on my wishes, and I have invoked his unwavering integrity to see to your safety and well-being, and to the arrangements for your journey to the Americas. Even now fear grips me as I think of sending you down a path I lacked the fortitude and courage to take. But even more, I fear what you will think of me when you discover the truth.'"

The last word came out in a rough whisper, and Jack sensed Véronique's anger. And her mother's regret.

"'Your father did send for us, my darling, many years ago. In my response to him I—'" Véronique read on silently, shaking her head, and then continued. "'I planted a thought that I knew his loneliness would nurture. I told him that while I loved him still, I had moved on with my life, for your sake—for both our sakes—and that we had found a home, and a solace, with Lord Marchand.'"

After a long moment, she continued. "'Know that I will be with you on that ship. I will be with you as you travel. And if I am able, and if God is willing, you will feel my continued love and presence.'"

She lowered the page. "I *have* felt it, Jack. In this very room."

He listened as she told him about the scent of white roses that had blanketed the room the morning he'd picked her up at the hotel three weeks ago. He was sorry he'd interrupted that moment, but noted that her attention had returned to the letter, so he saved his apology for later.

"'It strikes me as odd when I think of it now, but this time I am the one leaving first to prepare a home for us. I'll be waiting for you, Véronique. I'll be waiting for you both.'" She lowered her hand to her lap, looking spent and defeated. "And she signs the letter as my father signed all of his, "'My deepest love always, until we are joined again.'"

What could he say in light of this? Jack gently slipped the letter from her hand and stared at the words. Gradually he looked back at her. "Is there any question in your mind that she loved you?"

A familiar glint of rebuttal rose in her eyes.

"Just focus on that question, if you can, Véronique. And nothing else. Do you believe your mother loved you?"

For the longest time she stared at him. Then she slowly nodded. "*Oui*, of that I am certain. But I am also certain of this . . . what she did was wrong. I would never keep my child from her loving father. Not even if I had to cross a thousand oceans."

CHAPTER THIRTY-SEVEN

I HAVE GOOD NEWS, Mademoiselle Girard." Dr. Hadley leaned forward in his chair, holding up a piece of stationery in his hand. "At least I hope it is good news."

Véronique rose from her seat opposite the physician's desk. "The surgeon in Boston has responded positively to Lilly's case?"

"He has agreed to perform the surgery on Lilly, yes, mademoiselle. But I would not necessarily call his response 'positive.'" Gesturing, he invited her to be seated again. "I visited with the Carlsons last evening, and while I was there I told them—as we agreed—of a person who desires to speak with them about the procedure. I told them nothing more."

Véronique nodded. "*Oui*, thank you. This is welcome news, Doctor. I appreciate your coordination of these efforts and am aware of your depth of feeling for this family."

"You are most welcome, ma'am, but I did nothing that I wouldn't do for any patient who placed himself under my care." His expression grew apprehensive. "I've practiced medicine here in Willow Springs for nearly thirty years, and in the territory for much longer. I've healed many, and I've watched many go unhealed"—he looked away briefly—"despite my best efforts."

Watching him speak, Véronique thought of Miss Maudie. Several times on her visits to Casaroja in recent days, she'd overheard Miss

Maudie saying that Doc Hadley's prescribed bed rest was "just for spite." Véronique realized Miss Maudie had been jesting and was convinced that any action taken by the man before her on behalf of a patient was for the person's betterment.

Thankfully the doctor would be accompanying her when she met with the Carlsons later that evening. She wished Jack could be there too, but he'd left that morning on supply runs to mining towns farther away. They'd visited four new towns in the past week and a half, and since discovering her mother's letter, Véronique's earnestness to find her father had deepened—just as her hope was fading that she ever would.

"Dr. Hadley, I am certain you have served this community well. The people of Willow Springs should be grateful your abilities are available to them, as I know the Carlsons are."

His jaw tensed, and for an instant, Véronique thought she had spoken out of turn.

His eyes misted. "It is I who am grateful to the people of this town, Mademoiselle Girard. They have trusted me to deliver their children, and their children's children. I've doctored their ailments and have struggled, oftentimes in vain, to keep death at bay. While doing that, these people have taught me about life. I've seen the hand of God in their lives, many times. And I've discovered that He often moves in ways I didn't anticipate." He leaned forward in his chair. "I have always been honest with the people in my care, no matter the prognosis. And after much prayer on the matter, while I consider your offer most generous, ma'am, I still don't believe it's in Lilly's best interest to undergo this surgery."

Véronique wasn't certain she'd heard him correctly. But the resoluteness in his eyes told her that she had. He had expressed concern in their initial meeting, but surely not now—after the *chirurgien* had approved the *procédure.* "You would prefer to watch Lilly lose the ability to walk? To end up a cripple?"

"I would prefer to see her walk the path that God has chosen for her life, Mademoiselle Girard. Whatever that is. Playing the role of rescuer can be thrilling, and believe me, I've attempted that once or twice in my life." A gentle expression softened the frank remark. "However, I've discovered that rescue, the way we sometimes think of it, is not always part of God's plan."

Véronique stood, suddenly feeling judged and yet not knowing why. "One thing I must know before we meet with Pastor and Mrs. Carlson. . . . Will you counsel them against Lilly's having the surgery?"

"I will lay out the facts the surgeon has presented. I believe that, as their doctor, it is my duty. But to counsel them one way or the other . . ." He shook his head. "They will seek God's wisdom on that, Miss Girard. As well they should."

Sitting in the Carlsons' kitchen that evening, Véronique felt strangely at odds within herself, and in her purpose in coming. She'd seen Lilly at the hotel as she'd left earlier, and when she'd arrived had heard Hannah Carlson encouraging Bobby to play with a friend down the street. Perhaps it was the clandestine feel of the gathering that had her nerves unsettled.

As Dr. Hadley began the conversation, her mind kept returning to something he'd said that morning in his office. *"And after much prayer on the matter . . ."* But she'd given the matter a great deal of prayer as well. She'd prayed for Lilly's healing. She'd prayed for the *chirurgien* to say yes. She'd even prayed for Dr. Hadley's involvement in the correspondence. So why this niggling sense of having taken a false step?

She watched Patrick and Hannah's faces as Dr. Hadley laid forth her proposition to cover the costs of the *chirurgie*. Hannah's expression mirrored her surprise; her eyes welled up with tears. The pastor seemed to be battling his own emotions as well.

Patrick took hold of his wife's hand. "Mademoiselle Girard, your generosity is . . . overwhelming. On behalf of both of us, and Lilly, I extend our appreciation for your kindness. With the cost of the surgery, Hannah and I had given up on having a choice to make. We just figured God had made the choice for us."

"And we were working on coming to peace with it," Hannah added quietly.

Véronique inwardly flinched at Hannah's comment. "You are most welcome, both of you. I am pleased to be able to extend the offer."

Patrick nestled Hannah's hand between his. "Understanding what's at stake, Miss Girard, we'll need some time to discuss the situation with Lilly, and to consider what will be best for her."

"*Oui*, that is to be expected, of course."

Hannah reached over and gently squeezed Véronique's arm. "Your friendship to our daughter has been a gift in itself, Véronique. And now this . . ." She shook her head. "It's beyond belief. For the past few months Lilly has struggled, not only physically but with growing up as well, as I know she's confided in you. Children can be cruel. They don't mean to be, but their tendency to want to laugh can sometimes take a harsh turn."

Véronique recalled the day she saw the boys and girls making fun of Lilly behind her back. "*Oui*, it can be most painful. Both to Lilly, and to those who love her."

Hannah nodded, her tears renewing.

Dr. Hadley stood and reached for his hat. "The surgeon in Boston can perform the surgery on Lilly in October, but he needs your answer no later than the first week of July so preparations can be started. That's three weeks from now. Will that give you enough time?"

Patrick nodded. "Certainly."

"I'm not sure if you've had time to read through the materials I left with you last night." Dr. Hadley gestured to a large envelope on the table. "It outlines what steps will be done—during the surgery and afterward, during the recuperation. It states in very clear terms what to expect, and what the risks are. If you have any questions about the contents or what we've discussed, you know you can call on me anytime."

They said their good-byes, and Véronique was nearly back to her hotel room when the source of her concern became clear. Not once had she considered that it might not be within God's plan to heal Lilly.

Even now, with the *chirurgien* having agreed to perform the *procédure* and with the money available, she couldn't fathom that this orchestration of events wasn't part of God's plan. Everything had come together too perfectly.

Walking up the stairs to her room, she realized why that possibility bothered her so much. And the realization was bittersweet. If God would allow these events to come together, enabling Lilly to have the *chirurgie,* and yet it still not be His desire—what did that mean for her own situation?

Would God bring her halfway around the world on a search for someone He knew she would never find—only to lead her to someone she would never have found otherwise?

CHAPTER THIRTY-EIGHT

T HAT CANTANKEROUS MRS. HOCHSTETLER!" Véronique glared at the note left for her at the hotel's front desk. "Does the woman not believe that I will pay her?" The mercantile owner's note communicated nothing about whether her paints had arrived. Only that Véronique owed the remaining balance of her bill.

Lilly's grin said she was aware of the note's contents, and her violet eyes held a sparkle that hadn't been there in days past. "Would you like me to take your bank draft to her? So you don't have to see her today? I know Mrs. Hochstetler can be a little . . . abrupt at times. At least that's what mama calls it."

Véronique covered the girl's hand. "Oh, Lilly, would you do that for me? I am to meet Jack at the livery, and he is escorting me to Casaroja. Miss Maudie is expecting me for our Wednesday visit." She wrote out the bank draft for the amount quoted in the note and slid it across the desk. "I so appreciate your kindness."

Lilly stared at the bank draft and slowly raised her head. "And I appreciate your kindness, Mademoiselle Girard. So do my folks."

Just yesterday, Pastor and Mrs. Carlson had stopped by the hotel and informed her that they'd made the decision for Lilly to have the *chirurgie*. Véronique could not have been more thrilled. "Lilly, there is no need to keep thanking me. I am pleased to do this for you. And your parents seem happy, *non*?"

"Yes, ma'am. They sure seem to be. Doc Hadley was over at the house last night answering more questions."

Hearing that drew Véronique's curiosity. "And what did Dr. Hadley have to say?"

"Oh, nothing that we hadn't heard before. He just said he wants to make sure we understand all the risks." Lilly paused and tucked a dark curl behind her ear. "But I don't know . . ."

"What is it, *ma chérie*?"

"I get the feeling Mama's not for me having this done. That she's giving in because it's what I want. I can't really tell with my papa. He says that we've done all this talking about it, and that now God has done His talking—through the kindness of your gift—and that we ought to listen."

Véronique smiled. "Your papa is a wise man, Lilly. And your mother loves you without end. She only wants the best for you, I know this for certain."

No sooner had the words left her mouth than Véronique remembered Jack's question the evening she'd read her mother's letter to him. His gentleness with her, the way he'd stayed and listened, meant so much. She knew her mother's decision had stemmed from love. Despite everything else, of that she had no doubt.

But what that *love* had cost her was not something Véronique would soon forget. Nor easily forgive.

The rifle's report echoed across the plains east of Casaroja, and the wooden bucket went flying from its perch atop the rock some thirty feet away.

Jack looked from Véronique to the bucket, and back again. Her ghost of a smile told him she knew how well she was doing. Yet she said nothing.

She was a natural with the Winchester. He had suspected she might be with the way she handled the Schofield, but something else seemed to be at work behind her shooting this evening. An undercurrent that sharpened her desire to send that bucket sailing.

Maybe it had to do with her mother's letter. She hadn't said anything else about it since she'd read it to him in her hotel room, but he sensed an unrest within her. An anger—and a disappointment—

that she didn't know how to deal with.

When she'd asked him to escort her out here to see Miss Maudie, he'd gladly agreed. He hadn't expected time alone with her this evening, so this was an unexpected pleasure. And she seemed especially glad to be in his company, which only deepened that pleasure.

He studied her. "You're sure you'd never shot a gun before that morning I took you out?"

"I am quite sure, Jack. But thank you for the compliment. I have a good teacher, *non*?" She lowered the rifle and reloaded the chamber as he'd taught her.

Her smooth action with the firearm was a sharp contrast to the blue silk gown she wore. "I have been monopolizing your rifle, Jack. Would you like an opportunity to shoot?"

Purposefully staring, he said, "I'm doing exactly what I came out here to do."

She laughed. "To watch me shoot?"

"To spend time with you. Doesn't much matter to me what we're doing."

Her smile softened, and her gaze drifted from his.

His focus slipped to her bodice. The dress wasn't revealing, not indecent by any means, but his turn in thought was sudden. More and more, he found himself thinking about her these days, and in increasingly intimate terms.

Striding to the bucket, he picked it up, then repositioned it another ten feet out beyond the rock. She needed more of a challenge.

He wished he could be with her every day. That she could be the first thing he saw when he opened his eyes in the morning, and the last thing he saw before turning down his lamp at night. He walked back to her, aware of how her gaze followed him. Fine by him.

Some nights he lay awake in his room across the hall from hers and thought about her, wondering what she was doing. If she was asleep yet. Or maybe . . . if sleep eluded her too, was she entertaining similar thoughts about him?

She took aim again. Squeezed the trigger. And the bucket went sailing.

Unbelievable.

Later, after unhitching the wagon and getting Charlemagne and Napoleon settled at the livery, they walked back to the hotel. When they reached the third-floor landing, her pace slowed. He fell into step beside her.

"Thank you for today, Jack. For going with me to Casaroja, and for another lesson in shooting."

He stopped beside her door, took her room key from her hand, and inserted it into the lock. "Pleasure was all mine. You've come a long way since that day at Jenny's Draw." He laughed, remembering. "When you about scared the livin' daylights out of Scoggins, *and* me!"

She giggled. "I believe I scared myself as well."

He pulled his own key from his pocket. He'd never expected to be in a relationship like this again, and he certainly hadn't seen Mademoiselle Véronique Girard coming.

He noticed her watching him. "What is it?" he whispered.

"You have your key at the ready, and I am given to wondering . . . which room is yours."

"You mean you don't know?"

She shook her head.

"Lilly didn't tell you?"

Question slipped into her expression.

Slowly, he looked at the door behind him, directly across from hers.

Her gaze trailed his. Her eyes widened. "*Non*, it cannot be."

"*Oui*," he whispered, smiling. "I'm afraid it is."

"All this time, you have been across the hall from me. And yet you said nothing?"

Lacking adequate response, Jack shrugged and leaned down to kiss her cheek. At the last second she turned into his kiss and his lips brushed the edge of her mouth. Tempted to act on her encouragement, he stepped back. "Good night, Vernie. I hope you sleep well."

She scoffed and muttered something beneath her breath.

Jack slid his key into his own lock, feeling unexpected satisfaction at the exasperation in her tone. "Excuse me? I didn't quite catch that."

Her eyes narrowed the slightest bit. "I said . . . I think I will have much difficulty going to sleep now, imagining you are so close."

Laughing softly, he winked and nodded to her doorknob. "Best keep that locked tonight, would you please?"

Smiling, she closed her door.

Several seconds passed before Jack heard the lock slip firmly into place.

———

The mercantile bustled with Saturday shoppers. When Véronique saw the number of people pressing toward the front counter, it was clear she would have to wait her turn in line. The first day of July had arrived, and the heat of summer sauntered through the open doors of the mercantile, seeming bent on making itself at home.

The manner in which Madame Hochstetler had treated her when she ordered the paints nearly two months ago still grated on her nerves. But her excitement over the thought of painting again—or at least trying to paint—overshadowed her frustration with the woman.

As she waited her turn, Véronique noticed the other patron's stares.

The townsfolk in Willow Springs had proven kind and welcoming, and the attention they continued to show her wasn't bothersome. From a young age, she'd grown accustomed to people's attentiveness. Having lived and traveled with the Marchands meant you were on stage every time you walked out the door, or whenever someone walked in.

Thoughts of Jack trekking into the mountains made her wish she could have gone with him that morning on his supply runs. Yet for the first time, she didn't have that niggling feeling of being left behind that had so often accompanied his departures on these extended trips.

But come Tuesday, she would be ready for his return. Already they had plans to go to Casaroja to spend the afternoon and evening with Miss Maudie. Jack had seemed rather secretive about it, and she'd plied Miss Maudie for information on her last visit. But the woman could maintain her silence when she wanted to.

Véronique felt a sharp tug on her bustle and spun to discover a woman and child in queue behind her.

"I'm so sorry, miss." The woman gave a stern look to the little girl attempting to hide in the folds of her skirt. "My daughter's had her eye on your dress since the moment we walked in. It's very pretty, if you don't mind my saying."

"Thank you, madame. Your sweet daughter has done no harm." Véronique smoothed a hand over the rich plum-colored jacket and skirt and remembered the night she'd first worn it—to a parliamentary prayer vigil at the Cathédrale Notre Dame, with Christophe. Oh, how she wished Christophe would write, assuring her of his well-being, and that of Lord Marchand.

"I'm Susanna Rawlings, and this is Jenny, my youngest. I own the bakery here in town."

Véronique curtsied. "I am pleased to make your acquaintance, Madame Rawlings, and that of your daughter. My name is Mademoiselle Véronique Girard."

"Oh, I know who you are, Miss Girard. I don't expect there's anyone in Willow Springs who doesn't know that by now."

Looking down, Véronique noticed the enraptured expression on the girl's impish face. She bent down to be at eye level with her, but the dark-haired child once again sought the gathers of her mother's skirt.

"*Ma chérie*, would you like to touch the flowers?" Véronique kept her voice hushed and ran a finger over the appliqués on her jacket. "They are made of velvet and are very soft, *non*?"

The child peered up at her mother, who nodded her approval. Little Jenny took a cautious step forward. Stretching out a tiny hand, she gently touched the beaded center of one of the flowers and giggled.

Véronique smiled, about to encourage her to do it again when she spotted Madame Hochstetler some distance down the counter. If the older woman's expression was any indication, she was not having a pleasant day. Véronique didn't wish the woman ill—not severely anyway, any minor malady would do—as long as someone else waited on her when the time came.

She stifled a giggle at the *impolie* thought, chiding herself. She was becoming more like the Americans by the day!

Madame Hochstetler's eyes locked with hers, and narrowed.

The woman pushed her way down the aisle in Véronique's direction, the glare on her face not the least promising.

If Madame Hochstetler was coming to tell her that her paints were not in, Véronique was going to have to be more firm with her. This after the woman had given her such a difficult time upon ordering, *and* with Véronique already having paid the bill in its entirety.

Madame Hochstetler's face became an even deeper shade of

rouge than the apron she wore, and there was now no question in Véronique's mind that *she* was the object of Mrs. Hochstetler's wrath.

"Miss Girard!"

Startled, Véronique took a step back. "Madame Hochstetler, good day to you. I am here to see about—"

"Did I or did I not tell you that all those fancy paints you ordered were specialty items and couldn't be returned?" The woman braced her hands on her hips, standing much closer than was proper, or necessary.

The thrum of conversation in the mercantile dropped a level.

A thrush of heat spiraled up Véronique's chest and into her throat. How dare this woman speak to her in such a manner! And in public, no less! Véronique glanced about the crowded room. Most of the people she didn't know, but some were familiar to her.

And all of them were watching.

She purposefully kept her voice low, hoping to encourage Madame Hochstetler to do the same. "*Oui*, madame, you did explain this to me this, and I—"

"Did you have a problem understandin' my English?"

Véronique tensed at the condescension thickening the woman's tone. "No, madame. I speak your language quite well." *Better than you, in fact.* "Has the order we are speaking of arrived yet?"

"Oh, it's arrived all right, missy, but your second bank draft wasn't worth the paper it was printed on. So now my husband and I are stuck with a mess of paints we have to pay for. What do you say to that?"

Whispers skittered through the aisles.

Véronique felt the weight of the stares and sensed Madame Rawlings and her daughter, Jenny, inching back a step. "I am confident this error can be corrected, Madame Hochstetler. I will contact the bank immediately and will make certain you receive your payment." Heart pounding, she pulled herself up to her full height. "I would appreciate you holding my order until I return."

Madame Hochstetler scoffed. "Hold it?! What else am I going to do with it? As if anybody else in this town has the time to sit around and laze in that fashion. Or the money to throw away on such foolishness!"

Véronique clenched her jaw tight, no longer afraid of what she might say, because there was no possible way she could speak at all. Her entire body shook. She kept her eyes lowered as she picked her way through the crowded aisles. *"Pardonnez-moi, s'il vous plaît."*

Behind her, Madame Hochstetler's diatribe continued. It mingled with the murmured whispers of the other patrons and stirred a painful emotion in the pit of her stomach. She had nothing to be ashamed of. She had done nothing wrong.

So why did she feel so utterly disgraced?

For a third time, Véronique knocked on the double doors of the bank, ignoring the stares of passersby. She leaned closer to the window and tried to see inside. Seconds later, the door opened.

A bank clerk she recognized peered from around the corner. "I'm sorry, ma'am, but we're not open for business today."

"Oui, I understand. But I am in dire need of speaking to Monsieur Gunter, if he is here." She sensed the woman's hesitation and briefly explained her situation. "I will only take a moment of his time, I assure you. And I would be most grateful."

"Wait here, please. I'll see if he's available." The clerk returned minutes later. "If you'll follow me, I'll escort you to his office."

Once Véronique was inside, the young woman bolted the door behind them.

Véronique appreciated the relative privacy the bank offered in comparison to the humiliation she'd endured moments ago at the mercantile. Hands shaking, she could still feel the scorching stares of Madame Hochstetler and her customers.

As she'd walked out of the store, she couldn't escape her shortness of breath, or that split second sense of falling with no forewarning. Covering the brief distance to the bank, she'd felt a cloud of shame hovering over her.

She followed the woman through the maze of desks to the bank manager's office.

Monsieur Gunter had assisted with her account when she first arrived in Willow Springs and had appeared quite impressed with the amount of money deposited and awaiting her discretion. When she had informed him of the deposit amounts he could expect in the future, according to Lord Marchand's missive she presented him, Monsieur Gunter's behavior had become positively gleeful. Lord

Marchand's money had always carried a certain . . . influence.

But when Véronique entered Monsieur Gunter's office, a definite absence of glee defined the man's expression.

He rose from the chair behind his desk. "Mademoiselle Girard, how nice to see you again."

She curtsied and took the seat he indicated. "I appreciate you meeting with me, Monsieur Gunter. Especially on a Saturday."

"By all means. We have appreciated your business, mademoiselle."

Noticing his use of past tense, and how he remained standing, caution rose within. Véronique responded with a smile, but the gesture only went surface deep. The tick of a clock somewhere behind her counted off the seconds.

"Monsieur Gunter, moments ago I learned from Madame Hochstetler that my bank draft was returned to her . . . unpaid."

He nodded, his expression tentative. "Would you please allow me to come directly to the point?"

"*Oui*, I would prefer it."

"Your account with us is overdrawn, mademoiselle."

She shook her head. "How is that possible? I do not understand."

"What this means is that you have written bank drafts in an amount that exceeds—"

"I am aware of the meaning of the word 'overdrawn,' monsieur." She softened her tone. "What I do not understand is how this has occurred. Have you not credited the deposits from Lord Grégoire Marchand as I instructed?"

Monsieur Gunter studied the top of his desk. "Yes, ma'am, we have been depositing them as they have arrived. But all along your expenditures have come very close to depleting your funds, and then the deposit due this previous week, following the normal pattern, was never presented to the bank in New York. As recently as yesterday and again this morning, a number of bank drafts, written in your hand, were presented. Cumulatively, they have exhausted your funds, and quite beyond that I'm afraid."

She gripped the arm of her chair, and a similar feeling to that of peering down into a canyon swept through her. She suddenly wished Jack were there, then thought better of it. She wouldn't want him seeing her in this situation.

"Mademoiselle Girard, I wish it did not befall me to apprise you of this news. Know that I offer my deepest—"

She rose from her chair. "This situation can be easily corrected if you will but contact the depository in Paris. Surely you still have the address." Compassion moved into his expression, causing her to feel even more vulnerable. "Please, monsieur . . . would you check your files?"

Monsieur Gunter slowly opened a folder on top of his desk and withdrew a piece of paper. He laid it on the dark mahogany wood and gently nudged it forward. "I admit, mademoiselle, contacting the depository was indeed my plan. However, we received a telegram first thing this morning from the bank in New York City. I sent word to you at the hotel not even an hour ago, requesting an appointment with you . . . to discuss its contents."

Véronique caught the depository's name typed at the top of the telegram, and a cold knot of fear twisted her stomach. Her eyes moved across the page. Her vision blurred, and something inside her gave way.

Succinct in content, the dispatch stated that no future deposits would be issued to the account holdings of one Mademoiselle Véronique Girard—due to the recent death of Lord Grégoire Marchand. She searched the document for the name of the individual from whom the message had originated in Paris.

And when she found it, what remained of her fragile fortitude crumbled.

Looking at Monsieur Gunter became an impossible task. She thought of Lord Marchand, of his graciousness and generosity. Of how he had fulfilled her mother's wishes, at great cost to himself and showing personal favor to her.

A thousand thoughts cluttered the moment, few of them rational. She slowly lifted her gaze. "You stated that my account was overdrawn. By what amount . . . *s'il vous plaît* ?"

"Mademoiselle Girard, we do not have to do this now. I realize what a shock this is to—"

"I will be responsible for paying my debts, monsieur."

Hands shaking, she opened her *réticule* and began counting the bills and coins, laying them beside the telegram.

"Including the most recent drafts, mademoiselle, the amount owed is . . . over one hundred and fifty dollars."

She stilled, and stared at the paltry sum on the desk. Then thought of the vendors in town to whom she'd written bank drafts in recent days. To Madame Dunston at the dress shop, a sizable amount, but she couldn't recall how much. To Monsieur Hudson at the haberdashery, also a goodly portion. She owed the mercantile a handsome figure, of course, and would have to bear Madame Hochstetler's stinging ridicule. She'd also shopped at several other smaller establishments within the—

A trembling started deep within. "Monsieur Gunter . . ." She lowered her face, wanting to delay reading the answer in his eyes. "May I inquire about my request that your bank issue funds to a *chirurgien* in Boston?"

He opened the file on his desk, and she recognized the hotel stationery and her handwriting.

Pressure expanded inside her chest. *Oh, God, what have I done. . . .* The draft for the partial payment hadn't yet been sent to Boston, but that didn't change the fact that she had no money to cover Lilly's procedure—as she had pledged to do.

How could she face the girl? And Pastor and Mrs. Carlson? When she'd requested that the payment be sent, she'd assumed enough money was in the account. She'd never checked it. But all her life, money had simply . . . been there. How could she tell them what she'd done? What had her foolish actions cost Lilly?

Monsieur Gunter circled the desk and came to stand beside her. He gathered the money and put it back into her *réticule*. "We'll work through this, Mademoiselle Girard, in coming days. I'll hold the bank drafts in your file, and won't return them to the payees until you and I have spoken again. Let's plan on meeting together next week."

His voice held a graciousness that both employed her gratitude— and guillotined her pride.

"Is that agreeable to you, mademoiselle?" he whispered.

"*Oui.*" She nodded. "Your generosity is . . . much appreciated, monsieur." Tears slipped down her cheeks. As she walked to the door, Madame Marchand's face came to mind, then the matriarch's name being listed as the issuant on the telegram from the depository in Paris. In the end, the woman had had her exacting after all.

"One last question, mademoiselle, before you go." Kindness softened Monsieur Gunter's voice.

She paused, her hand on the latch.

"Do you own land in this country? Or a home perhaps? Any property that would be of worth that I could assist you in selling in order to help cover your debts? The bank's shareholders will require this information."

She thought of the only home she'd ever known—of Lord Marchand and Christophe, and her *maman* . . . and slowly shook her head. "I have no home. I own no property in this country, and none in France." As the reality of the words poised on her tongue took hold, fear yawned wider. She worked to hold herself together. "I possess nothing of lasting value, Monsieur Gunter."

He slowly nodded and looked down at his desk.

Opening the door, she suddenly remembered. "*Pardonnez-moi,* monsieur, but that is not altogether true. I own a wagon."

CHAPTER THIRTY-NINE

J ACK KNOCKED ON the door of Véronique's hotel room for a second time.

No answer.

He knocked again, harder this time. He'd returned to town early that morning, and now it was past the time they had arranged to meet. It wasn't like her to be late. It went against her "rules." Punctuality was nearly as important to that woman as having every seam straight and every hair in place.

He took the stairs down to the lobby and waited until Lilly finished with another patron. "Do you know if Véronique came through here earlier? She's not in her room, and we were supposed to ride out to Miss Maudie's together today."

Lilly glanced toward the stairs. "I haven't seen her since . . . Friday evening when the two of you were having dinner in the dining room. But I also haven't worked the desk the last few days. I got a note from her on Saturday though."

"I don't want to overstep my boundaries here, Lilly. But . . . did she seem all right to you? From what she wrote in the note?"

"Yes, she seemed fine. She said she wouldn't be at church on Sunday, that she was tired and had some things she needed to attend to. But I service her room, Mr. Brennan, so I know she's been here. She's probably been busy, that's all." The girl's eyes grew wide. "Did she tell you? My parents decided I can have the surgery."

Jack tried for a genuine smile. Véronique had confided in him, after the fact, about the offer she'd made to the Carlsons. It hadn't set well with him then, and still didn't. And he hadn't hidden his opinion from her. Yet if it was what the Carlsons thought was best . . . "Yes, she did, Lilly. Congratulations. When will the surgery be?"

"Not until October. We still have to work out a bunch of details with the doctor in Boston, but . . . I'm excited."

"That's real good, Lilly." Jack watched her, thinking she looked more nervous to him than excited. "I'm happy for you. Listen, before I leave would you mind checking to see if Véronique left me a note? Maybe she left it with Mr. or Mrs. Baird before you arrived."

Lilly leafed through the papers on the desk and the shelves beneath. "I don't see anything. But as soon as she returns, I'll let her know you're looking for her." She leaned closer and wriggled her brows. "Does she know about . . ."

He smiled. "No . . . at least I don't think so. I wanted it to be a surprise for her."

"Oh, I'm sure it will be, Mr. Brennan. And I know she'll love it! I can't wait to see her reaction."

Jack sighed. That made two of them. If he couldn't find her, the surprise might end up being on him. "Thanks, Lilly."

He walked on out to the front porch. His gaze roamed the faces of passersby, and places where Véronique might have gone ticked through his mind. He came up with nothing.

It wasn't as if she had to report her whereabouts to him every minute of every day, but they'd had an agreement to meet today. And he'd grown accustomed to being with her—from sunrise to sunset. When they were in town, he found himself looking forward to their next trip. And when they were on one of their trips, he knew contentment he hadn't experienced in years, and an excitement about the future he'd given up hope of ever feeling again.

He hadn't told her about his land yet. She knew he'd put a bid on it, but ever since the night of reading her mother's letter, the timing just hadn't seemed right for him to tell her. It was only land—why was he worried about timing? Yet something else came with the land in his mind, and he had a feeling she'd been thinking about it too.

At least he hoped she had.

Reluctantly, he walked back to the wagon and climbed to the bench seat. He'd spent the better part of a month getting all the details planned and set for tonight. And he'd worked most of yesterday afternoon and well into the night out at Casaroja making sure things were ready to go—though he'd intentionally led Véronique to believe he wouldn't return to Willow Springs from his supply run until after midnight. All part of the plan.

Jack glanced at the cloudless blue overhead; at least the weather was cooperating. He sighed, a great deal more concerned than frustrated, and finally signaled to Charlemagne and Napoleon to move out. Miss Maudie would already be looking for them. But first, he needed to make a quick stop by Mrs. Rawlings's bakery per Miss Maudelaine Mahoney's request.

———

Véronique stood at the edge of the cemetery, thankful no one else was there. She needed fresh hope, and why she had not thought to come here before, she couldn't say.

Dry twigs crunched beneath her boots as she walked the shaded rows of graves. Trees overhead whispered a song she'd come to expect since arriving in Willow Springs, and that she'd grown to cherish from their cousins in the higher country. Some of the graves had headstones with names and dates and loving epitaphs, while others bore only a simple wooden cross with the name of the departed carved deep into the wood.

Though none of the memorials on this sacred patch of earth came close to rivaling the extravagance of those in her beloved Cimetière de Montmartre, the same spirit hovered.

One of finality, to be certain. But also of expectancy.

And it was that sense of expectancy—of blessed anticipation—that drew her now. Perhaps it had drawn her to such places all her life. A truth had revealed itself in recent days, one that threaded through her life as far back as she could remember.

Life came from death. And death had less to do with endings and more to do with beginnings.

The churning waters of Fountain Creek beckoned her, and she walked a short distance, following the edge of the cemetery.

Reliving what had happened at the mercantile, then at the bank with Monsieur Gunter, and dwelling on what awaited her when she told the Carlsons there was no money for the *procédure*, made her want to run and hide again.

But she'd been doing that for the past three days, and it had changed nothing. Her conscience was bruised from the struggle and her honesty sore from wrestling with what she knew was the right thing to do.

She'd visited Madame Dunston at the dress shop, and Véronique still marveled at how the woman's forgiving spirit had been so convicting, while also so thoroughly healing. Véronique had offered to help in the dress shop to cover what she owed, and Madame Dunston had accepted with unexpected flourish. Most of the other vendors in town had shown understanding as well. Save Madame Hochstetler, whom she still owed a visit.

And the Carlsons—that would be the most difficult of all.

She looked down at her hands. Her nails were chipped and uneven. The scrapes and bruises from carrying the rocks with Jack the night of the thunderstorm had long since healed, but her hands looked nothing like those of a lady anymore. Jack had once commented to her about how she liked rules, suggesting that she was overly concerned with appearances and with what people thought of her.

Defensiveness rose within her—knowing he had been right.

It wasn't until she'd been forced from the safe haven of the Marchand home—from the far-reaching power of the family's influence and financial status—that she'd finally taken an honest look at who she was, separate and apart.

And she hadn't liked what she'd seen.

To think that Jack considered her spoiled or self-important in any way made her cringe inside. But what hurt her even more was knowing that, if he did think that, he was right.

She came upon a shallow place in Fountain Creek where the land leaned down to kiss the water, and she knelt and dipped her hands in the bubbling stream.

Maman . . .

A faint susurration from childhood echoed back toward her, and the voice was a familiar one. Even if it lacked some of its former sweetness. *"Maturity can often be measured by a person's response to success, Véronique. But it can* always *be measured by their response to failure."* In light of what Véronique knew now, the oft-spoken words from her mother rang truer. But she wondered, had her mother ever felt a check in her own spirit over her failures, her lack of courage, as she'd put it, as she'd offered this counsel to her daughter?

Remembering the day in the cave, Véronique knew God had granted her the wish of hearing her mother's voice again. And for that, she was grateful.

She dipped her hand again and cupped a portion of Fountain Creek in her palm. She mentally traced the creek's journey down through the mountains, knowing many of its twists and turns, and she felt certain the water before her had flowed past many of the mining towns she'd visited.

And perhaps one her father had once passed through.

Papa . . .

Though she had yet to travel to all the mining towns listed on her map, something within her whispered that her search was over. She had asked God repeatedly to answer her prayer. And He had.

Only not in the way she had expected.

She'd come to Willow Springs with the hope of finding her father and discovering who he was. And instead, had been shown who she was.

Or rather, who she was not.

Véronique took a deep breath and slowly let it out, and that's when she saw it.

Hidden beneath weeds and wild grasses was a small wooden cross—crude, held together by rope, it leaned to one side no more than four feet away from where she knelt.

She moved to the grave and began clearing away the weeds. Some were harder to remove than others, their roots going deep. But some plucked easily in her grip.

As the patch of ground became less unruly, she noticed the faintest outline of rocks surrounding the grave. They had been pressed into the soil to form an elongated circle, its circumference no more than two feet. She worked to remove the dirt covering the rocks, and with each sweeping pass of her hand, she pictured her mother's grave half a world away.

But even more, she pictured where her mother was now.

Véronique righted the cross, not an easy task, as the wood went deeper into the hardened soil than she'd imagined. There was no name. There were no dates. But from the size of the grave, she guessed it belonged to a *petit enfant.*

She stood and brushed off her hands. "'Death, be not proud,'" she whispered, "'though some have called thee mighty and dreadful. For thou ... art ... not ... so.'" She recited the sonnet with more feeling, more confidence, than she ever had before. "'For those whom thou think'st thou dost overthrow—'"

"'. . . die not, poor death, nor yet canst thou kill me.'"

At the sound of Jack's voice behind her, tears threatened. Unsure of whether he knew yet about what had happened to her, but knowing how quickly gossip traveled in a small community, she couldn't look at him.

"Would you like to continue?" He moved closer.

She closed her eyes at the tenderness in his voice. "*Non* ... I would rather hear you."

Jack came alongside her, and she listened as he quoted the rest of the sonnet. The words took on new life in the deep timbre of his voice, and she remembered something he'd said to her a while back. She waited as he finished.

"'One short sleep past, we wake eternally.'" Jack paused and took her hand. "'And death shall be no more; death, thou shalt die.'"

She stared at their clasped hands. "When first we met, I asked you if you had ever lost someone close to you. You did not answer me then. But I think you did just now. Who was it that you lost?"

The muscles in his jaw tensed. His hand tightened around hers. "My wife, and my son."

CHAPTER FORTY

J ACK'S WORDS HUNG in the air, and each second he waited for
Véronique to respond, they grew heavier.

Moments ago, as he'd passed the church on his way from
town out to Casaroja, he'd glimpsed a woman in the cemetery. At
first, he hadn't recognized her. But something had caused him to slow
down. Seeing the purposeful grace with which she moved, watching
how she brushed the hair from her face, he'd known.

This was definitely one place he'd not considered looking for her.

His gaze settled on the grave at their feet, and the freshly pulled
stack of weeds piled to one side. He gathered she'd been the one to
clear it off. Why she'd done it, he wasn't certain. But he suspected it
had something to do with her mother. Or maybe her father.

Véronique wore her mining-town homespun instead of her customary finery, and after his conversation moments ago with Mrs.
Rawlings at the bakery, he understood why.

Imagining the scene playing out at the crowded store on Saturday
morning as Mrs. Rawlings had described it, and knowing how it must
have affected Véronique, he'd wanted to march over to the mercantile
and throttle Mrs. Hochstetler—the old battle-ax. Though the woman
had reason to be frustrated, the way she'd chosen to handle the situation seemed intentionally vicious and meanspirited.

And from the woundedness he'd sensed in Véronique when he

first walked up, Mrs. Hochstetler had apparently accomplished her goal.

If only Véronique would look at him.

Wondering where to begin, and how to tell her that he knew, Jack opened his mouth—then promptly closed it when she lifted his hand to her lips.

Véronique kissed the back of his hand—once, twice—then pressed his scarred palm against the dampness of her cheek.

Emotions buried deep inside him rose unexpectedly, and Jack struggled to keep them in check. No words she could have spoken would have affected him more deeply.

After a moment, she lowered their hands but didn't relinquish her hold. "How long ago was this for you?"

"Fifteen years." The rush of the creek behind them filled the silence. "And another lifetime," he whispered. "I've been on the verge of telling you so many times before, but . . . just never did."

"I would like to know about them both, *s'il vous plaît*. If you are willing to share with me. . . ."

Warmth spread through him at her concern. Even with all she'd endured herself, her thoughts were for him. "I'm more than willing, Véronique." He wiped the tears from her cheeks, believing more than ever that what he had planned this evening at Casaroja would help lift her spirits. If only he could get her out there. "But would you mind if we continued this conversation in the wagon?" He winced, realizing that wasn't the smoothest of transitions. "Remember, Miss Maudie is expecting us, and I've got a delivery to make."

"Always it is this way with you, Monsieur Brennan." A faint smile touched her lips. "Must we be traveling together every minute?"

He heard the tease in her voice but saw the weariness in her expression. "Not every minute, no ma'am. But right now I've got a feisty little Irish lady who's waiting for her goods. And I know she'd love to see you too."

At her nod, Jack slipped an arm around her waist and they walked back to the wagon.

As he drove the familiar road to Casaroja, he told her about Mary and Aaron, their life together, the day of the accident, and about his life since then. "So I spent the next thirteen years guiding other families west. Trying to move on with my life while learning to accept what had happened."

She sat wordless beside him for the longest time. "How is it, Jack, that you can quote John Donne?"

He smiled and lowered his head briefly. "That would be Mary's doing. After she died, I found a book of sonnets in her trunk. Parts of that one had been underlined, many times. And gradually, I guess I just took it to heart."

"I also have that sonnet written on my heart. It was my mother's favorite, and I read it to her countless times." She gave a soft sigh. "But only now have I begun to understand its meaning."

"It took me some time too."

"Sometimes . . . it takes the better part of a life, *non*?"

Hearing the still-fresh grief in her voice, he took hold of her hand on the seat between them and remembered the day he'd spoken those same words to her. He slowly wove his fingers between hers, enjoying the privilege.

A warm breeze stirred the golden-gray stalks of prairie grasses growing on either side of the road, and Jack found himself counting the fence posts as they passed—and praying for her. He'd reached twenty-two when she broke the silence.

"Jack, I need to say something to you."

He slowed the wagon but she shook her head. "*Non*, please keep going on your way. I prefer it."

What she preferred, he knew, was not having him looking at her—something *he* preferred to do every chance he got. Yet he understood her request and gave the reins a gentle flick.

"Vernie, before you say anything else I need to tell you that I know about what happened at the mercantile on Saturday." He glimpsed the question in her eyes. "I stopped by the bakery in town earlier to pick up the—to pick up something to eat, and Mrs. Rawlings told me. My only question is . . . why didn't you seek me out this morning, to tell me?"

She looked at him as though his question were absurd. "I did not seek you out for the same reason you were not pleased to learn that I overheard your encounter with Monsieur Hochstetler. That is not too difficult to understand, *non*?"

He actually felt himself blush at her straightforward answer, and yet not a trace of sarcasm shaded her tone. Telling the truth was the same as breathing to this woman. He couldn't hide his smile. "If I remember correctly, I believe the word *touché* would be appropriate here."

"*Oui*, I have heard it used that way in this country." She smiled briefly, and gently withdrew her hand from his. "Saturday at the mercantile was a most unpleasant experience. However ... what happened following the confrontation with Madame Hochstetler was far more painful to me."

Protectiveness rose within him but he kept silent. Obviously Mrs. Rawlings had not been privy to this part of the story.

"After I left the mercantile, I went to see Monsieur Gunter at the bank. My account with his depository is severely overdrawn, and there will be no more deposits issuing from France." She bowed her head, and let out a deep breath. "But the worst news ... is that Lord Marchand, my former employer, has passed away. I do not know the details, but I am certain to get a letter from Christophe eventually. At least I am hoping for one."

She stared ahead as she continued, and Jack sensed each word exacting a cost. The hollowness in her voice reminded him of the loss he'd experienced after Mary and Aaron's deaths—as though he'd been set adrift without hope of finding anchor.

He quickly put two and two together. From his earlier conversation with Lilly, he surmised that Véronique hadn't yet told the Carlsons about her change in financial status. That had to be weighing on her something fierce.

The turnoff to Casaroja came sooner than anticipated, and he pulled back on the reins to negotiate the corner.

"I attempted to give Monsieur Gunter what cash I had remaining, but he would not take it." Her laugh came out hollow. "It was not nearly enough to cover the drafts I have written. He and I are meeting on Thursday to discuss what is to be done. As he encouraged, I have spoken to all the vendors except for Madame Hochstetler, and Lilly and her parents. I cannot fathom how great their disappointment will be. Both in the change of circumstance—" She paused. "And in me," she added in a rough whisper.

He searched for something to say, but nothing measured up. In the distance, at least twenty wagons were parked around the main house and along the pasture fencing. Wondering if Véronique had noticed, he stole a look beside him to find her gaze confined to her lap.

He stopped the wagon prematurely and set the brake.

That drew her attention.

He moved closer. "I know this makes little difference now, Véronique, but . . . I wish I'd been there with you when you got this news. About Lord Marchand, and about the money."

Her lips trembled. She reached up and touched the side of his face. "Would you have shot Monsieur Gunter for me, Jack? Like you threatened the miners?" She bit her lower lip, but the tiniest smirk still slipped past. "Or perhaps Madame Hochstetler instead, which would be my preference."

He couldn't help but stare at her mouth, and the image of Madame Hochstetler actually helped to curb his foremost desire at the moment. "Don't put such tempting thoughts in my head, woman."

Her eyes sparkled, but only for a moment. "Since all of this has happened, I have been given the opportunity to look more closely at myself, Jack." She shook her head. "And I have not liked what I have seen."

"That's where we're different, then, ma'am. Because I like what I see very much."

She bowed her head. "I was raised in a wealthy home, with privilege and opportunity not belonging to me by birth but by chance. Yet somewhere along the way, I lost sight of what I was, and I began thinking that all of that was mine. That I was deserving of it. In a way, it is ironic." She closed her eyes, and a tear slipped down her cheek. "All my life, I have been a servant . . . and yet I have never possessed a servant's heart."

Jack's chest ached as he watched the fullness of that realization move over her. She bowed her head, and a soft moan from somewhere deep inside worked its way up. He cradled her cheek, patient for her to look at him. When she finally did, he leaned close. "That might have been true in some sense before, Vernie. But it's not true of the woman I'm looking at now."

She took a quick breath and worked at forming a smile. "Must you persist with the use of that name?" Her lips parted and she looked at his mouth with clear intent.

Needing to ease the tension of the moment—not to mention his own—Jack drew back a fraction. "You're not about to be sick on me again, are you?"

His mouth went dry at the look in her eyes.

"*Non*, Jack. Rather, I am thinking what it would be like to kiss you again."

He could've fallen flat off the wagon right then and felt no pain. He actually had to swallow in order to speak again. "Is . . . is that so, Mademoiselle Girard."

"It is quite so, Monsieur Brennan."

She moved closer, and Jack did nothing to dissuade her this time. She seemed set on taking the lead, and he let her. Her kiss was tentative at first, her lips brushing against his until he encouraged her the slightest bit.

Her hands moved from his shoulders to the back of his neck, and she tilted her head into his kiss.

After a moment, Jack gradually grew mindful again of where he was. Caring so much for the woman in his arms, he took her gently by the shoulders. "Véronique," he whispered against her mouth.

She opened her eyes but didn't move. "*Oui?*"

Still able to taste her, Jack thanked God again for His foresight in creating the feminine gender. And this beautiful woman in particular.

She drew back slightly, as though reading his thoughts, a twinkle lighting her eyes. "Do we need to . . . be getting back on the road?"

Did the woman remember every single thing he'd ever said? Jack shook his head, enjoying her smile. It boded well for the evening ahead. "Yes, ma'am. We most certainly do."

CHAPTER FORTY-ONE

J ACK'S HAND BRUSHED against hers as they walked from the wagon toward the far side of Miss Maudie's home. He gave her hand a gentle squeeze, and Véronique smiled to herself, thinking back to moments earlier. There was so much more to Jack Brennan than she had first imagined, and still more she wanted to know.

She tried to imagine what sort of woman his wife, Mary, had been, and which parent little Aaron had resembled. Or had Jack's son been a blend of them both? Learning about Jack's previous marriage didn't change her feelings for him. Discovering what he'd been through, knowing what he'd lost—and yet witnessing what kind of man he was now—only made her appreciate him all the more.

They rounded the corner, and Véronique came to a halt.

Her mouth slipped open. When they'd first driven up, she'd heard faint laughter and the thrum of conversation, and figured there was a gathering—the number of wagons told her that. But she'd never expected this! Casaroja had been transformed!

Glittering cut-out stars crafted of red, white, and blue paper hung from boughs of trees, and streamers of similar colors adorned everything imaginable—from hitching posts to corral fences to clotheslines. Royal blue tablecloths covered long plank wood tables, and candles were arranged at intervals, waiting to be lit. And the number of people!

The entire population of Willow Springs looked to be in attendance. Which made Véronique want to turn and run—especially when she thought of facing Pastor and Hannah Carlson, and Lilly, and of having to explain what had happened. In light of that, asking pardon from Mrs. Hochstetler no longer seemed a great issue.

Already Véronique prayed the Carlsons would find the grace to forgive her, and that God would provide another way to heal Lilly.

Jack discreetly reached for her hand. "It's okay, Vernie. These are good people. They understand what it's like to go through hard times. And I'll be beside you when you tell the Carlsons, if you'd like."

"*Merci beaucoup*, Jack. I would be most grateful." She took a deep breath and gestured to the festive surroundings. "What is all of this about?"

"It's a celebration, of our country's independence. We do this every—"

"Fourth of July. *Oui*, I know of this. I have read of this celebration in a book from the library." It had simply slipped her mind in the events of recent days. She caught a whiff of something decadent. Apple pie, perhaps . . . "It very much resembles our Bastille Day."

Question shadowed his expression.

"That is the day my country celebrates the end of tyranny in France. Much as you do your freedom from Britain." She recalled something. "Do you remember what I told you about Louis the Sixteenth?"

A smirk tipped Jack's mouth. "He was the one with the nice house, right?"

She ignored his comment, but couldn't completely quell her smile. "The people stormed the Bastille—a prison in Paris—and that day was the beginning of the end for King Louis, and also for his wife." She let go of his hand and quickly slid a finger across her throat. "So we have similar histories in this respect, *non*? Fighting for our freedom?"

"*Oui*, mademoiselle." He bowed at the waist. "And on behalf of my country, may I offer my gratitude to yours for the aid provided in our fight against King George."

She curtsied. "You are most welcome, monsieur." She softened her voice. "My country is grateful for the alliance we have formed with yours. We cherish it, in fact."

Intimacy shaded his smile, telling her he'd understood the subtlety of her reference.

He tucked her hand into the crook of his arm. "Speaking of alliances, I'd like to explore how we might strengthen ours, Mademoiselle Girard. If you're open to that."

Something stirred inside her. *Oh, this man . . .* "I would welcome those negotiations, Monsieur Brennan."

With a lingering look, he covered her hand on his arm and drew her toward the crowd.

The first person Véronique spotted was Madame Dunston. Their eyes met and she tensed, anticipating the dress-shop owner's reaction at seeing her again. Madame Dunston had been gracious when Véronique had visited her about the overdrawn bank draft, but perhaps she'd had time to reconsider.

Madame Dunston made her way through the crowd. "Mademoiselle Girard, I've been looking for you." She gestured to the gentleman beside her. "I'd like to introduce you to my husband."

As the woman made the introductions, Véronique noted the sincerity in Madame Dunston's voice, absent of any trace of animosity.

Monsieur Dunston possessed a *gentil* manner that complemented his wife. "My wife tells me you've agreed to help her in the dress shop, Mademoiselle Girard. She's long boasted about your talent when it comes to fashion, ma'am, so I'm pleased this has worked out. She couldn't be happier."

Véronique looked at Madame Dunston. Warmth and acceptance filled the woman's expression, and it pained Véronique to realize that had the tables been turned, those were not emotions she would have demonstrated, prior to recent events. She curtsied, bowing low, feeling a depth of gratitude and humility in the gesture that she hadn't before.

Slowly, she rose. "It is I who am indebted to your wife, Monsieur Dunston. In many ways."

"Mademoiselle Girard!"

Véronique couldn't locate the owner of the voice in the crowd until Jack directed her.

She couldn't believe her eyes. "Monsieur Colby!" Excusing herself from the Dunstons, she wished it were appropriate to hug the man.

Bertram Colby grabbed her hand and bestowed a whiskered kiss.

He looked handsome with his freshly trimmed beard and ready smile. "Ma'am, you've come to mind so many times in past months. I'm glad to find you're still here." His gaze swept her up and down. "Looks like the Colorado Territory's been treatin' you well."

Jack clapped his friend on the shoulder. "Glad you got back in time to join us, Colby."

"Oh, I wouldn't have missed this for anything. It wouldn't be the Fourth without your show, Brennan." His attention swung back. "So tell me, ma'am, how are things goin' for you?"

As Véronique answered, she caught Jack mouthing that he would return in a moment. With quick glances, she followed his path, aware of people acknowledging him as he moved through the crowd. Men shook his hand, and women—single and married alike, Véronique noticed—made a point of touching his arm and thanking him for this evening.

Then she saw them—the Carlson family—and her stomach knotted. They waved, and Véronique did likewise, while attempting to listen to Monsieur Colby's animated conversation.

A bell clanged, and she felt a touch on her arm.

"It's time for dinner," Jack whispered, and relief filled her at his return. "Miss Maudie would like everyone to be seated."

Jack led her to a table with Monsieur Colby in tow, and the gentlemen flanked her left and right.

With a cane, and some assistance from Thomas Stewartson, Miss Maudie stood and addressed the crowd. "Welcome to Casaroja, dear friends. I'm so pleased you're able to join us for this evening's festivities. Let me tell you how the evening will unfold."

"Who's that fine-lookin' woman?"

Véronique grinned at Bertram Colby's whispered inquiry. "That is *Miss* Maudelaine Mahoney. Everyone calls her Miss Maudie." Véronique was certain she'd detected interest in the man's voice. "Casaroja is her home. And she is indeed a fine woman, Monsieur Colby. It would please me greatly to make an introduction on your behalf sometime during the evening."

"Not near as much as it would please me, ma'am." His focus never left Miss Maudie. "I'd sure be obliged."

After a delicious steak dinner, followed by an assortment of delectable french pastries made special by Susanna Rawlings in her bakery, the men pushed back the tables and the music began.

"May I have this dance, Vernie?"

Véronique didn't know what to expect, but quickly discovered that Jack Brennan had done his share of dancing, and was quite good. The song ended and another tune began, more lively this time.

She glanced around at the high-stepping dance the couples around them were doing. "I do not know this dance, Jack. Perhaps we should—"

He smiled and pulled her close. "Just hang on. You'll do fine."

Véronique stumbled once—no chance of falling with Jack holding her tight—and within a couple of minutes, she'd memorized the steps and was laughing along with everyone else.

The next melody was slower paced, and Véronique was glad for the chance to gain her breath. Jack didn't ask her if she wanted to continue to dance but slipped his arm about her waist and pulled her close.

As the music played, she knew she would remember every detail about this moment—the feel of his hand pressed against the small of her back, her fingers laced loosely through his, the shimmer of candlelight, the violins playing, the rustle of the evening breeze through the trees, and the knowledge that God had indeed had a plan all along. Even if it hadn't been hers.

"Thank you, Jack," she whispered.

His arm tightened around her and he kissed the top of her head. Bringing his mouth close to her ear, he whispered, "I got my land, Vernie."

She drew back. "Ah! *Magnifique!* I am so happy for you, Jack. You are most deserving of this."

"I'd like to show it to you."

"And I would like to see it . . . as long as there are no skunks."

"Can't promise that, I'm afraid."

The sound of his laughter took her back to the time she'd first heard it, when she'd seen him standing outside the hotel with Bertram Colby. She was as close to Jack as *étiquette*—and propriety—allowed, yet she wanted to be much closer.

A harmonica joined the blend of strings, and she couldn't remember a sweeter sound—not even in the opera halls of Paris. "When will you start building the cabin you have described to me?"

"I've already started clearing the land." His deep voice dropped to a whisper. "Larson Jennings is helping me. My land backs up to his. We're going to be neighbors."

"I am so proud of you, Jack. And of what you are doing."

The pride that shone in her eyes was more fulfilling than Jack could have imagined.

The music came to a close, and when another fast-paced jig began, he took her hand and led her through the crowd of onlookers to a table set up by the kitchen door.

Claire Stewartson started ladling something into a cup the moment she saw them. "Might I interest you two in some cool cider?"

"Mrs. Stewartson, you read our minds." Jack handed Véronique a full cup and spotted Jake Sampson heading toward them.

"Evening, Sampson. Glad you could make it."

Sampson took the offered cup of cider, nodding to the ladies. "Thanks, Brennan. Took me a while to get my work done. I tell ya, I got to have someone else in that shop or I'm going to work myself to an early grave."

Jack drained his cup. "I've been keeping an eye out but haven't run across anyone yet."

Bertram Colby approached, a most eager look on his face. "Excuse me, friends. Mademoiselle Girard . . . might I bother you to aid me with . . . what we were discussin' at dinner?"

"*Oui*, Monsieur Colby." A mischievous smile turned her mouth as she handed Jack her cup. "I would be honored. Gentlemen, Mrs. Stewartson, if you will excuse us, *s'il vous plaît*."

Jack watched her lead Colby through the fray, certain the two were up to no good. The demand for cider increased, so he and Sampson stepped to the side. "Sampson, I want to thank you for the good word you put in for me with Clayton. Whatever you said to him worked."

Sampson raised a brow. "You got your land?"

"Yes, sir, I did. Still can't believe it." He accepted Sampson's vigorous handshake. "I've already started clearing it off. Got a neighbor helping me with it."

A gleam slid into Sampson's eyes. The older man winked. "So that means you'll be stayin' around these parts, I take it? Gettin' settled down?"

Jack shook his head, smiling. "First things first there, my friend." He peered over the crowd and spotted Véronique and Bertram Colby . . . talking with Miss Maudie. Uh oh . . . what was that woman up to?

"So, Brennan, you have plans to start buildin' soon?"

"Yes, sir, I'd like to have at least a couple of rooms done before winter. I've got designs drawn for a cabin and have the perfect spot picked out. It's beautiful land. Best in these parts, in my opinion."

Sampson lifted his cup in a cheer. "With Fountain Creek runnin' through it, there's little doubt."

"Yes, sir. I feel privileged to have gotten it. My thanks to you again."

Then it hit him—he didn't remember telling Jake Sampson where the land he bid on was located. But Clayton probably had when he'd gathered the reference. Still, Jack's curiosity was more than a little piqued.

"And you don't owe me a bit of thanks, Brennan. Clayton never paid me a visit. Guess it was Bertram Colby's good word that did the trick."

Jack stared into his empty cup and, every few seconds, snuck looks beside him as Sampson watched the crowd.

It couldn't be . . .

He recalled the day in the livery when Sampson had first told him about Véronique. The man had alluded to gold prospecting in years past, and when Jack had questioned him about it, Sampson had given measured answers. Looking at Jake Sampson, Jack was hard-pressed to see anything other than a very talented wheelwright and a livery owner. But still he wondered. . . .

He decided to test the waters. "I've already met one of my neighbors. He's helping me clear the land, like I said. Maybe you've met him before. Do you know the families in that area?"

Sampson continued to watch the couples dancing.

"I said maybe you've met him before, Sampson."

"I heard what you said, son." Sampson tipped his cup back and wiped his mouth with his sleeve. Then he turned, a sage look in his eyes.

Jack held his stare. "You sold me that land . . . didn't you, sir?" he whispered. "You're the owner Clayton told me about."

Sampson frowned, and it almost looked convincing. "What on earth are you talkin' about?"

"I never told you where my land was located, Sampson. Yet you knew about Fountain Creek."

The man looked away, scoffing. "I hate to tell you, but half the land around here has Fountain Creek floatin' through it. You said your land was the best in these parts." He shrugged. "What else am I to assume?"

That wasn't true. And in his gut, Jack knew Sampson was hiding something. "I'll keep it to myself—I give you my word." He lowered his voice. "All I'd like to do is to thank the person who sold me the land, that's all. I've dreamed of having land like that for years. I'm not asking you to tell me why you did it, or why you don't want anyone else to know."

Saying nothing, Sampson turned back to watching the crowd.

Jack spotted Miss Maudie motioning to him from across the way. He started to question Sampson again, but stopped himself. The man must've had his reasons for wanting to remain anonymous, or he wouldn't have gone to such lengths to cover his trail. First with Larson and Kathryn Jennings when they bought back their land a couple of years ago, as Larson had described, and now with him. And *if* Sampson was the man, Jack had already accomplished his goal by giving him his thanks.

"Listen, Sampson," he said softly, regretting having raised the subject in the first place, "just so we're clear, I won't mention this again to you, or anyone else. You have my word." He started to walk away.

"You remember what I said about being contented, Brennan?"

The unexpected question brought Jack back around. He gauged his answer carefully. "Yes, sir. You said that learning to be content is hard. But that not learning . . . sometimes that's even harder."

A faint smile shone through Sampson's beard. "Having riches can change a man. Can change the people around him too—and not for the better. Makes it hard to tell the true friends from the false." Sampson shifted his weight and looked over at him. "Learnin' to be content was a costly lesson for me, and what I gained wasn't worth what I lost."

Shadows crept over Sampson's face, and even without knowing what loss the man was referring to, Jack felt the keenness of it.

Sampson cleared his throat. "But the Almighty has a way of bringin' good from the worst. And I believe a man will have to give account for what he's done with what God's given him."

Jack nodded. "I agree."

A gleam lit the older man's eyes. "Are you familiar with the phrase 'giving without lettin' your left hand know what your right hand is doing,' Brennan?"

Jack stared as the mystery of this man fell away in gradual shades. He laughed softly. "Yes, sir, I'm familiar with that Scripture." Miss Maudie motioned to him again, and he acknowledged her with a wave.

Sampson clapped him on the back. "Well, good, then . . . I believe that's enough said. You go on now, son. You've got a celebration to get underway."

———

Véronique followed the crowd of guests down the slope to the pasture, the well-lit path illumined by the soft glow of lanterns. She searched for Jack. The last time she'd seen him, he'd been speaking with Miss Maudie.

Oddly, she didn't feel uncomfortable walking by herself. Maybe the obscurity of darkness helped, but despite having seen several of the vendors to whom she owed money, she felt as if she was among friends this evening. Undoubtedly, Mrs. Hochstetler's lack of attendance bolstered that feeling.

Blankets were spread on the ground in a large circle, the circumference bordered by six-foot torches that bathed the ground in golden light.

Finding a place, she settled back, stretched her legs out in front of her, and arranged her skirt. The sun, now hidden behind the mountains, left a sliver of orange glow cradled in the cleft of the highest summit. Fistfuls of stars God had flung into the heavens at the beginning of time shone with a brightness she could not remember seeing before.

She heard laughter behind her and glanced over her shoulder. Miss Maudie was being carried down the slope . . . by Bertram Colby!

And they were headed straight for her!

Monsieur Colby gently situated Miss Maudie on the blanket beside her.

"Bless you, Mr. Colby." Miss Maudie smoothed her dress. "That was most kind of you, sir. And let me tell you—it was far more excitin' than that wheelchair Doc Hadley would have me careenin' down the hill in."

He removed his hat. "It was my pleasure, ma'am. And I'd be happy to carry you back up after we're done, seein' as you couldn't find your cane."

Miss Maudie gazed up at him with all the vim of a young schoolgirl. "Be careful, Mr. Colby. You do that and I'll start to think I've died and gone to heaven."

"Well, ma'am, seein' as I already consider myself there, I guess I'm one step ahead of you." Smiling, Monsieur Colby tipped his hat and excused himself.

Slack-jawed, Véronique watched the smooth-tongued *racaille* walk away, then giggled when Miss Maudie grinned at her.

The older woman leaned close. "How can I be thankin' you enough, Véronique, for introducin' me to that handsome man? Though I'm a wee bit peeved to think you traveled with him all the way from New York City and didn't breathe a word about him to me till now."

Véronique laughed. "If it helps to reinstate me to your good graces . . . Monsieur Colby requested an introduction to you as soon as you rose to speak tonight." She raised her brow. "He was quite taken with you from the very first."

Miss Maudie patted her arm. "You're forgiven of everything, my dear. And don't be tellin' anyone, but my cane is hidden beneath the shrubs by the kitchen."

The clang of a bell drew their attention, and Véronique spotted Jack walking through the crowd to the front of the gathering. He held a *torche* in his hand, and a flush of pride swept through her again. She sat a little straighter, wondering what he was going to do.

"Ladies and gentlemen . . ."

She smiled at the formal tone he'd adopted.

"On behalf of Miss Maudie, I welcome you again to Casaroja

this evening and want to share a few words before we continue our celebration."

Véronique wasn't certain, but from the way he kept looking in her direction, she wondered if he knew where she was seated.

"Though it's the first time I've done this at Casaroja, this celebration is something I've enjoyed hosting for the past thirteen years. And I wasn't about to let go of the tradition. My thanks to Jake Sampson, Patrick and Bobby Carlson, Bertram Colby, and Callum Roberts for their able assistance in setting things up."

At the mention of Callum Roberts, Véronique craned her neck to search the crowd for the pauper she'd met in town. Sure enough, there he was, sitting with the Dunstons a few blankets over.

"As Miss Maudie shared earlier, our country is ninety-five years old today, and—"

Applause and cheers rose from the crowd. Véronique found herself clapping along.

Once everyone quieted, Jack continued. "As we've enjoyed dinner and dancing tonight, and as we watch the festivities in a few minutes, I hope we'll pause and remember men such as Carter Braxton of Virginia. Braxton was a wealthy planter and trader whose ships were attacked and destroyed by the British navy during the fight for independence. Braxton sold his home and his properties to help finance the war . . . and he died penniless.

"Before being captured by the British, Richard Stockton of Princeton, New Jersey, managed to get his family to safety. But he was held prisoner for several years, separated from his wife and family, and lost all of his property during the British invasion."

Véronique sensed empathy and a common unity being woven through the crowd, and she wondered who of those gathered were related to messieurs Braxton and Stockton.

As Jack continued to speak, she couldn't help but notice how he commanded everyone's attention. Never demanding it, never coercing, and yet he held the crowd's unwavering focus.

"These men were among the fifty-six signers of our Declaration of Independence. They weren't wild-eyed, rabble-rousing ruffians. They were soft-spoken men of means and education. They had security, but they valued their liberty, and ours, more."

With little effort, she envisioned Jack Brennan guiding families across this country, and she imagined those families following him eagerly. What was it about him that inspired such trust? That made a person want to follow him?

And made her so grateful to be with him?

Miss Maudie reached over and took her hand, and Véronique realized Jack was leading them in prayer. She bowed her head.

"Father, would you make us more grateful for what you've given us in this country, and for the sacrifices of those who've spilled their blood. Would you make our government strong and keep us rooted in the faith of our forefathers. Help us to see our lives through eternal eyes and to realize that this life—though priceless—is but a vapor. And finally we ask . . . make us more like Christ, Father. No matter the cost."

An echo of amens trickled through the crowd, and Véronique added hers in a soft whisper. When she looked up, she couldn't see Jack any longer. The torches had been extinguished.

A resounding boom echoed and, instinctively, she looked skyward.

The night sky exploded with bursts of *rouge* and *blanc*. Another pop sounded and a streak of *bleu* shot straight up into the darkness, then blossomed into a plume and rained down toward the plains.

Miss Maudie joined others in clapping. "Isn't it beautiful!"

Gasps and cheers punctuated the explosions, followed by resounding applause.

Véronique had witnessed displays of fireworks before, but this experience captured something that none of the others had. Perhaps it stemmed from being in a new place, or from being overtired, or maybe anxious about what her future held. But with every burst of color that lit up the dark night sky, the slight ache in her throat grew more pronounced.

But it wasn't sadness she felt. Quite the contrary.

She'd never had less in her life in a material sense, she'd never had so little security in terms of her future, she'd never before seen herself so clearly, with all her faults and shortcomings—and yet she'd never been more content in all her life.

"Mr. Brennan!"

Jack turned to see Pastor Carlson walking toward him, with his daughter, Lilly, in his arms. Mrs. Carlson and Bobby trailed behind. Jack quickly scanned the area to see if Véronique was around. He thought he'd seen her and Miss Maudie head into the house shortly after the fireworks display. He knew she wanted to talk to the Carlsons tonight but wondered if waiting might be better.

Most of the guests had already left, or were preparing to leave.

"That was some show you put on. Our family really enjoyed it."

"I'm glad to hear it." With a nod, Jack acknowledged his appreciation, noting the fatigue on Lilly's face. "I enjoy doing it."

Carlson set his daughter down. "You okay, honey?"

"I'm fine, Papa." Lilly glanced at Jack before lowering her gaze.

"Brennan"—Pastor Carlson's smile was fleeting—"I'm wondering if you might know where Mademoiselle Girard is. We need to speak with her about . . . a new development."

Dread moved through him. Jack knew that delaying the discussion wouldn't make it any easier, but the Carlsons having heard about her situation secondhand would only make Véronique feel worse. "I believe she's with Miss Maudie."

He led the way inside. Miss Maudie was seated in the front room, her foot elevated on a table. Bertram Colby sat beside her and Véronique was nearby. Her hand went to her midsection when she saw the Carlsons.

"Miss Girard," Pastor Carlson said as he slipped an arm around his daughter's shoulders, "I know it's late, but we'd like to speak with you about something."

Véronique's face went pale, and Jack read her thoughts. "Certainly." She leaned down and whispered something to Miss Maudie.

Miss Maudie squeezed her hand and nodded.

"Pastor and Mrs. Carlson, and Lilly," Véronique motioned to the study, "we could speak more privately through here, if you prefer."

Jack knew this was hurting her. But it wasn't wounded pride he saw in her soft brown eyes. It was loving remorse, and determination.

"Bobby!" Bertram Colby stood and pulled something from his pocket. "I've got some fangs off a rattler I killed a couple of weeks back. Thought you might want to see them."

The boy's eyes went wide.

"Jack, would you join us too, please?"

Jack turned to see Véronique paused in the doorway of the study, waiting. He lightly touched her hand as he passed, and could feel her dread as she latched the door behind her.

"Miss Girard, we appreciate your time." Patrick Carlson stood with his wife by the sofa. Their expressions were gracious, especially considering the circumstances. Lilly sat on the sofa next to them. "I realize the hour is late, but Lilly didn't feel like she could leave tonight without speaking to you about this."

Véronique blinked, her throat worked. "I understand completely, Pastor. Please know that it was my intent to speak with your family this evening, before you learned this news from someone else. I should have come to you earlier, I realize, but . . . pride got in my way. And my dread at seeing your response once you learned the truth."

Jack saw the look that passed between Pastor and Mrs. Carlson and Lilly before Véronique did—because her head was bowed.

"I do not know what you have been told, Pastor . . ." Véronique lifted her gaze. "But I would appreciate the opportunity to state what happened, so that there are no misunderstandings."

"Miss Girard, I'm not quite sure what you're referring to." Pastor Carlson stepped closer. "We've asked to speak with you because Lilly has something she wants to say." He smoothed a hand over his daughter's dark hair. "She's afraid that her decision will hurt you or, greater still, will cause you to be disappointed in her."

Lilly bowed her head. Her shoulders gently shook.

Véronique glanced between them. "I fear it is I now who do not understand."

Hannah Carlson took a place beside her daughter on the sofa. "Lilly," she said softly, then whispered something Jack couldn't hear.

Lilly raised her head. "Mademoiselle Girard, I'm so grateful for what you've offered to do for me." Her lips trembled. "And please don't think that I haven't thought about this a lot, and prayed about it, because I have. But I've decided I don't want to have the surgery."

Confusion lined Veronique's expression.

"I've read all the material from the surgeon, mademoiselle, and I've had time to think about it. I know that if I have the procedure there's a good chance I may walk normally again. Or that I'll at least be able to keep walking as I do now. But there's also a chance I won't." Her hands shook as she spoke. "You're so brave, Mademoiselle Girard. You left Paris to come here to search for your father, to a strange country where you didn't know anybody."

Jack snuck another look beside him, knowing the conditions under which Véronique left Paris. Tears streaked her cheeks.

Lilly pushed to standing and walked to where Véronique stood. "But the more I've thought about doing this, the more I feel inside"— she touched the place over her heart—"that I just shouldn't. I can't explain it. I only hope you're not disappointed in me."

Véronique tucked a strand of hair behind Lilly's ear. "From the day I stepped foot into Willow Springs, I have admired your courage. I do not think it is possible for me to be disappointed in you, Mademoiselle Carlson." She hugged Lilly tight.

They parted, and a shaky smile turned Lilly's mouth. "I'll just leave it up to God whether I ever get to have that dance or not."

Véronique leaned close until their foreheads touched. "Oh, you will dance, *ma chérie*. Of that I am certain—in here." She touched the place over her own heart.

After seeing the Carlsons to their wagon, Jack returned to the house. Miss Maudie met him by the front door, cane in hand. "I thought you lost that." He pointed to her cane.

"Oh, Veronique found it for me, dear girl. Mr. Brennan, how can I thank you for all your hard work. 'Twas a night this old woman will be rememberin' for a long time to come."

"It was my pleasure, ma'am. And it did go over well, didn't it?"

"To be sure." Miss Maudie winked. "I won't be keepin' you long—these eyes are closin' fast—but I want to show Véronique somethin' before you leave, and I wanted you to be there when I did." She glanced to where Véronique stood talking on the front porch with Bertram Colby. "I'm convinced, Mr. Brennan, that if given the opportunity . . . those two could be trouble."

Jack laughed. "I've already had that exact thought."

Véronique and Colby glanced their way. And a smitten look covered Colby's face as he walked toward them.

Bertram took Miss Maudie's hand and held it between his. "Ma'am, thank you for this evening. And I'll look forward to seein' you Sunday for dinner."

Miss Maudie smiled as he kissed her hand and watched him as he walked to the stables.

Jack shook his head. Never in a million years would he have seen that one coming.

"Véronique, would you be so kind as to come with me, dear?" Miss Maudie held out her hand and led Véronique down a hallway. Jack followed.

Maudie nodded to the portraits adorning the walls. "I painted these. They're good, but they don't begin to measure up to your talent. And don't be tryin' to soothe me with flattery, child. If it's one thing a person knows at my age, it's what they're truly gifted at, and what they're not. I loved paintin', and I worked hard to learn the rules." She put her hand on Véronique's shoulder. "But I was never gifted like you are, Véronique."

She proceeded farther down the hall and paused beside a closed door. "You told me some time ago that, for a while, you thought God had taken away your gift. And He might have for all I know, for a time. Perhaps to teach you somethin'. He's done that with me on occasion. My point is that He has restored this precious gift within you, and I want to help nourish it."

Miss Maudie opened the door, and Jack saw it at the same time Véronique did. A canvas and easel were set up by a window in the corner and a full array of paints covered the top of a lace-covered table set against the wall.

Wordless, Véronique walked to the easel and ran a hand across the fresh canvas. Then she trailed her fingers over the myriad of colors filling the bottles of paints. She shook her head. "Miss Maudie, I cannot accept these. I have no way to repay you for—"

"It is a gift, Véronique. Like the talent God has given you to paint, and to draw. He gave you that gift so that you could make Him known, child. And so you could serve me while you're doin' it!"

Jack caught Miss Maudie's wink as she gestured to the paints.

"And there'll be no worryin' about payin' me back, lass. I've got several paintings I'd like to commission, if you're open to that agreement." She crossed the room and cradled Véronique's cheek in her hand. "You blessed me so much with bein' able to see the sweet faces of Larson and Kathryn, and their wee ones. Just don't ever be forgettin' that this gift you have is for the glory of the Giver, not for the one gifted."

Véronique nodded and slipped her arms around Miss Maudie. It struck Jack as he watched the two of them that these women were far more similar than he'd originally considered.

Nearly an hour later, he guided the wagon through the still streets of Willow Springs and up to the hotel. He gently nudged Véronique. She stirred against his shoulder, apparently not wanting to budge. But it was late, and he had to leave first thing in the morning for another string of supply runs.

He leaned down and kissed the crown of her head. "Vernie," he whispered.

"*Oui*, I am moving." She sat up and stretched, and accepted his assistance when he came around to her side.

He saw her to her room, and once she was safely inside, he started back down the hallway. He still had to see to the wagon and the horses.

"Jack?"

He turned at the whispered voice behind him. She leaned against the doorway, sleep softening her features, looking far too inviting for either of their sakes. "Yes, ma'am?"

"You are the kindest man I have ever known. I was proud to be by your side tonight."

He closed the distance between them, took off his hat, and took her in his arms. He kissed her thoroughly—slow and long—then summoned his resolve. "For the record, that's how we do it in America." The look on her face pleased him almost as much as had her response. "Good night, Vernie."

Nearly to the stairs, he heard her whisper his name again. Heart still pounding, he paused. "Yes?"

"Are you at all interested in buying a wagon?"

CHAPTER FORTY-TWO

I THOUGHT IT A rule that I was never to accompany you on an overnight trip, Jack. That I was too much of a . . . challenge." Véronique glanced beside her on the wagon seat, having waited to deliver that line all morning.

Jack looked away, but not before she saw his smile. "This is an exception to that rule. And you still are."

"Ah . . . so what makes this an exception?" Ever since he'd invited her on this trip, she'd tried to learn the reason behind his invitation. With no success. She'd even enlisted Bertram Colby's help. But the gentleman's skill at *espionnage* apparently needed honing. As did her own.

Jack had told her that the mountain pass they would cross today was one he'd not traveled before—which explained why he hadn't told her how breathtakingly beautiful it would be.

The September sun reflected off the snowy summit spreading out before them, and she snuggled deeper into the folds of the coat Jack had given her. A portion of the mountains off to her right resembled an enormous bowl that God had scooped out by hand and ladled to the brim with snow.

"The exception is that this mining town, according to Hochstetler, is actually a town, complete with a respectable hotel." Jack peered at her from beneath the rim of his hat. "I wrote ahead and secured our reservations."

She laughed softly, loving his forethought. "You have planned well, Jack. Which only deepens my curiosity." But her curiosity didn't have to work hard to guess what his plan truly was. She only hoped she was right.

It had been nearly a month since she'd last accompanied Jack on one of his regular supply trips. Though she missed the time spent with him, God had led her to a point of surrender in her search for her father. She still planned on inquiring about Pierre Gustave Girard in this town, and every other mining town she ever visited. But she'd learned—much through watching Lilly Carlson and her struggle in past weeks—that she'd rather be centered in the middle of God's will, whatever that meant for her life, than to be anywhere else.

This stretch of the Rockies was farther west and more forgiving than its rugged counterparts they'd journeyed before. And while the heights and depths still soared and plunged, the roads were wider and the inclines far more gradual.

Clusters of pine and aspen assembled along the interior slope of the mountain and stood sentinel on the gradual ascent. Boulders only God himself could have placed dotted the terrain, and even the land slanting patiently down to the canyon below was sprinkled with an occasional pine and wild flower.

A thought occurred to her as she stared out over the canyon. Perhaps—just perhaps—she was beginning to conquer her childhood fear.

"This doesn't bother you anymore?" Jack gestured to the edge of the road several feet away. "All those jagged rocks down there, just waiting to eat you alive?"

She cut her eyes at him. "Are you intentionally trying to scare me, monsieur?"

He shrugged. "I guess that would depend on what response I'd get for my trouble."

"And what if it means you will need a fresh change of clothes?"

He threw her a harsh look. "Has anyone ever told you how cruel you can be?"

She laughed. "*Oui.* I am certain Madame Hochstetler still holds that opinion of me."

Véronique remembered walking into the mercantile two days after the independence celebration at Casaroja. When Madame

Hochstetler saw her, the woman's feather duster paused in midair. A look came over her as though she'd just bitten into a rancid lemon.

Véronique stepped up to the counter. "Madame Hochstetler, I have come to offer an apology for ordering merchandise from you for which I could not pay." The animosity staring back at her tempted Véronique to take her apology and peace offering back out the door with her. But knowing Jack waited outside gave her the strength to continue. "I also regret the attitude I displayed to you when I was here last, and I ask for your pardon in that regard as well."

Madame Hochstetler's eyes narrowed. The resentment in them lessened as suspicion slipped into place.

Véronique's fingers tightened on the parchment in her hand. "I drew this for you, madame. It is a palace not far from Paris, called the Château de Versailles. It holds many precious memories for me. My wish is that it may bring a small amount of pleasure to you."

Madame Hochstetler glanced at the picture and huffed. "What were you over there, some kind of queen or somethin'?"

Warmth spread through Véronique's chest even two months later as she remembered her response to Mrs. Hochstetler that day, and the freedom that had come with speaking the truth. *"Non, madame. I was but a servant in Paris."*

Jack cleared his throat. "Mademoiselle Girard, would you do me the honor of having dinner with me this evening?"

Feeling his eyes on her, Véronique kept her focus ahead. "And for what purpose will we be having dinner, Monsieur Brennan?"

"Just answer the question . . . *s'il vous plaît.*"

She looked at him, appreciating what she saw. And from the satisfaction in his expression, he knew it. "I would love to have dinner with you, Monsieur Brennan."

Wordless, he reached over and pulled her close. She looped her arms through his and laid her cheek against his shoulder. The rumble of the wheels on the rutted road and the steady plod of the horses' hooves blended to form a melody unto themselves. And the jostle of the wagon moved her body against his in a way that was unintended, yet not without effect.

She could not imagine not knowing Jack Brennan. But at the same time, she could not deny the cost of having found him.

Without her father departing for the Americas so many years ago, without her mother's ill-fated decision and then her death, she would never have come to know Jack. How intricate were the stitches with which God was weaving the tapestry of her life. And how often did the blessings therein exact a price more dear, and further reaching, than she would ever comprehend this side of eternity.

A sudden jolt brought her upright. "What was that?"

Jack pulled back on the reins. "We'll find out soon enough." He set the brake and jumped down.

She climbed down and shadowed his path as he checked the wheels. "Another broken felly?"

"No . . . the wheels look fine." He peered under the wagon, then crawled beneath. And sighed. "But the main support for the bed is about gone. Cracked clean through. Which is putting more pressure on the axles. The front ones especially." Lying on his back, he scooted farther down. "With the load we're carrying, if we hit a good bump, we could lose the whole bed."

"Can you fix it?"

"Sure, with the right tools and two other men." He crawled out from beneath and brushed himself off. Exhaling, he looked in the direction they'd been traveling. "I say we try and make it on into town. We might if it's not too far."

He guided Charlemagne and Napoleon down the road at a slower pace, and with every bump Véronique sensed Jack tensing beside her. When they rounded the next curve, the town came into view.

Tucked in a protected valley, the mining operation appeared larger than most of the others she'd visited. And if the rows of businesses edging the main street and the tiny houses lining the side roads were any indication—the mining endeavor in this cloistered hollow had proven to be more profitable as well. And civilized. Not a dirty tent in sight.

Jack noticeably relaxed.

He maneuvered the wagon down the main thoroughfare leading into town and stopped beside the first pedestrian they came across.

Before Jack spoke, the little round woman beamed up at him. "Good day to you both, and welcome to Rendezvous. Tell me now, what brings you to this wee bit of heaven on God's snowy earth?"

Hearing the lilt in the woman's voice, Véronique immediately thought of Miss Maudie.

Jack tipped his hat. "Good day in return to you, ma'am, and ye've a beautiful town here. 'Tis a pleasure to be visitin'."

Véronique stared at him, and kept her voice hushed. "Where did you learn to speak like that?"

The wink he gave her brought a flush to her cheeks. "In a minute, you lovely lass," he whispered before turning back to the woman. "Could you tell me, dear woman . . . where might your livery be?"

"It'd be down this road, but only a street away, then turn to your right." The woman smiled and smoothed one side of her hair.

"And your supply store? Where would that be hidin'?"

Shaking her head at him, she motioned. "The McCrearys' place is on the far side of town. Peter at the livery can guide you there. He's a good boy."

Jack tipped his hat again. "Bless you, ma'am. And good day to you."

Once they pulled away, Véronique couldn't hold her laughter in any longer. "I will ask again, Jack, where did you learn to speak like that?"

"From me grandfather, you French beauty. Where d'ya think the fine name of Brennan would be comin' from?"

She pinched his arm through his coat, knowing it did no good. "No wonder Miss Maudie adores you."

"Aye, perhaps she does. But she's not the one I'm lookin' forward to dinin' with tonight."

She giggled. "I have much to learn about you, Jack Brennan." And she looked forward to every minute of it.

She was surprised to see women—respectable-looking women—strolling the boardwalk. Some had shopping baskets draped over their arms; a few even had children in tow. And though a number of miners in the street stopped and watched the wagon pass, this place was a far cry from what she and Jack had experienced before.

Jack maneuvered the wagon down the street and to the livery, and she accompanied him inside.

A shirtless young man she guessed to be Peter labored over an anvil by the forge. She couldn't help but think of Jake Sampson and wondered if this was what he had looked like in his younger years. She guessed the boy to be about Lilly's age, a year or two older, perhaps, though he came close to rivaling Jack's height. His tanned skin contrasted with his blond hair, and from the looks of him, he was accustomed to hard work.

The boy glanced up and saw Jack; then his gaze flickered to her and he reached for a shirt draped on a nearby bench.

"Good day, sir. Ma'am." He nodded, slipping another button through its matched hole. "How may I be of help?"

Jack stretched out his hand. "I've got a freight wagon out here that needs some work, and I'd be obliged if you'd take a look at it for me."

Jack glanced back as he walked out with the boy, and Véronique gestured that she'd be fine. The warmth from the forge felt good after the cold journey, and she hovered closer, holding her gloved hands out to soak up the heat.

Something on the far wall caught her attention. She squinted, unable to see it clearly through the smoke. She moved closer, her steps slowing as the painting came into focus.

It was the summit they'd passed earlier. The bowl God had carved out with His hand and packed full with snow. The colors were so vivid and real. The technique in the painting, while simple, was exquisite.

A door opened somewhere behind her, then the telling crunch of boots on hay.

Another painting drew her eye. Lower on the wall, and smaller. A scene with a bridge. She leaned close, recognition taking her breath with it. The bridge—that was *her* bridge. In Paris. She was certain.

"Good day, ma'am. How may I be of help?"

She couldn't look away from the painting—a true sign the artist possessed the *gift*. "*Bonjour,* monsieur. Peter is already helping us, *merci.*" Finally, she turned, gesturing behind her. "May I ask, who painted these?"

The man stilled.

She took a step toward him. If this man was Peter's father, he was the exact opposite of the boy's physique and coloring. Where Peter was tall and strapping, this man was of shorter stature, dark-haired, and the gauntness of his face made him appear weakened by illness.

His lips moved. But no words came.

He looked as though he were trying to form a sentence. His face grew paler, his expression pained. He murmured something she couldn't understand.

She held out a hand. "Wait here, monsieur, *s'il vous plaît*. I will retrieve your son."

She was nearly to the door when she heard it.

"Arianne . . ."

Her mother's name—a broken whisper, a fragile plea, and a wearied prayer, all in one.

She stopped short. Véronique closed her eyes and opened them again, fearing she would awaken and discover this to be a dream.

Slowly, she faced him, unshed tears threatening. In the instant it had taken for truth to register within her, his eyes revealed the same.

He walked toward her on unsteady legs, his arm outstretched, his hand trembling. "Arianne?" His voice grew weaker with uncertainty.

She shook her head. Her lips trembled. *"Non, Papa . . . je m'appelle—"*

"Véronique," he breathed, touching the side of her face again and again.

She blinked and tears slipped down her cheeks. Such love embodied in a single whispered name.

ÉRONIQUE STOOD AT the edge of the *cimetière*, her heart pounding. She couldn't believe this day had arrived, and so soon.

"Es-tu prête pour ce moment, ma fille précieuse?"

She slipped her left hand into the crook of her father's right arm, holding her bouquet with the other. Soon the ceremony would begin. *"Oui, Papa.* I am most ready for this moment."

The scene before her, reminiscent of her youthful wanderings at Cimetière de Montmartre, was surreal.

Morning mist hovered over the gravestones. It clung to the lingering shade beneath the bowers of tall cottonwoods, and rested with languid grace upon the shores of *La Fontaine qui Bouille.* A breeze stirred a stand of golden aspen, and their bright yellow leaves quaked, contesting winter's approach with the trill of a thousand tiny bells.

"Jack Brennan is a good man, Véronique. He is a man I would have chosen for you. He complements you, *mon chou."*

My cabbage. Véronique warmed at the term of endearment and tightened her hold on her father's arm, aware of his frailness even through the bulk of his coat. The distant sweetness of a single violin signaled the start, and other strings soon joined to frame the traditional melody.

"It is time, *non?"* he whispered.

The smile in his eyes was one she would not forget, and knowing how few days they had left, she cherished it. They took the first step together and walked slowly, as though the ground they covered on the way was as important as what awaited.

And in a way, it was.

She imagined Jack standing in the place Pastor Carlson had described to her earlier, tall and handsome, and she looked ahead to see if she could catch a glimpse of him. But the white-draped tent prevented it.

This setting had been Jack's idea, and she'd loved it from the start. Fountain Creek, near the *cimetière*. Their choice might raise a brow or two, but it fit them, for many reasons.

White rose petals marked the path she and her father followed, and their sweet fragrance lifted as they passed. Though she hadn't seen him do it, Véronique knew Jack was responsible. Desiring to walk the path before her, he'd said, preparing the way.

They'd not seen one another for the past week, at Jack's suggestion. He'd wanted her to have the time with her father before the wedding, and though she had initially protested, she looked forward to thanking him.

She could hardly believe it was happening—that the man she'd grown to love so deeply reciprocated the depth of her feelings. And that the man beside her was there to share her joy.

Her throat tightened. Only recently she'd found her father, and already he was giving her away.

In past weeks, as she'd gotten to know this man who had left such a quiet, indelible mark on who she was—far more than she'd realized—she'd continued to struggle with her mother's decision made so long ago.

Memories of her *maman* huddled close. The bitterness she felt had all but disappeared in light of finding her father. Fear had robbed them all of so much, and Véronique determined—with God's help—never to be ruled by fear of the unknown again.

She scanned the haze of blue overhead. "Do you think she sees us, *Papa*?"

Without looking up, he nodded. "*Oui*, I feel her presence." His hand came to cover hers on his arm.

His was cool to the touch, and Véronique covered it, sharing her warmth and recalling how they'd walked the canals of the river Seine so long ago.

"You mustn't blame her, Véronique. What your mother did, she did from love. Surely you know this."

Véronique didn't answer. She'd learned that, no matter how many times they discussed it, Pierre Gustave Girard would defend his beloved wife to his death.

Just as her mother had carried her love for him to hers.

As they walked the path, she spotted a grave on her left, adorned with fresh wild flowers, and when she read the name on the simple wooden cross, she warmed at the memory. JONATHAN WESLEY MCCUTCHENS. Jack had told her that if not for this man, he would never have come to Willow Springs. She whispered a prayer as they passed. "Until we meet . . . *Merci beaucoup*, Monsieur McCutchens."

"It was wrong, Véronique, for me to leave you and your *maman* behind, to separate our family. The weight of that mistake has worn on me every day of my life. But just as your mother made her choice, so did I, *ma petite*. I allowed my—"

He coughed once, and again more deeply.

They paused for a moment, and Véronique heard the telling rattle in his lungs. It was both difficult—and painfully easy—to imagine her father's impending death. Yet she still held hope that God would give her more time with him.

He finally regained his breath, and their muted footsteps again found rhythm with the stringed music.

"I allowed my shame over failed dreams to strip from me the treasure already in my possession—you and your *maman*." His voice grew softer. "But God, in His mercy, has seen fit to restore a portion of that treasure to me before I leave this earth."

Within view of the white-draped canopy, they stopped.

Hannah and Lilly waited with Kathryn Jennings outside the arched entrance, their smiles expectant. Mrs. Dunston stood with them, no doubt ready to make any last minute adjustments to the white pearl-beaded dress she'd sewn for this special day.

But even with such an exquisite satin gown, Véronique's favorite part of the day's ensemble was, by far, her bonnet. At least that's how Jack had referred to it in his note.

In reality it was a wedding *chapeau*, and a most stylish one. He'd sent it to her earlier in the week as a wedding present, along with a note. Under playful duress, Mrs. Dunston confessed that she'd ordered it from New York City weeks ago, at Jack's request.

Véronique fondly remembered Jack's analogy long ago about the desire to purchase a bonnet. She'd thought of his story's meaning many times in recent weeks as she'd anticipated becoming his wife. A coy smile tipped her mouth. She looked forward to thanking him for his thoughtfulness later that night.

Her father gently lifted the front of her veil. He placed a soft kiss on her left cheek, then her right, and repeated both again. "So many nights I dreamed of you, *ma petite fille*. I prayed for God to keep you strong, and that my faults"—his smile was gentle—"and those of your precious *maman*, would not keep you from following the course He had set for your life. No matter the cost."

His words took her back. And in her mind, Véronique knelt again by her mother's grave. *"If somehow my words can reach you, Maman . . . Know that I cannot do as you have asked. Your request comes at too great—"*

"A cost," Véronique answered within herself, truth knifing what bitterness remained. How could she not have seen the similarity before? "She knew, *Papa*. She knew I would not leave Paris to come to the Americas on my own. I would be too afraid . . . just as she had been. So *Maman* removed any chance of my staying." Véronique slowly shook her head. "I wish she could have known . . . it was her unwavering confidence in me that gave me strength to make this journey."

Her father studied her for the longest moment. "I believe she does know. But if not, I will tell her soon enough." Tender longing shadowed his expression. "I am most eager to see her again."

Hannah motioned them forward. "You look positively beautiful, Véronique. And, Mr. Girard, you do her proud, sir."

He squared his shoulders and raised himself to his full height, being only slightly taller than she was. Recognizing the all-too-familiar mannerism and the teasing in his smoky-brown eyes, Véronique chuckled.

With each day, her appreciation for her father's kindness of character deepened. When she'd first believed that Peter was her father's son, her reaction had been hurt and disappointment. But learning that her father had adopted the one-year-old Peter when the boy's parents died only increased her affection for him.

Pierre, the French form of Peter. She smiled to herself, pondering the not-so-subtle sign of God's working.

The boy was fifteen, only a year younger than Aaron would've been had Jack's son lived. Peter spoke of Jack constantly, his admiration unquestionable. And she didn't have to ask Jack if his feelings for the boy were mutual. Seeing them together was enough.

Kathryn squeezed her hand before situating Véronique's veil. "Hannah's right, Véronique, you look radiant. Like a queen befitting the grandest palace in Europe. And if I might say, your husband-to-be looks quite dashing himself."

Lilly nodded, giving a subtle wink. "A mite easy on the eyes is how I'd phrase it, Mademoiselle Girard."

They all laughed, and Véronique hugged each of them. "*Merci beaucoup.* I cannot imagine this moment without all of you."

Mrs. Dunston pulled back the gauzy curtain veiling the entrance and held up a hand when Véronique stepped forward. "Not just yet, my dear. You and Jack are to see one another at the very same time." She grinned. "I've been sworn to make certain of that."

Véronique's excitement wrestled with her patience, yet she didn't dare move an inch under Mrs. Dunston's watchful eye. From where she and her father stood, she could only see the last few rows on the right hand side. But every seat was occupied.

Larson escorted Kathryn down the aisle first, followed by Hannah and young Bobby. When it came time, Lilly stepped forward and accepted Peter's waiting arm. Lilly smiled up at him and the sparkle in both their expressions was impossible to miss.

Before the veiled curtain fell back into place, Véronique glimpsed white-silvered hair reflecting the filtered sunlight—Miss Maudie. The dear woman sat on a chair closest to the aisle, with Monsieur Colby by her side. Miss Maudie was hosting the wedding brunch at Casaroja afterward, and Véronique could hardly wait to see what her friend had planned.

At Mrs. Dunston's approving nod, her father led her closer to the veiled opening of the canopied tent. The music continued for several heartbeats; then the final notes hung in the air, slowly fading until all Véronique could hear was the bubbling water of Fountain Creek.

Patrick addressed the gathering of friends, and time seemed to slow.

She couldn't see Jack yet, though his face filled her mind. She scanned the crowd. What blessings God had given her in this new country. And what blessings she would have forfeited had she not followed God's lead. She only wished her *maman* could see what her daughter's journey had wrought.

Briefly bowing her head, Véronique touched the cameo at her neckline and went back in her mind to a world away, one more time, to a day treasured in memory—to the day when she'd painted the picture of Versailles. And she strolled the gardens, hand-in-hand, with her beloved *maman* and sat by the canal where the two of them had feasted on bread and wine and cheese. She imagined her life as a canvas and the events of it, miniscule brushstrokes. Seen up close they meant little. But when given perspective, each splash of color, every dab of paint, however small or large, dark or light, was meant for her eternal good. God had proven that in recent months.

And she prayed she would always remember.

The violin music resumed. The veil across the entrance parted. And Véronique lifted her gaze to see the rest of her life waiting for her at the end of the aisle.

———

Jack stoked the fire, wanting to give his new bride the time she needed. He'd checked the chimney twice to make sure smoke wasn't leaking anywhere, and he resisted the urge to go back outside into the cool night air and check it again.

Their cabin was sound—what he'd built so far, anyway. Only two rooms, but he would add another before winter came, for Véronique's father and Peter.

He glanced at their bedroom door, wondering how long she'd been in there. It felt like hours, yet the clock on the mantel told him that not much time had passed.

The wedding that morning would reside in his memory as nothing short of spectacular—all credit going to his new bride. It looked as though everyone in town had been in attendance, but he actually remembered very few faces.

As soon as Véronique had started down that aisle, everything and everyone had faded from view.

He glanced at the bedroom door again, then pulled out a chair and straddled it. He was debating whether to pour himself another glass of Miss Maudie's cider, when the door opened.

He jumped to standing.

Véronique stepped out, and he swallowed, suddenly wishing he had something stronger than cider.

Her nightgown was fancier than anything he'd imagined her wearing tonight. Not that he was complaining. The way the gown hugged her in some places, while draping from others, brought a single overriding thought to his mind—marriage was a good thing.

"Would you like to have time to change, Jack?"

He stared at her, unable not to. "I don't really . . ." He shrugged. "I don't really have anything to change into."

"In that case, when you are through in here"—she glanced behind her—"I'll be in th—"

"I'm through in here."

She smiled, looked away, and then looked back again. Her tiny hands gently fisted and unfisted at her sides. Her gaze couldn't seem to settle on any one thing.

Oh, how he loved this woman. He took her hand and led her into the bedroom. The room was warm, but he left the door ajar to share the heat from the hearth.

He walked to her side of the bed—or what he guessed was her side; they'd have to figure that out later—and turned down the covers.

Close beside him, she looked at the bed, then at him. "I am not yet ready for sleep, Jack."

The tease in her voice prompted a grin. "That's a good thing, because sleep's about the last thing on my mind."

He faced her and ran his hands slowly down her arms and back up again, letting them rest on her shoulders. He stepped closer until their bodies touched, and he kissed her like he'd wanted to since that first time on the trail.

She tasted like cider and cloves and something else sweet. Her hands moved over him, tentative at first but growing more confident as the kiss progressed.

She suddenly drew back and gazed up at him. "Jack?"

"Yes?" he whispered.

She ran a hand over his chest, lingering on the buttons of his shirt. "I have been considering something."

He quelled a groan. He loved talking to her, but talking wasn't exactly highest on his list right then.

She pressed close and wove her arms around his waist. "Some time ago, I passed by a shop window and . . . something drew my attention. Since then, it is all I think about. In fact, I can think of nothing else."

He would agree to buy her just about anything right now if they could just continue what they'd been doing.

"I was not looking, you understand." She slowly raised a brow. "But it caught my eye."

And that's when he understood. Jack pulled her closer, doing his best not to smile. Starting at the nape of her neck, he traced a feather-soft path down her back with his hand. "Is that so?"

She shivered and a promising look moved into her eyes. "If it is agreeable to you, Monsieur Brennan," she whispered, "I would very much like to . . . buy a bonnet. One that was made especially for me."

Jack tilted her face so her mouth would meet his. "That was made especially for us both, *mon amour.*"

⇥ A C K N O W L E D G M E N T S

To Jesus, your mercy is immeasurable, and my need for it—the same. To Joe, thank you for spending the better part of a day meandering through Cimetière de Montmartre with me. I'll never forget that experience, and what came from it. Kelsey and Kurt, God gave you both to us, and I couldn't be more thankful. It's with eager anticipation that your dad and I look forward to the unfolding of your lives.

To Deborah Raney, your wonderful critiques are better than Iced White Chocolate Mochas! I love the way you push me. Don't ever let up! To Lauren Miller Gonikishvili, thanks for sharing your knowledge of the French language. Blessings in your new marriage, and any mistakes in French . . . are my own. To Karen Schurrer, my editor, if books are "babies" then this one sure had a long birth, my friend. Thanks for your patience and for being open to my changes in the story upon my return from Paris. To Charlene Patterson, Jolene Steffer, Ann Parrish, and Sharon Asmus . . . your touches are all over this book, and your encouragement means the world to me. To Doug and June Gattis, my parents, my thanks for reading this manuscript in varying stages, and for always asking for more! To Dr. Fred Alexander, my favorite father-in-law, my appreciation for donning your editor's cap once again. You wear it well! To Virginia Rogers and Suzi Buggeln, your comments while I write always challenge and encourage! To Naila Kling, my unofficial "Publicist Extraordinaire," your "word of mouth" skills are unmatched, my dear! And your check is in the mail!

I offer my deepest thanks to you, my readers, who have written numerous letters and e-mails asking to know more about Larson and Kathryn Jennings, Matthew and Annabelle Taylor, and most of all . . . sweet Sadie. My appreciation for how you've embraced these characters and their stories. You could not pay me a greater compliment. Until we meet again in the next series (coming in 2008), I pray God's richest blessings upon you and would love to hear from you!

———

Winner of the Gayle Wilson Award of Excellence and triple RITA Award nominee, TAMERA GATTIS ALEXANDER has a background in business management and corporate conference coordination. She has led women's ministries for many years and is active in music ministry, facilitating small groups and Bible studies, and mentoring other women. She lives with her husband in Greeley, Colorado, where they enjoy life with their two college-age children and another important member of their family—a seven-pound Silky named Jack.

Tamera invites you to write her at tameraalexander@gmail.com or at the following postal address:

Tamera Alexander
c/o Bethany House Publishers
11400 Hampshire Ave. S.
Bloomington, MN 55438

Looking for More Good Books to Read?

You can find out what is new and exciting with previews, descriptions, and reviews by signing up for Bethany House newsletters at

www.bethanynewsletters.com

We will send you updates for as many authors or categories as you desire so you get only the information you really want.

Sign up today!